Strangers in Time

BY DAVID BALDACCI

Travis Devine series

The 6:20 Man • *The Edge*
To Die For

Amos Decker series

Memory Man • *The Last Mile*
The Fix • *The Fallen*
Redemption • *Walk the Wire*
Long Shadows

Aloysius Archer series

One Good Deed • *A Gambling Man*
Dream Town

Atlee Pine series

Long Road to Mercy
A Minute to Midnight
Daylight • *Mercy*

Will Robie series

The Innocent • *The Hit* • *The Target*
The Guilty • *End Game*

John Puller series

Zero Day • *The Forgotten*
The Escape • *No Man's Land*
Daylight

King and Maxwell series

Split Second • *Hour Game*
Simple Genius • *First Family*
The Sixth Man • *King and Maxwell*

The Camel Club series

The Camel Club • *The Collectors*
Stone Cold • *Divine Justice*
Hell's Corner

Shaw series

The Whole Truth
Deliver Us From Evil

Other novels

Absolute Power • *True Blue*
Total Control • *The Winner*
The Simple Truth • *Saving Faith*
Wish You Well • *Last Man Standing*
The Christmas Train • *One Summer*
Simply Lies • *A Calamity of Souls*
Strangers in Time

Short stories

Waiting for Santa • *No Time Left*
Bullseye • *The Final Play*

Vega Jane series

Vega Jane and the Secrets of Sorcery
Vega Jane and the Maze of Monsters
Vega Jane and the Rebels' Revolt
Vega Jane and the End of Time

DAVID
BALDACCI

Strangers in Time

MACMILLAN

First published 2025 by Grand Central Publishing, USA

First published in the UK 2025 by Macmillan
an imprint of Pan Macmillan
The Smithson, 6 Briset Street, London EC1M 5NR
EU representative: Macmillan Publishers Ireland Ltd, 1st Floor,
The Liffey Trust Centre, 117–126 Sheriff Street Upper,
Dublin 1, D01 YC43
Associated companies throughout the world
www.panmacmillan.com

ISBN 978-1-0350-1578-8 HB
ISBN 978-1-0350-1579-5 TPB

1 3 5 7 9 8 6 4 2

A CIP catalogue record for this book is available from the British Library.

Printed by IVE

To the memory of Abner Stein, a wonderful agent and friend,
who taught me much about the publishing business, and life

Only the dead have seen the end of war.

—*George Santayana*

There are no strangers here
Only friends you haven't met yet.

—*attributed to William Butler Yeats*

A Boy Called Charlie

IT WAS WELL PAST the midway point of 1944 when Charlie Matters clambered over the piled-up debris that littered much of London, while doing his best to fade into the lingering edges of the night-time. Charlie would be fourteen on his next birthday, and years had passed since his parents had been alive. Eighteen thousand souls had died violently in the eight months of the Blitz alone, and one in six Londoners had been left homeless at one time or another. Sometimes there seemed to be more fallen buildings than ones left standing. A person could easily become desensitized to such profound loss. Yet while the war years had tried their best to rob him of it, Charlie was still resolutely in possession of a heart.

He hurried along streets lit mostly by hazy moonlight. The blackouts were still in full effect, and the electricity that was permitted was reliably unreliable. It was the same for the bluish plumes of gas, while plump fists of contraband coal were but a distant memory for most, especially folks like Charlie. They were all still steeped in the hostilities that had engulfed the world and struck particularly fiercely at the city of Charlie's birth. Yet he didn't mind the darkness; it was actually an aid to him right now.

He continued to skitter over bricks heaved up like stilled waves, and weaved around the stark warning signs of possible unexploded ordnance. Charlie had seen a defused bomb once. The crude lettering on the device was written in a language he couldn't actually read, but he still knew exactly what it said:

GOTT VERDAMMT DIE ENGLISCHE

Well, God would choose which people to damn, and it certainly wouldn't be the English, he believed. Things were actually appearing far more hopeful than a year ago, at least according to the snippets coming through on the wireless, and conversations Charlie overheard on the streets, and the bits of newspaper headlines he managed to glimpse.

He tugged up the waistband of his tattered trousers with the cuffs turned up three times. Until last week they had resided in a shop that gave out worn castoffs for a few shillings in return. The queue had flowed out the door and snaked down the pavement, as desperate East Enders sought to augment their meagre piles of necessaries. His grandmother, her ration book allotment for clothing nearly exhausted, had dutifully waited for hours on tiring pavement to get her grandson a proper pair of trousers that he could at least grow into over the next year or so.

At the bottoms of Charlie's long, knock-kneed legs were shoes that were too small and caused him to step gingerly even in haste, which was often how he was compelled to move.

As the wailing wind—which darted through wide, ominous gaps where buildings had once stood—quieted for a few moments, Charlie heard the sputtering belch of a motorcar approaching. He quickly scooted behind a dustbin filled with the bombed-out wreckage of the building it fronted. When Charlie saw who was coming, he was glad he had hidden.

The pair of bleary-eyed constables puttered by in their rickety Morris. They were looking for people like Charlie. People up to no good, with the West End's accusatory finger pointed doggedly towards the likes of Bethnal Green, Stepney, and East Ham.

I am up to no good, but for a very good reason, thought Charlie.

The poor cherished their possessions, because they could invariably see all of them at the same time. The rich did not miss that for which they had four spares. Thus, Charlie had no compunction relieving from affluent folks a bit of their surplus.

The Morris receded into the night as Charlie stepped clear of the dustbin. He passed by one bombed shop with no windows and no door and eyed the sign out front, which read MORE OPEN THAN USUAL.

Charlie's goal tonight was straightforward: shoes. Footwear for boys his age were in unusually short supply in London. But for those with enough money, they could be had. Well, he didn't have the money, so Charlie's process was a smidge different, though on a legal scale it was rather more significant than that.

St. Saviour's, a prominent school, was his destination. The majority of the students were enrolled there because of the influence of money and peerage. The remaining few had gained access based on actual merit.

Charlie lacked the money, the peerage, and the merit. He wasn't travelling to this school for a privileged education or for future glory, but simply for reasonable footwear. He would have preferred a steady job to outright theft, yet he was apparently too young, too uneducated, too *common-looking*—a term he'd heard more than once—for gainful employment as, say, an assistant shop clerk or a butcher's boy. And even with the odd job he occasionally found, it seemed that when it came time to pay the wage, folks conjured all sorts of reasons why they couldn't part with their shillings.

The rain fell and embellished what appeared to be shiny layers of frost lying everywhere. It was actually powdered glass from windows shattered and then fused by the heat of the bombs. In the heavy drizzle, this coating gleamed like the metal wreckage of a plane, something Charlie had also seen. Aircraft had been in abundance in the skies over London, and not all had remained there.

Night after night Charlie, his gas mask on, had huddled with his body clenched like a fist, while steel, explosives, and detonators collided with laid brick, mortared stone, and, more than occasionally, fragile flesh. One never knew when something dropped from above would strike and that would be the end of you. So far he had survived all that.

He licked his thin lips and took a deep breath.

I'm not a boy.

I'm a man.

Act like it, Charlie.

This had been his mantra for a while now. It might be so for the rest of his life, however long or short that actually turned out to be.

St. Saviour's School

As the rain picked up, Charlie felt drops of it creep inside his threadbare coat, which was missing half the material and associated warmth it had started out with. He passed by a building where the façade was gone, revealing a twisting staircase leading to an upper floor that was no longer there. He glanced at a sodden newspaper lying on the street. There was a blurry photo of a stocky, balding man with burned bits of coal for eyes and a pugnacious jaw. He was holding a fat cigar, his waistcoat fronted by a stout timepiece on a chain.

Charlie knew that this man was the prime minister. He had told his people to be strong, and calm and patient, while the world fell apart all around them. And they had, for years, mostly done just as he asked. Yet there were limits to people's willingness and ability to sacrifice, and for Charlie and many like him, these limits were growing steadily nearer.

For tonight's task Charlie had reliable information that St. Saviour's rear door had a lock that could be defeated with the right tool and skill, both of which Charlie possessed. Just inside this door was a till with the money students paid for their meals. Maybe a few quid. Maybe many pounds. Certainly it would be enough to purchase secondhand shoes.

He calculated the timing of his operation. His grandmother would not be up until five. Each morning she left him his school lunch tin, and the food in the icebox for his breakfast. Then she went to work at the bakery shop. She believed that Charlie awoke, ate his breakfast, and then hurried off to school with his lunch tin and a heart eager to learn.

Instead, over a year ago, he had forged a letter in her hand, informing his teacher that his grandmother and he had moved to the country. The woman had freely accepted this because many people had traded dirty rubble and wretched loss for trees and open green fields, along with a centuries-old drafty stone church in which to pray for something better than what was currently available in London. He had been afraid that he might run into his former teacher at some point, which would reveal his lie. However, Charlie had learned that she had died in a bombing a month later. It was emblematic of the world they lived in now that Charlie had not been devastated by the woman's violent passing. There were simply too many people dying all around him, from bombs and even more from sickness, to dwell long on any one of them.

Yet it was not the same experience for everyone. Rich people's shelters weren't in coal cellars, tube stations, an Andy bomb shelter, or under-the-stairs cupboards. They went to the Ritz or the Dorchester or the Savoy for pampering and full English breakfasts before being whisked off to country estates in chauffeured motorcars. At least that was what Charlie had often heard, including from his gran, and therefore fully believed.

He nimbly clambered over the school's low gate and dropped quietly inside the darkened grounds.

St. Saviour's was two storeys tall and built of only the finest forged brick and quarried stone. For some inexplicable reason, as with St. Paul's, no bomb had ever scored its hardened, noble hide.

Imperious white columns fronted the entrance. Dramatic mouldings soared horizontally overhead. An elegant fanlight topped the pair of imposing solid oak front doors. A statue of a solemn-looking gent clad in a frock coat and gripping a walking stick and a book stood as weathered guard outside. Whether this chap was St. Saviour, Charlie didn't know. He *did* manage a smile at the thought of a hallowed saint in a ridiculous coat destined to stand in the rain and muck for all of eternity.

Charlie would not be going in the front door. For East End blokes like him, the tradesman's entrance would be the expected one for all their natural lives.

Unfortunately, he found the rear portal had *two* locks fronting it, stacked one on top of the other. This was an unexpected dilemma.

Charlie took out a sturdy piece of metal with a precise bend at the end and a protruding bit of blackened iron on its top side shaped in the form of a rectangle. He had been given the tool by his mate Eddie Gray. Eddie said his father had claimed it could defeat 90 per cent of the locks in all of England. One like it had passed to Eddie when, years before, his father had died during a botched armed robbery. Eddie, who was good at making things, had fashioned a second lockpick and given it to Charlie. Eddie had also patiently instructed him on how to overcome a lock with it.

Charlie worked away intently, twisting the metal this way and that, while feeling through his fingers the guts of the lock moving around. It would be easier and simpler to pinch things from the open stalls of Brick or Petticoat Lanes back in the East End. Yet he didn't like stealing from his own kind, and they had no spare boots there anyway.

He finally heard a soft click. Charlie turned the knob and it rotated freely. However, when he tried his instrument and skill on the top lock, Charlie could make no progress. After a few minutes of concentrated effort, he withdrew the pick in despair. This must be one of the 10 per cent of the locks his tool couldn't conquer.

Bloody well figures.

The high-set windows on the sides of the building were iron-barred. There was no iron left in the East End; it had all been stripped and melted down for the war effort. But this wasn't the East End. One ventured "up" to the West End, but "down" to the East End, and those terms were literal in all possible senses. He had been told by one constable that in Charlie's world you had your costermongers, fish curers, and thieves, with the latter adding up to about nine in ten of the population, the bobby reckoned. And he had included Charlie in that criminal group, although the lack of hard evidence at the time had sent Charlie on his way with only a stiff caution instead of the darbies put on with a swift ride to the clink to follow.

Charlie clutched the bars, hoisting himself up and peering through the glass. Looking in instead of out was his lot in life, it seemed.

Then he let go and fell to the damp earth.

He'd been lied to. There was probably no money in the till here. There was probably no till. The two boys who had told him about this opportunity didn't have parents and had stayed with a hodgepodge of distant relatives, friends, fosters, and child minders. Recently, they had been sent to an orphanage just outside of London, but had broken out, they had informed Charlie, after telling him how awful it had been.

"You ain't even got a name in there, Charlie, just a number," said Lonzo Rossi. "I was bloody T207 or some such, but I always just been Lonzo."

Eddie Gray, Lonzo's best mate, had said nothing, but had looked off into the distance with an expression that spoke to Charlie of traumatic experience.

Charlie jogged back to the east and soon found himself in the heart of Covent Garden. A minute later the rain was bucketing down so hard that he could barely see; his sore feet felt encased in stone. And he still had a four-mile trek ahead of him to Bethnal Green. He stumbled along until he saw a bit of light coming from an alley. He peered down its mouth, conscious of the silence all around him, except for the *drum-drum* of the falling rain. In the drench, he saw a glimmer of light from a shop. At this hour that was truly remarkable. And it drew Charlie like metal to a magnet.

A Sly Pot of Gold

CHARLIE CREPT DOWN THE alley until he reached the soft glow of feeble light. Darting under the green awning and out of the rain, he looked at the neat, gilt-lettered sign on the dirt-streaked plate glass window:

THE BOOK KEEP
I. OLIVER, PROPRIETRESS

Below that were adverts that looked hand-stencilled.

A book a day keeps the bombs away.

And:

Reading books is far better than burning them.

Scrim tape had been applied to sections of the window to prevent the glass from shattering and becoming a weapon itself during a bombing. Triple-layered black curtains fairly covered most light from inside. However, the owner hadn't pulled them all the way closed. There was a gap through which Charlie could see into the space. If an air warden came by, the shop's owner might be given a tongue-lashing and even a caution. Yet Charlie also knew folks had grown lax about such things.

When he peered through the gap the first things Charlie saw were books. He had been in a library before. Most recently to get out of the rain and avoid the accompanying chill and pneumonia that often followed. There, every single volume had been properly shouldered next to its neighbour.

Charlie had actually resented the clean, regimented lines of these books. Nothing in the world should be that uncluttered, he had thought. It simply did not seem right when the world itself was all sixes and sevens. Yet here teetering book stacks were haphazardly placed on the floor. In crevices and corners balls of dust rode alongside feathery cobwebs. A rickety ladder with brass rollers ran along a slender, cylindrical tube attached to shelves which bulged and flinched under the weight of leather tomes that were stitched to their wooden-framed hides, wordy ships yawing in storms on dry land. The overhead naked bulbs popped and wavered and seemed indifferent to their intended purpose.

It was then that Charlie saw the two men, who were a study in remarkable contrasts.

The first one was in his forties, tall and too thin, and harried looking, like everyone these days. His longish full hair was brown; his skin was pale, and, like Charlie's, it had the odd freckle strewn here and there. The man wore an old, rumpled grey woolen vest, and a white shirt stained with a long day's grime. The rolled-up sleeves revealed bony forearms spotted with thickish moles like the eraser bump on a pencil. There were also some deep burns on his skin that looked quite painful. His trousers were as worn out as his vest, his shoes shabby, the heels uneven from constant wear over rumpled pavements. Rimless specs covered hazel eyes.

This gent must be the shop's owner, I. Oliver, thought Charlie.

The other man was short and squat and had on a slouch hat, pulled low. He wore an expensive black waterproof, and new-looking stout wellies against the foul weather. He was jowly, with a bit of stubble on his weak chin. He handed the shop's owner a packet of papers bound with black ribbon, and said something that Charlie could not hear.

The other man took the papers and put them away in a drawer that he then locked.

When the shorter man turned and headed to the door, Charlie hid behind a handy dustbin overflowing with bomb debris, of which there were thousands in the city. The man opened the door, which caused the tinkling of a bell, and stepped out. He gave a searching look right and left, making Charlie shrink down farther. Then the gent turned up his waterproof's collar and hurried off.

Charlie waited a few moments to make certain the squat man was not coming back. He stole up to the window once more to see the shop owner bent over a fat ledger behind the counter and right next to the till. His long finger moved down the columned page as he made small ticks on the paper with a pencil. After a minute or so he put the pencil down and drank from a chipped porcelain cup set next to his elbow. Beside that rested a plate holding a few slender biscuits.

Charlie eyed the biscuits as his empty belly commenced speaking to him in the form of bold protest.

Next the man picked up a curious cylindrical-looking device. Parts of the contraption seemed to rotate, because he was moving things around on it. He continued manipulating it for a few moments before returning to his pencil and ledger.

A minute later, the man lifted up a box labelled *Simpkin & Marshall Book Wholesalers* and disappeared through a curtain into a backroom. Charlie instantly seized the doorknob. Fortunately, it was unlocked. Unfortunately, the little bell tinkled when Charlie wrenched open the door; he had forgotten about that.

He quieted the bell, scurried behind a tower of books in one corner, and waited. Momentarily, the man appeared and looked around, his eyebrows touching in confusion, his spectacled gaze bouncing around the small space. He rushed over to the drawer where he had placed the packet of papers and unlocked it. He took out the sheaf of documents and examined them. Satisfied, he locked them back up, used the lift gate on the counter to pass through, strode across the floor, turned the door latch, and then retreated the same way, disappearing back through the curtain.

Quick as a ferret, Charlie came out of hiding, grabbed the biscuits, and thrust them into his pocket. He examined the odd device that lay on the counter. The thing was wood and metal with little rotating disks on which letters were imprinted. Setting it down, he rushed over to the ancient till. He pushed one of the metal-dipped keys, pulled back the large lever, and the wooden drawer popped open like a cuckoo from a clock. Paper and coins disappeared into one of his other pockets. He also grabbed a book off the counter, figuring it might be worth something.

Charlie thought his escape had been unseen. However, as he looked back, he saw the man bracketed in the curtained doorway, his mouth open perhaps in disbelief or dismay, or both. The next instant Charlie had unlocked and flung open the door, and was sprinting down the rain-slickened alley.

He had just turned wretched defeat into splendid triumph.

It was about time.

Down to the East End

Charlie followed the kerbs, trees, and lamp-posts that had been painted white to help folks navigate the city at night. There were no exterior lights permitted on buildings, and vehicle lights had to be concealed, except for a small crack in the covering. The traffic lights were also shrouded, again save for a small slit so drivers could view the necessary colours. All streets other than the main thoroughfares were dark, and these roadways only possessed a small starlight filtering downwards so as to give no aid to the Luftwaffe above.

The buses had signs that read LOOK OUT IN THE BLACKOUT. Yet even with these aids, people were still regularly struck and killed by cars, taxis, lorries, and double-decker buses lurching out of the darkness at them like leaping predators on the prowl. Charlie had had more than his share of close calls. Thousands of others had not been so fortunate and currently lay six feet under the earth for their effrontery at taking a walk in the city.

The blackout had been difficult for many Londoners, who had been used to a city brilliantly lighted at night. Charlie could still recall when the blackout had been instituted. He had watched with his grandfather from atop a building as, sector by sector—including the mighty Big Ben—the great city went dark. And with the absence of light came a deluge of fear for many, because everyone knew that terrible things always tended to happen in the dark.

Along the way home, the sore-footed Charlie was still nimble enough to latch on to the rear end of a full bus that was shepherding folks engaged in the round-the-clock war efforts to either their homes or places of work. He had been taught how to expertly perch on the outside of buses by Lonzo. It required strong fingers and exceptional balance, with the bottoms of your feet pressed against the vehicle's metal hide, as well as the ability and courage to safely jump off a moving bus if the ticket conductor spied you and angrily came for the freeloader with his club.

At his ramshackle building in Bethnal Green, Charlie entered his tiny flat the way he always did after one of these night-time forays. The overturned dustbin in the alley led to the bottom of the frayed rope attached to the lowest rung of the fire escape ladder. A tug on the rope brought the ladder down. After a quick clamber up the steps to the landing above and resetting the ladder, he was in through the window that, unlike the back door to St. Saviour's School, had never latched properly.

Charlie slid into the wooden crate that represented his bed inside the space that had once been a small storage cupboard. When they had first moved here, it had been cosy. Now, with his quickly lengthening limbs and torso, it felt akin to a coffin. Yet at least he had a room of his own. He had many mates who did not.

Charlie had learned that his crib had once been an egg box, where as a wee thing he'd spent much time lying in nappies. As he'd grown, his digs had been replaced with an orange crate. He didn't know what his current box had once been, but at least it was larger, because so was he.

Despite the cramped quarters, Charlie knew he and Gran had it better than most around here. Many East Enders lived multiple families to a few rooms with exterior toilets and no kitchens, with the fronting streets barely ten feet wide. And being jettisoned into those same streets was, for many folks, only an illness or death of a husband and father away.

His grandmother had once told him in front of a meagre fire and lukewarm tea, "There was a workhouse in Whitechapel, Charlie." She had shivered at the memory. "Bloody awful place. Nearly a thousand helpless souls. And the whole family had to go and share in the shame of being destitute. Shaved your head to keep off the lice. Fed you but not really with what I would call food. And they separated husbands and wives, and their children too. It was hard labour every day, and the law said the living conditions had to be worse than that of the working poor. And that's saying something, Charlie, because we're working poor, aren't we? And look at us! And if you were old and your family couldn't take you in, you went there, too. Bread and soup, and one day out so you could do your begging on the streets." She had paused, lips quivering with emotion. "You hear anyone ever speak of the workhouse *howl*, luv?" she said in a fearful tone.

Charlie had shaken his head. "What's that?" he'd said, with dread in his voice.

She had settled her despondent gaze on him. "Well, Charlie, it's hard to describe. It's . . . it's when folks have been so beaten down by life and all the hardships that go with it, least for our kind, that . . . that all that sadness and, well, anger too, just comes out of your mouth and you howl away, like some poor, suffering beast. Because that's what folks can become who haven't ever had a decent turn in life. You still see it often round here," she'd added bitterly.

"Have . . . have you ever had to howl like that, Gran?" he'd asked.

She had hurriedly changed the subject and didn't answer him.

Charlie knew he never wanted to go to the workhouse. And he never wanted to be so sad that he howled, though some days he could see it happening.

He tugged a single tattered sheet over his wet self, felt in his pocket for the biscuits, and broke off a piece. He pushed it into his mouth and quickly chewed. He wanted to eat slowly, but he was too ravenous for that.

With his other hand, he felt for the paper money and coins. Food *and* proper money, instead of a shilling or mere pence. His prospects had gone up quite nicely with a single night's larcenous labour.

He lit a candle stub, angled it into the crevice between the wooden box and several old pillows that constituted his mattress, and pulled the money out. His soiled fingers rubbed over the countenances of the august royal images imprinted on the notes and then touched the coolness of the coins. On the penny farthing was the image of Britannia on one side and George the Sixth on the obverse.

In total there was thirty-eight pounds in paper, plus an assortment of coins adding up to around another four quid. He had never held such a fortune. He slowly put it all back in his pocket and turned his contented attention to the book. In the dim light Charlie noticed for the first time that there was nothing printed on the cover or the spine. When he turned to the first page his hopes of more bounty from this stolen article fell. He quickly flipped through all the pages; every single one was blank.

"Bloody useless," he commented to the darkness. He hid it under the pillows, snuffed out the candle with moistened fingers, and listened to the quiet outside. It was interrupted only by the occasional passing of a sputtering car belching dodgy petrol, or the sharp strike of regulation boots on pavement, heralding a weary constable or an air warden performing their important rounds.

As time passed, there came the frail echoes of a wireless from the flat next door. Charlie and his gran had once had an Ekco brand radio, but it had gone to pay bills. Charlie missed listening to the BBC. The radio broadcasts reported the war-related news, certainly. But there were also programmes that made him laugh, and *Children's Hour*, one of his favourites, which came on every day. Sometimes, he would sit out in the hallway at night and listen to the wirelesses of other people, hoping to hear well enough to chuckle at something—anything, really, to take him away for even a few moments from the desperation of his daily life.

At three in the morning he heard the gong of a tower clock. A minute later this was followed by a bullhorn blast from a ship, either navigating up or down the long, winding thread of the mud-coated Thames. The 215-mile-long river essentially defined Charlie's world, becoming tidal at Teddington, and sliding into Greater London at Thames Ditton. It fanned wider and ever more winding as it headed east. All the fine bridges were to the west because of that. The unmistakable loop around the Isle of Dogs made the East End and the all-important docks easily visible from the sky for German bombers, especially on moonlit nights. And the Luftwaffe had taken advantage of that unique topographical quirk, with devastating results.

A moment later the sharp cry of a train whistle cut right through him. Charlie tried to think of which station it could be but then gave up. And when would he ever be on a train? He had been born in this city and he felt quite certain that he would perish here as well without ever once travelling anywhere else; the only unknown was how many years from now. Or days. And whether his end would be natural or violent. These thoughts were not the result of an overactive imagination. Charlie had seen much that was unthinkable and terrible in every conceivable way.

Yet nothing, for him, could ever take away the horror of that late summer's day.

The Day the Bombs Came

Black Saturday, Charlie had often heard it called afterwards. Before that, sirens had sounded for many months with few German planes accompanying the warnings. Because of that folks had started calling it the "Bore," or "Phony War." But that had not been the case on that first Saturday in September 1940.

It was a lovely warm, sunny day, fairly rare in England.

At 4 p.m. British radar stations picked up a fleet rendezvous between German bombers and fighters above the French coast. About fifteen minutes later the frontal edge of the twenty-mile-wide Luftwaffe armada, which rode over ten thousand feet in the sky, crossed the English coast and was spotted by an Observer Corps post. The RAF was then scrambled.

By then, it was far too late.

It was around five when the city's bomb warnings went off, building in volume. The sirens sounded to Charlie like high-pitched screams from the sky. Charlie and his gran, and his mother and his grandfather, for they had been alive back then, had hurried to their agreed-upon shelter, a cupboard in the windowless back room of their old flat. Folks with rear yards often fled to their hardy Andy bomb shelters, half dug into the ground with their thin hides of corrugated arched aluminium set next to flower beds that had been turned into Digging for Victory gardens. However, many poor folks without yards went to public shelters; others headed to the Underground. Most, like Charlie and his family, ventured straight away to the cupboard.

Gripped in his mother's hand was her gas mask, a device they all had been issued. She helped Charlie to put on his, then aided her parents, and, finally, donned her mask.

At first, there had been no sounds other than people rushing here and there outside, and the warbly sirens. Then Charlie looked up at his mother.

"They're coming," he heard her say, and in a tone that captured her son's full attention. She helped Charlie tighten his mask. In her skirt pocket was a tube of No. 2 Anti-gas Ointment. It was supposed to help burns on the face and relieve the eyes of the gas's sting, and perhaps return one's mustard gas-stolen sight, though even young Charlie was highly doubtful that any cream could actually accomplish that.

Plymouth and Cardiff had already been struck by the Luftwaffe, but not London. The city had seemed protected by some divine power that kept great metropolises from the inconvenience of wholesale destruction.

That delicate fantasy was about to come to an end.

First came the unnerving drone of plane engines as they neared Dagenham, Rainham, and Barking. Charlie would learn later there were three hundred and fifty Junkers, Heinkels, and Dorniers massed in this particular Luftwaffe fleet, escorted by six hundred fighter planes. Next came the scream of bombs, high-pitched walls of wails that brought a terror to Charlie far greater than any nightmare he'd ever endured. The target was the East End around the U-shaped bend in the Thames. Known as Silvertown, it was a collection of massive warehouses, and workers' homes, all muddled topsy-turvy together next to the labyrinth of docks that were critical to the war effort.

The Ford Motor Works was hit first, then the enormous Beckton Gasworks. The Woolwich Arsenal, the country's largest, was also struck. After that the three Royal Docks, loaded with foodstuffs, were levelled; the stench of incinerated fruits and cheeses would linger for months. Barge tethers burned away, sending the freed boats gliding down the Thames, only to return later with the tide. Barrage balloons designed to entangle German planes instead simply burst from the ensuing heat of detonations and soaring fires. As the bombs went off, the very foundations of the city seemed to vibrate as explosion after explosion produced a tsunami of terrifying sound.

Disrupted dust settled over Charlie and his family. Windows cracked, roof trusses groaned, floorboards quivered. And each subsequent blast of concussive force seemed more powerful than its predecessors. They never heard the big ack-ack guns fire back, and had no idea it was because British gunners on the ground feared they would strike their own planes in the air.

The Germans returned that night and dropped still more bombs, using the fires caused by the first attack as handy illumination for the second. Wholesale evacuations by thousands of people from the stricken East End had some dub it "Dunkirk in London."

After the all clear siren sounded around 4:30 on Sunday morning—one elongated note to distinguish it from its counterpart of short separate blasts—nearly four hundred and fifty Londoners had perished. Sixteen hundred more were seriously injured, and many would eventually die. And countless structures had been levelled, leaving the poor in the East End, who had little to begin with, with even less now.

Infernos raged along the obliterated docks as the Auxiliary Fire Services courageously battled them. The Thames became a pumping station of last resort when the hydrants ran dry. A conflagration fire meant that a hundred-plus pumps were needed to extinguish it. There were *nine* such fires that night.

The Isle of Dogs was mostly gone. Both sides of the river in the East End had been reduced to rubble. Bow Road Station no longer existed. Stepney Green looked like a blackened carpet, denuded of trees. People as far off as Reading thought they saw the sun set in the *east* that day, because the Blitz fires burned the sky just as brightly as did the descending sun.

By the end of the month more than six thousand Londoners were in premature graves. They had had ashes to ashes and dust to dust sprinkled over them by legions of religious men, who all looked stunned that their god would allow such devastation despite sincere prayers, thundering sermons, and the frenetic fingering of rosaries.

In his box in the cupboard, Charlie opened his eyes, and the sounds of death coming for them all vanished.

Gran

Right on schedule, Charlie listened to the dull dings of the battered windup alarm clock followed by the sounds of his grandmother lurching up from her hard mattress. The dings ceased, and her bare feet scuttled across the cold planks until he heard the bathroom door close. A minute after that the toilet gave a pathetic flush. Next the sink water began its feeble run.

She would dress as quickly as she could, having few items from which to choose: basically the one skirt and blouse or the spare, and the old, scruffy shoes, with the low chunk of worn heels, and stockings now so threadbare they were near transparent against her swollen, veiny calves. After that he would hear her trudge a few truncated steps to the small kitchen. The only other space was the front room, which held a chair for her, a wooden stool for Charlie, and a small square of faded Wilton rug. A chipped porcelain shepherd's lamp with precarious wiring perched on a wobbly table. On the fireplace mantel was a pair of tarnished brass candlesticks, often minus any candles; and then there was the fireplace itself, a blackened brick opening about two feet square, that rarely had anything to do.

On twin pegs hung their respective gas masks. They were two of nearly forty million handed out by a government terrified that the Germans would continue their World War I tradition of deploying mustard and other poison gas, only this time dropped from the sky. Gran used to always carry her mask, but as memories of the Blitz receded, she, like many others, left it behind more often than not. She *did* carry her ID card, as did Charlie. They had been issued by the National Registry to every person living in all of the United Kingdom, and the Isle of Man. If people were to be blown into unidentifiable pieces, perhaps this bit of paper would survive to tell folks who had perished. Only Charlie couldn't see how.

After a cup of lukewarm tea and bread with margarine and jam and perhaps a slice of fried Spam, she would be off to her job at a bakery shop one jarring bus ride away from here.

He firmly shut his eyes when she opened his door and leaned down to kiss him on the forehead, which she always managed to do despite her rheumatism. She touched his head and then brusquely cuffed him on the ear.

He sat up, annoyed. "Eh, what was *that* for, Gran?"

"Wet hair, Charlie," she exclaimed, looking very cross. "You've been out again. Tell me, and no fibs now."

"Had lice in my hair and ran the tap to get 'em out," he said defiantly.

"Lice!" she gasped. Her fingers automatically started to search his head. "I best get the Lysol then."

"It's okay, Gran. The matron at school give me somethin'."

He was pleased with this lie, since it not only explained the wet hair but also reinforced the equal untruth about his still attending school.

Her fingers left his hair as she straightened and looked down at him. "You worry me, Charlie. If only I could keep up with you. If only I weren't so . . . *old*!"

"You ain't so *very* old, Gran," he replied kindly.

"Even if we do win this bloody war, there's so much out there that can hurt you."

"I'm strong, Gran." He made a muscle with his arm.

"If you were fed proper, you'd be stronger still."

"We'll get by, Gran, we always do."

She rubbed absently at her mouth where he knew she'd recently had a tooth out. She didn't have the shillings necessary for the gas or cocaine used by the dentist to dull the pain. They pulled teeth for free so long as you could endure the trauma of having them forcibly yanked.

"You deserve proper parents, luv."

Charlie's still forming Adam's apple quivered at this unexpected comment. "Well, I ain't got none, whether I deserve 'em or not." Before she could reply to that he added, "You'll be late, Gran. And me too. Workin' on some mathe-matics at school. *Very* interestin'."

She looked him over. "You're growing ever so tall, Charlie, like your father was, while your mum was such a wee thing." She eyed the diminutive space. "This cupboard—you need something bigger."

"Why, it's more space than I know what to do with, really. And we got a kitchen, and a lav all to ourselves. We're practically rich."

"Well, you can thank your granddad for that. Many around here respected him. And we got this flat because of that respect. Your dad's people lived in Whitechapel with six families to two rooms and no lav. Lord, I don't know how they did it. Now, you're quite sure you didn't go out last night?"

The way she looked at him—a bit mournfully, he thought—took all the fun out of his lying.

He eyed her squarely. "Things are different, Gran. They just are. And we need to do what we need to do to keep goin'. And I'm almost grown now."

"No, you're still a boy, and providing for you is *my* job."

Charlie's defiant look melted into an even grimmer one. "I ain't been a boy for a long while now, Gran. And I can leave school when I turn fourteen next year."

"No, Charlie, education is too important. You need to stay in school, luv."

"We need to eat too," he replied. "And if the war keeps goin', I can join up."

"They can't conscript till you're eighteen," she countered, her expression full of dread.

"They didn't have to make Dad go, did they?" retorted Charlie, making Gran's lips quiver. "And I hear boys are fakin' their ages. They carry the rifle at seventeen, maybe sixteen. Bet we're still fightin' the Germans when I'm sixteen."

"No, Charlie. Pray to God the war's over long before then. There'll be nothing left of us. And you're all I do have left."

His expression softened and he touched her hand. "See here, Gran, the Yanks have got the Jerries on the run, ain't they?"

"Yes. The *Americans*." Her look did not seem to hold the same positive view of their chief ally as Charlie clearly did. "Well, your packed lunch is in the tin in the box, because I know they don't feed you enough at that school though they say they do. But you're getting the third of a pint of milk every day, aren't you, Charlie? They're supposed to give you *that*."

"Absolutely, Gran. It's quite delicious."

"Good, good. Now, there's some dried fruit, and a bit of marge and bread for your breakfast, and a cup of cereal with the powdered milk. And there's a little of the tinned sausage meat. Use the salt so it doesn't taste so foul."

"Yes, Gran."

"Our new ration books just came in. And the pink books' coupons look very nice indeed. There're things we can sell or trade off to folks."

"That's good."

She frowned. "The butcher says a rabbit for Christmas, but he won't look me in the eye when he says it. I might have to start breeding my own."

"The Savoy's got chickens. I seen 'em."

"I heard they had a farm outside of London where they keep their fowl, but I didn't know they kept them at the hotel, too." She shot him a sudden suspicious look. "Eh, what were you doing at the Savoy? You've no business in the West End. Like crossing a border. It's not a good place for our kind."

Charlie didn't miss a beat. "We took a school trip there."

Her doubting look deepened. "Is that where those extra eggs came from? You said I miscounted."

He stared resolutely back at her. "That would be nickin', Gran."

"Hmmm." Her expression changed. "Do you know they dance at the Savoy while the bombs drop? Got some kind of reinforced basement or what not." She suddenly smiled proudly. "But East Enders went there for lunch once and then opened their coats and showed off their 'Ration the Rich' shirts. Now that's the proper spirit. Boo-hoo to those money-bag blokes. Churchill goes there right regularly, I've read, so of course they get all they want. And movie stars stay there too. John Wayne, Frank Sinatra. *And* Clark Gable! Oh, what I would give to meet Clark Gable," she tittered, turning a bit pink before focusing back on her grandson.

"If only I could have a proper garden, Charlie. We'd have cabbages and runner beans and peas. You could pop cherry tomatoes right in your mouth. Sweet and filling, they are. Had 'em once when I went out to the country on a visit with your granddad. Here we just got the allotments and they're always taken. You'll die of old age before you get one, much less me."

"Tell me about before the war. Sometimes I forget, Gran."

This was a little ritual of theirs, and Charlie reckoned it did as much good for Gran remembering as it did for him hearing it.

She smiled warmly. "Shops full and vendors in between with their wheeled carts with lemonade, and *sandwiches*, Charlie. And the muffin man with the tray on his head. And the Indian toffee fella. And the okey-pokey gent with ice cream in the summer and chestnuts in the winter. And the pie and mash shops. You could smell the scent of fish and chips from here clear down to the Thames."

Charlie's belly gave such a rumble that Gran looked guilty.

"Well, no need to speak of what we don't have. The past is past. But our lot gets the dregs. You know what dregs are?"

He shook his head.

"Well, they're nothing much, I can tell you that. Now, I would imagine there are those who manage to get whatever they want in this city. I don't begrudge the likes of Churchill anything because the man needs to be at his best." She added huffily, "Although Winnie did tell us that the German bombs would never reach London, didn't he?" Her features softened. "Well, he was no doubt trying to build up our stiff upper lips, eh? But they say rationing is equal? Don't you believe it. Got to register our ration books at just a few shops, limits what we can get, don't it? But others drive their fancy motors and eat at the Dorchester and go to the country for '*weekends*' like there's no bloody war going on. I hope they feel some guilt in their hearts, though I don't hold out much hope for *that*. Now, you have a good day, luv, and fill up that head with knowledge at school. And no more *lice*."

She kissed him again and lumbered from the flat to catch her bus.

Memories on the Wall

Charlie lay in his box staring at the small patch of mildewed ceiling. Part of him felt bad for lying to his grandmother. The other part believed that she *knew* he was lying, so somehow that eased the deception. His gran had grown up poor in the East End, which made Charlie think that she had indeed been familiar with the workhouse howl. But she was exceptionally bright and had read many books and educated herself, Charlie's mum had told him.

"She should have been a teacher or a nurse," she had told her son.

"How come she weren't, then?" he'd asked his mother once.

"Sometimes it has nothing to do with you and what you can do, and everything to do with where you're from, Charlie."

"That ain't fair."

"No, son, it's not." She had tousled his hair and added, "And maybe the likes of you can change that one day."

Charlie had since learned that the sorts of jobs for women like his gran and mother were few in number and usually involved getting on your knees and scrubbing floors and hearths, cooking and sewing for others, or working in a bakery, greengrocer, or fish shop.

Gran had helped teach Charlie things outside of his schooling, just as she had Charlie's mother.

Helped me with my elo-cu-tion, he thought with a sudden grin. She had managed, after much work, to resettle his Cockney-subtracted *h*'s to where they needed to be, but he still had some difficulty corralling his *g*'s. His speech had got so *polished* that his East End mates had taken to asking him why he was talking so funny!

So what would he buy with his newfound wealth? He needed shoes, of course. But that would not cost anywhere near what he had. His coat was nearly done in and the cold was coming. But he didn't want to spend the money just on things he *needed*. He wanted to buy something he actually *wanted*.

He lay there half dozing for another few minutes and then rose, washed his face at the tap, pressed down his helter-skelter hair, and stepped into the kitchen. In the tin his grandmother believed would constitute some of his meal at school was a slice of day-old bread from the bake shop, a hard-boiled egg, a few chips fried in drippings, and a nodule of Government Cheddar.

He ate it all, including the cereal and tin of dried fruit, and the bread, with the smear of marge that tasted like machine oil, and the sausage with lots of salt, which wasn't rationed because people needed it to make the food taste passable. He washed it all down by putting his mouth under the tap in lieu of a cup of tea. That was strictly rationed as well, and was only to be taken at dinner, though Gran had old leaves for her morning cup.

His clothes were still wet, so he took them off along with his shoes and laid them over the back of a chair in the kitchen to dry for a bit. It was lucky that Gran had only felt his hair and not his clothes, which would have been proof positive of his night-time excursions.

Wearing only his tattered undershorts he walked into his grandmother's small bedroom and looked around. Her bed was neatly made; she did so every morning. He knew the mattress being on the floor made it hard for her to get up, with her aches and pains and rheumatic knees. But the bedframe had long since been sold to pay bills that apparently would always come due before the money was had to pay them.

She would sometimes pawn her wedding band on Monday, pay bills with the money, and then retrieve it on Friday when her wages came in. During the week he would catch her frowning and rubbing anxiously at the empty space on her finger where the ring, for many decades, represented a solemn vow to her late husband.

His grandmother had a small wardrobe and a tiny matching vanity with a mirror cracked during the Blitz. When she had come out from shelter and first seen the damage, Gran had sobbed inconsolably. Young Charlie couldn't understand why, since they were all alive, and it was only a bit of glass, and you could still see yourself just fine in the reflection. But then his mother explained that sometimes it was the small things that set people off. Charlie's mother had soon made things right, telling her mother that the crack gave the mirror *character*, and that she would be able to tell everyone later that it had proved superior to the worst the Nazis could chuck at it. His mother had always come up with sayings like that, to make folks feel better.

He looked at the single window and saw black, because even a fraction of light constituted a target for the Germans. In their old flat Gran had sewn blackout curtains. But it had been bombed, and later demolished because the structure was no longer stable. They had survived in their cupboard that night, but it had been a close thing. Now, a neighbour had just applied tar over the windows in their current building. It was effective but smelled quite awful.

Like his mother had said, it was the small things that seemed to bother folks the most. And not being able to look out a window was one of them for Charlie.

He studied the lone picture hanging on the wall and containing the images of two people. His father was a fading memory for Charlie. Robert Matters had been tall and lanky, with a long, perpetually sad face, restless eyes, and a trim moustache. Charlie could imagine his father tipping back a pint or two on a pub stool in the snug and thinking of what he wanted from life. Robert Matters had worked long hours at a physically demanding job at the docks in return for slim wages. It had always seemed to Charlie that those sorts of jobs were the only ones available to blokes from the East End. At home his father usually fell into an exhausted sleep, but he had been kind to his son, kicking a ball with him in the street, showing him how to ride a bike that he'd borrowed from a mate with a son Charlie's age, or taking him for long walks in Vicky Park, Charlie's small hand in his father's large, callused one. His father would tell him stories of his life as a kid growing up in Whitechapel, and they would sit on a bench and watch the world go by and point out funny images that the clouds made.

His father had also taken him to work on Saturdays and driven him around on a dray horse-drawn cart. He'd even shown Charlie how to manage the reins and care for the horse after its work was done. Charlie had been gobsmacked at the size of the beast as he scrubbed it down, but also at how gentle it was. His father had said the horse's name was Puff because the equine walked with its big chest puffed out. He would even ride Puff bareback around the docks. His father had told Charlie that he was a natural with horses and he might want to think along those lines when he grew to be a man. Charlie had loved those times with both his father and Puff.

Then the war had started and his father was gone along with millions of other men, many of whom never managed to make it back to British soil. And the dock where Puff had laboured was no longer there, and neither was the horse. The Germans had seen to that.

Charlie hoped they had given his father a proper Christian burial at Dunkirk. He sometimes wondered about how his father had died: bullet or bomb or knife. But when he dwelled too long on this question his insides became as squirmy as worms after a hard rain.

He next cast a furtive, anxious glance at his mother's image in the photo. Charlie had ventured out with his mother one day, and only he had eventually returned home. And though it had been more recent than his father's passing, precise recollections of her were unnervingly remote in his mind. That may have had nothing to do with memory and everything to do with sorrow.

I don't want to forget her. But it hurts so bad in rememberin' Mum 'cause I know what I lost when she died. I lost . . . everythin'.

Charlie had lived with both his grandparents after his mother was killed. Then his grandfather had died during a tragic incident at the Bethnal Green Underground Station. There had been a stampede on the stairs and bodies had fallen like tenpins and over one hundred and seventy people had been crushed to death, including his grandfather.

The loss of his grandfather had been traumatizing to Charlie because he had become a surrogate father to his grandson and Charlie knew that his grandfather also took good care of his wife.

Now Charlie tried not to think about what would happen to him when Gran died. Whenever she got the cough or wheezed too often or moved creakily he would watch her closely, and do his best to nurse her back right. He was terrified that the sun would rise one day, and his gran would not; yet he worried the same about himself.

Charlie turned away from the photograph and went to check on his clothes. He pronounced them reasonably dry, as were his too-tight shoes. He dressed and, noting that the rain had passed, he stepped briskly out into the narrow street fronting his building.

And that was when Charlie saw him, his brown hair covered by a battered felt hat. He was walking slowly along and looking up at the numbers.

It was The Book Keep's owner, I. Oliver.

Honourably Disreputable

What was the bloke doing in Bethnal Green? wondered Charlie.

If the man had walked he had got an early start since it was at least a ninety-minute trip by foot from Covent Garden to here, what with all the debris and other wartime obstacles. He couldn't possibly know where Charlie lived. He'd just got a glimpse of him. And everyone knew boys like Charlie were six a shilling in London.

Thus, he watched in growing dismay as the man halted in front of *his* building and peered up at the number.

Charlie's first inclination was to run. This was often Charlie's first impulse, because people looking for him was never good. Instead, an idea occurred to him. He reckoned he could just make it, given the slow pace of the gent. He raced around to the alley and to the fire escape. He scampered up the steps, snuck in the window, and hurried to his front door. He opened it and peered out. The hall was clear, so Charlie slipped out, fled down the hall in the opposite direction, and took up a place around the corner. He looked back to see the man clear the last riser and step into the hall.

The chap made his way along, glancing at the flat numbers as he went.

Still, Charlie thought, *He can't be here for me.*

He stopped thinking that when the gent halted in front of his door. Now Charlie's heart started to beat so rapidly he felt the rush of blood and then the throb of a pulse in his ears. His face flushed, and his breaths became shallow as his small chest heaved. For one awful moment Charlie thought helmeted and brass-buttoned constables might rush up the stairs and find and arrest him. He would be led away in shackles, with Gran somehow appearing and sobbing in his shameful wake.

The fellow—*It must be I. Oliver,* thought Charlie—rapped on the door and then waited before knocking again. When no one answered, he took something from his pocket and, using a thumbtack also taken from his pocket, stuck it to the door. Then Oliver turned and slowly left the way he had come.

Charlie had glimpsed the man's features and noted that he looked both upset and sad.

He ran to the door and saw what Oliver had tacked to the wood. Charlie lifted up his jacket and examined the lining. He saw the ends of broken thread there. What Oliver had returned was the name-and-address tag Gran had sewn into all of Charlie's few pieces of clothing. The tag had obviously fallen off in the man's shop; that was how he knew where Charlie lived. He stuck it in his pocket, his spirits sinking through his sore feet.

He knows who I am. What if he goes to the bobby on the beat?

Moments later he was out of the building and fleeing down the alley. From there it was only a short distance to a tradesman's street-level rear entrance into one of Bethnal Green's many bombed-out buildings. On the side of the partially collapsed brick wall was an advert for Chesterfield cigarettes. Charlie knew it had been put up prewar, because the elegantly dressed man in it looked too jolly.

He flung up the metal flaps of the door level with the street, then skittered down the steps after closing the metal wing flaps behind him. He pulled on the string of a solitary light bulb and his prayer was granted, for the light somehow crackled on. He sat on an old vegetable crate, with miniature spud remnants growing in its crevices.

From his pocket he slipped out the identification tag.

THE HONOURABLE CHARLES ELIAS MATTERS
FLAT 4A, 13 DAPLETON TERRACE
BETHNAL GREEN LONDON E2

He always smiled at the word "Honourable." Foremost, he was not "Honourable," either by title or nature. And he was simply Charlie, not Charles, though he knew Charles was his full given name. That was a formality, and surely everyone knew formalities had no place left in a world at war. And he was a common thief. There was nothing remotely honourable about that. Yet Gran apparently had a far higher expectation for her only grandson than Charlie had for himself.

He felt for the money in his pocket. It seemed far heavier now than when he had taken it.

With a sigh Charlie rose from his crate seat and headed back to daylight.

Though Charlie was not above thievery when necessary, he had a set of principles to which he adhered. In that spirit, there was something he needed to find out. And he set off to do just that.

The Shadow of I. Oliver

THOUGH HIS SCHOOLING HAD ended prematurely, Charlie's reading and writing skills were acceptable, even if his spelling wasn't the best. And despite their poverty, Charlie's mother had always managed to have a few books in the flat. And after she got off from work she would often take Charlie to the small library near their home, where they would sit and read together, if only to have a place with some warmth, quiet, and comfortable chairs. Afterwards, when the twilight was commencing, they would occasionally venture to a café near the library, where Charlie would have a small cup of steaming cocoa while his mother would indulge in a pot of tea. And they would split a thick buttery scone when buttery scones were still possible.

He passed where that library and café had once stood. All that was left was a pile of bricks, twisted metal, charred timbers, and the mingled smells of doused plaster and bomb particles, along with a lingering melancholy.

Charlie spotted a milkman, wearing a cream-coloured jacket and carrying his metal rack of full bottles, scampering nimbly over the wreckage with a practiced artistry. Charlie and many others felt, however improbably, that so long as the milk kept being delivered, the world was not going to end.

Across the street a woman sat on a three-legged stool painting on a large canvas the scene of destruction in front of her. Charlie learned that these folks had been hired by the government to capture the devastation for "posterity," whatever that meant. But he had to admit the artists he'd seen were quite good, even if the grim objects they painted made him quite ill.

As he kept walking, Charlie passed motorcars that jerkily dodged obstacles in their path, their exhaust pipes emitting smoky breaths. On the side of one bus was an advert for Doctor Carrot, a campaign devised by the Ministry of Food that was meant to remind folks, particularly children, to not only eat their carrots, but like them. The only time Charlie had ever heard his gran use a foul word was when they had been out walking and she had seen a sign for Doctor Carrot. She told Charlie that while she liked carrots and they *were* good for you, she didn't like the "wily" Ministry of Food trying to pull the wool over the eyes of its citizens.

"They want us to eat carrots and the like because they've muddled up the food supplies so badly, Charlie. Bungled the whole thing, so to speak. See, they don't have to bring the carrots in from somewhere else. Now, I don't mind sacrificing and we've all done our share of that, but don't lie to me. Don't treat me like I'm a damn fool. Tell me the truth, even if it does make *you* look the fool. Otherwise, we're all thinking one thing: What else are they keeping from us? Trying to make us believe everything's tickety-boo, when we all can see it's not. Do they think we're all bloody doolally? Right, Charlie?"

"Right, Gran," he had said back, as he always did after one of her little tirades against the government, particularly the Ministry of Food, a popular target of hers.

Even short journeys in the city involved detours, traffic blocks, rubble piles, and cratered streets. The walkers bested the motors pretty much every time. Up ahead he saw Oliver gliding along the pavement, as he passed a soldier guarding the personal inventory of a bombed building that had been piled on the street.

Charlie fell in behind Oliver and followed the man down one street and then another on the long walk back to Covent Garden. When Oliver turned into a narrow lane, Charlie became puzzled, because this was taking the man in a different direction from The Book Keep. Perhaps he was just combining another errand with his visit to Charlie's digs. Oliver stopped at a ragged doorway, rapped on the wood, and was admitted.

Charlie waited in hiding, and when Oliver came out, he was putting some papers in his pocket. In the opening stood the same short, squat man who had been at The Book Keep the night before.

I wonder what all that's about, thought Charlie.

As Oliver reached the main street again and turned back in the direction of Covent Garden, Charlie decided to take a shortcut, quickly making it back to the mouth of the alley where The Book Keep was located. This was possible only because the last quarter of the journey he nimbly hung on to the back of a blustery, fast-moving double-decker Covent Garden–bound bus while evading the eye and grip of the conductor, as well as other passengers, who didn't much care for those who took advantage when they had to pay the full fare.

Charlie sprinted down the alley and then stopped as he saw a slender woman, whose grey hair was curled into a bun, wielding her broom at the kerb of the shop across from The Book Keep. Over the top of her head and bolted to the wall was a sign that read THE SECRET GARDEN. Displayed in the window were teas and cakes and other things that Charlie dearly loved but could not afford.

He doffed his cap. "Hello, Miss."

She turned and eyed him with an unfriendly look. "Hello, boy."

"I was just wonderin' 'bout the gent at the bookshop there."

"What about him?"

"Tall, thin fellow with glasses? I. Oliver?"

"That's right. *Ignatius* Oliver."

"He must like books."

"I suppose he does, running a bookshop," she said condescendingly.

"Has he been here long?"

She straightened and held the broom in a defensive posture. "Why? What's it to you?" She ran her gaze over him. "Wait a mo', where are you from?"

"London."'

"Don't be daft. I meant what part."

"East of here."

She gave him a knowing look. "I thought so, though you don't exactly talk like your kind."

This ruffled Charlie. "Right, Miss, East End, part that got bombed."

"We *all* got bombed, Mister Cheeky, thank you very much." But she shivered a bit. "My younger brother worked at the docks. He was killed in the Blitz."

"Sorry to hear that," said Charlie quite sincerely.

She shivered again, and looked at the slice of sky visible in the alley. "Let's hope we never see the likes of that again."

"So, is Mr. Oliver nice, then? See, I was thinkin' 'bout askin' him for a job."

She squinted at him. "A job? You're still in school, aren't you?"

"I'm all done. Have to make my own way now."

"Then you can go work in a factory or on a farm."

"No farms round London, least that I've seen. So, *is* he a nice bloke?"

"Nice enough. I mean, he's not what you would call outgoing. But I've seen him smile now and then. Today, that counts as downright loquacious."

When Charlie looked at her funny she added, "Means 'talks a lot.' He's also one of them air raid wardens. Goes out in his tin hat, with his torch, and cape all glowing, and looks out for planes and bombs and helps folks what needs it. Takes 'em to the bomb shelters and like. Knows everybody's name hereabouts. Has to so's he can keep track of who's in the shelters and who's not. Tries to roust me every time, but I usually stay in my basement when the sirens go off. He's quite brave. Won the George Medal. Pulled some folks from a bombed building that caught fire. He's still got the burns from that. Then he managed to turn off the gas before it took the whole block out."

"How come he's not in the army? He a conchie?" asked Charlie, referring to a conscientious objector.

"He's too old." She pointed to her face. "And his eyes aren't so good. Wears the specs. But the war keeps going, they'll come for the likes of him, blind or not, I imagine. Won't be no men left here, young or old. Bloody Hitler. I know the wireless says we're winning now, and the war might be over soon, but it don't seem like it."

"Has he had the shop long?"

"Oh, it wasn't his shop."

"No?"

"No, it was . . . Oh, here he comes now."

Charlie looked to see Oliver turn down the alley. He said quickly to the woman. "I best be gettin' on."

"I thought you were going to ask about a job?"

"I am. But I need to get cleaned up first, put on my best shirt and all."

"Well, good luck, though most of us aren't hiring, I'm afraid. Few customers and not much to sell to the ones we do have. But we get by."

"And don't tell him 'bout our little talk, Miss. It might be bad luck, for *me*."

She watched curiously as Charlie flitted down the alley.

The Book Keep

Ignatius Oliver waved to the tea shop owner.

"Hello, Desdemona," he said.

"Morning, Ignatius," said Desdemona Macklin. "Where you been off to?"

"Oh, I took a walk over to Bethnal Green. Had an errand to run."

"Bethnal Green! Well, you were up and out early then. It's not half eight yet."

"Yes, it was quite early. How're the teas and cakes selling?"

"Oh, it's bloody wonderful," she said, her voice liberally doused with sarcasm. "Why, if I knew it was so good for business, I'd wish we were at war all the time."

"Well, we must do our part."

"That was a bad bit of bombing the other night," she said. "You look like you made it through all right."

He rapped his knuckles against the wooden door. "For luck," he said.

"Saw you had a late-night visitor last night."

He turned to the woman. "You did?"

"Yes, I did."

"Sharp eyes, you have," he said, unsmiling.

"Isn't that what the government tells us? Lots of dodgy things going on in wartime."

"Yes, I suppose there are."

"Funny time for a bloke to be wanting a book, considering it was after midnight. Little stout bloke. Saw you open the door for him before I nipped off to bed."

She waited for him to respond.

"Yes, well, he's a collector of sorts who came into town late, from the north. He was leaving very early this morning and last night was the only time he could meet."

"So he was after a book, then?"

"They're the only things I sell after all," he replied.

She sniffed and didn't look convinced. "Book blokes are funny, aren't they?"

"I consider myself a 'book bloke' and I'm not at all funny. Now, if you'll excuse me?"

He lifted a set of keys from his pocket, inserted one in the door, and opened it. The bell tinkled and the door closed behind him.

Charlie waited until Macklin returned to her shop and then hurried back in time to see Oliver take off his jacket, hang it on a peg, lift the hinged countertop, and disappear through the curtained doorway.

Charlie squatted there, trying to decide what to do. He could leave here and purchase himself shoes and a coat, and Gran a hat because hers was disintegrating on her head. And fresh spectacles because she told Charlie she had the cataracts. And Charlie could take her around to the pub near them and they could have a meal prepared by someone else for once.

Yet how would he explain to Gran where the paper pounds and coin had come from? Gran *was* old, and there were things he could get away with, but she wasn't stupid.

But there was one thing Charlie needed to know first, which was why he had come back here.

He slid over to the door and, wary of the tinkling bell, slowly opened it just enough to slide his nimble fingers through and stifle the ringing before it could commence.

He ventured near the till. Next to it was a framed photo he hadn't noticed the previous night. The woman pictured was quite pretty, with large, intelligent brown eyes, full lips, and an angular face, which all promised goodness in abundance, if features could actually manage that. The clothes she wore were like what Charlie's mother had worn. Oliver's wife, maybe?

There was a black gauzy material wrapped around the frame. He gingerly touched it. The correct term came to him from some distant part of his brain.

Funeral crepe.

This person had died.

He eased by the framed picture and noted the coat hanging on the peg. It was as threadbare as his. The old felt hat next to it was stained and carried several tears and holes.

Charlie felt a thickening lump form in his throat. He could sense poverty when he was looking at it. And the man had walked halfway across London to return Charlie's clothes tag, and probably enquire about his missing money and book. And he had risked his life to save others and earned the George Medal.

He slowly withdrew the pilfered paper and coins from his pocket and looked down upon them. Swimming across his mind were visions of shoes and a coat for himself, and a hat and specs for his gran, and a meal free of watery cabbage soup. They abounded in neat, linear frames of his imagination. And then, like loose sand in a tide, they were washed from his thoughts. Even thieves, at least those like Charlie, had principles. And empathy for others also badly off.

He only took from those who had spares. This man clearly did not.

Charlie placed the money next to the till and stepped away. He would have returned the biscuits, too, but he'd eaten them all. And there was also the book. He reached into his pocket and placed it next to the money.

"You weren't home earlier."

Charlie turned. Ignatius Oliver was standing in the curtained doorway.

A nimble and lightning-quick Charlie leapt to the door, his hand on the knob.

Oliver made no move to stop him; he simply glanced at the money on the counter and then looked at Charlie.

"Why?" Oliver asked.

Instead of answering, Charlie said, "So the 'I' on the glass is for Ignatius, then?"

"No, it's for Imogen," he said, surprising Charlie. "My wife. This was her shop. I—" he looked around as though seeing the space for the first time "—I was never much of a reader. I just took it over . . . when." His gaze travelled to the funeral-creped photo.

"Never knew no bloke named Ignatius."

"Saint Ignatius of Antioch. I was named for him."

"What'd he do to be a saint?" asked Charlie with genuine curiosity.

"He was fed to wild beasts as his martyrdom."

"Wild beasts! Who woulda done that?"

"People who did not agree with him. It happens, you know. Awful things occur all the time. This war is a prime example. Do you go by Charles?"

"No, just Charlie. You sell lots of books, do you?"

"Not many, no. If folks have spare shillings, it probably won't be going for books. I have sold a number of book *tokens* as part of a national scheme, so that helps. Rather good idea, actually. Yet not that many have been redeemed. I think people are rather . . . tired. But maybe that will turn around as the war continues to move in a positive direction."

"I guess your wife liked books."

"Yes, indeed. She said they were a wonderful way to get through troubling times, though my sales of late do not necessarily support that conclusion. Perhaps it's the location. This alleyway can be rather hard to find."

"*I* found it," said Charlie.

"Indeed you did." He paused and glanced at the pile of paper and coins on the counter.

"You must'a dropped it out on the street," explained Charlie. "I just found it and brought it back."

"Clumsy of me. But I can be clumsy."

Charlie looked in the direction of the drawer where Oliver had placed the packet of papers from the night before. When he looked up, Oliver was studying him closely.

Charlie said, "Heard you got the George Medal. That you're brave."

"Many people are brave. Why I got the medal over others, I'm not sure."

"For not sellin' many books, that's a lot of quid."

"That was for many months' worth of sales, I'm afraid," replied Oliver. "So not so very much." He eyed the book next to the money. "Ah, yes, I thought that was missing as well."

"It ain't got no words in it," said Charlie.

"Well, it's like a diary or a journal. My wife filled up many of them with her . . . thoughts."

Charlie spied the odd device he had seen before lying on the counter. "Eh, what's that thin'?" he asked, pointing.

Oliver picked it up. "It's a replica of Alberti's Disk. Have you heard of it?" Charlie shook his head. "Alberti was an Italian polymath from the fifteenth century."

"A polly what?"

"It means he was quite accomplished at a great many things: poetry, languages, art, architecture, and *cryptography*, of which this is an example." He held it up. "It has two concentric rings. The outer ring is imprinted with a standard alphabet, and the inner one the same, but with the letters out of normal order. When you rotate the inner ring and line it up with letters from the outer, you can create an encrypted, or secret, message."

"Why would you wanta do that?"

Oliver set the device down. "Oh, just for a bit of fun."

"I gotta go now," said Charlie.

They stood there staring at each other for a moment.

"Charlie, why don't you keep the book?"

"What?"

"Take the journal and . . . well, you can write things down in it, like my wife used to do."

"What things?"

"Imogen would describe things that she saw. A man walking. A bird on a tree branch. A pile of rubble that used to be a home. A woman bringing food to people who needed it. And then she would write down what she thought about all that."

Charlie used his sleeve to wipe his runny nose. "Is that really somethin' folks do with their time?"

"At least certain people, yes. You strike me as observant and curious. So you might find it . . . *worthwhile*, I guess is the word I'm looking for. Ironic that a bookshop owner has difficulty finding the right words."

"Bet you know a lot more words than me."

"I daresay you'll catch up and pass me. But please take the book. I have so many others, as you can see for yourself." He picked up the book and held it out to him.

Charlie came forwards and his grimy fingers closed around the journal. "Thanks."

Oliver said, "And thank you for returning the money. It's very fortunate you found it. In fact, I would imagine a finder's fee is in order."

Charlie stared at the money, but then he held up the book. "You give me this. And thanks for fetchin' my tag back. Must'a dropped it round here."

"Exactly where I found it, around here."

"Saw a short, fat bloke here. Was he buying books?"

"He was a friend with a manuscript for me to read. I'm afraid it's not very good."

"Well, goodbye," said Charlie, wondering if the same man had given Oliver another manuscript, whatever that was, earlier that morning.

"Goodbye," said Oliver, not looking pleased.

The bell tinkled freely as Charlie left Ignatius Oliver and his shop.

A moment later he slid his head back inside the door. "And I ain't bloody *honourable*."

"Well, you were today, Charlie."

A Girl Called Molly

MOLLY WAKEFIELD WALKED OUT of Liverpool Street Station and gazed around at a city she had not seen since 1939. All these years later, London was in an unrecognizable state, shocked by war, and perhaps stunned at its own resilience. You never really knew what you were capable of, Molly believed, until the moment came to be capable of it. Since leaving London, Molly had had a great deal of experience along those very lines.

She had got up especially early this morning to begin her long journey back. There were three rail stops in between the coastal village where she had been sent to live at the start of the war and her hometown of London. She should have been exhausted, but was far too excited to succumb to weariness from the long trip.

Molly had travelled to the country after the war had broken out in a scheme set up by the Ministry of Health and given the unofficial name Operation Pied Piper. Well over a million people—more than half of them children—had been evacuated to the countryside during this process, though most had returned long ago, she knew.

Molly, who would turn sixteen the following year, had not seen her family during the whole of this time. She had been smiling until the train slowed and started winding its way through the outlying suburban areas and then into London proper. All she could see were jagged remains of toppled buildings that looked like shorn and blackened fingers reaching skywards, stacks of rubble, grimy and litter-strewn streets, few cars, and anxious men and women walking with singular if cautious purpose. A twisted double-decker bus was wound around the remains of a structure whose roof was gone, its insides open to the bleak, overcast skies.

There were no cabs in line outside the train station, so she carried her cloth satchel with her as she walked down the street, hopefully in the right direction.

She saw a church with its front all gashed open, the pulpit visible from the street. Despite that, a wedding was taking place inside. Molly stopped to watch the ceremony happening amid all the chaos of war. The sight brought a hopeful smile to her face. She then left and continued her journey home.

On a side street a family of four sat on a pile of smouldering bricks. The little girl was staring at a partially crushed and singed dollhouse, which had obviously been pulled from the wreckage. Molly stopped and asked if they were all right. They looked back at her blankly and didn't respond. Molly could not know that a squadron of German Junkers and Dorniers had stolen into London during the night and reduced homes on this street into drifts of shattered building materials perched at odd angles. When she saw the smoke rising from the wreckage, Molly realized that the residual heat from the exploded bombs was the only thing keeping the now homeless family warm.

She hurried on, using various familiar landmarks as her guide. While London was the city of her birth, this was not an area in which she was all that accustomed to being. And the interceding years of devastation had severely altered how the city looked, at least to her.

A group of ragged children was gathered around a brazier in which a small fire was burning, warming themselves. They looked curiously at the primly attired Molly as she marched along, as though she were a ghost from the distant past when the world was at peace.

Sandbags were stacked all over, and it seemed every substantial building had a sign out proclaiming it as a designated public air raid shelter. The windows were uniformly painted black with scrim tape crisscrossed over the glass.

The pubs were open and doing a brisk business. Mostly old men or younger ones missing limbs and displaying medals and ribbons pinned to coats spilled into the cratered streets with their pints and pipes, gossip, and grousing.

Molly saw a troop of perspiring soldiers working hard clearing debris from the streets, their smart tunics draped over a low wall.

She passed several storefronts that had "business as usual" cards taped on window frames that no longer had any glass in them. One blackened, gutted structure, which she remembered as being a well-known emporium, had a sign out front saying it was REOPENING IN A WEEK'S TIME, NAZIS OR NO NAZIS.

There were lines of housewives in queues outside the butcher and bakery shops with their open baskets, pinched, impatient features, and short lists.

In her village, Molly had been told little of what had occurred here. But she had glimpsed snippets of wartime events in London in local newspapers. She had also heard things on the wireless in the home where she lived with her hosts, the Coopers. The BBC's news programmes also gave updates on the war. For years the prognosis for Great Britain's survival had been bleak. However, lately, the tide had seemed to turn.

The Coopers had received eight shillings and sixpence each week from her father as a billeting allowance while she stayed with them. Her father had also sent at yearly intervals fresh sets of clothing for his daughter as she had grown. The Cooper children had watched in envy as Molly had opened elaborate packages from Harrods and Selfridges filled with costly outfits Herbert Wakefield had selected for her. In turn, Molly had given her old clothes to the younger Cooper girls.

The family had treated her very well, even providing her a modest birthday party each year. Mrs. Cooper was a schoolteacher and a most capable one. Molly had been precocious from an early age, with her mother and her nanny reading with her regularly. And she had attended a private girls' school before leaving for the country. Mrs. Cooper had followed that up with a rigorous education over the course of Molly's time there, in addition to her regular schoolwork. A great many books were read, extra lessons learned, and boxes of stubby pencils used up putting both thoughts and mathematical calculations to paper. Mr. Cooper was a vicar and quite scholarly, with a well-stocked library. And he had delighted in expanding Molly's academic horizons. Being naturally bright and curious, Molly had flourished in such an environment.

The vicar's spinster sister, Eleanor Cooper, was a highly trained senior nurse. Transport ships carrying men injured in the war routinely docked at the coast two miles from Leiston, the largest town very near Molly's village. Wounded soldiers were then transported over land to the hospital facilities set up in Leiston. Eleanor had gone to one of the hospitals each day to help care for the wounded. Then, when Molly turned fourteen, she began taking the girl with her.

At first, Molly was only allowed to roll bandages, clean up sick, and help with the parcelling out of food and the cleaning of beds, laundry, and toilets. But because there was a shortage of medical staff, Eleanor began to rigorously train Molly on how to help with the wounded. Due to her age and relative inexperience, Molly was at first only allowed to help with those men who had lesser injuries. But as it became clear that, in addition to being exceptionally bright, she had a distinct aptitude for this sort of work, Molly was given a great deal more responsibility.

Part of Molly was appalled at the terrible injuries that she had witnessed and helped treat. And she had been immensely saddened by the men who had left the hospitals in makeshift coffins, and others who had gone home with fewer limbs than they had started life with. But a large part of her felt proud and fulfilled to be assisting in the war effort.

Eleanor Cooper had once told Molly that she would make a fine nurse when she grew up, to which Molly had replied, perhaps a bit immodestly, that she thought she would make a fine *doctor.* And her mentor had immediately agreed, with a sly look at her surprised ecclesiastical brother, who had been only half listening to the conversation until it had got around to Molly's liberal retort.

Molly was understandably sad to leave the Coopers, but most of her was far happier to be going back to her real family. Now, as she gazed at the rubble and blight, and at the grim, ill-clothed and too-thin figures slowly navigating through deeply stricken London, Molly sensed her high spirits at returning home dissolving.

A Brief Education

Molly passed one place where the windows were shattered and the door had been knocked down; the inside looked gutted, with tables and chairs overturned and broken up, although there was no sign of an actual bomb's having exploded there. Then she looked up and saw that someone had painted "Tally" over the name, Edoardo's Café.

Molly had no idea that "tally" was an anti-Italian slur.

She finally managed to flag down an old, puttering, stiff-bonneted black cab, and it wheeled to the kerb as the driver rolled down the window. He was grey and sallow-cheeked, and the etchings on his moustached face looked like a swarm of railway lines all coming together. He wore a pair of thick specs that unduly magnified his eyes. He had military ribbons and medals on his jacket, and painful-looking scars etched on his battered, gnarled hands, all surely from fighting in a previous war, she assumed.

"Where you headed, Miss?" he asked.

She gave him the address of her home in Chelsea and his eyebrows edged higher.

"Nice enough," he said. "You got the fare, right? I ain't workin' for free, luv."

She opened her small purse and showed him a handful of coins. "I just got off the train at Liverpool Street and walked here. I know this is sufficient to get me to where I'm going."

He harrumphed and said, "Right, Miss, just checkin'. Strange times they are."

They started off slowly and the speed never picked up.

"Where you comin' from, Miss?" he asked, giving her a look in the glass.

"Suffolk."

"What you doin' here then?"

"London is my home. I was sent to the country at the start of the war and now I'm back."

"Thought all you kiddies was long ago back," he said in surprise.

Molly's cheeks reddened. "Yes, well. I see you have medals. Was it from the last war?"

He pressed down the accelerator judiciously, no doubt conserving precious petrol, and slowly shook his head. "No, Miss. This one."

Molly looked startled. "Oh, I'm sorry, I . . . I thought."

"I've just turned thirty-four, Miss. I knows I looks a bit older. But, well, war does that to a bloke. Mustered out a year ago. Can't hold a rifle worth nothin' no more, and me eyes, well, they ain't what they used to be 'cause of a mortar round hittin' close by. Though I can sees well enough with the specs to drive in the day if I don't go too fast. And then there's me bad leg. Got metal in it. Aches with the weather, I can tell you, and walkin' ain't so easy as it once was. So's drivin' a cab is 'bout all I'm good for, Miss."

"Of course, I'm so sorry."

His wiry moustache bristled. "Not lookin' for no sympathy. I'm alive, ain't I? Many lads can't say that. I did my job, that's it. I'm alive."

He focused on his driving and they both fell silent for a bit.

"Did they really bomb the palace?" Molly asked. "I heard on the wireless that they did, but I couldn't believe it."

The driver nodded. "I was in uniform then, but my missus told me. The King and his family is fine. Just a bit of bother, really. And they're still here, waitin' it out with the rest of us."

"Well, that's a proper spirit."

"It will take more than that to beat the Jerries. It will take more men than we got and more planes and tanks and bombs and bullets, too, by God."

"Well, the Americans have been fighting with us now for several years. They actually share an air station with the RAF at Leiston near where I lived. I would see Spitfires and American Mustangs flying over the town. It made everyone feel quite hopeful."

He frowned. "Folks think the Yanks are the ticket. That we can lay down our guns and let them win it for us. Well, it'll take all of us to beat the bloody Germans, from what I seen."

"Yes, I'm sure you're right."

"So how was it in the country, Miss? Was you bombed out there?"

"We never were, although I heard that Leiston had been on several occasions. I never even heard any of the bombs strike, though. They came at night, apparently." Molly hesitated. Part of her wanted to tell him about her job helping the wounded. But she felt certain that he had seen far more horrors than she had, and had suffered a great deal. She simply added, "And I'm very glad to be home."

"And what *did* bring you back, then?" he asked.

Molly didn't know exactly how to answer that straightforward query. The fact was the billeting allowance was no longer being paid by her father. The Coopers had offered to keep her on in spite of that but, after all this time, Molly had wanted to come home. She had written to her parents with the date she was returning. Molly was worried because she had not received a reply and no one had come to greet her at Liverpool Street Station.

"It was just time, I suppose."

She sat back and wondered what would be awaiting her in Chelsea.

Mummy

From her purse Molly retrieved a letter her mother had written her. It was full of love and anticipation for her homecoming.

Dearest Molly,

Your father and I will only feel like a real family again once you are home. It still breaks my heart that we allowed you to be sent away. You know we didn't want to do it, Molly, dear, but your father said it was for the best and he's very nearly always right. Still, I can only count each minute until you arrive back safe and sound into your mummy's arms. My mind can venture to think of nothing else. Until I hold you once more and cover your sweet face with kisses,

All my love,
Mummy

Molly carefully folded the paper and slid it back into her purse. Despite the kind, loving thoughts in the letter, there was one element of it that truly disturbed Molly. The letter was from *nearly five years* before, fairly soon after Molly had left home. She had received none since from her mother, though her father had corresponded with her infrequently. In the interim, she had written to her mother whenever the Coopers had been able to buy stamps. Her mother had never once replied.

A year ago, Molly had gone into the village and called her home in London from the phone box in the square. Her father had answered, informed his daughter that her mother was resting, but that he would tell her of the call. Her father instructed her to keep up her courage, and to not be any bother for the Coopers. And then he had rung off before she could ask him why he had not brought her home after all this time.

Molly fingered the chain necklace she wore that held a locket. She took off the necklace and opened the locket, revealing a small photograph of her mother. She wondered how much she would have changed since Molly had last seen her. And clearly, she would be astonished at the change in Molly over the last five years.

She put the necklace back on as the cab turned onto a main road and drove at a sedate pace through more wreckage and ravaged streets until they reached her neighbourhood. Here, there was damage, but not nearly as much as Molly had seen previously. Still, there was a silent and omnipresent gloom in the air that she could understand if not yet fully identify with.

The cab pulled to a stop in front of a large white-painted brick two-storey home. Twin pilasters painted alabaster bracketed the eminently respectable front door with its brass knocker.

"Nice place, Miss," said the driver. "Only been to Chelsea to drop folks. No other reason to, you see."

He carried her satchel as he limped behind Molly to the front door. She was surprised that it looked shabbier and far more worn than Molly had remembered. The scratches and cracks and missing paint surely hadn't been there before. And the brass knocker, too, was not nearly as shiny as she recalled. The small patch of grass was nearly all dead, and there were no flowers in the cracked pots on the small porch. The windows were grimy and the curtains behind them appeared the same.

Yet at least the door was still there, and her home along with it. She knew there were many in Britain who could not claim that.

Molly Wakefield drew a long, excited breath.

"Here you go, Miss," said the driver, setting the satchel next to her.

As Molly turned to look at him, her gaze carried across the street. A man in a long coat and hat was staring directly at her with what seemed a strange expression. As she focused on him, he turned and hurried off.

How very odd, she thought. But maybe London had become quite odd, what with the war.

Molly turned back to the door and prepared herself for what lay on the other side.

Home Again

Molly knocked and waited, for she did not have a latchkey.

Presently, the door opened. It was not her mother or father standing there, but her old nanny, Mrs. Pride.

She looked at Molly curiously. "Yes, Miss?" As her gaze fixed on Molly something flickered behind the woman's eyes.

"Mrs. Pride, it's me, Molly. I wrote that I would be returning today."

Mrs. Pride was now close to sixty, large in stature, and respectability itself in the cut of her stiff, wide tweeds that managed to conceal any trace of female figure beneath the pleated folds. Her hair had gone white since she had come to oversee Molly, but her full cheeks still carried a robust dash of girlish pink. She looked at the young woman with a mixture of emotions that surprised Molly. Surely, she thought, happiness would be the only order of the day for her homecoming.

The next moment Mrs. Pride hugged Molly so fiercely that the girl thought she might crack. When Mrs. Pride let go Molly saw clusters of tears attached to each corner of the woman's sunken and anxious eyes.

"Molly, dear, how you've grown. Has it been years or decades, child? Come in, come in." She glanced at the driver, who stood there unsteadily on his gimpy leg; he picked up Molly's bag.

"Here, give me that, cabbie." She took the bag while Molly paid the driver.

He smiled at the generous tip and doffed his cap. "Well, good luck to you, Miss."

Molly walked in and Mrs. Pride shut the door. "Let me look at you. My goodness, you're such a young lady."

Molly stared around at a space that she had known intimately for the first decade of her life. It appeared remarkably unchanged, but as she ran her gaze around the boundaries, it did look decidedly smaller and shabbier than she remembered.

Situated against one wall next to the door were pegs to hang hats and coats with a mirror set above, and a long metal canister where walking sticks and umbrellas were collected. She picked up a hat that was hanging from a stout wooden peg.

It was her father's homburg, Molly knew. She noted several strands of grey hair clinging to the liner. This startled her because her father's hair had been a dark brown when she had left.

Years aged one, obviously. She thought of the taxi driver. *War* years accelerated all that.

Next to the hat hung a gas mask on another peg. From the size of it, she reckoned it belonged to Mrs. Pride. And of course her father would no doubt have his with him, wherever he was presently. She didn't see her mother's mask, though.

"Where is Mr. John? I thought he might pick me up at the station in the Singer."

"Well, we never did get a letter from you, dear, but that's hardly unusual. The post hasn't been what it was."

"And Mr. John?"

"He's no longer with us, dear."

"What! Is he all right?"

"Yes, yes, I'm sure that he is. But he got another position, you see."

"I'm surprised Father let him leave. He was very fond of Mr. John. And Father doesn't like to drive."

"Yes, well, everyone has had to make sacrifices," replied Mrs. Pride firmly.

Molly felt a sudden twinge of guilt for voicing concern over no longer having a driver for their luxurious car. "Yes, of course. Oh, before I forget." She reached into her purse and drew out a small pamphlet. "My ration book. You'll need that with one more mouth to feed."

Mrs. Pride took it and said, "Thank you, dear. By law the shops where you register have to stock the things you registered for, but I'm not sure the law has been round the shops lately."

"Yes, there were shortages in our village, too."

"Have you eaten, dear?" said Mrs. Pride. "I can prepare something."

Molly gaped. "*You?* Is Mrs. Brand no longer with us, either?"

"No, no she's not. She lost both her grandsons in the war, poor dear. And, well . . . working here no longer suited her."

"I'm so sorry to hear that. I remember her grandsons. They would come by sometimes when I was very little."

"Yes, yes they . . . would." Mrs. Pride's voice dropped to almost nothing.

Molly noted her distress and thought it better not to speak further of Mrs. Brand's loss. "I had some food on the trains."

"Then perhaps a cup of tea?"

"Yes, thank you." Molly looked around. "And Mother and Father?"

It took a considerable length of time for Mrs. Pride to answer this simple query. "Your father, bless him, is at work. He's at the Ministry of Food now. If we knew you were coming, of course he would have met you at the station. He'll be back in time for dinner, I'm almost sure." She wrung her hands as she said this, and didn't look remotely sure of anything.

"And Mother?"

Once more Mrs. Pride didn't respond right away. "Yes, well, actually your mum's having a bit of a lie-in. Now, you can have your tea and then we'll see what's what, shall we?"

Mrs. Pride took Molly's coat and hat and hung them up, then flitted out of the room. Molly started to follow her.

Mrs. Pride turned back and said, "I'll make the tea, dear. If you want to go to your room and put your things away? I'll be up directly with your cup."

Molly carried her bag up the stairs. Her room was on the right at the end of the hall. Her parents' room was on the left just at the head of the stairs. She eyed their door and then leaned over the stair railing. She heard the kettle clattering against the stovetop and imagined she could hear the sharp strike of the match and the whoosh of ignition as Mrs. Pride heated the water.

Molly went over to her parents' door and listened at the wood. Hearing nothing, she eased the door open and peered in, expecting to see her mother asleep. However, the bed was made and there was no one there. She looked around. The furniture was all the same, at least that she remembered. The square of rug was a bit ragged with a few odd loops of thread sticking up. She saw one of her father's coats hanging on a peg along with a set of frayed brown braces. The room held a mustiness that she had never noticed before. The light coming through the windows was weak and diffused, throwing all she saw into shadowy relief, which somehow seemed ominous to Molly.

Surely Mrs. Pride had said that her mother was having a lie-in. And where would she be doing that other than in her own bed?

Molly continued to her room, opened the door, and stood there for a few moments taking it all in. Her room was exactly as she had left it, as though time had ceased passing. Lying in the centre of her bed was one of her old dolls. And it had something in its hands. She hurried forwards and saw that it was a letter. She eagerly unfolded the crisp paper.

It was on the official letterhead of the Ministry of Food.

Dear Molly,

I wish I could have been here to see you when you arrived back from the country. I have been quite busy as of late. I will be home as soon as I can.

With affection,
Your Father

Molly recalled that her father had worked in a position that required frequent trips to the continent. Now he had apparently taken a job with the Ministry of Food, as Mrs. Pride had said.

Yet there had been one puzzling omission in his letter: There had been no mention of her mother.

And Mrs. Pride had said they hadn't received her letter. So how would her father have even known that she was coming home today?

Her head full of disquieting thoughts, Molly put the paper in her pocket as she heard the whistle of the kettle. She was still putting away the clothes from her bag when the door opened and Mrs. Pride bustled in with her tea, a small jug of milk, and a plate with two thin and cracked biscuits and a spoon.

"Here you are, dear," she said, setting the cup and plate of biscuits down on the table next to her bed and pouring the milk into the tea and spooning it around. "I can't tell you how pleased I am to have you back home, Molly. So very, very pleased. I mean, I can scarcely believe my eyes." She handed the cup to her.

Molly smiled and took a sip of her tea. "I, um, found the note from Father."

Mrs. Pride's features tensed. "Oh, yes, I suppose you did."

"I checked Mummy's room, but no one was there. You said she was having a lie-in?"

"Well, I should have told you that while she *was* having a lie-in, it wasn't here."

Molly very carefully set her cup down and, with panic rising in her, said, "Not here?"

Mrs. Pride's hand flew to her mouth and worried at it a bit with her index finger. "The truth is, dear Molly, that your mother has not been well as of late. She has left here to convalesce at another . . . place."

"Place? What place?"

"A sanatorium," she replied, her gaze now averted from the girl's.

Molly gasped. "A *sanatorium*?"

Mrs. Pride dropped her hand. "It's a place where people with unsettling troubles travel to get some peace. It's in . . . it's in Cornwall."

"Cornwall! Are there no sanatoriums in London?"

"Well, London has been right hard hit, and though they don't come every night like they used to, the Germans do still come. There was an odd bombing or two last night, in fact."

Molly felt her throat tighten. "I want to see my mummy straight away."

"Yes, I suspected you would want to do that. The fact is, Molly, your father should be the one talking to you about this."

"Is she all right, Mrs. Pride? Please tell me."

The woman finally met her gaze. "The war has been hard on all, Molly, from the King on down. But it has been far harder on some, and unfortunately, your mother is one of them."

And on that rather ominous note, Mrs. Pride fled the room.

A Glimpse During Uneasy Quiet

Molly heard Mrs. Pride take to her bed later that night. Her nanny's steady tread was still recognizable to her even after all this time away.

Molly lay in her nightclothes with the bedcovers pulled up to her neck. The fireplace yawned empty of coal or wood. And though she listened for it intently, she never once heard the latch-key followed by the creak of the front door announcing the return of her father from his official duties at the Ministry of Food. Nor had Mrs. Pride offered any explanation for his absence other than saying, "It's the war, Molly. Everyone works such long hours. Not to worry."

This was certainly not the joyful homecoming Molly had anticipated.

The long journey and accompanying fatigue finally overcame her anxiety and Molly fell asleep. Later, she awoke with a start and looked to the window. She had heard something out there, or at least she thought she had.

She rose, parted the heavy blackout curtains, and looked out. A glowing light emerged from across the street. As Molly continued to watch and her focus sharpened, she saw that it was a man with a cigarette. She kept observing, expecting to see him walk off, but he never did. He just stood there.

Was he watching their house? Of course not, she concluded.

You're imagining things, Molly. You're tired and confused and is it any wonder after the day you've had?

A moment later she sensed movement to her right. When she looked that way a lanky boy a couple of years younger than Molly appeared and secreted himself behind a small row of hedges on the Wakefields' tiny patch of dirt. Molly next turned her head to the left and saw a police motorcar pass by. The boy waited until it was gone before stepping into the open. Then he glanced upwards, and Molly saw his face. She drew back a bit because he seemed to be looking right at her. The next moment he was running off in the direction opposite of the police vehicle.

She thought, *He looks quite thin.*

As she peered at the dark sky, filled with barrage balloons, a few clouds, and the luminous moon, Molly reflected on having never heard the roar, whine, and screech as explosive-laden metal fell to earth with a gravity-fuelled fist. As she had told the cab driver earlier, she had never even heard a bomb explode. She wondered if the boy had experienced those things. He looked as though he might have.

She went back to bed, but could not sleep. She was used to complete quiet in the country, but no matter how late the hour, the great city, with some of its teeming millions scurrying on their way at odd hours, could never truly be silenced.

Molly finally sat up and made a decision. She dressed and, after checking to make sure her father was not in his bed, ventured downstairs.

She carefully opened the front door and closed it just as quietly behind her. She found the spare latchkey where it had always been kept—under the statue of a mournful cocker spaniel with a cracked right paw that sat at indifferent attention on the top step. She had not thought to use this key when she had come home, but rather had wanted to knock on the door and see the happy faces of her mother and father when they appeared. At least that had been her plan, a dashed one now.

After locking the front door, Molly looked around and wondered how she would get to where she needed to go. She had no idea where the Ministry of Food even was. She of course knew where the nearby Downing Street was. But that was where the prime minister worked. Then there was Whitehall. That might be a possibility, since lots of government types laboured there.

She knew London well, at least certain parts. Before she'd been sent to the country Molly had gone on a great many picnics with her parents. They had either walked with their basket or else been driven by Mr. John in the well-appointed Singer. They had gone to Regent's Park and also to nearby St. James's, Green, and Hyde Parks. She especially loved the Serpentine in Hyde Park, the "upside-down tree," and all the beautiful statuary. Then there had been boat rides on the Thames, visits to the British Museum, plays in the West End, concerts at the Royal Albert Hall, and chocolates and teas at Fortnum & Mason in Piccadilly. And, of course, there was Harrods, where one could purchase positively anything. Much to her poor mother's horror, Molly had become lost for a time in the labyrinth of the store when she'd just topped five years old, and had thought it quite the best adventure of her young life. And there had been lunches at Claridge's in Mayfair, with broad, colourful hats and frilly frocks and vast stacks of delectable delicacies served by the most professional of staff.

Thus, she knew London. The amusing parts. The expensive parts. But as she looked doubtfully up and down her street in Chelsea, she began to feel that such a London no longer existed. This place, this world, had surely been transformed over the years she had been gone.

And so must I be, thought Molly with some trepidation.

Boy Meets Girl

"Hullo?" she said suddenly, having just now spotted him once more, lurking this time behind a sickly, leaning maple instead of a hedge.

The same boy turned to stare at her.

"Hullo," Charlie Matters said back.

"Why are you hiding behind that tree?"

"Just takin' a rest," said Charlie, stuffing his grimy hands into his dirtier pockets.

"Come now, were you hiding from that police motorcar that passed by earlier? Are you in trouble?"

He looked her up and down and came away annoyed. "Just out for a stroll. No law against that. And if I find somethin' along the way, what business is that of anybody 'cept me?"

She looked over his thin frame and shoddy clothes, and her expression softened. "I could provide some food for you."

Charlie took a hand from his pocket and waved this offer away. "I don't take charity."

"But it would be no trouble. I live right here." She pointed to the door of her home.

Charlie looked up at the tall white brick face. "What, you mean in all 'a it?"

Her eyes narrowed at his very odd query. "I don't understand. In all of what?"

He pointed at her home. "I mean do you live in all 'a it or just one of them rooms?"

"Well, I have my own bedroom, but my parents own the whole house."

"Blimey, you must be rich then, Miss."

Molly blinked. "What's your name?" she asked.

"Charlie."

"Charlie what?"

"Charlie Matters."

Molly glanced across the street. She didn't see the man who had been smoking earlier. But part of the darkness seemed a shade darker, as though someone . . . Her gaze dropped to Charlie's right hand, where there was a long, reddened cut.

"That's infected," she admonished. "You need to wash it thoroughly with soap and then apply topical medicine and cover it with a bandage."

"Why, I've had worse'n that," scoffed Charlie.

"I have experience with such things and I'm telling you that it *is* infected. You don't want it to turn into septicaemia."

"Septi-what?"

"Septicaemia. It's an infection of bacteria in your bloodstream. That bacteria can then be swiftly carried over your entire body from within. You can actually die from blood poisoning."

Charlie now stared down at the cut with interest. "How d'you know stuff like that?"

"I just *do*. Now, were you hiding from the constables because you've stolen something?"

Charlie frowned under this interrogation. "Look here, what's *your* name?"

"Molly Wakefield."

"So why are you standin' outside your house when you should be in bed, eh?"

"I'm not sure that's any of your business," she replied primly. "But never mind that. My father works at the Ministry of Food. Do you know where that might be? I would like to go there. It might be in Whitehall, but I'm not at all certain."

A bemused Charlie said, "So there really is such a thin'?"

"What thing?"

"A Min-stry of Food."

"Well, people *do* need *food*."

"But if there's a bloody min-stry of it, then *where's* the food got to? You sees my point?"

"You shouldn't say 'bloody.' It's coarse and disrespectful, especially in the presence of a lady," she added firmly.

"I beg pardon. But I'm not the only one wonderin' 'bout the food, I can tell you that."

"Well, I *am* sorry. Where do you live?"

"Nowhere's near here and I'll leave it at that."

"Well, if you can take me to the Ministry of Food, I can give you something in return."

"Somethin' like what?" he said, now clearly intrigued.

Molly withdrew from her coat pocket a coin. "This."

"What's that, a farthin'?" he said in a deprecating tone. "I daresay my time's worth more'n that."

"Does this *look* like a farthing?"

Charlie peered more closely. "A half crown! Where'd you get it?" he demanded. "Did you steal it?"

"Of course not! My parents gave it to me for emergencies when I left here."

"Left?"

"To go to the country. But I never had an emergency where I was sent to live."

"You left before the bombs, then?" he asked.

She nodded. "Yes. Did you?"

He shook his head. "Mum wouldn't put me on the train. Wanted me to stay with her," he added with a touch of defiance.

Molly's face went pink. "I see" was all she could think to say. She held up the coin. "So, can you take me to the Ministry of Food? I suppose they have an office in London."

"Surely you know where it is if your father works there?"

Molly started to shake her head, but then something occurred to her. She took out the letter her father had left. The address was right there at the top of the stationery. She silently chided herself for not thinking of this before. She held it out for him to see.

Charlie read off the address under the illumination of the moonlight.

"Do you know where it is?" she asked.

He nodded. "But it's quite a ways off, Miss."

"You needn't call me Miss. I'm simply Molly. And it doesn't matter to me how far it is. Can we get there somehow? We used to have a driver, Mr. John, but he's no longer with us. And I obviously can't drive our car."

"What kinda car is it?" Charlie asked quite eagerly.

"A Singer."

"You mean one of them big'uns with the long bonnet?"

"It *is* quite large, yes," replied Molly.

"You say it's yours?" he said.

"Well, it belongs to my father. It's in the garage behind the house."

"Well, then there's no doubt a'tall, is there?"

"About what?" she asked.

"That you're rich."

"Well then," she said. "Take me there and the money is yours." She suddenly looked at him warily. "But I know London well enough to figure out if you're taking me to the wrong place." Her eyes narrowed and her jaw set firm. "And you won't be able to take the money from me by force, I can assure you. I'm older than you and quite strong."

"I never would do such a thin'," said a shocked Charlie.

She replaced the coin in her pocket and eyed him expectantly. "Well then, how can we travel there? I've never been on the Underground. How about that as a way?"

Charlie gaped. "What, never on the Underground?"

Molly now looked embarrassed. "My parents preferred the car, you see. And my mother didn't care for being . . . down there with so many people."

"Fact is, most stations close after 'bout nine or so. Last trains leave and folks settle in for the night in case the Germans come. But there's a bus stop not too far off that goes near where your dad works. It's a shillin' each."

Molly pulled from her other pocket two coins.

"You got money in all them pockets?" said Charlie.

"Shall we?" replied Molly.

A Trip Taken

As they paid their fare and received their tickets and boarded the double-decker bus, the grey-whiskered uniformed conductor looked suspiciously at the pair.

"Here now, what you two be doin' out at this hour? Should be home in yer beds, eh? Where yer parents, eh? You think I'm daft and ain't notice, eh?"

Molly seemed frozen by his aggressive attention. Charlie, though, was not at a loss.

"Our mum's charrin' at the Min-stry of Food office. We're goin' to help her. Got her dinner in me pocket." He added, with a sly glance at Molly, "'cause they ain't got no food at the Min-stry of Food. *Eh!*"

The conductor snorted at this comment as he poured out a cup of tea from a dented metal thermos. He gazed at the unkempt Charlie and then eyed the properly attired Molly. He said to Charlie, "Now *you* look you got the char ma, but not her. Think yer having me on, boy? You sure you two even got the same ma?"

"Ain't think we don't know our own mum?" said a seemingly outraged Charlie.

"Oi, which one of you's older, then? Tell me that, you young scamp!"

"We're ruddy twins," replied Charlie. "Who got the coins to ride this here bus, right?" This was directed at the young, female driver, who nodded and told her colleague to stand down.

The beaten conductor turned away, took his seat near the front, and quietly sipped his tea as the bus pulled off.

Charlie and Molly sat side by side while tired-looking people sat all around them. However, one young man in a sailor's uniform and what was likely his girlfriend were energetically kissing. Molly primly looked away.

"How long a ride is it?" she asked.

"A bit," replied Charlie, scratching his cheek. "Make sure you don't lose that coin now."

"I've got it right here in my pocket," she replied firmly.

"So why didn't your dad come home?"

"He works very long hours. His job is very important. As you know, it deals with getting food to folks who need it."

"Bloke needs to work harder, then," said Charlie as he tipped his cap lower over his eyes.

The bus bumped slowly along, and it seemed to Molly that they could have travelled far more swiftly on foot. They passed through several stops where people got on or got off, and never once did Charlie stir. Finally, he lifted his cap and said, "This here's our stop."

As they alighted onto the pavement, Molly said, "Are you sure? I'll be very cross if this isn't the right place."

"This way," said Charlie confidently.

They walked down one street, made a diagonal through another intersection, and wandered over to a broad thoroughfare that was dimly lighted.

"I think we're lost," said an angry Molly, coming to a stop because Charlie had halted.

"Look at the street name on that buildin'," he instructed.

When she did so, Molly knew that he was right. "Oh, I see. Now we just have to look at numbers, of course."

"It's that one," said Charlie, pointing at a flat-faced, sad-looking building with dark windows. They walked over to it.

"You're very quick to spot things," said Molly.

"Blokes like me got to."

"Do you ride the bus a lot? I thought that would be expensive."

"It is if you pays for it. The buildin's dark. You sure your dad's here?"

She knocked on the door three separate times, but no one came.

Molly frowned. "It might be that my father has already headed home. We might have passed him, do you see?"

Charlie scratched his chin and nodded half-heartedly. "S'pose," he said.

She took out the coin and held it up. "But you still earned your wage," she said.

Charlie looked at the half crown and his fingers rubbed together in anticipation of seizing it. But his hand stayed by his side.

"Well, take it," urged Molly. "It's yours now."

"How do you figger to get back?" he asked.

"The bus, of course," she said. "I have more coins. We just reverse course. Well, *I* do. I've no idea where you might be going."

He shook his head and pointed at another clock tower. "Don't think so, seein' as how we were on the last bus to come through here tonight."

Molly whirled round to look. "Then what do I do? I have to return home."

"We can walk," opined Charlie, looking down at her fine, buckled shoes with a doubtful expression. "Though they don't look too good for walkin'."

"Your shoes don't look so comfortable, either," countered Molly.

"They ain't. They pinch somethin' fierce."

"Well then?" she said.

"We can take 'em off."

"That is quite ridiculous. I have *stockings* on. They'd be absolutely ruined. So I cannot countenance your suggestion."

"Now, don't take this the wrong way, Miss, but you sound quite educated."

"I *have* received a very good education. And I have also read a great many books, which is like receiving another education in itself."

"I know a place with lots of books."

"Where?"

"The Book Keep, down an alley in Covent Garden. It's got a green awnin'. Man called Ignatius Oliver is the owner. He's named after a saint that got et up by wild beasts. Least that's what he says. Bit of a strange bloke, he is. The shop's over near St. Saviour's School. Do you know it?"

"I know Covent Garden, of course. We used to do some shopping there."

"But books won't help you get home," he said crisply.

"Do you have another idea?"

Charlie glanced over her shoulder. "That."

She turned to look at the bicycle leaning against a lamp-post.

"What about it?"

"It's the way you get back home."

"But it doesn't belong to me."

"Oh, we'd just be borrowin' it. We'll ride it to your place, see, and then I'll come back here with it, all in a jiffy."

"But then how will you get home after that?"

In answer, he pointed at his feet. "With these. Only a few miles. I've walked a lot farther'n that."

"But the bicycle, isn't that stealing?" she said apprehensively.

"It's stealin' only if you don't brin' it back. And I figure whoever left it there done it so's if another fellow comes along and needed a ride somewheres he'd have one. See how it's not even locked up or nothin'?"

She looked at the bike and back at him. "But how can we *both* ride it? It only has one seat!"

"Me on the pedals and you on the handlebars."

"The handlebars!" said a shocked Molly. "I'm wearing a dress."

"Well, okay, you can do the pedals and me on the bars."

"No, we'd crash. I . . . I, you see, I never learned to ride a bicycle. Father didn't think it important, and the family I stayed with didn't have one."

"Then better me on the pedals and you on the bars."

They set off and Charlie kept to the middle of the road and tried his best to avoid the numerous holes so as not to jostle Molly too much.

In what felt like a fairly short period of time they pulled to a stop in front of Molly's home. His feet planted firmly on the pavement, Charlie clutched the handrail of her front steps and held the bike steady so Molly could safely dismount.

She turned to him and once more held out the coin.

He eyed it again, his top row of teeth clenching over his bottom lip. "Better you hang on to it," he said at last.

"Why?"

"It might come in handy, even for rich folk like you."

Before she could say anything, he had whipped his wheels around and was pedalling furiously down the cobbles.

"What a very unusual boy," she said to herself.

Molly used her latchkey to enter the house. She quickly saw that they had not passed her father after all. His coat and hat were not where they should have been, and when she peeked into his room, he was not in his bed. She even called out to him in the toilet.

Her thoughts had then turned from her absent father to Charlie Matters. She had been fortunate to run into him. Yet she doubted she would ever see him again. It was just not likely in such a large city where there were many such boys.

And with that thought she undressed and climbed under the covers.

Not realizing how very wrong about that she was.

A Decision Made

The rain pitter-pattered against the window as Charlie slowly ate his tinned meat along with a small carrot and half a boiled potato. His gran looked over at him as she used the last of the ration butter mixed with margarine and a bit of beef drippings to dab on a chunk of stale bread she'd brought home. She cut it in two and passed the far larger portion to Charlie.

He noted this act of kindness, but it didn't make him feel any better. He said, "Gran, you needn't always do that."

"Young gentlemen need their nourishment, Charlie. Though who could call *this* a proper meal? They cut the weekly bacon from four to three and the cooking fat by half. I've got a full pound of sugar on both our ration books and what do I get? Two ounces. Not enough to make your lips pucker. And *your* book is due a packet of dried eggs and three ounces of cheese, but the shops don't have them, do they? Why, it's been so long since I've had a proper bacon butty, I wouldn't know it if I smelled it. And mind you I haven't seen an onion at the greengrocers since 1940. And I think I'd faint dead away if I ever laid eyes on a banana or an orange, the latter of which apparently comes from the Yanks, who I don't consider all that reliable."

"Yes, Gran." Charlie heard this diatribe at pretty much every meal.

She then smiled and looked pleased about something. "Now, I've saved up enough, and in a week or so, Charlie, we're going to the canteen at the church hall. A nice meal we'll have with a pudding and custard after."

Charlie looked chuffed by this. "That's amazin', Gran."

Her smile broadened. "And later this week I'm picking up a meat pie from the chippie."

"A meat pie?" repeated Charlie, who thought that life was finally starting to look up.

"From the chippie, yes. Fish and chips used to be just what our kind ate, now the uppity in Kensington and Mayfair eat it, too." She beamed. "Even saw a photo of the King having a bite of one, off the newspaper and all. But we were ahead of them, Charlie. We knew it was good before they did, right?"

"Right."

"And the royal family have the same ration books we do. Think about that. Shared sacrifice, it is. Though their digs at the Palace are a bit nicer than ours." She tittered at her little joke. "Blitz Spirit they call it, though that was years ago; feels more like a century. Blighty Blitz Spirit I call it. But good thing they feed you some at school in addition to your tin. Otherwise I'd be even more worried about you."

Charlie did not bat an eye. "I get more than I need. It's very good, too."

"Why, that's so fine to hear, Charlie."

The light sputtered and then went out, casting them into darkness, but neither reacted to that. Gas and electricity had been rationed since 1942 and quite often their building went dark. That's why Gran kept a torch on the table. She turned it on and they continued their meal.

Two minutes later the power returned and Gran started up again, as though she needed proper lighting to vent her complaints.

"I mean, shelves as empty as if they'd been robbed. It's a scandal! Why, I had more nourishment from a jar of fish paste when I was your age than I get from a full meal today. Shippams was the paste I liked, but your granddad swore by Bovril. Now let's hope to heaven they're feeding the poor soldiers better than this. We're all doing our bit to fight the Huns, mind you, but for the love of God can't we have something that tastes good? And if Lord Woolton of the high and mighty Ministry of Food lectures us one more time about how we should be delighted with nibbling carrots like rabbits, well, I might forget I'm a lady and tell that man a thing or two. A right old bust-up we'd have."

"On the way home from school, I met a girl whose dad works at the Min-stry of Food," said Charlie.

"A girl whose father works at a ministry goes to *your* school?" Gran said in disbelief.

"No, I just met her on the *way* home. She was with her mum. They were . . . givin' clothes at the shop. 'Cause they got so much extra stuff."

"Well, it's so nice to see people giving a toss. I hope you told her so," said Gran.

"I did, Gran. So I guess the Min-stry of Food is quite big?"

"Oh, 'tis. They also do the rationing books and the 'cooking programmes.'" She rolled her eyes. "Oh yes, like I have time in the middle of the day to motor over to Harrods for a two-hour cooking demonstration on *legumes*. The nutters! Bloody codswallop if you ask me. And they say one packet of dried eggs comes up to an even dozen of the real thing. Well, maybe it does, but it surely doesn't taste like eggs to me. And then you got to have something to mix 'em with, Charlie. And well, you mix 'em with *powdered* milk. Powder this and powder that and what's in the blooming powder?" She pointed her fork at him. "Did you know that Lord Woolton says sausages must contain at least ten per cent meat? *Ten per cent*, Charlie! Well, the question is, what's the other nine-tenths, eh? Tell me that and you're smarter than I am, because I haven't found one ruddy bloke in all of the East End who can answer that."

"Yes, Gran."

"Oh, they *minister* things all right. Paper shuffling and official regulations and lots of tut-tutting. And mind you they have secret warehouses full of food spread all over Britain in case of invasion. Well, the Huns aren't coming, are they? So I says, give us the food. But no, they won't do that, will they? If you can muddle that bit out, then Bob's your uncle."

Charlie helped her with the few dishes. Afterwards, Gran made them two cups of weak loose tea, and they settled in the front room. The fireplace held only woebegone howls of the wind and the idle drips of rain coming through their cracked chimney pot.

"Now, Mr. Abernathy did promise more coal," Gran said, her tone frustrated. "But I suppose it hasn't come in yet. And my old bones tell me this coming winter will be a positive corker. Chills already set in, least with me, but I'm old as Methuselah."

Off this remark Charlie produced two lumps of coal from his pockets.

"Where on earth?" she began when she saw them. "Charlie!"

Charlie set about to turn the lumps to heat in their small fireplace opening. "Fell off a lorry," he explained. "And I was there when they did."

"Didn't the driver want them back?"

"Bloke didn't notice. I yelled and yelled but he must'a been deaf or somethin'. Lot of that goin' round what with the bombs and all."

Charlie had actually stolen the lumps after using his metal tool to defeat a lock on a door where the coal was stored. The two pieces were all that would fit in his pockets. He breathed life into the small flames with a pair of bellows and his gran drew closer to the hearth.

"Damp gets in your bones, don'it, Charlie?"

He rubbed his hands together near the bluish flames. Their chimney flue had never worked properly, but he didn't mind the smoke collecting around the room and settling over him, though it did make him hungry. Well, just about everything made him hungry.

"I . . . found somethin' the other day, Gran."

She put down her tea, picked up her ball of yarn and needles, and took up working on what would be a winter sweater for him, if the yarn and her rheumatic fingers held out.

"Found something? What would that be, I wonder."

Charlie took out the book and held it up to her.

"The pages are empty," he said.

She laid aside her clacking needles and took up the book. "You said you found it? Where?"

"Down an alley. I was taking a shortcut to school," he added quickly. As a rule, his grandmother did not care for him being in alleyways.

She flipped through the pages. "What are you going to do with it?"

Charlie shrugged. "Could sell it. Folks want paper."

"So, you don't want to keep it, then?"

He scrunched up his bony face. "Keep it? What for?"

She eyed him suspiciously. "Hang on a tick, your schoolwork requires no writing?"

Charlie had been ready for that one. "They give us copy books, Gran. You got to use *theirs*, see?"

She looked at him frowning. "Oh, I see, yes, indeed I do." She handed the book back and picked up her knitting once more.

"I'm all knackered, Gran, goin' to bed," he announced with a yawn.

She immediately looked at the small windup clock on the mantel that matched the one in her bedroom, and then glanced in surprise at her grandson. She put a hand to his forehead. "You feeling poorly, Charlie? You do look a bit peaky, luv."

"Just tired. Tired in the *head*. Mathe-matics," he added with feigned fatigue.

And with this final lie of the night he went to his cupboard and lay down in his small box after closing the door so that it was very dark. His fingers skimmed the edges of the book. He hadn't a pencil or a pen, though he might be able to pinch one. Yet what would be the point of writing things in it? He set the book on the floor and deliberately faced away from it.

He would sell the book. Paper was useless to him. But coins weren't. As he had told Molly Wakefield, they could come in quite handy. And with that thought he focused fully on the girl. Charlie had been out trying to pinch some useful things when he had run into her.

Like a hunter who expanded his range when game became scarce, one had to go to the part of the city that crowned kings and queens to get the good stuff. Chelsea was a long trip for him from Bethnal Green, but he had perched on the back of a late-night lorry, hopping off when it slowed to make a turn when he neared his destination. That had led him to Molly's street, and yet he had ultimately come home mostly empty-handed. A lock had been too difficult, a window a bit too high, a pair of suspicious eyes a tad too watchful.

As he drifted off to sleep the rain started to bucket down. In the receding mists of consciousness, he thought that at least the Germans wouldn't bomb them in such poor weather.

Charlie always prayed for the worst possible inclemency. Nothing terrified him and the rest of London more than a clear, windless night.

Lonzo & Eddie

The kiss on his forehead told Charlie that Gran was off to work. A couple hours later he blinked himself awake and slowly sat up. As usual, he had slept in his clothes for the added warmth. He rose, washed his face at the tap, tamped down his hair, and ate his breakfast and the contents of his lunch tin for his first meal with no idea or prospects for his second. Later, he set off with the book tucked into his coat pocket.

He had no more reached the next street over when he heard the gleeful voice.

"Why, 'tis Charlie Matters, ain'it?"

Charlie turned to see the two boys heading his way.

Lonzo Rossi was a half foot taller than Charlie and nearly three years older. His face was long and narrow, but his nose was wide and short and held a pair of aggressive nostrils.

It was Lonzo who had spoken. He was always the first to speak of the pair.

Eddie Gray was shorter than the lanky Charlie, though he was much the same age as Lonzo. Charlie suspected that Eddie was tougher than his larger friend by half again.

Eddie also had the more interesting face: thick eyebrows and long, upturned lashes, deep-set brooding eyes, and a grim mouth. Eddie never said much, but one tended to listen when he did venture to speak.

Charlie got along fine with Eddie.

No one really got along with Lonzo.

"'aven't seen you since you went lookin' for *shoes*," continued a smiling Lonzo as the pair came to a stop in front of Charlie.

Both were dressed as he was: hand-me-down trousers, shirt, coat, cap, and shoes that were always too small. Yet while his gran kept Charlie reasonably clean—she required that he take a hot bath each Saturday night and regularly clipped his fingernails—no one in Lonzo's or Eddie's lives had ever seemed to do the same for them.

They, too, had been orphaned. Lonzo had eventually been heaved from his third family and Eddie his fourth. It wasn't necessarily anything they did, Charlie knew. It was called *war nerve*. As boys got older and ate more and required fresh clothing as arms and legs grew, it got to be beyond the pocketbooks of most. They were then chucked out in favour of the legal offspring.

Both boys now lived in a burned-out shell of a building, hunting and scraping for what they needed to survive. And while doing so they had to stay one delicate step ahead of both the bobbies on the beat and the orphanage folks. The latter would dearly love to catch the pair both for the government pence and also for the perceived good deed of taking hooligans off the streets.

Lonzo gazed down at Charlie's small slipshod shoes, his wide grin displaying nearly all of his irregularly placed and yellowed teeth.

"Well?" said Lonzo, as Eddie hovered next to him, his intense eyes threatening to swallow Charlie whole. "See you got them same shoes on your feet. So, what gives, eh?"

"I got the money," said Charlie.

"Liar," bellowed Lonzo. "And we know that door was double-locked and them windows barred, right, Eddie? See, Eddie already tried his pick on the second lock and it ain't budged. And Eddie's way better at pickin' locks than you are. Right, Eddie?"

Smiling, he nudged Eddie's arm, but his partner just kept peering at Charlie.

"I *got* the money," said Charlie stubbornly. "And bought *this* with it."

He held up the journal.

"You spent shillin's on *that*," Lonzo barked. "Are you daft or—"

Eddie interrupted. "What's it a book of?"

Lonzo snatched it from Charlie's grasp and flipped through the blank pages before tossing it back.

"Why there ain't a single word in it." He added spitefully, "You're barkin', you are. Does your gran know you wasted money on nothin', you prat?"

Charlie put the book in his pocket and started to walk on until Lonzo halted him with a hand on his shoulder.

"Where you think you're goin'?"

"I got business to tend to."

Lonzo snorted. "What *business* you got?"

"I'm goin' to sell the book, that's what," Charlie replied.

Lonzo looked at him incredulously. "Who would pay for a book with nothin' in it?" he said derisively.

Eddie answered. "For the paper. People need paper."

Charlie nodded, while Lonzo suddenly looked interested.

Eddie said, "How much you think you can get for it?"

Charlie shrugged. "Hopin' for maybe a quid."

"A quid!" exclaimed Lonzo. "For *that*?"

"I gotta go," said Charlie. When he glimpsed a certain look in Lonzo's eyes that Charlie had seen before, he took off running.

"Oi," cried out Lonzo. "We want a word with you. We *knows* you're lyin' 'bout—"

They started to run after him.

"You come back here," screamed Lonzo. "We knows what you really done that night—"

Charlie heard nothing else because with his long legs he was exceptionally fast, even in bad shoes, and he had turned a corner and fled down the pavement. He entered an alley that was a shortcut to the next street, and looked back, but they had given up the chase.

Okay, now to business.

Satan Dwellers

As Charlie walked down the street the city slowly awoke. The rain had stopped, but the blackened, scudding clouds and screaming wind threatened more inclemency.

Charlie muddled through in his mind what Lonzo had said. *They know I was lying? They know what I really did that night?*

He had no idea what Lonzo meant by that.

Charlie refocused on the task at hand. He had never really tried to sell anything before. He nicked things he or his gran needed; he didn't part with things. But he'd told Lonzo and Eddie he was going to sell the book, so he had no choice.

He passed through one distinctive part of the city and then another. Charlie had found that London was like a large puzzle where every piece was completely different from its neighbours, at least in some ways. The farther he ventured west the more affluent and posh the surroundings became. He gazed at shop windows as he went by. Some were closed; others were just opening for business. Windows were being cleaned, doorways swept, awnings wiped down. Deliveries were occurring, though even here the supplies he saw coming off the trucks were meagre. Yet he appreciated that folks were trying their best to keep things as normal as possible when life was anything but that.

There was a mobile canteen usually set up on the next street over, he knew. They came to bombed-out areas and set up shop at regular mealtimes. They fed both citizens and rescue workers.

Charlie made this detour, helped the women to pass out food, did a bit of sweeping and wiping up, and was rewarded with a cup of powdered milk, brown toast with a smear of marmalade, and Spam masquerading as sausage. Charlie didn't mind. He actually quite liked Spam.

"Now don't drop none 'a that on the pavement, boy," the canteen lady had warned him. "If a bird comes along and steals it away a constable could put you in the clink for feeding a poor animal *human* food."

"Is that really true?" asked a clearly disbelieving Charlie.

"I'd like to say it's just a bad joke, lad, but 'tis the law all right."

Careful to not drop even a crumb while he ate, Charlie returned to his journey. His book *would* make a fine ledger. Perhaps at a counting house of some kind. Charlie had heard his gran use that term. What they "counted" there Charlie did not know.

A column of uniformed schoolchildren passed him with their tall, officious teacher leading the pack. Charlie eyed the students, who were not much younger than he was. When Charlie noted the teacher staring suspiciously at him, he tugged his cap down, tried to appear taller and bigger than he was, and hurried on. You could leave school at fourteen, but Charlie wasn't quite there yet. And Gran would probably need to sign something and he doubted she would because education was important to her. But schooling could come in many different ways, he believed. And living by your wits and skills was one of them.

At Trafalgar Square, in the centre of London, he passed a monument on a long pillar of stone with a man in archaic garb at the very top, and four huge lion statues at the bottom. The stone chap was an old war hero in His Majesty's Navy or some such, Charlie recalled hearing. Like St. Saviour's and St. Paul's, how the bombs had missed him, Charlie didn't know.

As he stepped gingerly over and around rubble that lay in piles throughout the city, Charlie heard the clang of a fire engine bell and the accompanying screech of tyres. It was coming closer, its sound painfully loud. It would have been terrifying had Charlie not heard it so many times before. Indeed, he was sometimes startled when he *didn't* hear it. At least the air raid sirens weren't bellowing. *Those* still scared him.

He came to an abrupt stop as a tall, burly constable stepped in his way, arms spread wide, blocking Charlie and several people behind him from proceeding on the pavement.

"What's the trouble, Constable?" asked a man in a wrinkled suit and bowler hat and carrying a battered leather satchel.

"Just stay where you are till I says otherwise," replied the officer dutifully, his helmet strap wedged under his pointy chin.

Charlie peered past the bobby to see the fire engine navigate the corner just up ahead. He turned to go back the other way and had gone about twenty paces when he heard it.

"It's probably 'nother 'a them *UXBs*."

Charlie looked down to see a bedraggled man sitting on the pavement against a crumbling wall of brick. In front of him was a small glass cup of matchsticks set next to a tin cup with a few coins in it. He was wild-eyed and bushy-haired with a long, unruly beard.

Charlie knew that the man was a person of the pavements. There were many of them, and Charlie also knew he was perilously close to becoming one himself.

"A what?" said Charlie.

"UXBs, boy. An *unexploded bomb*," said the creature in a hoarse whisper.

Charlie nodded. There were many of those around here, he knew, half sunk in the streets or in the sides of buildings, or, even more dangerous, hidden entirely from view.

"You know how far down Satan dwells, lad?" he said.

Charlie blinked, shook his head, and slowly edged away from the man.

"Sixty-four feet, six inches."

"How's that?" said a startled Charlie.

"Jerry bomb named Satan. Thirteen and a half feet long, 'tis. Damn thing burrows down sixty-four feet, six inches. Makes a crater big enough to fit two bloody double-decker buses, it does. We got it out, though, yes we did."

"*You* did?"

The creature looked past Charlie, perhaps all the way back to the Blitz. In a calmer voice he said, "Was with the Royal Engineers, back then. Bomb disposal. Tricky business. Delayed fuses, photoelectric cells, booby traps. Most bombs go in at an eighty-degree angle. Burrows down only twelve feet or so, but not the Satan. It goes down over five times deeper. Then you dig, that's the hardest part 'cause digging can make vibrations and that can make the bomb go off. Can't think about it too much. Dead before you know it anyways, so what's the bother? The Jerries, they were cunning, give 'em that. But we outsmarted 'em." He paused and patted his upper thighs.

Charlie could then see that there were no legs below them. He next noted the square board and attached wheels the man was sitting on.

"Till a bomb hit East Ham but didn't go off," the man continued in a more subdued tone. "Sent us in to defuse it. But it blew up while we was working on it. Jerry got three of us that day. And half 'a me. Only reason I'm still here is I went to get some water for my mates. Blew when I was coming back."

Charlie mumbled, "I'm sorry," but the man waved this off.

"No rules to war, though they lie and say there is." He looked Charlie up and down. "I bet your dad is fighting, eh, lad?"

"Dunkirk" was all Charlie said.

The man's expression dimmed with this response. "Aye." He looked at the journal in Charlie's hand. "Is that a proper book, with words in it and all?" he said in wonder.

Charlie shook his head. He opened it so the man could see. "I'm lookin' to sell it," he said, eyeing the few coins in the cup.

The man stroked his filthy beard. "Got no use for it, then?"

"Got more use for money," replied Charlie, still staring at the coins in the cup.

"Don't we all," said the man. "But don't look at me cup of coins. Got none to spare. But *they* use quite a lot of paper."

"Who does?"

The man pointed across the street. "*Them.*"

Charlie looked that way. It was a brick building stained dark with time and war. There was one wooden front door painted the red of the telephone boxes. Next to it were windows with black shutters. There was a brass plate set on the brick next to the door. Charlie couldn't make it out from here.

"King & Chauncey, Solicitors," said the pavement man helpfully.

"What's a so-lis-tor?" asked Charlie.

"For His Majesty's fine court 'a law," said the man. "Barristers do the talking in court. But the solicitors, well, they write all legal things up, see? Wills and deeds and the like. *Paper*, lad. Loads of it, they need. You go there to sell your book and a fine price you should name, too. Pen and paper over bombs and bullets."

Charlie thanked the man and rushed across the street, dodging a motorcar, a jerky bus, and finally a dray horse pulling a cart of milk cans along with a sleepy driver.

King & Chauncey

Charlie buttoned his patched coat, removed his cap and smoothed down his hair, used spit to clean the dirt off his face, wiped his hands on his trousers, and knocked smartly on the wood. He leapt back when the door was instantly wrenched open by a tall, thin, severe-looking woman dressed in starched collars and cuffs that looked as stiff as she did. A monocle was inserted into one eye, the red ribbon attached to it pinned to her milky white blouse.

"Yes?" she said quite aggressively, eyeing him with disdain. "We do *not* encourage visitors without an appointment, young man."

The way she looked at him clearly said that it would be impossible for Charlie to have an appointment at King & Chauncey, Solicitors.

Charlie held up the book. "Got this to sell, Miss. Paper. *Blank* paper. That, um, gent over there said you used paper. So's . . ."

The woman looked over Charlie's shoulder at the pavement man who was busy handing out matches to a well-dressed man for a half-penny in return.

"Oh, he did, did he?"

"He did," replied Charlie. "And there's not enough paper. Rationin'. Quite awful, 'tis."

The monocle lost a bit of its aggressiveness. "Do you know that authors are having to wait years to get their books published for lack of paper on which to print them?" she said. "When more books should be read during a war than at any other time. How terrible is that, young man?"

"Now that's a real shame."

"Let me see it," she demanded.

Charlie handed it to her and she flipped through all of the pages, seemingly to make sure they were indeed blank. She passed it back.

"Come," she said, turning sideways and motioning Charlie in.

Charlie followed the woman down a broad hallway that was well lighted with both electrical lamps and flickering wall candles. The smell of a wood fire reached Charlie's nostrils, and he wondered where they'd got the timber. That was even scarcer in London than the coal.

He grew more comfortable as he looked around at the plush interior. His belly was reasonably full thanks to the canteen lady, and good prospects seemed to inflate with each step he took. The idea of a single quid was pushed to the back of his head. He reckoned these people might actually have *pounds* to spend on fine paper such as his. And wouldn't it be sound justice if his boast to Lonzo turned out to be more than true?

She led him to a room with a desk, sturdy shelves full of weighty volumes and packets of papers with red ribbons around them, and wood-backed chairs with striped, cushioned seats. A painting of a bridge hung on one wallpapered wall. A cheery fire burned in the fireplace. Charlie took all this in and then glanced at the woman, who was watching him closely.

"Nice place, Miss," said Charlie.

"Thank you." She pointed to a chair for him to sit in. Charlie took off his cap, brushed off the grimy seat of his trousers, and sat while she settled in behind the desk.

She looked at Charlie and he stared back at her.

"So, are you King or Chauncey, Miss?" he asked in his politest voice.

She seemed startled, and perhaps pleased, by this query. "I'm neither. Mr. King and Mr. Chauncey are both elsewhere today. They are solicitors. My name is Virginia Woodley, and I assist them."

Charlie nodded. "This solicitin' bit seems to pay quite well."

"It takes years and years of rigorous education to become one."

Charlie's face fell. He reckoned there had to be some catch.

"And what is *your* name, young man?"

Charlie started to answer, but then thought for a moment. "The Honourable Charles E. Matters, Miss."

Her eyebrows knitted and then proceeded to hike up her long forehead like a building lift in motion. "And where did you get the book, Mr. Matters?"

"Didn't nick it, if that's what you're thinkin'. Someone give it to me."

She ran her monocle over his unkempt appearance. "You're certain? Because I will absolutely not entertain the purchase of stolen goods."

Charlie never broke eye contact. "It was given me," he said.

"By whom?"

"Why's that matter?"

"Things like that simply do."

"Ignatius Oliver, who owns The Book Keep over by St. Saviour's School. He was the bloke what give it to me."

She gazed at him wide-eyed. "You most assuredly do not attend St. Saviour's?"

"I most 'ssuredly does not, Miss."

For a moment Charlie thought her twitching lips might lift into a smile, but they didn't quite manage it.

"And why would he give you the book?"

Charlie shrugged. "He . . . he said his wife used to write down . . . thin's in hers. And he supposed I might like to do that, too."

"Then why are you here attempting to sell it?"

"'Cause I could use the money more than I can the writin' down what I'm thinkin' and such. I doubt it's worth the bother."

She gazed uncomfortably over his tattered clothes and thin frame. "How much, then?"

Charlie bit his lip. "I was thinkin' five quid, but for you I'll let it go for only two."

"And why give me such a *bargain*?" she asked with suspicion.

He decided to simply tell the truth. "'Cause we been havin' a nice talk and all. It's warm in here," he added. "And this chair's the softest I ever sat in. These thin's count with me, Miss."

She placed her hands in front of her, but did not look unduly put off by the stated amount. "All right. But two pounds is still quite a lot of money."

"Well, it won't all go to me."

"Oh?"

"Yeah, the bloke across the street told me about you, so I figures he deserves a tanner. He helped take care 'a the bombs till his legs got blown off down East Ham way. And Gran needs a hat and specs. Then some of it would go for some shoes and a coat for me, if I can find 'em at the right price, or if I can find 'em a'tall. Anythin' left over, well, my gran, she likes a puddin' sometimes."

"Your 'gran'? Do you live with her?"

Charlie nodded.

"And your parents?"

Charlie shrugged. "Just got me gran."

She cleared her throat and without looking at him said, "I think *five* pounds is the going rate for a book such as this. It *is* quite a large amount of paper. Let me just nip off and see to it."

As she rose, Virginia Woodley dabbed at her eyes with a handkerchief pulled from her cuff. As she started to pass by him Charlie said firmly, "There's no need for pity, Miss. Lots of folks worse off'n me. I got Gran, and a roof."

"Of course, Mr. Matters. And may I say that St. Saviour's probably doesn't deserve a fine lad like you."

She patted him kindly on the shoulder and then hurried off.

Charlie continued to sit in the chair and look around the room.

If such a place as this existed here amid all the loss and rubble, then perhaps one day they could all put the war behind them and push on to better times. It was a nice thought at least.

His gaze settled on the book. It was no longer paper stitched together with a leather hide. It was five pounds! He flipped through the pages, and as he did so Charlie suddenly didn't simply see blank pages anymore. He wasn't exactly sure what he was seeing, perhaps possibilities of an unforeseen or even unknowable kind.

The prospects that lay with five pounds were quite clear enough: hat and specs for Gran, coat and shoes for him, and a tanner or two to the tin cup bloke, with perhaps a bit left over for the pudding.

And on the other side of the ledger? Invisible things. Wispy phantoms of the mind, even.

Charlie leapt from the chair, sprinted down the fine hall, and was out the front door before Miss Virginia Woodley ever came back with the fiver.

Independence Day

"I . . . I CAN'T THINK WHAT happened," said Mrs. Pride. "Perhaps your father had to travel out of town? And he obviously doesn't know that you're home, or else I'm sure he would have written or phoned. And I don't know how to reach him."

Molly stared at Mrs. Pride as though she were deliberately speaking in a foreign tongue. They were in the kitchen, and Mrs. Pride had just set down a plate of breakfast and a cup of powdered milk in front of Molly.

And by the woman's helpless expression it seemed to Molly that her nanny knew this farce had to end sooner rather than later.

She added nervously, perhaps reacting to the stony look on Molly's face, "Now, I know you must be disappointed and frustrated. I would be if I were you. But the war has . . . has changed so much."

"Granted, but I've been home now for well over a week and I still haven't seen him once. I'm beginning to believe that, like Mother, he no longer lives here."

"This is his *home*, Molly," Mrs. Pride retorted indignantly.

"Then you would think he would actually make *use* of it," she snapped back.

"As I said, the . . . the war has changed many things."

"Where does he work?"

Mrs. Pride smiled anxiously. "I told you that, Molly."

"Yes, yes, I know, the Ministry of Food, but *where* exactly?"

"Oh, I'm not sure. Many different offices and the like, I suppose. That's why I have no way to contact him. It's quite large. I would imagine all the ministries are enormous. Look at the Exchequer. Or the Ministry of Pensions." She added in a huff, "Though I doubt there's many about anymore with pensions. Hold on to one's wages with both hands, I say."

"But what about Mummy? I want to see her. Today."

"I expect you do. But she's in Cornwall and we can't just nip off to Cornwall, can we? Now, eat your breakfast before it gets cold. There're many hereabouts who don't bother to sit at the table because there's nothing *to* eat once they get there."

A clearly flustered Mrs. Pride bustled off before Molly could ask another question.

Molly looked at her plate of food. There was one powdered egg, a single slice of brown toast with a dollop of margarine, a tiny slice of some sort of meat, and a morsel of cheddar.

She buttered the toast, ate it and the egg and meat and cheese, and drank her powdered milk, which tasted nothing like actual milk. Once she was done, she felt something she never had experienced before coming home: hunger.

This also made her think of Charlie Matters. He might be one that didn't sit at the table because there was nothing to eat, as Mrs. Pride had said. The coin that still rested in her pocket? He really had earned it, and perhaps he could use it to buy some food. But she had no idea where he lived. Or whom he lived with. Maybe no one. The war had turned many children into orphans.

And at least right now I apparently have no mother and father, either.

She took out the half crown and fingered it. Then she put on her hat, coat, and gloves, and told Mrs. Pride that she was going for a walk.

"Do you think that wise?" her old nanny said.

"I think it wiser than waiting here for my father *not* to show up."

"Molly, dear, I really must protest."

"Yes, Mrs. Pride, I imagine you must. Goodbye."

Molly closed the door behind her, gave a sweeping look around, and got her bearings. She was heading to Covent Garden. It wasn't that far, and it was a lovely morning with no bombs falling. And, she mused, during a world war, why waste such a glorious opportunity for some adventure?

A First Lie

On her way Molly passed the enormous Hyde Park on her left and the much smaller Green Park on her right with the Palace to the south-east. The quite fashionable areas of Mayfair and Soho were ahead of her along Piccadilly. Covent Garden was off the Strand to the east of Soho.

As she walked along, the city was coming fully awake. The sky was clear, and the rising sun was already lending warmth to the chilly air. Along the way she stopped and asked people if they had heard of The Book Keep in Covent Garden. No one had. Perhaps there was no such bookshop. Charlie Matters might be far too glib than was good for him. And that glibness might cost him a half crown, she thought.

When in the country she had walked miles at a time, but doing so here, she had to admit, was different. There were more people to dodge, as well as rubble to bypass or climb over, and there were motorcars, bicycles, buses, and the occasional horse-drawn cart to look out for, as they occasionally left the roadway and invaded the pavement.

As she widened her search and trekked towards the Thames, Molly stopped at one corner near the Savoy, where she had taken tea, and also had a dress fitted at a shop on the short drive into the hotel. Now it looked gloomy and barren, though there was a suited doorman in front and a few cabs were idling at the hotel entrance. A large wall had been erected that blocked the view to the river. And there were sandbags stacked everywhere. She supposed it must have to do with protecting the hotel against bombs. Molly didn't know that directly below the hotel was an air raid shelter exclusively for the Savoy's guests that was quite luxurious and unlike any shelter most Londoners would flee to when the bombs came calling.

As she turned back around, she noticed a two-door Riley with a pair of men inside parked across the street. There was nothing unusual in that. But what *was* odd was that Molly was certain she had seen the same car with the same two men across the street from her house as she had stepped out that morning.

Either I'm quite going mad, or I'm being followed.

When the car abruptly pulled off, she decided, as before, that she was simply unsettled by her current plight and was thinking nonsense. She refocused on her mission, determined to see it through to a successful conclusion, as she had tried to do with all her endeavours. Molly had always been an exemplary student. Her mother had told her that she could grow up to be anything she wanted. Her father had said the same, so long as it was a teacher or perhaps a secretary to a powerful man. And, of course, there was the inevitable marriage to just the right sort. But Molly wanted to go to university. Which made her think of something that Charlie had mentioned that might aid Molly in her search.

St. Saviour's School. Surely someone would know where *that* was. And indeed, one gentleman she encountered did. He graciously tipped his hat, stroked his respectable moustache, and volunteered that he had been a student there himself, before telling her the way. Although he seemed puzzled at her query, since St. Saviour's School, as he informed her, was only for males.

"My brother," said Molly. "I'm meeting him there."

The man smiled and said, "Ah, well then," before gliding away.

Well, that was the first lie I ever told.

And Molly was surprised at how satisfying it had felt to carry it off.

She hurried off in the direction of St. Saviour's but never arrived there. As she was passing the mouth of an alley, she happened to look down it and saw the green awning that Charlie had described. Now, to be fair, she knew there were a great many green awnings in the city. She rushed down that way and gave an exclamation of pleasant surprise—like one does when one receives the actual present one wanted for a birthday instead of the gift the giver *believed* the person wanted.

THE BOOK KEEP
I. OLIVER, PROPRIETRESS

There it was, plain as the day. And that meant Charlie had not lied to her, which made Molly feel quite comforted. But she was also confused.

Proprietress? Surely Charlie had said . . .

When she peered through the dirty glass and saw the jumble of books, Molly was immediately taken aback. She had been in many London bookshops, and none had looked like this. Had the war simply changed everything? She hoped not. There were standards, after all, that should be observed.

As he had put her on the train to the country, her father had warned her, "Anarchy must be avoided at all costs." The Germans preach about efficiency and method, he had said. This pertained to their trains, their uniforms, even their Blitzkrieg, which Molly had understood to be war in a hurry against a far weaker foe. But what the Nazis really wanted, according to her father, was anarchy. Anarchy of the *soul*, he had further explained, which was the very worst anarchy of all. And then he had kissed her on both tear-stained cheeks, patted her head, smoothed down her braids, and seen her off. That was the last time she had ever been with her beloved father.

Her mother had been too distressed at Molly's leaving to accompany them to the train station. And that was probably a good thing. There were so many mums and dads saying goodbye to so many children with identification labels pinned to their coats, and gas masks in hand and small bags over quivering shoulders holding all that they possessed. It was a necessary flight of innocents from coming evil, to be sure, but certainly one of the saddest in all of history.

She opened the door to the shop, the bell tinkled appreciatively, and Molly entered The Book Keep of I. Oliver, with the unwieldy comingling of trepidation and hope in her heart.

A Second Visitor

Molly took a few moments to look around and concluded that her second impression of the shop differed from her first. Yes, it was cluttered, but it was jumbled like one's mind was when one had too much to think about. That was not always a bad thing, was it? She actually found herself smiling as she took in the swollen shelves and the teetering towers.

The next moment the curtain parted and there he was.

"Yes, Miss, may I help you?"

He looked kind and eager and not remotely like the "strange bloke" Charlie had described.

She began crisply, "You are Ignatius Oliver?"

"I am."

"I understand that you know a boy named Charlie Matters?"

He lifted the hinged countertop and came to stand next to her.

"I *do* know him. May I ask the reasons behind your enquiry?"

"He helped me do something and I promised to pay him. But then he was off before I could. I was hoping that you could tell me where he lived, so I could follow through with my pledge of compensation."

Oliver took off his specs, cleaned them on his sleeve, and

replaced them. "I could see why that would be a predicament for you, Miss . . . ?"

"Molly Wakefield."

"And your home is in London?" he asked.

"Chelsea."

"Yes, of course."

She frowned at his words. "What do you mean by that?"

"Just that it's a fashionable area, and you yourself are clearly fashionable."

"I suppose," she replied, looking down at her very proper and expensive clothing.

"Charlie is a good lad."

With a sideways glance at Oliver, she said, "From the looks of it the war has not been kind to him."

"As it has not been kind to many."

"That's why I want to pay him what I owe. It was a half crown." She took it from her pocket and held it out.

"That is a small fortune these days to someone like Charlie," said Oliver, admiring its shine. "And do you live with your parents?"

She frowned again, and decided to answer less than truthfully. "I live with my mother and father and my nanny."

"Your parents are well?"

"My father works very long hours. The Ministry of Food," she added, as though that would explain all.

"And your mother?"

"Is a bit under the weather," Molly replied cautiously.

"As many of us are."

"Is it just you here, then?" she asked, deciding to learn some things about the man.

"Yes."

Molly glanced around and saw the photo of the woman with the funeral crepe. "Is that . . . ?"

"My late wife. As I told Charlie, this was her shop."

"Ah, that's why it says 'proprietress' on the glass," noted Molly.

"Yes, the *I* stands for 'Imogen.' After she died, I took over running it. I haven't done such a good job, and the war certainly has not helped."

"I'm sorry about your wife. May I ask what happened to her?"

"The war happened to her, unfortunately." He followed her gaze as it swept across the shop. "I see you are an avid reader," he noted.

"How did you know that?" she asked in surprise.

"The eyes of a bibliophile are competent guides. They essentially sparkle when they alight upon books, as do a gourmand's when he samples a chef's fine creations, or those of a wine connoisseur when he is presented with a row of dusty Bordeaux bottles."

"Do *you* read a great many books?"

"Imogen read positively everything. And she would tell me about all that she read, in the greatest detail. She would also read aloud to me, in the most vivid voices. So, through her, I guess I am remarkably well-read, yes."

"I *do* love to read books. And you evidently have a great many here."

"With little organization, I'm afraid. This was Imogen's doing. I like to be a bit more orderly. But do you know what she once said?" he added eagerly.

"Tell me."

"If you know where everything is, there is never a sense of surprise or discovery, which she believed were the most delightful sensations. Hence, the jumble here. It allows people to be freed from their areas of comfort, I suppose." He eyed her nervously. "Am I rambling on?"

"No, not a'tall. I agree with getting out of one's comfortable surroundings and discovering new things. I mean, isn't that what life is for?"

"Undoubtedly."

"Getting back to Charlie, do you have his address?"

He took up a fat pen and wrote something down on a slip of paper and handed it to her.

Molly gazed down at the writing:

The Honourable Charles Elias Matters, Flat 4a,
13 Dapleton Terrace, Bethnal Green, London E2

"I understand that Bethnal Green has been badly damaged by the bombings."

"Yes. The whole of the East End was heavily targeted during the Blitz," noted Oliver.

"At least the bombing is not so bad as it was. I heard that on the wireless."

"But the planes do still come. And people still lose loved ones. And along with them, perhaps they lose hope as well."

"Charlie seems to have hope," said Molly.

"I think Charlie has more hope than anyone."

"Do you know him well, then?"

"Some people you can read more easily than others. But you also said just now that you *heard* of the bombings lessening on the *wireless*?"

Molly explained, "I was residing in a small village in Suffolk very near the water. I was sent there during the evacuation scheme. I'm just back." When he looked puzzled, she added, "I know most have long since returned, but . . . but my circumstances were a bit . . . different."

"As you say," he replied graciously.

She gazed around at the wealth of books once more.

He said, "Please, set forth and discover. Imogen always said that there can never be too much reading of books. It's like saying that too much bracing air to breathe is a problem."

"I *will* take a look around, thank you."

"And now, would you like a cup of tea and a piece of toast with Golden Shred? I had just put the kettle on. I know tea in the morning is not condoned by the Ministry of Food, but I have quite a lot of it. We purchased it *before* rationing," he quickly added. "So I don't believe I am breaking any laws, at least in spirit."

"No, you needn't—" Molly paused as her belly rumbled. "Well, toast and a cup of tea would be wonderful. Thank you. And how do you know Charlie again?"

"Well, he dropped by one night."

"One *night*?"

"Yes, you may have noticed that he quite likes the night-time."

"I *have* noticed that."

He disappeared behind the curtain, leaving Molly to browse.

She slowly made her way around the place, turning books over, flipping through pages, reading snatches here and there, and twice reciting out loud a particular passage.

She eyed a stout wooden door down a short flight of steps. She went to it and turned the knob, but it was locked. She ventured back to the main floor of the shop and recommenced her wanderings. A book finally seized her attention.

When Oliver came back in with the tea and toast she said, "I'll take this one." She held it up. "How much is it?"

"My gift to you, Miss Wakefield."

"No, really, that isn't necessary."

"Oh, but you came here with good intentions for another. So please, it would make me quite happy."

"Well, thank you." She pointed to the locked door. "What's in there?"

"A special room," he said. "For special moments in time."

"So, you have books in there, and such?"

"And such."

"It's a Jane Austen," she said, holding up the book once more.

He handed her the tea and plate of toast, then squinted at the cover. "Ah, *Mansfield Park*."

She nodded. "I've read several of her others. I think she's quite good."

As Molly drank her tea and munched on the toast and marmalade, she said, "While I believe I understand Austen's intended irony, I do not care to endlessly speculate about whom I shall marry one day."

"I think as you grow older the sharpness of her wit, the refreshing satiric quality of her barbs, and the sophistication of her underlying meanings will impress you far more. And I think you will find some commonality with *this* particular story, since, as you are just back in London, it deals with a young lady in unfamiliar territory."

"So, you've read it?" said Molly.

"Imogen read it to me. She had of course already read them all herself."

"What, all these books?" Molly said in amazement.

"As she said, what else does one do with books besides read them and then wonder about what one has just read? And, even more pleasurably, what one will read *next*?"

"Well, she was the proprietress of a bookshop, so she could *sell* them."

"Ah, and Imogen was very keen on this. She said, 'Without reading them first how shall I decide what is worthy to sell and what is not?'"

Molly thought about this. "She makes a fair point."

"I always thought so," said Oliver—a bit sadly, concluded Molly, who also thought it a little disturbing that the man seemed only to echo his wife's philosophy of life rather than espouse his own. Perhaps Charlie had been correct that Mr. Oliver was a *strange bloke*.

"Then I shall visit Charlie and make the required payment."

"Is that the only reason you seek him out? To pay him his wage?" asked Oliver.

"Well, no, not the only reason. I think . . . we could be friends."

"I believe you may well be right about that."

"He looks like he might need a friend, actually," noted Molly, glancing at Oliver hopefully.

"And if you permit me to say so, I think you may as well."

"Thank you, Mr. Oliver. I hope that we shall meet again."

"I am almost always here."

She turned to the door but then looked back at him and held up the paper with Charlie's name and address. "Why do you refer to Charlie as 'Honourable'?"

"Because he has the potential to be," replied Oliver. "As do we all."

A Small Knifepoint in Time

After a filling supper at the church hall where Charlie devoured a custard tart and had a spoonful of Gran's pudding, they walked back to their flat. Gran had been strangely reserved during the special meal, so Charlie knew that something was amiss.

Gran led Charlie into the front room and asked him to sit down. She would not meet his eye, which made Charlie fear what she was about to tell him.

She placed an aged hand on one of his bony knees. "There's no easy way to say this, Charlie."

"Are you s-sick, G-Gran?" he stammered.

"What? No, Charlie, no. I'm fine, luv. But there *is* some . . . bad news. The thing is, the bake shop hasn't been doing a'tall well. Can't get enough to sell and when we do, folks don't have the money to pay for it. And while I wasn't made redundant or anything, my wages, well, my wages have been cut in half."

"What does that mean?" said Charlie, though he knew it could mean nothing good.

"Well, for one thing it means we can't stay here. We're going to have to move."

"Move where?" asked Charlie with dread in his tone.

"Well, I haven't quite figured that out yet. I only learned of all this today. But people will help us, Charlie, I'm sure of it. And I think there is a ministry to assist folks with housing and the like. Now, we might have to go to a place where we'll have to share with others, but there'll be a roof over our heads. I'm sure we'll be fine."

"How much would it cost to stay here?"

She blanched. "Charlie, this is my problem to figure out and I will. Now, you just go off to bed and get a good night's sleep. Things will look better in the morning."

Gran rose and lumbered to her room while he hurried to his cupboard and lay in his box thinking all of this through and settling on a plan.

He didn't even wait until Gran was asleep. He rose, exited quietly out the window, and skittered down the alley. He needed to get some money and do so quickly. His plan was to go to Molly's house and see if she could give him the half crown. That was bound to help Gran. He hoped it wasn't too late for him to visit her.

When he turned the corner, he stopped when he saw Lonzo and Eddie standing there. Lonzo had the butt of a cigarette in his mouth; thin wisps of smoke rose off it to join the fog that clustered around them, blurring their images.

A few moments later Lonzo ground the finished cigarette into the pavement with the heel of his thirdhand boot. His hands in his pockets, he stared at Charlie.

"We 'eard 'bout yer gran. Got her wages cut. What you gonna do?"

"I'm goin' to get some money."

"How?" This came from Eddie.

"Dunno yet," Charlie lied. He didn't want Lonzo anywhere near Molly Wakefield.

Lonzo stepped forwards. "Thin' is, we seen you go to that bookshop 'cause we followed you to the school." He poked a finger into Charlie's slender chest. "We tried tellin' you that the other day, but you run off, didn't you? And then we followed you the next mornin' and seen you give back the quid to that bloke. Are you barmy or what?"

A thin line of sweat broke over Charlie's forehead despite the chill.

"It was a lot 'a money, Charlie," added Eddie. "Nuff to help yer gran."

"And help *us*, mate," said Lonzo with a malicious grin.

Charlie backed away and shook his head.

Lonzo took out something from his pocket. Charlie saw that it was Lonzo's flick-knife. He opened it to reveal a small, lethal blade. "Now, your gran's a nice old biddy, ain't she, Charlie? Shame if somethin' happened to her."

A furious Charlie leapt forwards to attack Lonzo. But Eddie grabbed him and held him tightly while Lonzo edged the blade against Charlie's quivering neck.

"So we're all goin' to get the money you took back to that bloke. Then we splits it, three ways, all fair, like we always done. 'Cause you ain't one to let the side down, are you, Charlie?"

Charlie struggled against Eddie's grip, but the older boy's strength was greater than Charlie's.

"Don't be daft, Charlie," urged Eddie breathlessly. "He won't even miss it."

"He will," exclaimed Charlie. "He don't got much."

Lonzo said, "Well, he's got mor'n we got. So let's go."

Charlie finally burst free from Eddie's grasp. "I won't help you do it."

"Okay," said Lonzo, folding up his blade. "We'll go and you get nothin'. But if the bloke tries and stops us . . . ? Well, he's goin' to get cut, ain't he?"

Thinking quickly, a desperate Charlie said, "Okay, I'll go with you. We can get in and out without him even knowin'."

Lonzo grabbed Charlie's arm. "Let's go."

The Parting of Death

After hitching a ride on a lorry making deliveries and helping the driver unload boxes of produce at a warehouse near Covent Garden, they reached the alley and Charlie saw the green awning. He prayed that the door would be locked. When they got there, the light was off, and the door was indeed secured, and the blackout curtains drawn.

However, Eddie pulled his lockpick from his pocket and began to work away on this problem, while Lonzo kept a tight grip on Charlie's arm. He bent low and whispered, "When Eddie gets that door open, you go in, all quiet-like, get the quid and brin' it 'ere, you got that? No tricks." Lonzo held up his knife.

Charlie nodded.

However, when the door would not yield, Lonzo barked, "Oi, what gives?"

Eddie said, "Dunno. Got the lock open, but 'e must 'ave it latched on the inside."

"Well, I ain't goin' off empty-'anded after we come all this way!"

Lonzo shoved Eddie aside and put his shoulder against the door, once and then twice and then a third time. The wood cracked and the door popped free.

"Oi," the voice called out as the beam from the torch fell upon them.

The copper was at the mouth of the alley. "You lads hold up right there."

He started to run towards them.

The trio of boys did not hold up right there. They sprinted in the other direction, just as they had done in all encounters with the police.

When the constable passed by The Book Keep's window the light inside came on, and Oliver appeared in his robe and pyjamas from behind the curtain. He spotted the damaged and partially opened door, flipped up the hinged countertop, and ran to the entrance. He looked down the darkened alley in time to see the backs of the constable and the three boys in full flight.

"Stop!" called out the officer. "You boys stop. Or it'll go hard with you."

They burst from the alley with the swift-footed Charlie in the lead, Lonzo right behind, and the shorter-legged Eddie bringing up the rear.

When they reached the street, Charlie shot across it, and Lonzo did so a moment later. They both looked back when they heard the squeal of wheels, the gnashing of brakes, the blaring of a horn, and, more distressing, the impact of flesh against metal. And, most horrifying of all, the screams.

The lorry had slammed into the constable right as he reached Eddie, hurling his body a good ten feet in the air. He landed with a sickening thud. Eddie had seen the truck coming and had ducked down; the lorry's wheel rolled over his head.

Charlie had stopped so fast that Lonzo ran into him. They went down in a tangle of arms and legs. Charlie saw that the constable and Eddie were lying in the street a good many feet apart; both were motionless, their blood staining the road. The driver of the lorry climbed out and looked at the bodies with a dazed expression.

Charlie got to his feet and cried out, "Eddie!"

He was about to go back when Lonzo violently grabbed his arm. "No, Charlie. We got to run for it."

"We got to go back," protested Charlie.

"We go back there they'll put us in prison for sure."

"But—"

Lonzo pulled his knife. "I'll gut you right 'ere. And then I'll do your gran. Now move!"

"Hey, you there, you come back here," the lorry driver, a bearded, beefy man, called out when he spotted them.

Charlie turned and sprinted away with Lonzo right behind. They ran for what seemed miles through much of sleeping London. Finally, they stopped, bent low, and gasped for breath. When Lonzo straightened he said haltingly, "You . . . you reckon Eddie . . . ?"

Charlie said breathlessly, "I . . . I don't think it's good. I . . . I think he's . . ."

"Shit." Tough Lonzo looked to Charlie like he might start to weep.

Charlie understood this. Eddie was all Lonzo had.

Lonzo looked angrily at Charlie. "This is your damn fault."

"It was *your* idea to go there, Lonzo."

"But if you 'adn't been so *stupid* as to brin' the quid back," he snarled in his misery. "And a copper done for on top'it. That's . . . that's a bloody 'angin' job."

Charlie had not considered this. "They won't hang us, Lonzo. We ain't old enough."

"You stupid git! We're just a pair of East End blokes, not worth nothin'." He grabbed Charlie's arm. "You keep your mouth shut, you 'ear me? You say one bleedin' word 'a this, I'll cut you up *and* your gran, too. I swear it on me mum's grave."

"I ain't sayin' nothin', Lonzo. I don't want to hang."

"You better not." He let go, turned, and disappeared into the night.

Charlie, his limbs all still quivering, swiftly made his way back to Bethnal Green.

When he returned to his flat he opened Gran's door and stood there staring at her lying on her mattress for the longest time. An image flashed through his mind of Lonzo breaking into their home, his knife raised, Gran screaming, and the blade coming down . . .

Trembling with fear and shock, he fled to his cupboard. He lay there fully dressed, his mind full of a darkness far blacker than the tar on the windows.

Eddie was dead. And a copper, too. A *hanging* job. What they had done tonight was a hanging job, thought Charlie.

His eyes were still open when Gran rose in the morning and kissed him goodbye. He leapt up and followed her, making sure she got to her bus all right and that Lonzo was nowhere around.

When Charlie got back to his bed he finally fell into an exhausted sleep, until the knock came hours later. He rose, thinking it must be the coppers and he would have to flee out the window, until he heard *her* voice.

A Fleeting Meeting

"Hello, Charlie Matters," she said.

He stared at her through the width of his shabby doorway.

Molly looked triumphantly back at him. She had on a light green dress with a white hat and beige coat. Her shoes were also beige. In one hand was a purse and in the other a very proper wicker picnic hamper with a lid.

"How'd you know where I live?" he said darkly.

"I had a nice chat with Mr. Oliver. He gave me your address." She looked over his shoulder. "Aren't you going to invite me in?"

"Don't see why I should."

"It would be rude if you didn't. I've come all this way, haven't I?"

"How'd you get here anyways?"

"I walked part of the way and then I took a cab. It's a nice day." She noted his disconsolate expression. "Is anything wrong?"

"No, why should there be?"

"You just look different. Are your parents home? Though it's Saturday I suppose your father might be off to work?"

Charlie hesitated and then said, "He's in the army, Miss."

"Yes, of course, how very stupid of me. So does your mother work, then?"

He didn't answer right away, his mind moving swiftly. He didn't really know Molly. And what business was it of hers about his parents?

"Yeah, she does the cleanin' at some buildin's and such, like I told that bloke on the bus."

"You mean at night?"

"Yeah. She's asleep. Just got home a bit ago."

Molly set down the basket, opened her small purse, and took out a bottle of ointment and a bandage. "Let me see your hand."

"What?"

"The cut there."

Charlie slowly held out his hand.

"Have you cleaned it like I told you to?"

"Um . . ."

"I thought so. Hold still." She took a bottle of soapy water and a cloth from her purse, poured some onto the cloth, and thoroughly cleaned the cut and dried it. "Now some ointment and a bandage. Don't worry, it won't hurt."

"I ain't worried," he muttered, thinking guiltily of dead Eddie with his smashed head.

She glanced at him as she applied the ointment and then tied the bandage around his hand, finishing with a sturdy knot. "There, that should do for now. You should have your mother change the dressing daily until the redness goes away and the wound begins to heal. You can take the ointment and I'll leave you with several more bandages."

She handed all this to Charlie, who put them away in his assorted pockets. "Thank you, Miss. So, did your dad pass us?"

"What?" she said, clearly startled by his query.

"Your dad? Was he home when you got back that night?"

"Um, no, actually. He worked very late and didn't come home a'tall."

"Does your mum mind him workin' so late and all?"

"Everyone has to do their part," said Molly stoutly.

"So you've seen him, then?"

"Um, yes, yes I have. He's quite . . . well, if . . . tired."

Charlie now glanced at the hamper. "Do I smell *meat*?"

"Mrs. Pride, my nanny, did some shopping. I passed Victoria Park on my way here. I thought we could have a picnic, though there were some barriers up at the entrance."

"Vicky's closed on 'count of the war. They got the big ack-ack guns there now."

"Well, if you don't mind a long walk, we could go to Hyde Park. Although we could take a cab. I don't know if the Underground goes that far right now."

Charlie slipped his cap and jacket off the pegs by the door. "I don't mind walkin' when I need to. And I never mind eatin'. And like you said, it's a nice day." Charlie looked down at his achy, pinched feet. "But if you can spare the coins, a *bus* to the West End would be good."

Charlie was finishing the last bit of fried sausage, tinned fish, and dried fruit, along with a chunk of cheddar.

Molly sat across from him on the blanket drinking from a cup of water.

She eyed the empty tin. "They had actual fish where I was staying along the coast."

"Just got the tinned fish here," said Charlie.

"Why is that?"

"U-boats. You don't want to get sunk by no torpedo while you're fishin' in the Channel."

"Oh, of course."

"My gran says the shops got stuff that don't look or smell like a fish. Maybe whale meat that's, well, if you never have any in your whole life, that would be just fine."

"Well, people have to make do with what they have. The ladies in my village used leg makeup because nylons are no longer available. Liquid Stockings, it was called. Came in a bottle. The women would even draw in hosiery seams with a black eyeliner pencil."

Charlie looked up from his food. "*Leg makeup?* Why, I never heard of such a thin'."

"Does your grandmother live with you and your mother?"

Charlie said smoothly, "Yeah. My granddad died a while back and she come to live with me and Mum."

"Does your father come home on leave often?"

"Not too often, no," said Charlie, looking back at his plate.

Molly glanced over at a nearby statue. "I remember seeing that when I was much younger," she said. "Do you like it?"

Charlie turned to see a naked boy atop a large sea creature. He frowned and shook his head. "Looks like he's hurtin' whatever that is."

"It's a *dolphin*. I read all about it. It was sculpted by Alexander Munro. He was a friend of Lewis Carroll's, who wrote *Alice's Adventures in Wonderland*. Although Lewis Carroll was his nom de plume. His real name was Charles Dodgson. And do you really think he's hurting it?"

"How would you like someone's knee on your back?" replied Charlie heatedly. "And look how he's twistin' its tail and pushin' down on its head."

"You don't have to get so upset by a statue, Charlie."

"I'm not upset," he said irritably. He looked back at the statue. "But I don't like it when people hurt thin's that ain't done nothin' to them."

"Yes, of course," said Molly, taken aback by his retort. "I . . . I wouldn't, either."

She glanced over at several large anti-aircraft guns with camouflage draping nestled in the middle of what had once been a pristine flower bed. She could see at least a dozen other guns like those, some stationary and fixed, and others on wheeled carriages. Soldiers with cigarettes in hand lingered here and there, ever at the ready if the sirens sounded and the German planes appeared. The nearly sixteen-foot-long gun barrels were aimed at the sky like enormous metal fingers pointing at something of interest there.

Molly had read that these weapons could heave twenty-eight-pound shells eight miles into the sky. Although the guns were not very accurate, the hope was that in skies crowded with German aircraft they would at least hit something, or drive the Luftwaffe fleets to ever higher altitudes, where their bombing accuracy would be sharply diminished.

Molly looked over at the paved walkways and remembered when vendors would be there selling every flavourful delicacy one wanted, like plump muffins and moist tea cakes and ice lollies. And back then there were comfortable sling chairs set around the park, where one could putter away the afternoon sunning one's face or napping in serene contentment.

Now there were ugly holes in the earth and battered fountains and felled trees, and large guns instead of flowers.

Molly was startled when a man across a section of lawn pointed a camera at her and took a picture, the camera bulb heating up and then cooling down within the length of a breath.

She rose. "Excuse me, what are you doing?"

Charlie turned to look at the man. "What's wrong?"

"He took my picture."

As Molly headed over to him the man hurried off and soon disappeared among a crowd of folks walking along.

Charlie said, "Maybe he was taking a photo of that statue."

"Maybe, but—"

"But what?"

"Oh, I don't know. It will probably sound quite mad to you, but I think someone is following me. Watching my house, that sort of thing. And now this man with the camera."

"But why would they do that?"

"That's just it, Charlie, I don't know why." Molly shook her head. "Well, there's nothing I can do about it now." She glanced up and said, "It looks like it might rain."

Charlie played with a corner of the picnic blanket. "So, you went to see Mr. Oliver?"

"Yes, I needed your address."

"Why?"

She took out the half crown. "Because I mean to give you this."

Before last night Charlie would have taken the coin. But now, the sight of the money made him think of the dead copper. And Eddie. The large truck rolling over his small head. Lonzo's threats. He made no move to take the offered payment.

She said, "I promised this to you in return for services rendered. You performed those services. Hence, you deserve to be paid. It's only fair."

"I don't deserve nothin'," said Charlie, his eyes starting to tear up.

"Charlie, what is it? What's wrong?"

He wiped his eyes dry. "We best get on. You can get a taxi over there."

"I can walk. It's not so very far from here. And I can nip into Harrods on the way. I haven't been there since I went to the country."

"But not with the rain comin'. And a taxi's better what with your basket and all."

"But what about you?"

He shrugged. "I'm wet mor'n I'm dry. And I don't mind walkin' long ways. I do it every day."

"Is your school that far from your home?"

"It's . . . no, it's not that far. But I walk other places, *after* school."

They picked up their things and put them back in the hamper. At the taxi stand next to the park, Molly said, "I would like to meet your mum."

"Okay, and I'd like to meet yours," he shot back.

Molly turned a bit pink. "I . . . she's not been well."

"Your dad then."

"Right. Well, we'll have to see, won't we?"

As they were waiting in the queue Molly glanced down at a newspaper that had been left on a bench. "Oh, how awful."

She picked it up and showed Charlie the front page. There was a picture of a lorry with two bodies under sheets in front of it.

Molly read, "'A constable and a boy were killed in a tragic

accident. The constable has been identified as Ambrose Tapper, age thirty-one. He was married and had two young children. The name of the boy is, as yet, unknown. The driver of the lorry reported to police that the constable was chasing three youths when the accident occurred.'" She glanced at Charlie. "Isn't that terrible?"

Charlie was staring at the bodies under the sheets and did not answer.

Molly continued to read. "'The driver has given descriptions of the other boys to the authorities. And they are looking into reports of crime in the area, under the belief that the three lads had been engaged in some illegal act. The constable had been doing his duty in chasing them down when he met his sad end.'"

She looked at Charlie. "Some people simply have no respect for the law and the lives of others. Oh, listen to this." She continued reading: "'*They just run off*, the lorry driver reported. *Just run off and left their pal dead. What sort of person does that?*'" She folded the paper and put it back on the bench. "Well, I hope they catch those other boys. And I hope they feel wretched for leaving their poor friend behind."

Gazing over her shoulder, the cold grip of the hangman's noose latching on to his throat, Charlie managed to say, "There's your cab, Miss."

She got into the taxi and then held the coin out the window. "Please take it."

Charlie said, "Thank you for the picnic. It was very nice." Then he turned and walked off.

As the cab drove away Charlie snatched up the paper and tucked it inside his jacket. He walked all the way back home in the rain, wondering how he could have left Eddie lying dead there like that.

I deserve to be hanged.

The Remains of Jane

THE NEXT NIGHT CHARLIE ventured, as he sometimes did, to the sacred place. Several years had passed now, but the crater was still filled with rubble. And yet plants like hollyhocks, buddleia, and willow herbs, from fledgling straight on to robust, had reclaimed the land where the school had been, producing life from where once had occurred sudden, violent death.

It had been Charlie's first day at the new school—they had moved to another neighbourhood after their other home had been bombed. He and his mother had walked, holding hands, down the street. However, the closer they had drawn to their destination the more nervous Charlie had become, until he was tugging forcefully against his mother's grip, pleading with her to let them stay together, and not to leave him in this strange place.

His mother had squatted down in front of him so they were eye to eye, smoothed down his hair and tidied up his clothes, and told him how the other children would welcome him as their new chum. They would read together and play together and learn so much that his head would be as full as his belly after a good meal, and how so very wonderful that would feel.

And because he loved his mother more than he loved anything

else, and because she had never, ever spoken to him an untruth, they had continued on. A hug in the front corridor of the school and then they had said their final, tearful goodbyes.

Neither one at the time could have realized that an eager Bremen-born Luftwaffe bombardier riding in the belly of a Dornier 17, and following the distinctive line of the Thames, was about to end his mother's life and transform her son's future in ways unimaginable.

Charlie perched on a section of brick that had once been part of a wall of the school, slipped off his cap, rested his bony elbows on his slender thighs, and closed his eyes. He remembered the sirens, and then after that the whistle of the falling bombs.

Charlie thought a boy had been doing the whistling. He had no idea that it was the wind being pushed through a set of organ pipes riveted onto the bomb fins by the Germans to instill even more fear in the people down below. Jericho's Trumpets, they would be dubbed.

For some reason, the warning sirens had been quite late in sounding, and thus they were told there was no time to go to a proper shelter. Wearing their gas masks, they had all frantically rushed back into their classroom and the teacher had shut the door. They crouched under their desks shaking with fear, as the sounds of the planes filtered through the ceiling.

When the wave of bombs struck, Charlie's memory of the day vanished, but returned when his eyes opened. Above him was only darkness because he had been buried in the collapse of what had once been a safe haven for children. For the longest time Charlie had thought that he was dead and that this was what the Heaven promised by the vicar looked like. He could feel neither his arms nor his legs. His small chest was compressed; his lungs were full of things they shouldn't be. His ears contained nothing but a piercing, dull hum that apparently no other sound could penetrate.

The darkness was finally lifted off him when anxious hands reached down and pulled him back into the light. One searing odour hit him intently, but he didn't recognize it: cordite, ubiquitous in all explosives.

Charlie was carried on a stretcher to a bus with many other wounded because the ambulance fleet had been overwhelmed ferrying other victims to hospital. His injuries—a broken arm, a shattered collarbone, a wrenched ankle, bruises over his entire body—were relatively minor compared to those of other victims, he had been told. And his head wasn't filled with horror from the ordeal because it had happened so fast. Sustained, suffocating blackness, then a burst of light, like being born all over again.

How he and some others at the school had survived was anyone's guess. A miracle, the newspapers had said, no doubt thrilled to have something positive to report amid the tragedy.

Charlie forgot about everything else when two men in baggy suits came to visit him in hospital along with his grandparents that night. Gran looked like she wanted no more part of living, while his grandfather merely stared at his shoes. Sobbing, Gran had gripped Charlie so tightly all of his injuries screamed in protest. But Charlie's sole focus was the men, who stared at him with an odd mixture of sincere sorrow and professional weariness.

It was they who had told him that his mother had been among those killed. When the late sirens had finally started, she had ignored her personal safety and rushed to the school to retrieve her son. Right before she got there, a bomb had landed barely ten feet from her, witnesses had said.

And then she, like the building, had ceased to exist. Jane Matters had been transformed into a mere memory, simply because she had wanted her son to go to a proper school and had walked him there on his first day because she loved him so.

Charlie had known his mother was dead long before he had been told. Else she would have been sitting next to him all that time, holding his hand, cooling his brow, and whispering things that would matter greatly to the only child she would ever bear.

And now, all this time later, the underlying shock remained such a part of him that Charlie didn't even realize it *was* a part of him. Just as a heart thudded in synchronicity, lungs inflated, and kidneys filtered, the shock continually palpitated throughout him, as though he had grown a new organ, of unceasing, debilitating anxiety.

Charlie's last image of his mother was her walking away down the hall. She had turned once and smiled, managing to calm, with just her look, the fear of her only child's being left there without her. Then she had turned back around, and gone to her death.

He stared across the width of the road where lay the nearest Underground station, which had been miraculously undamaged by the bombing that had destroyed the school. There Charlie and his grandparents had slept, night after night, either on the tracks or on the platforms with hundreds of others as explosives dropped all over the city. Incendiary devices or parachute flares had often fallen first, in large clusters called breadbaskets, igniting buildings, and also lighting the way for the wave of long bombs that would do most of the damage and take most of the lives.

The incendiaries were nasty things, made of magnesium that burned hot enough to melt solid steel. They crashed into buildings and caused conflagrations that were nearly impossible to put out, because magnesium was impervious to water. The ingenuity of killing via warfare was often beyond belief, Charlie sometimes thought.

Lying on the tracks or suspended over them in a rude hammock made from a slit burlap bag, Charlie had closed his eyes and tried not to listen to what was going on overhead. Then came the shaking of the earth in a way that bled uncontrollable terror among all down there. Charlie would listen intently to the return fire from the ground and pray that every single British shell would find its mark.

Someone had set up a piano in the station, and the crowd would engage in singalongs each night. The Women's Voluntary Services, or WVS, would also provide tea and sandwiches, which Charlie very much looked forward to, because it was often the most expansive meal he would have. And libraries donated books, so he would sometimes sit and try to read to keep his mind off the bombs. But it was not easy, because waiting to die like that was not natural, Charlie felt.

Along their way home, after the all clear had sounded, he and his grandparents had circumnavigated holes where something had once been, and averted their eyes from crumpled, blasted bodies that had, not too long before, been living. It was a field of debris spawned by the depravity of humankind, minus the human.

The new school Charlie had ended up going to after his mother's death was a room in the basement of a disused and shabby government building. It contained a single chalkboard, a few chairs, and one weary teacher for forty children. Most students sat on the floor wearing their gas masks, which was a stark reminder to Charlie of what had happened to both him and his mother that day.

Every time he drew close to the basement his heart seemed to seize up, his muscles tensed, and his vision blurred. When he was actually inside the dank, gloomy room with his mask on, his mind shut down and the teacher would look at Charlie, who always sat hunched over in a little ball, with pity. Then she moved on to those children who could still learn.

Then one day Charlie had written out the letter in Gran's hand and delivered it to the basement before anyone arrived there. And that was the end of Charlie's formal education, and the commencement of his informal one.

Charlie's thoughts returned to the present and he rose from the wall and left the place where his mother had died. He spent the rest of the Sabbath cleaning out a shed by the river for two bob and a soft apple. The apple constituted both his breakfast and his lunch, for Gran had had next to nothing to put in the icebox for his breakfast, or for his Sunday lunch. Her reduced wages had been late in coming—and besides which, the market shelves where she could shop with her ration book and few coins were bare.

After a meagre supper that night, Charlie gave Gran his shilling and explained that on his way home from a walk, a man in a shiny hat had been inclined to be charitable.

Gran said, “Well, it does the heart good to know that there is still decency out there. That people *do* care. The rich and the poor in the fight together, eh, Charlie?”

Shortly after her gentle snores reached his cupboard that night Charlie had gone down the fire escape.

“Oi, Charlie.”

He turned to see Lonzo standing there, waiting.

So Long

Charlie looked to see whether Lonzo was holding his knife or not. He wasn't. Lonzo came forwards while Charlie stood his ground.

"Eddie's dead," said Lonzo sombrely.

"I know, I saw it in the paper."

Lonzo looked down at the ground. "See, blokes know me and Eddie was mates. If the coppers think . . . then they'll know . . . And that lorry driver, 'e got a good look at me, I reckon."

"What are you goin' to do?" asked Charlie.

"Dunno. I could leave 'ere, but I got nowhere's to go, and no money to get there."

"Would a half crown help?"

Lonzo stared at him. "*You* got a 'alf crown?"

"I can get it. Then I'll give it to you."

Lonzo looked dumbstruck. "Why . . . why would you do that, Charlie?"

"We didn't want Eddie or the copper to die, Lonzo. It just happened."

"I'm no good, Charlie. I know that. I . . . I used to be before . . . the war. Me mum, she was nice, did her best. And when me dad got in the damn pints and took off 'is belt to beat me, she wouldn't let 'im. And then the war took 'im. And then Mum . . ." He looked back down at the ground. "I don't want yer money, Charlie. Give it to yer gran."

"But then what will you do?"

"I'll think 'a somethin'. I always think 'a somethin', even without Eddie round. 'e was a good bloke. 'e had it worse'n me. 'e really did. At the orphanage and all. What blokes done to him 'cause 'e was little."

"Right," said Charlie.

"Might join up. Fight the Jerries. I looks old enough." He put out his hand. "Good luck to you, Charlie."

Charlie shook his hand and then Lonzo was gone.

Charlie passed by the wreckage of a Dornier aircraft, its severed snout resting half inside an abandoned building and its shattered tail with the German Cross on it lying a dozen feet away. An RAF sergeant had guarded it for a bit after the plane had first come down. But once it was stripped of everything, the sergeant no longer came. Folks would take pictures in front of it or throw rocks at the ruined hull. He studied it for a bit, imagining the airmen inside it plotting their bombings. Charlie was glad they were dead.

Two corners over he received a shilling from a man in return for shovelling dead rats from a building that was being *rehabilitated*, or so the man said. Charlie didn't know what that meant, but he scooped skinny grey carcasses and earned his money. Charlie didn't know what the man had used to kill all those rats, but he could smell something strong that might have managed it. It was actually making his belly feel funny.

After he was done shovelling and got his coin, he had rushed to the river and thrown up the bile in his stomach, as did four other boys who had scooped rats with him. The man with the shillings had never ventured into the building. He had stayed well away smoking his pipe.

In the blissful peace of the cluster of hours caught between darkness and true dawn, Charlie stared at the black ribbon of the winding Thames. A great city lay half in ruins. The hearts of the survivors were just as damaged. Millions of men had fallen on battlefields all around the world, and the clash of countries was far from over. He wondered what they would call the next world war other than number three.

He tossed a flat stone into the dark water but was unable to see the ripples.

I really can't see me, either, but I'm here, for now. Until maybe they hang me for Eddie and the copper. Or a bomb does the job.

He made his way along the river, heading west.

He liked to keep moving. For lads like Charlie, it was always a good idea.

Mother Wakefield

Mrs. Pride was still under her bedcovers when a fully dressed Molly had marched down the hall and opened the door of her parents' bedroom without bothering first to knock.

As had been the case since she had arrived home, there was no one there and the bed was untouched. Molly had previously placed one of her gloves under the sheet and then smoothed everything back over. If her father had slept in the bed, he would have surely noticed that and removed the glove.

She found the glove exactly where she had placed it.

Next, she opened the door to the bathroom. The bathtub had not one smidgen of stain; there was no bar of soap. A towel lay over its holder, but it was dry to the touch and Molly was convinced it had not touched human skin in a very long time.

She walked down the steps to the main floor and surveyed the space. Hat and stick by the door. No clink of the latchkey, no creak of the door the previous night. Or any other night.

Molly went into the kitchen. There was not a whiff of recently cooked food. Not a plate or cup was out of place; the sink and stove were scrubbed clean, and the kitchen's wooden worktable was pristine. No one had obviously set foot in here since she and Mrs. Pride had taken their final meal last night and Molly had helped her nanny to clean up.

That meant her father could have partaken of no food or drink, even on the off chance that he had slept in a bed with his daughter's glove under his backside, and washed up in a bathroom while leaving no signs of having done so. She stepped outside to the garage and saw through the dreary window the Singer parked there. Using her latchkey, she unlocked the door, went inside, and ran her finger over the Singer's bonnet. Her finger came away covered in grime. She opened the car door and was immediately hit with the musty odour of a long-enclosed space.

She went back inside just in time to see Mrs. Pride clatter down the back stairs from her small flat that was directly over the kitchen. Her old nanny was just securing an apron around her waist when she saw Molly and came up short. "Molly! My, you're up early. Couldn't you sleep?"

"I slept," said Molly tersely. "Just not well."

Mrs. Pride pushed a strand of her hair back into place. "I believe that your father—"

"He's not here," interrupted Molly. "In fact, I know that he never came home last night."

"Well, I don't know about that, dear. I really couldn't say."

"I *can* say. His bed hasn't been slept in. Last night after you were asleep, I also checked the laundry. None of his clothes were there, and all his clean clothes are still hanging in his wardrobe. So, unless he has got into the habit of leaving the house without wearing clothes, something surely is amiss. And nothing in the kitchen has been disturbed. His bathroom looks untouched. Why would a person bother to come home if not to eat, sleep, make his toilet, and dress? And the Singer has clearly not been driven in a very long time."

Mrs. Pride gave a tremulous smile in response to all this. "Well, surely you must be mistaken, dear."

"I am not mistaken. And I listened for him until three in the morning."

"Well, there's a simple enough explanation. He might have stayed at work all night. He does that, you know. The Ministry of Food—"

"I already went to his place of work and he wasn't there."

"You . . . went to the Ministry of Food?" said an astonished Mrs. Pride.

"Yes, I did. The place was dark and empty."

"That was not very wise, dear, to go there all by yourself. Think what might have happened."

"I didn't go alone, and nothing happened."

"Well, as I said before, he might be out of town all this time."

"No, Mrs. Pride, he's not. What you've been telling me is clearly rubbish and I'm sick of it. So I am asking you to end this absurd farce right now and tell me the truth."

Mrs. Pride shrank back under this direct assault. "Molly, dear, this doesn't sound like you a'tall."

"I am quite nearly sixteen years old. I am a young *woman, not* the little girl you remember."

Mrs. Pride put a hand to her mouth and her eyes widened. "It has been a difficult time, Molly. Desperately hard."

"Well then?"

"Are you certain you want to hear this?"

"I am very certain that I *have* to hear it, whether I want to or not. I should have heard it from you long before now."

Mrs. Pride dropped into a chair. "You always were a most practical child."

Molly sat down and looked expectantly at her.

"What I told you about your mother is true. She *is* in a sanatorium in Cornwall. I really hesitated to tell you."

"Why?"

"Well, some might consider it shameful. And I have always been so protective of your mum. The dearest lady to walk the earth . . . before her . . . odd ways came on."

Molly drew a breath. "And how long has she been at this sanatorium?"

"About four years now."

Molly's jaw went slack. "Four years! What on earth happened to her?"

"She started acting a bit strange before that, but your father believed we could manage things here. But then . . ." She stopped and looked down at her hands.

"Please just tell me!" implored Molly.

Mrs. Pride gave Molly a ferocious look. "It was the bloody Germans, at least partly. They came one night with their bombs. I was visiting a friend; it was my night out. But your father got your mother to the tube shelter not that far from here. And . . ." Mrs. Pride once more looked down at her hands.

"And what? Was the shelter bombed?"

"No. But in all the rush, your mother and father became separated. He looked all over for her, but the station was chock-a-block with folks, and it was also very dark. When the bombs stopped he kept looking for her. And he finally found her." Mrs. Pride stopped speaking and traced her mouth with a shaky hand.

"Where was she?"

"He found her in a little room down a long, dark corridor, he told me. Some . . . excuse my language, *bastards* had brought her there, no doubt taking advantage of her fear and confusion."

Molly put a hand to her chest. "Some . . ."

"I don't want to call them men because they certainly didn't act like men, more like animals."

Molly's eyes began to fill with tears.

Mrs. Pride saw this and gripped her hand. "Oh, Molly, you don't want to hear this."

Molly composed herself as best as she could. "I'm afraid I need to hear everything, Mrs. Pride. No matter how . . . awful."

"Well, when your father found her, she was dishevelled, and

battered and bruised and crying. Her purse taken, her clothes . . . torn . . . her . . . *dignity* stolen."

Molly let out a small moan.

"Your father was, of course, beyond furious. Here they had come for safety from the damn Germans and she's attacked by her *own* people."

"What did Father do?"

"He found a policeman is what he did. And tried to get him to take a report, to go after the men who'd done it."

"What do you mean *tried*?"

"Your father was sitting in the chair you're in now when he told me this, while Mrs. Wakefield was upstairs wailing her head off. The constable tried to ask her some questions, but she was too distraught to answer, of course. Hysterical, really, and your father said the constable seemed more frustrated and bothered than concerned or helpful. When your father tried to explain that, the bobby didn't want to hear it, did he? Had other things to do, didn't he? A war was going on, he had the impertinence to say. How could he know that anything happened a'tall? She might have got lost and fallen and torn or lost some of her clothes that way, he had the gall to suggest. She might have dropped her purse. As if," she added with a scowl.

"What did Father do?"

"Oh, he didn't stop with that bobby. He went to a detective chief inspector, and then to the chief superintendent, and then, when he got no satisfaction there, he took it up with the assistant commissioner at Scotland Yard."

"And?"

"And nothing seemed to matter, Molly. To them, it was a bit of odd bother during a war. Women get attacked all the time, they said. Men too. Unfortunate, yes, but many things were unfortunate during such troubling times. They didn't have the manpower to run down every report, did they? Half their force was in the military, they told your father. They were dragging old men out of retirement, and young men who didn't qualify to carry the sword for Britain were now wearing a bobby's uniform. It's a scandal is what it is."

"So nothing was done?"

"No. As far as I know they never even looked for the men."

"And Mother?"

Mrs. Pride looked pained. "Well, your mother was always an excitable, nervous person, even before that. You saw that while you were here. Fretted over you in some ways that weren't so healthy, I guess, looking back on it. And when you left she fretted even more, certain that you were never going to return."

"She could have come and seen me."

"Well, she wanted to, but it wasn't that easy to leave London at the time. And, to tell the truth, I don't think your mum was up to travelling that far. And after what happened to her in that shelter, well, things rapidly became very bad."

"How bad?"

"We would try to get her to take a walk, even offered to go with her, but we would get her to the front door and she would start to scream and fight us."

"My God."

"It was like she withdrew into a little shell. She'd walk around here like a ghost."

"Didn't Father try to get her help?"

"Oh, yes. But you can't find a doctor these days to set a broken bone, deliver a baby, or take your temperature, Molly, much less the sort of doctor she needed. Where expectant mothers would be without midwives, well, I don't know. But it'd be no place good."

"I'm sure," said Molly in a hollow tone.

"She *would* write you letters and slip them under your bedroom door, like you were still with us, things like that. Or sew a new collar on an old dress of yours and hang it in your room for you to wear the next day. She would even have afternoon tea and talk to you as though you were there."

"You mean my mother was going quite mad?" said Molly dully.

"I would never say that. She's the gentlest, sweetest creature."

"One can be gentle and sweet and still be quite mad," replied Molly.

"Well, I wouldn't know about that," said Mrs. Pride, glancing at her hands. "But I believe that she was trying to go back to a time when there was no war and her family was all together and happy. That was a safe place for her. So she pretended that was where she was. And who could blame the poor woman?"

"I think you may be right about that," said Molly thoughtfully.

"Well, I'm no head doctor or anything, but I *do* have common sense."

"So how did Mother end up in Cornwall?"

Mrs. Pride took a few moments to clear her throat and wipe her eyes with a tissue. "One morning she got up before any of us. She came down to the kitchen, put some cooking fat in a pan on the stove, lit the gas, and apparently forgot all about it. When she realized her error, she came in and chucked water on it to stop the smoke. Well grease and water don't mix too well, and we nearly lost her *and* the kitchen. Luckily, your father heard her cry out and came down in time to stop any further damage. When she'd seen what she'd nearly done, your mother, well, she went a bit berserk, I guess one could say. Shouting and punching your father, and tearing at her clothes and hair, and well, *raving*."

"My God, Mrs. Pride," said a visibly shaken Molly.

"That was why Mrs. Brand left. See, your mother went after her too when she came to your father's assistance. 'Who do you think you are, taking liberties with Mr. Wakefield, you dreadful hussy!' she screamed at her. And Mrs. Brand was sixty if she was a day. Anyway, she gave her notice that very morning, and we had a devil of a time getting a replacement because your mother insisted on interviewing them. And, well, most of the ladies ran out of the house after a few minutes of being shouted at and berated by her. So then, it just fell to me."

"My word," exclaimed Molly.

"And then poor Mr. John had several rows with her. She'd order the car and then while it was moving down the road, she'd climb out or try to. When Mr. John would stop and try to get her back in she would fight him, saying he was trying to kidnap her, do terrible things to her. After the third time he handed in his notice. Said his nerves and his knees could take it no longer."

"I would imagine not."

"Any man that came near her—the milkman, the postman, it didn't matter—she flew into a rage. She was uncontrollable. Then the decision was made to send her to the sanatorium in Cornwall, where they have a very nice place by the seaside. Your father took her by train and got her settled in, then came back here. He visited her as often as he could."

"And did he say how she was doing?"

"He never spoke of it," said Mrs. Pride. "And it didn't feel right for me to ask if he didn't want to volunteer it."

"And where is Father now?"

"He's . . . he's, um, gone, Molly," said Mrs. Pride apprehensively.

Father Wakefield

"What do you mean, 'gone'? Is he . . . is he dead?" asked Molly.

"I don't know."

"How can you not *know* something like that?" Molly cried out.

Mrs. Pride pointed towards the front of the house. "I watched him one morning come down the stairs with his suitcase, put on his hat and coat, and pick up his umbrella, for it was raining like a monsoon. He turned to me and said, 'Mrs. Pride, please take care of things while I'm away.' Now, this surprised me because he hadn't mentioned taking a trip. So I says, 'And where might you be going, Mr. Wakefield? And when might you be back, sir?' As the housekeeper I needed to know things like that, of course."

"And what did he say?" asked Molly breathlessly.

"He said, 'Mrs. Pride, if I had the answers to that I'm not sure I would tell you. But I don't, so that becomes an unnecessary decision.' That was what he said, word for word. I'll never forget it till my dying day."

"So you just let him walk out?" asked Molly incredulously.

"What was I to do, Molly? He's the master. If he wanted to leave, what right did I have to stop him?"

"And when did all this occur?"

"Six months ago, almost to the day."

"Six months! But what about the letter he left me on my bed?"

Mrs. Pride looked deeply troubled. "Please don't be upset, Molly, but it was me that put that there the morning you came back."

"But you said you hadn't got my letter and thus didn't know I *was* coming back."

Mrs. Pride looked even more ashamed and kneaded her bony fists into her thighs. "It was true that we never got your letter, but I saw you from the upstairs window when you knocked. I knew it was you straight away though you'd changed so much. I got the letter and put it on your bed before I answered the door and . . . pretended I didn't recognize you."

"But it was Father's handwriting. He wrote that note, I'm sure of it!"

"Indeed he *did* pen that note. He handed it to me before he walked out that door. He said, 'Just in case, Mrs. Pride. Odder things have happened, of course, but just in case, for dear Molly, upon her arrival back. Thank you.' Then he tipped his hat, opened the door, and stepped out into the rain. I've never laid eyes on him since."

"But as time passed, why didn't you communicate with me?"

"I would never bother you with such a thing, Molly. And besides . . ."

"Besides what?" she said sharply.

"Your father made me promise not to tell you. He didn't want to burden you with it. And I could not go against his wishes. He's the—"

"—the *master* of the house, yes, I know. But at some point why didn't you go to the authorities and tell them that he had disappeared?"

The woman looked shocked. "Molly, that would have been a betrayal to your father. He never said I could do such a thing. And there's a war going on. Lots of people have disappeared without a by-your-leave. You may not have seen that where you were, but here in London it happens all the time." She paused and seemed to gird herself.

"But, with that said, after four months went by without a word from him I . . . I actually went down to the police station near here with the mind that I might say something about your father being gone."

"And what happened?"

"There were literally hundreds of adverts up in that one station about missing people, and have you seen them and such." She grew quiet and looked down. "And . . ."

"And what?"

Mrs. Pride looked up, her face now full of tears. "If I told them Mr. Wakefield was gone and the missus was in a sanatorium and you was in the country, well, what would they do with me? Would I lose my position? Would I have no roof over my head? Would I be chucked out on the street? There're too many there as it is."

She started to sob into her hands and Molly rose and perched next to her, patting her back and saying soothing things into her ear until the woman calmed.

Molly resumed her seat. "I suppose this explains why he never summoned me to come home."

Mrs. Pride blew her nose into her handkerchief and gave Molly a pained expression. "With your mother the way she was and all, it would not have been a good situation for you."

"Meaning Father wouldn't have wanted me to see her like that?"

"Yes. And he sent the Coopers money each month for your care."

"But the Coopers told me the money stopped coming recently. Regardless, they offered for me to continue staying with them, but I wanted to come home. It was time, you see."

"I knew nothing about that. But after he walked out I had to keep up the house and all. He had left some funds, and I paid the bills from that."

"But why didn't he tell me what was going on? He could have written. I could have come back and helped with Mother. Father could have had me to talk to and think things through with. If I had been here, he might not . . ."

"He might not have gone away, you mean?"

"Yes!" said Molly.

"Well, I'm sure he did what he thought was best for you. But . . ."

"But what?"

She glanced up at Molly. "Your mother wasn't the only Wakefield changed by what happened that night. Your father was too. He would come into the kitchen and start ranting that he was an Englishman, faithful to the Crown, paid his proper taxes, did what was expected of him, performed his duties selflessly, a true patriot. And yet this had been allowed to happen to his wife. It was like his belief in the whole of England had just been washed right from him. I don't know, really, who was affected more by this terrible thing—your mother or your father. But Mr. Wakefield was a different man after that, root and branch. When the police would do nothing? When no doctor could be found in London to help your mother? When no one seemed to . . . care? It broke him, Molly. I don't think he ever held his head up after that. It wasn't just the rank unfairness of it all. It was, well, I think he blamed himself for what happened. It was like he had failed your mother. That all of this was his fault. And that is simply too big a burden for anyone to carry, in my opinion."

"Poor Father," said Molly miserably. "I feel terrible for thinking so unkindly of him."

"Well, you weren't to know, were you?" said Mrs. Pride firmly.

After a few seconds of silence Molly sat up, trying to look as composed as possible, even as her runaway nerves threatened to paralyse her.

"Mrs. Pride, can I continue to live here without my mother and father? Isn't there some . . . I don't know, *law*? While I am nearly sixteen I still am considered underage, am I not?"

Mrs. Pride rubbed her hands along her apron; nervous fingers smoothed away errant wrinkles in the fabric. "I . . . I don't know, Molly. I suppose you might be. Heard somewhere that you had to be twenty-one to be considered an adult. Yet I was married when I wasn't much older than you, though my parents did have to consent. And your father may walk back in that door anytime," she added stoutly.

"And he may not."

Mrs. Pride went back to smoothing out wrinkles and said nothing.

"Do we at least receive regular information from Cornwall about my mother?"

"Your father had quite a number of letters and I believe he left them here."

"Can I see them?" Molly said anxiously.

"I can fetch the first one he received," said Mrs. Pride. "I know right where 'tis."

"Do the letters say that she is getting better?"

"I . . . well, I'm not versed in medical terms. But I'm sure if you write to them, they'll answer any questions you might have."

"I *will* put questions to them, Mrs. Pride," Molly said decisively.

"And I know all you want is for your mum and dad to be here. I dearly wish I could make it so," she added in a quavering voice.

"Well, wanting something and having it are two very different things, Mrs. Pride. They often are in life. Now, the letter?"

Mrs. Pride rushed from the room but was back presently with it and handed the envelope over to Molly.

Molly rose and said, "I will read through this, get a better picture of her condition, think on things, and then we'll go from there, shall we?"

"You . . . you sound ever so grown up, Molly," said Mrs. Pride hesitantly.

"Do I have a choice otherwise?"

Before Mrs. Pride could answer, Molly retreated up the stairs, fled down the hall to her room, shut and locked the door behind her, collapsed on her bed, and pushed her face deeply into the pillows so that no one other than herself could hear the wails.

Cedric

Ignatius Oliver had fixed the front door himself because he could not afford a proper repairman. He also took the bell off the inside of the door and screwed it onto the outside wood. The police had questioned him about the attempted robbery. They had told him about the accident with the lorry and the two deaths. And about the pair of boys who had got away, one taller and older, one smaller and younger.

He kept the door locked now with a handwritten sign on the glass to ring the bell if you wanted service. He didn't think he would have many such requests. There had been unsettling word from the BBC that the Germans might soon commence their regular bombings again, day or night. It seemed Hitler was becoming increasingly unhinged with the war turning against him and had decided to kill as many people as possible before all was lost.

How a single madman could do so much damage to the world, Oliver thought. God was indeed testing them all.

Oliver religiously listened to his wireless, an old Philips radio that sputtered and buzzed, but the BBC still came through with sufficient clarity. If he had the choice between sleeping and listening to the wireless, he would choose the latter. Folks would fixate on the BBC weather forecast with as much intensity as they did their King's speeches, to see if a bombing seemed imminent.

Yet it wasn't all bad tidings. They had programmes to lift the spirits and make folks laugh, which was quite important, for otherwise there was nothing much at all to find funny with the world at war.

Later, he took his ration book around to the shops and collected his food for the next few days. Back at the bookshop he dusted off some tomes and replaced them on the bulging shelves as he thought about his duties as an air warden.

The shelters provided refuge for those terrified of the bombings. But they were often not safe places, and it had nothing to do with the Germans. The air was unhealthy with so many bodies packed together. There were also mosquitoes, lice, and rats; scabies outbreaks were numerous. And other germs that spread in those places were sometimes more deadly than the bombs. There were also always some men who filled up on pints before going there and who often brought hostility and active fists to the congregations. Oliver had had to break up many fights in the shelters, often getting pummelled in the process. People were simply not designed to sit calmly and peacefully while others were attempting to kill them with bombs dropped from the sky.

And then there was one poor young woman who always showed up at the same shelter with the same doll in hand, to replace the daughter she had lost in the war. Oliver would sit with her and stroke the doll's hair and talk to it at the woman's urgings, to keep her "child" calm during the raid. Oliver didn't know if he was actually hurting or helping the woman by doing so, but he did as she asked.

Folks brought electric fires, and also wirelesses and sometimes hand-cranked gramophones to the shelters, so they could listen to something other than bombs exploding. Little boys with "medals" and Home Guard bands on their slender arms would run around with their tiny air guns playing war and always convincingly defeating the Germans. Nurses would come to some of the shelters and instruct new mothers on how to properly knit clothing, while their newborns were safely tucked away on overhead bins.

As the bombings went on, some stations had planks put over the tracks to accommodate more people, and other stations even added bunks for folks to sleep in overnight.

Oliver would sometimes perform simple magic tricks for the youngsters to keep their minds off what was going on above them. White lies were also told to try to make the experience easier for the kiddies. Yet Oliver had seen that once the children passed the age of five, those lies and distractions no longer worked.

And the worst task of all: helping to compile the list of victims that would be posted on government buildings in the area so that people would know what had happened to loved ones.

The bell tinkled, interrupting these thoughts, and Oliver looked up to see the man there through the window. He walked quickly over and unlocked the door, looking across at the Secret Garden tea shop where Desdemona Macklin, as always, was watching through the glass. She was smoking a cigarette. She was always smoking a cigarette, it seemed. He couldn't imagine how she managed the ration book on her Player's brand of tobacco.

Oliver smiled at her and waved. She waved back, but her interest was clearly piqued. And not in a good way. At least for Oliver.

Once a busybody, always a busybody. And she had already questioned him about that late-night visit. He didn't care for that, not at all.

Oliver locked the door behind his visitor and drew the short man out of Macklin's line of sight. He was the same man Charlie had seen in the shop right before Charlie had nicked the money and the biscuits from Oliver.

He said irritably, "Cedric, I didn't expect you today, and certainly not at this *time* of day. It's not safe. And Desdemona saw you when you came by last time. And just now as well."

"Desdemona?"

"Desdemona Macklin. She runs the tea shop across the alley. She asked me about your visit. She was suspicious. It's not good. She's quite the nosy one."

"It could not be helped, Ignatius," Cedric said with a shrug and a significant look in the direction of the tea shop. From a compartment of his long overcoat he lifted out a sheaf of papers and handed them to Oliver and said, "Things have accelerated. You need to take great care and deal with this in the usual way."

Oliver locked the papers away in the same drawer as before. "Exactly *what* has accelerated?"

"The war, Ignatius. You British have shown more pluck than we anticipated. And the Americans have become something more than bothersome. We have reached a critical point."

"I thought it all critical, every moment of it, except for the funny parts, of course."

"You will have your little joke. So what do you have for me? You are always prepared. That is what we like about you."

In answer, Oliver walked over to a bookcase, reached up, and plucked a tome off a high shelf. "This is quite a good one. I think you will enjoy it." He handed it over.

Cedric took the book. "*Consuelo* by George Sand?"

"Many consider this her best work."

"*Her?* But the name is—"

"George Sand is a pseudonym. Her real name is Amantine Dupin, a Frenchwoman. She died in the last century."

"French, eh?" said Cedric, looking mildly disgusted. He opened the book and looked at the papers secreted inside the space where the pages had been cut out. They contained numbers, symbols, and letters in long columns. "My superiors tell me that your encryption technique rivals that of Enigma in its cleverness, Ignatius."

"High praise indeed."

"It is fortunate for us that you chose to work for our interests. Cheers, as you English say."

"I'll see you off," said Oliver, holding the door open for him. When Cedric disappeared down the alley, Oliver glanced over at

Macklin. She was behind the counter completing a purchase for a customer, but her eyes were directly on Oliver. He smiled and waved again.

She smiled back, but there was nothing save suspicion behind it.

When she finished with her customer she came out to the alley and said, "So your *collector* is back in town, I see."

"Yes, yes he is."

"Another book then?"

"He's quite fond of certain French writers."

She folded her arms over her chest. "Oh he is, is he?"

"He is," said Oliver. Then he went back inside his shop and locked the door.

The Lofty Domain of Another

Later, Oliver checked his watch; it was time. He placed the closed sign in the front window, poured a cup of tea, and pulled on an old woolen cardigan against a clammy chill that had overwhelmed the shop. He took the fat key from his pocket, glided down the short flight of steps and over to the door. He set the cup and saucer down on a small table set against the wall, drew an uneasy breath, and unlocked the door. He swung it open, replaced the key in his pocket, and picked up the cup and saucer. He ventured through the opening and closed the door behind him.

He took a few moments to look around the space.

This had been Imogen's study. They had lived in the flat over the shop, where there was situated a small bedroom, a smaller kitchen, a miniscule sitting room that almost never had anyone actually sitting in it, a tiny guest bedroom, and one lavatory. It was all spare and common, the pipes forever rattling and the water never warm and the stove never that hot. It was cold when you wanted heat, and insufferably hot when you desperately sought coolness.

However, the study made up for all of that and was Imogen's pride and joy. It had been her father's before her. John Bradstreet had been a highly respected public official, serving in important capacities in several governments. He was the author of a shelf full of learned books and had received a number of illustrious prizes for his writings. Imogen had revered him, and she had bitterly missed him after he passed away.

After his public career was over, her father's private one had begun with this bookshop. This room had been his particular province, and he had furnished it in a way that Imogen thought perfect, for she had changed nothing when she had inherited the business and along with it her father's cherished sanctum.

First, there was the desk. Solid oak with bountiful carvings on the sides, and a large work surface with tooled hunter green leather overlaid on the wood; brass tacks surrounded the leather pad, like columns of steadfast ants. The highbacked chair had a faded brown leather backrest. Along three walls were shelves bulging with Imogen's and her father's personal collection of books, many of them autographed. Against the fourth wall was a stout fireplace with a brick surround and wooden mantel. Fires would regularly simmer there before the war. Now it was a luxury to burn anything in it.

The rest of the space was a comfortable clutter of old chairs with worn seats, rickety tables, and a life's worth of collected objects, along with a rug that was as wonderfully aged and worn as everything else in the room. The floor underneath was darkened walnut planks that had absorbed the mingled scents of countless cheery fires and smells from her father's Barling briar pipes.

In the middle of the desk, and situated directly on the leather, was a fine Crown typewriter with a blank piece of paper wound into its maw. Next to the typewriter was a tin dispatch box. In front of the typewriter was an open journal with elegant writing in pen flowing sumptuously across its pages. And next to the journal was the pen that had done the markings. It was an Onoto work of art with a golden-tipped nib that Oliver had bought Imogen for their first wedding anniversary. It had cost him a packet, but it represented a physical specimen of his love for her cast in delicately crafted metal and lustrous mother-of-pearl.

He took some paper slips from a vase on the mantel, placed them in the fireplace, then drew two lumps of coal from the scuttle and tossed them in there as well. He lit the match, ignited the slips, and let the damper draw, until a meagre bit of soothing warmth and delicate glow invaded the space. He settled in the chair, looked over the writings in the journal for a few minutes, and carefully positioned his fingertips on the Crown's keys.

This was always the hardest part. Well, all of it was difficult, but this . . . this was Oliver's long-standing nemesis. His Waterloo, as it were.

The half-finished and as yet untitled manuscript was Imogen's. She had written one hundred and sixty-five pages before her life had ended. They were in the tin dispatch box next to the typewriter. He had read every single page. The story was good—no, it was better than good; he actually thought the unfinished manuscript exceptional. In those mass of words was his late wife's perspective on the war, or at least the war's effect on the city of her birth woven into a novel and told through various points of view, rich to poor, Mayfair to Stepney, pacifists to military heroes, larger-than-life leaders to prosaic followers, Tory backbenchers to energetic anarchists. She had completed page one hundred and sixty-five, placed it in the tin box, wound the next blank paper into the Crown in preparation for the next day's labour, then rose from this desk, walked out of her study, and never walked back in due entirely to the cruelty of war.

Page one hundred and sixty-six was still curled into the typewriter awaiting the imprint of the keys.

Nearly a year without her. Nearly a year since that page was placed into the typewriter by her capable fingers. Nearly a year since she left me behind for ever. Alone. And utterly bereft.

Oliver came here every day at this same exact time. He came here hoping for inspiration, intending to finish his dead wife's novel and see it in print under her name. And every day he sat in this chair, took in long whiffs of the long-ago remnants of coal fires and pipe smoke, drank his tea until it turned cold, and not a single word came to his mind to transfer to the paper. He did all the right things, he assumed. He placed his fingers on the keys, composed his thoughts, and waited for the organized epiphanies to come. They never ventured within a mile of him.

His dilemma was clear enough. When he tried to compose the words, Imogen's face crept into his mind and would not leave. With that visage confronting him, Oliver could not encounter revelation or experience inspiration or whatever it was that occurred when what was in one's thoughts was transmitted to words, and placed dramatically on paper.

In his anxiousness he took the Alberti's Disk from his pocket and manipulated it, swiftly creating one encrypted cipher after another. He had always been far more comfortable with numbers and puzzles than he was with written tales crafted from scratch.

When he had been a child, his father, a university professor of mathematics, had challenged him with figuring out encryption techniques after Oliver had shown some promise in the field. His father had said, "This is the Vigenère Square, Ignatius. To give you a bit of a hint, it is based on the Caesar Shift, which I tested you with previously."

Oliver knew the Caesar Shift had flummoxed the brightest of minds for over three-quarters of a millennium, and it had taken eight more centuries to find a better method of encryption. Oliver had been tasked by his father to unlock its secrets and had done so within a very few minutes.

"No pressure now, but the Vigenère Square remained unbreakable for three centuries, Ignatius," his smiling father had told him before giving him the encrypted message.

He had quickly figured out that the Vigenère encryption was based on *sequences* of various Caesar Shifts. The cipher presented by his father had been a question about a birthday gift for his mother. Oliver had presented his own coded answer to his father that afternoon.

"You have a gift, Ignatius," he had said after decoding his youngest son's response. "Do not waste it."

But did I waste it? No, I lived the life I wanted, with the person I wanted to live it with. Just not for nearly as long as I hoped I would.

Next he did what he always did. He opened the tin box and read the first chapter Imogen had written and then the last one. The principal character in the first chapter was a young girl full of brilliance, grit, but also heartbreaking loss. The last chapter held the fate of a boy wondering whether he would live much longer while the bombs fell all around.

Then, as though following an instruction manual for beleaguered scriveners, he closed his eyes, and his thoughts wandered back to the conversations he had had with Imogen about her book, what she was thinking, her possibilities in plot, and "character arcs," as she termed it. This invariably led to a conversation with his beloved wife that Oliver would never forget.

The Last Inkling of Dreams

THEY HAD EATEN THEIR dinner, the remains of a meat pie, tins of dried fruit, and a small potato each, all fortified by cups of strong tea. Then Imogen had pulled out a bottle of port from a cubby that Oliver didn't even know they had. She had poured out small portions into two glasses, and they had sat in this very room swirling the amber liquor and leisurely talking about things that did not seem of any particular significance: the weather, the assortment of books that had just come in, the disreputable state of the kitchen. Next, the loud cat in the alley. Then the odd bit of gossip each had heard about this or that person. Lastly, how Desdemona Macklin was not very nice, although he recalled that the word his wife had actually used was "cow."

And then Imogen had wanted to talk about dreams. Oliver had adjusted his specs as she ventured into that subject. He was a mathematician by training, so dreams that had nothing to do with numbers—and what dreams really did?—were not part of his experience or interest.

He had taught at a private boys' school in London right up until the start of the war, when it had closed. Because of his abilities with numbers Oliver had been recruited to work for the war effort in various official capacities, before being offered a full-time position at Bletchley Park, where the British were attempting to break the German encryption system. But that would have realistically meant being away for years from Imogen, and thus he had, with some reluctance, declined the offer.

He had instead, over Imogen's protests, become an air warden. He had gone to duty at his warden's post waiting for the sirens to erupt. Yellow alert meant the bombers were twenty-two minutes away and the red alert—known colloquially as the "Wailing Winnies" or "Moaning Minnies"—cut that time nearly in half. When the yellow alert came the wardens would put down their darts and cards and rush to help folks to shelters. However, as part of their duties and long before any sirens sounded off, wardens would also patrol their official sectors to check and see that windows and doors were covered and up to snuff, that logbooks were up to date, and that the latrines in the shelters were cleaned and water canteens in place, even ensuring that lending libraries located there were well stocked. As the husband of a bookseller, Oliver enjoyed performing that particular task.

Oliver had very nearly died in the course of his warden duties, and he still felt he wasn't doing enough. However, others obviously thought he was performing up to snuff, and had even honoured him for his service to King and Country.

He opened the drawer of the desk and withdrew the George Medal. On the face of it was King George the Sixth, who had originated the honour to commemorate civilians who had shown exemplary bravery during wartime. On the obverse side was the eponymous Saint George slaying the dragon. The ribbon to which the medal was attached was crimson with five blue stripes. It was to be worn on the left side by men. Oliver had never worn his after it had been given him by the King, because why him and not others, especially those who had died? He put it back in the drawer.

He had looked at Imogen that night and said, quite sincerely, "I am living my dream by being here with you, my dear."

She had smiled tenderly at his words and said that dreams were such starkly contrary things. He asked her what she meant.

"Dreams are never in context, are they? That's the point of dreams, of reaching for something so impossible, so impractical, often something so undeserved, that the act of wishing for it defines more about us than the actual dream does."

"But people can work towards their dream," he had said. "You are writing a novel. That is *your* dream. You work very hard at your craft, to realize that dream. Thus, if you do, you are certainly deserving of it. And that, my dear, puts the whole thing into the context which you argue is lacking."

Oliver knew that his wife possessed a first-rate intellect, and was a superb debater, a skill she had demonstrated when they were at university together. Thus, he well knew his argument, however sound or well-intentioned, would not carry the day.

"My novel may be the best writing in the world, but if someone who can manage to have my jottings published does not like what I have written, my dream will never be realized. However, if what I have written is utter drivel, but lands in the hands of someone influential who loves such deplorable writing, I may see my book read by a great many. My dream will be realized, but so what? It's all dependent on the whimsy of others."

"You think too deeply of things, Imogen," Oliver had responded, trying to draw his wife back from one of her *moods*. "Dreams, either asleep or awake, can be silly and happy, or sad and sometimes frightening, but they are part of what makes us human. I daresay it can make an unbearable life at times tolerable. Is that so wrong?"

She had finished her port before answering. "It is not simply a question of wrong or right, Iggy." This was her nickname for him, which he loved, because of the intimacy it implied. "It is a question of honesty. To dream is often to deceive oneself. We may dream so often about another sort of life that we forget to live the one that we already possess."

"There is nothing wrong with aspiring to better things," he had countered.

"And that is where the context is lost, because who is rightfully to judge what is better? Will a million pounds make things right?"

He had smiled. "Well, I, for one, would not decline such a sum if offered."

She had glanced at the tin box and, he understood, to the pages within. "I do not wish to live an uninspired life. I also do not wish to live a life not of my own making. I do not want to spend my time seeking something because someone else tells me that what I have is not good enough."

"But you enjoy writing," he had said.

"Does anyone really truly enjoy anything?"

He was about to make a flippant remark in order to ease the increasing tension he was sensing from her when he, instead, finished his port and replied, "I see exactly what you mean, Imogen. We must make the best of what we have. To seek out something different merely because it is perceived better by standards laid out by people we may not even know? I would say *that* is the height of self-deceit."

She had gripped his hand and given him an imploring look. "Do you really mean that?"

"Yes, Imogen, I do."

It was sometime later that she had had another conversation with him, in this very room. It was a talk that had changed his life dramatically. No, that word was hardly potent enough. It had changed *everything* about him and his world. And, most critically, his relationship with Imogen.

Not too very long after that, she was dead.

And he had acceded to what turned out to be her final wish, fully and completely.

So, as he did every time he came in here, Oliver rose and left the study, locking the door after him, without having added a single word to the work in progress that constituted the only thing of his wife he had left.

Oliver did not dream anymore, either while sleeping or being wide-eyed awake. He apparently no longer had the stomach for it.

And perhaps that was why it was impossible for him to add a jot to his wife's unfinished work.

He used his Alberti's Disk once more to nimbly encrypt a message that represented all that he felt, and all that he had endured every second of his life since her passing.

I will forever love you, Imogen. And that love is matched only by how deeply and terribly I miss you.

Breathless

THE DAY WAS NEARLY done when Molly finally sat up in her bed with her cheeks stained reddish pink, her hair matted to her head, and her breathing sickeningly lopsided. She felt slow, feverish, and doddering, as though an illness had overtaken her. Mrs. Pride had knocked on the door several times, but Molly had simply not answered, and finally her old nanny had gone on her way. And then Molly had fallen asleep, apparently from mental exhaustion.

You must get a hold of yourself, Molly, because what good does crying ever do?

Ignoring the ache in her belly and head, for she'd had nothing to eat all day, she opened the letter from the sanatorium in Cornwall. The stationery was peculiarly stiff, and Molly thought she could detect an odd chemical odour from within its folds.

The letter was addressed to her father, Herbert James Wakefield.

The words were stark and antiseptic, constituting a blunt assessment of her mother's condition. The author of the letter was Dr. Thaddeus P. Stephens. It was his decided medical opinion that Eloise Mary Wakefield was suffering from an acute anxiety neurosis. But Dr. Stephens felt that with certain treatments her prognosis might improve. Stephens did not say precisely what the treatments were, but he did bandy about certain abstruse medical terms.

Molly needed to see the other, more recent letters from Dr. Stephens to which Mrs. Pride had referred. And she also needed something to eat. She had never been without food this long. As she washed her face at the bathroom tap and smoothed out her hair, Molly looked in the glass above and, in her mind's eye, she saw a much older woman there. She went downstairs, her hand holding tightly to the banister, as she still felt wobbly in her legs.

"Mrs. Pride?" she called out.

To her surprise, the woman didn't answer.

Molly went up the back stairs to Mrs. Pride's small flat and knocked. There was no response. She eased the door open and looked inside. The bed was made and no one was there. She ventured to the toilet that was Mrs. Pride's, but it was empty as well. Molly walked to the kitchen and looked through the pantry. It was quite bare. She opened the icebox and found a slice of bread, some margarine, and cheese. She put the cheese on the bread, placed it on a plate, set the kettle on, and boiled the water, then had her tea and cheese and margarine sandwich at the kitchen table.

After she finished, Molly wondered what to do. Should she search Mrs. Pride's room for the letters? Or were they perhaps in her father's study? She hadn't been in there since she had returned, though it was a room that as a child she had adored. It held shelves of old books and the sweet smells of her father's strong pipe tobacco and the nuanced aromas wafting from old inkwells. Comfy, cracked leather chairs and a small couch with worn upholstered cushions with images of horses and buggies from another era sat in one corner. The room also had a sturdy fireplace and a decanter of whiskey with glasses on a wooden sideboard with a granite top that, as a little girl, she had dared not touch.

It was her father's sanctum. It reeked of him.

She had vivid memories of opening the door to that room and seeing her father at his desk writing a letter on crisp, monogrammed paper with his favourite pen, a Conway Stewart trimmed in herringbone with a gold nib. He had allowed her to practise her letters with that very pen. It had felt so wonderful, so important and weighty, in her small grip.

It was then that she heard the latchkey in the kitchen door and looked around in time to see a hatted Mrs. Pride briskly walk in with her market basket.

"Oh, Molly. I thought you'd still be asleep." When she saw the dirty plate and empty cup on the table she exclaimed, "Oh, luv, please tell me you didn't prepare a meal for yourself. I went out with the ration books to get the makings for your dinner."

Though Molly's stomach was still quite empty, she said, "Oh, that's all right, Mrs. Pride. I'm quite full up. You can use what you purchased for your meal."

Mrs. Pride looked at her nervously. "I hope you had a good lie-in. And I'm sorry if . . . if the things we discussed upset you."

"They absolutely *did* upset me. And while I wish you had sent word to me about all of this, I can understand why you might have been hesitant to do so."

"Well, thank you for saying that, dear."

"But Father should not have left you in the dark, and without a word to me. And what of Mother? Does she know that he's gone?"

"I . . . I don't know."

Molly closed her eyes for a moment. She had revered her father all of her life. She had never questioned his judgement about anything. Now she was both hurt and disappointed by him.

Molly opened her eyes. "Now, the other letters from the sanatorium? Could you bring them to me? I'll be in Father's study." It seemed to Molly that she had adopted the tone of the mistress of the house. And she supposed she was now.

But for how much longer?

The Sanctum of Sanctums

Molly hurried down the hall and entered her father's study. She closed the door and gazed around the book-lined space. Crossing the room, she drew aside the curtain, and gave a searching look up and down the street. There were no passing motorcars and no people out walking. Over the tops of the opposite houses Molly could see the night coming as the sky burned gold and red before the sink of the sun snuffed it out.

Molly sat at the desk. The green leather high-back chair swivelled. As a little girl, she had sometimes spun around in it till she became dizzy. Once she had nearly become ill, but fortunately had made it to the toilet before desecrating her father's sacred place with her sick. Ignoring the electric switch on the wall, she lit a candle, drawing a match from the same box her father had used to light his myriad pipes that perched in a wooden rack on the desktop.

On one side of the desk was the fat black telephone that no doubt Herbert Wakefield had made important calls on. As a child she had lifted the receiver and pretended to call the King and ask him over for tea. Her father had showed her how to make a trunk phone call to her now-dead grandmother in Shrewsbury on the occasion of her birthday.

She took up the Conway Stewart pen, which Molly was certain had lain in perfect parallel to the letter opener since the very day her father had walked out the front door. She held the pen over a sheet of crisp paper monogrammed with her father's initials. The pen now felt small and rather insignificant in her grip, but then again, her hand was much bigger than the last time she had held it. Yet nothing came to her that was exceptional enough to mar the page, so she set the instrument aside.

What if he left here and was killed somehow?

She closed her eyes and lay her throbbing head on the desk until, about ten minutes later, she heard bustling out in the hall and the door opened. She lifted her head in time to see that it was Mrs. Pride with a meal tray.

"Shall I put it on the table over here, dear?"

"But I told you that—"

"A bit of cheese and bread is no proper meal for you," her nanny said quite firmly. "Now here's a nice plump sausage, some chips, mustard, bread and cheese, and a carrot. And a quite nice parsnip, which I literally had to fight a so-called *lady* over. And a fresh cup of tea with *real* milk, and I got our sugar rations."

"Thank you, Mrs. Pride, so very much."

"Oh, Molly, you shouldn't be sitting in the dark like that with just the one candle." She moved to turn on the light after setting down the tray, but Molly said, "Please don't. I actually prefer it darker right now, Mrs. Pride. I have a bit of a migraine."

"Well, if you're sure."

As Molly watched, her nanny set out her silverware and a cloth napkin. This made Molly think back to her childhood. Mrs. Pride would come to her room every morning and make sure her charge was suitably clean. Then, after Molly's hair was thoroughly brushed, she would help her dress and then bring Molly downstairs in a presentable state.

Molly's mother and father would usually be seated at the small breakfast table in the sunny, windowed nook just off the kitchen:

her father quietly absorbed in the *Times* over a cup of coffee, porridge, brown toast, and two poached eggs, her mother doing a bit of embroidery while awaiting the sounds of her daughter's approach. Then Eloise Wakefield would instantly toss aside whatever she was doing, and she would be Molly's faithful companion for as long as the little girl so desired. Sometimes Mrs. Pride would literally have to snatch Molly away in order to get on with her tasks having to do with the child.

Molly remembered that her mother never looked happier than when her gaze was on her daughter. And Molly had always loved to be the centre of attention. But now, looking back on it with a more mature perspective, she could see the difficulties such a prolonged separation might have caused a mother so devoted to her only child. That must have been what Mrs. Pride was referring to before. And after what had happened to her mother at that shelter? That would have devastated anyone, whether they had any previous mental issues or not.

She took her locket from around her neck and opened it to reveal her mother's picture once more. That kind, sweet visage. What would she look like now? More important, what would her mother *be* like?

"Do you need anything else?" Mrs. Pride asked.

Molly came back to the present with a bit of a start. "What? I'm sorry, no. That's fine, thank you."

"Are you sure you're all right, dear?" said Mrs. Pride in a voice that made clear she did not believe Molly to be in any way "all right." She glanced anxiously at the locket.

"I'm perfectly fine, thank you. Oh, Mrs. Pride, have you . . . um, I know this will sound strange. But have you noticed anyone watching the house?"

Her nanny's eyebrows lifted. "Watching the house?"

"Yes. Some men. Perhaps in a car?"

"Well, come to think, a few times it did seem that I saw the same man standing across the street and smoking a cigarette. I thought he was just loitering. But he wasn't dressed as such. He seemed, well, like a gentleman, not one of them rascals on the street. Have you seen him, too?"

"I think I have."

"Do you think we should tell the constable?" asked Mrs. Pride.

"I think we should, yes. It might be nothing but . . . well, one never knows, particularly nowadays."

"All right, Molly. I'll tell the bobby next time I see him. He's a young lad, quite conscientious. Now, nothing else you need?"

"Oh, I would like the other letters from the doctor in Cornwall."

"Yes, of course, thank you for reminding me," she replied with her gaze averted. It seemed clear to Molly that her nanny would rather not face this family dilemma.

Mrs. Pride took her leave and Molly sat down at the table to eat. She slipped her napkin over her lap, readied her silverware, gave everything a pinch of salt, and tucked in. The simple fare was wonderful, but then really anything would have been, so ravenous was her hunger.

The door opened as she was finishing her dinner, and Mrs. Pride came in carrying a stack of letters.

"They were in your parents' room. It took a bit of searching."

"Thank you."

Mrs. Pride deposited the letters on the desk, took the tray, and shuffled out, closing the door behind her.

Arranging them in chronological order, Molly picked up the first letter. It was on the same stiff notepaper. The contents were brief but to the point. Her mother was undergoing treatment and handling it well.

The next letter and the next said the same thing.

Then, in subsequent communications from Dr. Stephens, the wording changed slightly, but Molly was still able to grasp the meaning behind the fancy medical terms.

There were certain *challenges* in her mother's diagnosis, proclaimed Dr. Stephens. Another letter cautioned that extreme "mood swings" were to be expected. Then in another letter dated fourteen months ago came an ominous warning that her condition had *deteriorated*, only to be revived in the next letter to a better state of prognosis. Still more letters carried this theme through, with more ups and downs. The last missive simply said that Mrs. Wakefield was responding to certain treatments and that Dr. Stephens was cautiously optimistic that they had hit upon the *correct course* this time.

As she laid aside the last letter, Molly was well aware that the correspondence from Dr. Stephens had ended just about the time that her father had walked out the door. She wasn't sure if the two events were connected, but they certainly could have been.

She had an idea and lifted the fat telephone receiver. She dialled for the operator, and a voice came on and asked what she needed. Molly gave her the phone number for the Beneficial Institute that was imprinted on the letterhead. "It's in Cornwall," she added.

"Hold, please, you'll need the trunk operator to ring that."

There was silence for the longest time. Then another operator came on the line. "I'm sorry, the number is not answering. The lines may be down. Please try again later."

Molly sighed, returned the phone to its cradle, and watched the candle on the desk burn down to a mass of wax. It was quite dark outside now, what with the gas streetlamps no longer being lit. She obviously could not travel to Cornwall tonight. And she had no idea where her father had gone, or if he was even alive.

Molly needed someone to talk to. And perhaps she knew just the person.

Parallel Conditions

A FARAWAY CLOCK TOWER struck the hour. Charlie looked up at the murky sky as he turned down the familiar alley. He had made up his mind to tell Ignatius Oliver that he was one of the lads who had left Eddie and the policeman dead. He didn't know if Oliver would call the constables on him or not. He hoped not. But he could not keep this inside himself any longer. And he couldn't tell his gran. He didn't want to see the crushing disappointment on her face. Charlie wasn't sure he could survive that.

He stopped as soon as he saw her. "M-Miss?"

Molly turned to look at him as she stood by The Book Keep's dirty window.

"Charlie? What are you doing here?"

"I wanted to ask Mr. Oliver somethin'. What are *you* doin' here?"

"I have some letters I want him to read."

"How'd you get here?" he asked.

"I took a taxi."

"You shouldn't be out alone at night."

"And *you* should?" she retorted.

He waved this off. "I can take care of myself. But you're quite different."

"Because I'm a girl?"

"No, because you don't know the ways of the city no more."

"Well, as you can see, I made it here just fine," she said with spirit. Then she put her hand in her pocket and held up the half crown. "You're going to take this."

"No, Miss."

"If you don't, I'll throw it in the gutter drain over there."

"You wouldn't do that!" said a shocked Charlie.

"Watch me!"

Charlie slowly reached out, took the coin, and put it in his pocket. Then he tried the doorknob but it was locked.

"What happened to the door?" asked Molly, suddenly noticing the repaired damage.

"Dunno," lied Charlie. "And he put the bell on the outside."

"It says to ring it for service. Even though the closed sign is out the lights are on, so let's do so."

Charlie tinkled the bell and waited. Presently, through a crack in the drawn curtains, they saw Oliver come out from behind the counter. He walked quickly over and unlocked the door.

"Molly, Charlie, what an unexpected pleasure. Please, come in."

They did so.

"It's quite late. Is anything wrong?"

They shook their heads.

"Would you like some tea?"

They both shook their heads once more.

Oliver looked at his front window and said, "Here I am, an air warden, and I haven't pulled my blackout curtains all the way. I should give myself a notice-of-light-showing card." He pulled them fully shut before turning back to the pair. "Now, what can I do for you?"

Molly looked at Charlie. "Would you like to go first?"

"No, you go on ahead," he replied in haste.

Molly took out the letters and explained to Oliver what they were and her mother's being in a sanatorium in Cornwall. She glanced nervously at Charlie as she did so, her cheeks turning slightly red with this admission.

"Perhaps you could read them and provide some advice," suggested Molly.

"If I can be of assistance, but I'm certainly no doctor."

He put on his specs, took out the letters, arranged them, and read the missives from first to last while Charlie and Molly looked on.

Finished, he put the correspondence back in their respective envelopes and passed them over to Molly. He took off his specs and wiped them on his sleeve.

"It does seem serious, Molly. Again, while I'm not a doctor, my brother is. Thus, I have heard the terms 'social phobia' and 'neurosis.' They can be quite difficult to overcome. And with any illness of the mind it's not as simple as taking a teaspoon of castor oil or wrapping one's hand with a bandage."

"But she *could* get better?"

"Oh, certainly. I don't know exactly what sorts of treatment they are referring to but I'm sure they are taking her best interests into account. Now, what does your father think of all this?"

Molly glanced at Charlie to see him staring earnestly at her.

She looked back at Oliver and said slowly, "He . . . he is very concerned as well. He has been in constant contact with Dr. Stephens, as you saw from the letters. He went out to Cornwall to take my mother there and has visited her often."

"Then I'm not sure exactly what it is you want me to help you with. He's in a far better position to answer all of your questions or take any needed action."

"The fact is, my father is consumed with work at the Ministry of Food. He sometimes doesn't come home at night. I felt that if I could relieve him of that burden, then it would make things better."

Oliver frowned and shook his head. "You're quite young to be relieving your father of such a responsibility, Molly. For instance, no doctor would take direction from you with regard to your mother's treatment. I'm not sure they would even discuss the case with you."

"I *am* her daughter!" Molly replied heatedly. "And I'm not a child. I'm quite nearly sixteen."

"And if it were up to me, I would tell you everything about her condition. But, unfortunately, it is not up to me. And if my elder brother is any indication, members of the medical profession can be quite patronizing to members of the fairer sex."

Molly's spirits dipped. "But do you think it's possible that I could visit her?"

"I'm sure if there is a way to do so, your father will arrange it and go with you."

Molly said slowly, "The thing is, he is very busy. Days go by when I don't see my father at all. I don't think that it's possible that he will be able to get away."

"Perhaps you can ring them?" suggested Oliver.

"I tried but the line was not working."

"Yes, that does happen very often now. But I'm not sure what I can do."

"Is it such a long trip to Cornwall?" said Molly.

"Fairly long, yes. Oh, it's the most beautiful country. People often go there for their health and to take in the sea air. Now, there are trains that leave from Paddington, but there are several transfers along the way, at least there were. But what with the war, I have no idea how long it would take or if it's even possible right now. The last I heard, all rail lines south were out of commission. Whether that strictly includes Cornwall or not, I'm not certain."

"So you've been there?" asked Molly excitedly.

"Well, in Plymouth in Devon, very near Cornwall. My wife and I honeymooned there."

"You might have stayed near where the Institute is located," said Molly.

"We might have done, but I don't recall any such place. I don't know how long it's been there, either. And our honeymoon was fifteen years ago." His face fell as he said this. "Fifteen years ago . . . yesterday. We had always planned to go back, but . . ."

"I'm so sorry for bringing this all up," said Molly, noting his despair.

"Please. You couldn't possibly have known."

"Then I guess I won't be able to see my mother," said Molly.

"You really should speak to your father about this," urged Oliver. "I'm certain that even though he is terribly busy, he would perhaps make a call to the Institute and let you talk to the doctor, or even your mother, if she is able to. Or he could possibly arrange a trip there with his government contacts."

"Yes, yes," said Molly dully. "I . . . I will talk to . . . Father."

"Good," said Oliver, although he looked puzzled by Molly's clear lack of enthusiasm at his quite sensible suggestion.

"Mr. Oliver?" she said. "There's one more thing."

"Yes?"

"I know this will sound quite silly, but it seems that, what I mean to say is, there might be people watching my house. And following me."

"Following you?" he exclaimed.

"Yes. When I first came here to see you, two men in a car followed me. I'm sure of it. And I've seen another man watching my house. And so has my nanny."

"And don't forget 'bout the bloke that took your picture at the park and then run off," interjected Charlie.

"Took your picture?" parroted Oliver.

"Well, at least I think he did," said Molly.

"Have you told your father about this?"

"I . . . No, but I suppose I should."

"Yes, Molly, you absolutely must. It might be nothing but, then again, one can never be too careful. Particularly these days."

"Of course, yes, I will tell him straight away."

"Good." He turned to Charlie. "And how are you, Charlie?"

"I'm fine, guv."

"And what brings you here?"

"I . . . saw your door was all banged up."

"Yes, it seems that someone tried to break in. I didn't see who. It was a group of boys, I think. It turned quite tragic. You might have heard about it? Two people died after being hit out on the street by a passing lorry."

Molly exclaimed, "Oh dear, do you mean the constable and the boy? Charlie and I did read about that in the paper."

He glanced at Charlie. "I have no idea why out of all the shops around here they would choose mine."

"Maybe they weren't all that smart," said Charlie, while looking away. "Or maybe they might have wanted books, you reckon?"

"Perhaps," said Oliver. "But surely you didn't come here for that. You would have only seen the state of my door when you got here. What was the reason for coming in the first place?"

"I . . . I . . ." Charlie glanced at Molly. "I was wondering if you had a pencil."

"A pencil?"

"Yeah, so's I can write in the book you give me."

"But don't you have a pencil for school?" asked Molly.

"Yeah, but you have to leave it there. They won't let you take it home."

"But don't you have schoolwork to do at home?" she persisted.

Charlie looked at her crossly. "Readin' and such. But not writin'."

"I have something better than a pencil." Oliver walked over to the counter, opened a drawer, and withdrew from it a pen. "This was the pen that my wife used to write with before I bought her a new one for our first anniversary."

"You don't want to give that away, surely," said Molly.

"Let's just call it a *loan*, shall we, Charlie? When you're done with it, or have acquired another writing instrument, you can simply bring it back."

He held it out to Charlie, who did not reach for it.

"It's okay, Charlie, really. I would like you to have it."

Slowly, Charlie took the pen and curled his dirty fingers around its glistening skin. "Thank you," he mumbled.

"I'm sure that whatever you write down will be important," said Oliver.

"I doubt that," said Charlie.

"Even if it is only important to you," amended Oliver. "Which is often the most important thing of all."

"Very fine thoughts," said Molly.

"It was Imogen who said them."

"I'm sure you miss her terribly," she said.

"Something more than terribly, actually," replied Oliver, looking away.

"Was it the bombin's?" said Charlie. "How she died?"

"Charlie!" said Molly in an admonishing tone. "That's none of our business." Of course she had previously asked Oliver the very same question.

"No, no, that's all right. What I will say is, it was the bombings, but it also wasn't the bombings. And more than that, I just can't . . . reveal. I feel like it's as much as I know, frankly."

In a lighter tone, Oliver added, "Anyone care for a cup of tea now?"

A Fresh Plan

Three nights later, Charlie peered straight up at the ceiling of his cupboard and wondered about things. It had rained on him coming home from a night-time excursion where he had cleaned debris from a boat docked on the Thames for two shillings plus a quarter-loaf of bread and a wedge of cheddar to line his empty belly. He had dried off as best he could so Gran wouldn't know he'd been out. He doubted he could use the lice excuse a second time.

He eyed the journal with the thought of transforming it into five quid. Would Miss Virginia Woodley of King & Chauncey still give him the money? If he went back there full of remorse with a packet of glib lies to tell?

From his pocket he drew out the pen Oliver had given him. It was a fine thing, firm in his hand, quite pretty and delicate with a golden nib. That might be worth something, too, he thought, but then quickly chastised himself.

You're not sellin' his dead wife's pen, you git. It ain't yours.

Charlie's thoughts had turned back to selling the book because things were quite desperate now. In two days' time, they would no longer be able to live in the flat, and Gran had so far failed to find another place for them to live. She had begun boxing up her few possessions and agonizing over what was to become of her vanity and chair. She had gone off to her room tonight grim-faced and stiff-limbed. Charlie had had no such issues about his possessions. He had nothing, really, to box up other than a few odd bits of spare clothing.

So he would go directly to King & Chauncey in the morning after cleaning himself up and making sure his clothes were presentable. Then he would plead his case to Miss Woodley, get the five quid, rush back here, and wait for Gran to return home from work and announce grandly that the sale of the book had saved them. He would hand her the five pounds, and the half crown earned from Molly, along with the shillings from cleaning the boat, and he would see the smile break across her face like the sun did coming through the clouds. And they would be all right again. And it would be Charlie who provided for them after only being a burden to his grandmother for ages and ages.

With a roof securely over their heads, Charlie would seek gainful employment. At very nearly fourteen he was strong with lots of energy. He could surely do things worth real wages.

Charlie shifted slightly in his box. He had to sleep diagonally and curled up, and still he felt the wood on his head and toes.

The rain had started to fall even harder now; he could hear it beating against the darkened panes of the window in the other room. It would be chilly and damp tomorrow, and he worried about Gran getting the cold in her chest. Most medicines were going to the soldiers, as was proper. He would have to watch her carefully. And maybe with some of his future wages he could buy her some cough syrup from the chemist down the street.

Then his thoughts turned to Molly and their meeting with Mr. Oliver. She had lied to him, Charlie believed. Her father wasn't at the Ministry of Foods; he was gone, Charlie was convinced of that. So even with her very fine home and her nanny, and a Singer, she had no parents, really, while Charlie at least had Gran. Still, Charlie put a hand over his eyes and thought about how nice it would be to have parents. Maybe Molly was lying awake in her bed thinking the very same thing. It forged a definite bond between them, he suddenly realized, which was startling because they came from such different worlds.

And while he liked Ignatius Oliver very much, he was quite odd. And those packets of papers? He said it was a manuscript or some such. He thought about the place in the alleyway where Oliver had been given some other papers by the same bloke he'd seen the first night at The Book Keep.

Yeah, quite odd.

He got up and spent some time using his spit to rub the stains off his clothes like a cat did its fur, and making sure his cloth cap was in good shape. He would manage his hair in the morning and use the tap and the soap bar to scrub his face and hands pink.

The meagre cleaning of his clothes finished, an exhausted Charlie got back into his box. The beats of the rain slowly grew so melodic that once Charlie closed his eyes he succumbed to a slumber that carried him past all possible waking points. When he finally opened his eyes it was still pouring outside. He sat up and stretched in his bed, sensing that it was later than usual.

Then it occurred to him: He had not heard the footsteps, or the shuffle to the lav, or the activity in the kitchen as Gran prepared to leave for work at half wages. And he had not felt the kiss on his forehead.

I must'a been sleeping hard!

Suddenly Alone

"Gran?"

He rose from his bed.

"Gran?"

He went in search of her.

Her bedroom was empty.

The bathroom was not.

Charlie stood in the doorway looking down at the floor.

There was only one eye showing because of how she was lying there. It was open and seemed to stare back at him a bare inch above the cold floor. The pupil seemed dulled and unusually large.

He took one cautious step inside the room.

"Gran?"

She might have fallen, he thought. And then passed out. One of her slippers was off and he could see the full extent of her swollen calf, the blue veins prominent like ink marks of a meandering river enshrined on a cartographer's survey.

What if she had cried out for help and he had slept through it?

He inched closer. "Gran? Do you need help to get up?"

The eye did not blink. The bare foot did not move, not even a tremor.

He knelt down beside her, reached out, and touched her shoulder. She still had on her nightdress. Her white hair fell around her shoulders; it was longer than he imagined it would be—she always wore it tied up. The strands lay haphazardly around her neck.

He felt that neck.

Cold and stiff, and as unlike Gran as it was possible to be. She always gave off heat; he had warmed his slender bones next to her many a frigid night.

He sat down next to her, his knobby knees touching, his hand resting protectively on her cheek, which was chilled, too, as though she had been outside in weather and had just come in seeking warmth before taking a serious fall.

"Gran? Are you okay? Are you hurt?"

As the rain fell outside, Charlie felt a fragile part of himself rise to the ceiling and then look down at the pair of them there on the scuffed bathroom floor. The beating rain took on the elements of a mournful tune, like the organ in church produced.

His "floating self" merged with what was left on the floor and a familiar refrain abruptly assembled in his head.

I'm not a boy.

I'm a man.

Act like it, Charlie.

He managed to roll Gran over on her back and put his ear to her chest, his finger to her neck. He had seen the ambulance men do this to the bloodied people on the streets after the dropping of bombs.

Heart beating.

Lungs swelling.

Gran had neither.

He put his finger over her lips, trying to detect breath.

He felt her cheek. She was even colder now.

He sat back and looked at her as she lay there, helpless—no, dead, he had to admit. The body limp, the mouth sagging, the eyes unblinking.

He tried to close her eyelids, but they refused to fall. He needed to tell someone of this, but his mind wouldn't inform him as to whom that might be. Then he finally had a spark of decision.

There was a neighbour upstairs, a man who worked at the butcher shop two squares over. He had been kind to Gran, occasionally giving her a bone to drop in the soup pot, finding meaty scraps here and there for them when he could, always a cheery hello when passing by, checking on them when the Jerries had finished their business in the skies for the night.

Charlie opened the front door and hurried up one flight of stairs. He kept knocking until he heard the man say, "All right, all right, 'ang on, I'm comin'."

Charlie said just enough to fully engage the man. The fellow's bare feet raced down the stairs and Charlie followed slowly. He knew what awaited him in the bathroom and was in no hurry to embrace it once again.

Later, a constable came along with a dark-suited, bowler-hatted gent carrying a black bag, who spent a little time in the bathroom with Gran still on the floor. He pulled out a stiff-backed official-looking booklet, filled out something on one of its pages, signed it, neatly tore out the sheet, and handed it to the policeman.

Charlie thought he heard the man say something about Gran's heart.

The bobby had asked Charlie where his parents were. He said, almost automatically, that his father was in the army and his mother was at work. The bobby had nodded and told Charlie to give his mother his condolences. Then the two men left.

The neighbour man had asked Charlie if there was someone to contact, somewhere for Charlie to go. A fearful Charlie told him there was, though he couldn't think of who or where that was right now.

A while later a long, black motorcar came with men in respectably sombre suits and tall hats and holding umbrellas against the inclemency. One of the dark-suited men told Charlie that the doctor who had declared his grandmother dead had alerted them as to the need for their mortuary services. Charlie had dully nodded and shown them where Gran was.

As they carried her body down the stairs on a stretcher, a sheet placed over her, Charlie thought of the address for some reason: Flat 4a, 13 Dapleton Terrace, Bethnal Green, London.

It was no longer his home.

Neighbours stood outside the building and watched Gran being loaded into the back of the long motorcar. Some crossed themselves, others bowed their heads, and still others shed tears because life was so hard here and Gran had been kind and helpful to all. Knitting a cap or gloves for a neighbour's child, bringing up a bowl of hot soup, freely giving away hunks of crusty bread from her shop throwaways, producing a plaster for a wheezy chest, or simply offering another pair of sturdy, loving hands and a soothing voice to help a weary mum with her newborn.

The long motorcar pulled off, and Gran was gone for ever. A bewhiskered man in a high hat had given Charlie a card with the name and address of where they were taking her. He had told Charlie to have his parents come around the next day. He had not asked for payment. He had not asked for anything. He had not asked if Charlie even *had* parents or where they might be right now. It was apparently just that way during a war, particularly where Charlie lived.

His family had not buried his father because there had been no body with which to do so. And Charlie was still in hospital when they had laid his mother's remains in the ground. He could clearly recall attending his grandfather's funeral, a matter that his gran had handled. Now it was Charlie's turn, and he wasn't at all sure how to manage it. For the longest time, he just stood there on the top step of Number 13 Dapleton Terrace, as the folks passed by to go back inside and move on with their day. Some touched his arm, said a few commiserating words, or tousled his hair. Two women gave him hugs. Another pressed in his cold hands a piece of cheese between two thin slices of coal-warmed bread. Still, he stood there because 4a was no longer his home.

He had no home.

He had no gran.

He had nothing, really, except himself, and what was that worth, he thought.

Charlie's mind, for some reason, could recognize all this, yet it appeared to have no effect on him emotionally. He hadn't cried. He hadn't fallen to the ground paralysed. He hadn't really done anything, and he felt terrible guilt for not viscerally reacting properly in the traumatizing wake of Gran's passing. Her death had deserved far more from him, and yet he had failed to live up to his responsibility to her in death, just as he had when she'd been breathing.

He had not got her the hat and specs, or the rent money. He had never really given her anything, except trying times. And she had left this life probably thinking that her only grandchild never would make anything of himself.

He returned to their flat and gathered the only clean formal dress that his grandmother had. He collected her stockings and underthings and her church shoes, though neither of them had been religious after his mother's death. But these constituted her burial clothes and they had to be proper. He put them all in an oilskin bag he pulled from under the sink in the kitchen.

He put on his coat and his cap and left the flat with her things in the one bag and all his possessions in another.

He walked out onto the street where the rain had mercifully ceased, at least for a bit. He hoped they had got Gran's eyes to close. It didn't seem right that they remained open if she couldn't see anything with them.

He hoped the four shillings and six pence were enough for a proper burial, but something told him it would not be. And then what would happen to Gran?

Charlie ran down the street to the only place in all of London he could think to go.

A Gathering of Particulars

"Yes?"

Mrs. Pride stared at Charlie, who looked back at her with an oilskin bag slung over each slender shoulder. The rain had begun to pour again halfway here and he was soaked through. He put down one bag, doffed his cap, and said, "Please, ma'am, I was wonderin' if Miss Molly Wakefield was here."

"Supposing she is, what would your business be with her?"

Before he could answer, the door opened wider and Molly appeared.

"Charlie?" she exclaimed. "What's wrong?"

"You . . . you know this . . . *boy*?" said Mrs. Pride.

"Yes. He's my friend. Come in, Charlie, quickly, it's starting to rain harder."

She reached past Mrs. Pride, gripped Charlie's arm, and pulled him, wet as he was, into the front room.

Mrs. Pride closed the door and looked askance at what she no doubt considered a nearly drowned street urchin in her mistress's fine home dripping all over the Wakefields' handwoven carpet.

"I'll take things from here, Mrs. Pride, thank you. Wait a moment, though, Charlie, have you eaten?"

He simply shook his head. He had given the bread and cheese the woman had handed him to a pavement man he had passed on the way here. It was the only time Charlie could ever remember giving food away. Now his hunger was painful.

"Mrs. Pride, can you prepare some breakfast for Charlie, please? And put the kettle on?"

"Yes, Molly. If you're quite sure," she added, glancing questioningly at her.

"I'm absolutely sure."

As a thoroughly flustered Mrs. Pride hurried off, Molly turned to Charlie. "How did you get here?"

"Run," he answered.

She looked astonished. "All that way? In the rain?"

He nodded.

She studied his stricken features. "What's happened?"

Charlie pointed his face down like the weight of the world was tugging on his chin. "My gran. She . . . she died this mornin'."

Molly put a hand to her mouth. "Your . . . your grandmother *died*?"

Charlie slowly nodded, even as he shivered. Not from the cold but from saying, out loud for the first time, that his gran was no longer with him.

"Oh, I'm so very sorry, Charlie. Please come and sit down over here. And let me bring you a blanket."

She did so and wrapped it securely around his shoulders before sitting beside him. "What happened to her? Was she ill?"

Charlie rubbed his wet nose. "Dunno. I found her on the floor of the lav. Her eyes were open and she weren't breathin'. The doctor said somethin' 'bout her heart. They . . . the men took her away in the motorcar."

"You mean the undertakers?"

"S'pose, yeah," sniffled Charlie.

"Do you know where they took her?"

In answer Charlie handed her the card from his pocket.

She read off it. "Yes, of course."

"They says to come round tomorrow."

"Yes, I suppose that's right," Molly said. "They would need some time to . . . to organize things properly." She looked at him and asked tentatively, "Did you live with your grandmother?"

Charlie nodded.

"And did you . . . live with anyone else as well?" she asked in a delicate tone.

Charlie shook his head. "No. My mum's dead. And Dad died at Dunkirk. I'm . . . sorry I didn't tell you before but . . . I don't like to . . . talk 'bout not havin' 'em."

Molly sat back, her guilt increasing tenfold over keeping her own secret about her father from him. "I'm so sorry. But it will be fine, Charlie."

He lifted an angry gaze from the floor to her. "It ain't fine. Gran's dead!"

"I meant that things will be taken care of. *She* will be taken care of. I will help you to do so. Losing . . . someone you love is hard enough without having to worry about such . . . details."

Everything you said to him could just as easily apply to you.

Charlie rummaged in his pocket and pulled out the half crown she'd paid him, and his shillings from the night before. "Got this to bury her proper."

Molly looked at the coins and said, "I'm sure that will be enough."

"You really think so?" Charlie said dubiously.

"Yes, absolutely. Now, what are in the bags?"

He had set them on the floor beside him.

"This one's Gran's things, to be . . . to be buried in. And this one is, well, all what I got 'cause we . . . see, *I* can't live there no more . . . the rent . . . Gran's wages got cut, so's we couldn't . . . pay it." He stopped abruptly and looked deeply ashamed.

"We'll worry about that later. For now, while you eat, I'm going to go through these things and see what's what."

Charlie looked embarrassed. "I took her underthin's and such because . . ."

"And that was perfectly sensible for you to do."

Charlie's expression suddenly turned frantic. "My book, I forgot my book!"

"That's all right. We can go back and get it later."

"It might not be there later!" exclaimed Charlie.

"I'm sure it will. Now, let me just nip in and check on your breakfast." She hurried off.

Charlie sat there, forlorn, because he knew that things at Dapleton Terrace tended to go missing when left behind by folks who died or couldn't pay their rent. But he couldn't hurry all the way back there now because he was so very tired, not so much from running, but from losing the only family he had left.

He stood and looked around the room. He had never been in a home such as this, full of furniture and paintings on the walls and thick carpet underfoot. And over there was a towering fireplace with a proper mantel and a fine brass-and-wood clock perched on top of it. He knew that some lived like this, but he'd had no firsthand knowledge of it.

Then the realization that he was all alone in the world hit him so incredibly hard that he sank back onto the couch, all of his strength withered away. He had always tried to overcome adversity with a proper spirit, somehow consistently seeing the good in the bad. But now he could glimpse nothing save misery ahead.

Molly returned and said, "Your breakfast will be ready presently and the kettle is nearly hot. Why don't you come and settle at the kitchen table while I take the bags to my room and go through them?"

She led him into the kitchen, where Mrs. Pride was preparing his plate. There was one fried egg, a slice of toast with actual butter and a wedge of cheddar, a bit of ham, a small bowl of porridge, a stewed prune, and a cup of what looked to be real milk. Molly would have once looked askance at such a shabby meal, but Charlie, his grief dissipating for a few moments, looked astonished. "Goodness, Miss, do you eat like this every meal?"

She could neither meet his eye nor answer his query. She simply fled the room.

While Charlie took up his cutlery, Molly carried the bags to her bedroom and looked through the first one. She carefully folded Gran's clothes and hung in the wardrobe what needed hanging, after first smoothing out some wrinkles. Mrs. Pride could iron them properly later. Her inventory showed that Charlie had missed a few essentials, which Molly was sure she could provide from their own stock of clothing. When she opened Charlie's bag she had to gasp. The smells emanating from within were quite overwhelming. All she could glimpse was a hodgepodge of rough, blackened garments.

She took nothing out, but hastily carried the bag at arm's length down the back stairs, found Mrs. Pride, and instructed her to have it all thoroughly laundered.

Mrs. Pride looked in the bag and said, "My Lord, I don't see much worth saving in there, Molly. It's for the dustbin, I'd say."

"When we go to get his book I can stop and purchase a few essentials for him. At least that'll do for now. Where do you keep the household funds?"

"I used to keep them in the cabinet in the small sitting room at the back of the house. But now I just keep them in a box in a cupboard under the stairs."

She showed Molly the box. When Molly saw what was there she said, "This really is all we have?"

"I should have told you this earlier, but I didn't want to worry you."

"Tell me what?" asked Molly, looking curiously at her nanny.

"I went to the bank last week to get some more pounds. Hadn't had to do that since your father left. But with you back and all. Anyway, the accounts he set up, well . . ."

"Well what?"

"The bank manager himself came out, took me to his office, and told me that the funds were no longer available."

Molly looked perplexed. "Did he say why?"

"No, but he was quite rude about it. Why, he looked at me quite suspiciously."

"What in the world?" said a bewildered Molly.

"And then he called in another man who asked me, bold as brass, where was Mr. Wakefield? And why didn't *he* come in to enquire as to his account?"

"This is all so confusing," said Molly.

Mrs. Pride gave her a side-eye look. "It . . . well, it was almost like he was suggesting that your father had committed some act of, I don't know, theft, or larceny, or whatever they call it."

"Father would never," replied Molly fiercely.

"Oh, I know that. I'm just telling you what I think that bank person thought. War does funny things to folks, Molly," she added.

Molly didn't know if she was referring to the bank people or her father.

"Mrs. Pride, you said you had also seen a man watching the house?"

"Yes. And I told the bobby on the beat about it. He wrote it down and promised to keep an eye out for him." Mrs. Pride stiffened. "Wait, do you think it could be connected to this bank business?"

"I don't know. It's just very puzzling. I mean, why would the *bank manager* have met with you over a single account?"

"That *did* seem quite odd to me." She suddenly looked even more worried.

"What?" asked Molly quickly.

"Well, I'm sure it's nothing, but . . . but a few weeks ago I sent a letter to a friend of mine, she lives up in Norfolk. Hadn't written a letter for the longest time. Had to go to the post office for a stamp."

"What of it?" said Molly impatiently.

"Well, my friend wrote me back. And she said that it looked like my letter to her had been steamed open and then resealed."

"Opened and then resealed?"

"Yes. It was quite odd."

"Mrs. Pride?"

"Yes?"

"Was my father also going mad? Leaving without explanation to you or a letter or a call to me? And it might be connected somehow to the men watching us, the odd behaviour by the bank, and perhaps the reading of your letter. In his despair he . . . he might have done something . . . *careless*."

Mrs. Pride drew herself up and said firmly, "Your father was, *is*, the sanest man I have ever met. If he was going mad, then the whole world has, too."

Molly pocketed sufficient money, tidied herself up to go out, and rejoined Charlie, who was just finishing up his meal.

"How was the food?" she asked.

"I . . . I never tasted nothin' so good. And there's so much of it."

This praise almost made Molly weep. *But then I may not be far behind.* "Oh, Charlie, I didn't see your gas mask in the bags."

He looked up at her ruefully. "Me and Gran, we sold our masks a few days ago."

"Sold them?" she said, looking startled.

"There was bills comin' due and a bloke give us money for 'em."

"I see. All right. Well, my father, I mean, we have a spare here for you."

"Thanks." He finished his porridge and put on his cap.

"Charlie, where are you going? Your clothes are still wet!"

"It's all right, Miss. The book is more 'portant. It's five quid."

Too Late

Molly insisted that they take a taxi to 13 Dapleton Terrace. When they arrived, Charlie ran up the steps, tugged open the front door, and they clattered up the stairs to Charlie's floor.

They hadn't yet reached the door to his flat when Charlie cried out, "I closed the door when I left. I swear I did. And now it's open."

"Well, maybe someone came in after just to check on things."

"Maybe," said a wary Charlie.

Once inside Charlie immediately ran to his cupboard and Molly hurried after him.

"You . . . you slept in here?" she asked, looking down at the bedding in the box. She could have reached out and touched both sides of the space at the same time.

He didn't answer. Instead he searched through his bedding and cried out, "It's gone. It was right here." He kicked the box. "Bloody hell!"

"Charlie! Language!" she admonished.

Charlie heard a noise and poked his head out of his room. He saw the open window in the kitchen, the one he always used when going and coming late at night. He ran to the window, looked out, and saw him.

It was Lonzo leaping off the ladder and onto the overturned dustbin. He hit the ground, running fast. And he clearly had something under his arm.

Charlie leaned out the window and shouted, "Oi, Lonzo, you come back with that. It's *mine*. You hear me?"

Lonzo simply ran faster, until he reached a corner and was gone from sight.

"Who was that?"

Charlie turned to see Molly peering out the window beside him. "Lonzo."

"So he has your book?"

"Yes," replied Charlie bitterly.

"We'll have to report this to the police."

"The police?!" exclaimed a shocked Charlie.

"He stole from you, Charlie. That's a crime."

Charlie mumbled. "We . . . we don't need no police. I'll set things right."

"How do you know this Lonzo?"

"He's just a boy what lives round here."

"So we can speak to his parents, then?"

Charlie rubbed his nose. "He ain't got no parents."

"*Doesn't* have any parents," corrected Molly. "Grandparents, perhaps?"

"No, he ain'—he doesn't have none of them, neither."

"Who, then?"

"Well, nobody. He only had a mate—" Charlie shut his mouth.

"Why would Lonzo have taken the book?" asked Molly.

"'Cause I told him I could get a few quid for it, that's why. And now Lonzo'll be the one gettin' the money. And I won't be able to bury Gran proper," he added miserably.

"Well, we must go to his house and demand the return of your book."

"Lonzo don't live in no house! And he's goin' to sell that book." Charlie shook his head in despair. "Damn!"

Molly didn't have the heart to scold him this time over his coarse language. As they walked outside, she said, "So, your parents? You said your father died at Dunkirk?"

"Yeah."

"And your mum?"

"A bomb."

"I'm so very sorry."

Charlie looked at a blown-apart building down the street, where children played games amid the rubble.

He let out a sigh. "Seems like everybody's sort of dead, Miss. Only some just don't know it yet."

The Complicated Business of the End

They stopped at a secondhand shop and found two sets of clothes, underwear, and socks for Charlie and a pair of boots that were in decent shape, along with a felt cap. Charlie protested at first when Molly explained her plan, but he finally relented and carefully packed his new clothes in a box provided by the shop's assistant. Back in Chelsea, Charlie performed a rigorous bathing in Molly's parents' claw-foot tub. He came out of it scrubbed pink and feeling cleaner than he had ever thought possible. He put on a set of his new clothes, and they and the boots fit him well.

Later, he and Molly sat in her father's study.

Charlie looked around in wonder at the shelves of books. "Have you read 'em all?"

"When I left here, I was really too young to read them, though when I was in the country I read every day. I went through the vicar's library and then visited the library in town every week. It's a true pleasure losing yourself in another's imagined world. And you can spend time with so many different people from so very many places, places I may never actually go."

Charlie looked at her knowingly. "My mum and I would

sometimes go to the café and I'd have a little book and she hers. It was nice."

"Your mother. You mentioned a bomb?"

Charlie glanced upwards. "I guess nobody expected the Jerries to bomb a school."

"And were you at the school, too?"

"Yeah, but I was just a bit jumbled." He looked around. "So you got no parents, either?"

She said quickly, "I *do* have parents. My . . . my father is away on business presently. And as you know, my mother is in a sanatorium in Cornwall."

Charlie rubbed his now very clean nose and nodded. "So, when's your dad comin' back from his . . . *business*?"

Molly couldn't meet his eye as she prepared her lie. "I don't expect it will be much longer, now that I'm home."

"Were you and your mum close?"

"My mother was the closest friend I had. But she loved me perhaps too much."

"How can you love somebody *too* much?" he asked.

"It's not really important." She added wistfully, "I so looked forward to seeing both her and my father when I got home. And I've seen neither."

"Wait, not even your dad. I thought you said—"

"I was not being entirely truthful, Charlie," she said, looking guilty and pained by this admission. "I have *not* seen him. And I've no idea when I will. That . . . is not the sort of homecoming I envisioned." She glanced at him. "But you have it far harder. At least I'm reasonably certain my parents are still alive. I wish your parents could come back to you, Charlie. I know that they would want to more than anything."

"Well, wishin' for somethin' never works. Least not for blokes like me." He rose and said, "I guess I'll be takin' my leave now. Thanks for the food and the clothes."

She looked surprised. "I thought you would stay here, at least for now."

"Why? I'm not family or anythin'."

"But you're my friend."

"Still, don't think it's a good idea. We're, well, we're different."

"We do have to take care of your gran. I can help with that."

Charlie gave her a searching look. "Why? I mean, I ain't done nothin' for you."

"You led me to the Ministry of Food."

"And you paid me a half crown for that," he replied.

"Which you wouldn't accept at first. Why was that?"

Charlie shrugged. "I was goin' that way, so why get paid for goin' somewheres I was already goin'?"

"I think you should stay here, at least for a bit. We'll make the arrangements for your gran. Do you know where she—I mean, for the burial?"

"Same place we buried my mum and granddad, I guess."

"Where is that?"

"At a church near where we used to live over in Stepney. We'd go there regular when my mum was alive. Got a little graveyard behind it."

"It would be nice for her to be with family."

"Do you reckon them undertakers can help with that?"

"People do die all the time, and they are taken care of with proper dignity and respect. This is England, after all."

In her mind's eye, Molly glimpsed rows of coffins containing the remains of soldiers lined up outside the hospital near Leiston.

Charlie said, "You woulda liked my gran. Now, she said her mind when she wanted to, but she took good care 'a me."

Molly shook her head clear of coffins. "I'm sure she did, and I'm certain I would have very much enjoyed knowing her."

The next morning, they took a taxi to Wilkinson & Dunn, Undertakers, which wasn't that far from Charlie's old flat. It was a dour, sooty brick building with two front doors painted black and a tall, round chimney with thick smoke belching from it. Since a sign posted outside said the building also housed a crematorium, Molly kept her eyes averted from the stream of smoke escaping into the sky.

They met with the gentleman who had given Charlie his card. He was Wilkinson the Second, son of the now-dead principal founder of the firm, he explained. When Charlie mentioned the church graveyard where his mother and grandfather were buried, Wilkinson stroked his whiskers, nodded, and said that could be arranged. He asked no questions about Charlie's parents, or even Charlie's age. With tens of thousands perishing in London from the bombings, many more having been left homeless, and untold numbers having succumbed to sickness, it apparently wasn't unduly critical whether one was left alone or not, because so many had been.

They gave Wilkinson the bag with Gran's burial clothes. When the man started to discuss his fees, Molly frantically looked through her pockets and then said that she believed she had dropped one of her gloves outside. She asked Charlie to go and fetch it for her.

When he returned with the glove that Molly had indeed dropped near the front door of the building, Wilkinson told him that the sum total for the burial would be four and six, which was the exact amount that Charlie had collectively earned from Molly and the gent with the boat. And he would make the arrangements with the church Charlie had mentioned for Gran's plot near her husband and daughter.

Charlie duly paid over the money, and the matter was left at that. The burial would take place two days hence, they were told.

Wilkinson rose, thumbed the fat silver watch that fronted his vest, and said, "Would you like to see your grandmother now, young man? We have not yet prepared her for burial. It's right down this hall."

Charlie stared up at him, his eyes frozen in their hollows. "S-see Gran?"

"Yes. Or you can wait until the day of burial."

"I'll wait," said Charlie quickly.

On the journey back, Charlie glanced at Molly and said, "Surprised you ain't notice you dropped your glove."

"I'm terribly fuzzy about things like that." She shot him a look. "You needn't have a look at your gran if you don't want to."

He gave her an appraising glance. "You seen someone in the box, too?"

Molly's mind once more flashed to the rows of simple pine coffins containing the bodies of soldiers who would never again see their loved ones.

"One of the sons of the family I stayed with. It was very sad. He was only nine when he died. He looked . . . very peaceful. Just like he was sleeping. And he was no longer sick. I tried to focus on that, but I still cried. It's perfectly acceptable to cry."

"I guess," said Charlie. "Though I tries not to, if I can help it."

"Why is that?"

"'Cause once you start, you might never stop." Charlie thought of his mum and his gran and his cheeks trembled. "Leastways I won't."

Confessions

The morning of the burial emerged cold, with fringes of dreary, moistened clouds wrapping the city like clingy wisps of gossamer. The long hearse sat at the kerb. Wilkinson & Dunn had supplied the men necessary to carry the coffin.

The graveyard was a small parcel of dead grass coated with leaning, aged, lichen-coated tombstones of varying degrees of embellishment. A rusted wrought iron gate attached to a tilting stone column constituted the sole entrance. The short parade of people made its way to a rectangular hole already dug to the requisite depth.

Wilkinson the Second was in front wearing formal tails and top hat, commensurate with the sombre occasion. Behind him were Molly in a black dress and Charlie dressed in the other set of clothes that Molly had purchased for him. And behind them were the two columns of men, their broad shoulders holding aloft the coffin with Gran's remains inside.

Earlier, Charlie had viewed Gran in her coffin back at the undertakers. Molly had stood resolutely with him, gripping his hand. She had been right, Charlie had told her. Gran looked quite peaceful, like she was merely sleeping. Her eyes were closed, her small hands resting one on top of the other at her chest. Her dress looked very fine, her skin was paler than Charlie thought possible. And her face and body seemed compressed, as though the firm of Wilkinson & Dunn had released something buoyant from within the woman.

As he continued to stare at her, Charlie's face screwed up and the tears slid freely down his cold cheeks. Molly said nothing, but she squeezed his hand and kept her gaze respectfully downcast, as tears trickled down her face.

The church's vicar was waiting at the gravesite with his sombre vestments and worn Bible. He read from the Scriptures and said some spirited words over the dead that no doubt he'd said many other times, especially with a war going on. And then he tossed a handful of dirt into the hole, where it landed on the coffin.

The man of God nodded at Molly, gripped Charlie firmly by the shoulder, whispered some words clearly meant to be helpful and healing, then took his leave, perhaps scurrying off to preside over another interment, without even asking Charlie where the rest of his family might be.

Wilkinson doffed his hat, gave them both a curt, officious nod, and left with his men in tow and his fee fully paid. This left Charlie and Molly alone, other than a big, rough-looking bearded fellow with huge, callused hands sitting on the ground with his back against an ancient tombstone three over from Gran's grave with a dented shovel resting next to him. He took a swig of something from a flask, closed his eyes, and dozed off before it came time to place the English earth over the old woman.

Charlie's attention was not on the freshly dug hole, but on a pair of grave markers. He pointed at one, a small affair where the engraving was still reasonably clear.

"That's my grandfather."

Molly leaned in and read, "Elias Jacob Wilson. That's a very fine name."

"My second name comes from him. He told me he got a bullet in the arm fightin' the Jerries the last time. And he had one eye not work proper 'cause 'a the gas they used."

"That's terrible."

He nudged the other marker with his boot. "And this here is my mum."

Molly looked at the inscription: *Jane Alice Matters, Cherished Mother and Daughter.* She glanced at Charlie. "I'm sure you miss her so very much."

Charlie slipped off his cap and stared down at the sunken dirt and his face screwed up once more. "I was still in hospital when they buried her. But then I come here and told her I'd never leave her 'cause I can't leave my mum. I don't want her to be alone. Not ever. Wouldn't be right after all she done for me."

Molly drew a breath and looked at the grave marker. In her mind, she scrubbed clean what was there and replaced it with: *Eloise Mary Wakefield, Devoted Wife and Mother.*

A tear formed in the corner of her right eye and she suddenly felt lightheaded as her thoughts swirled on a southwesterly route all the way to Cornwall and the Beneficial Institute.

She envisioned her mother wrapped in blankets and sitting on a gothic, windswept terrace looking out over a countryside vista that would seem quite foreign to a woman used to calling London home.

"You okay?"

Molly broke from these thoughts and looked at Charlie, who was staring curiously at her.

"You can leave from here and still never, ever leave *her*, Charlie."

"How's that?" he said doubtfully.

In response, she gripped his hand and guided it to his chest. "You will always have her inside you, no matter where you go. That's how powerful love is. She carried you inside her for nearly a year. That bond is unbreakable. Wherever you go, she will be there with you. It's . . . it's like a law—no, a *covenant*, that's the word. It's for ever."

She let go of his hand.

"You really think so?"

"I *know* it is so. Do you believe me?"

Charlie thought about this for a moment. "Yeah . . . I do."

"I have something to tell you. A confession, really."

"What?"

"My father is *not* away on business. He left home months ago and no one has seen him since."

"What? And you've no idea where he went?"

"None. So, like you, I do not have parents right now."

"I'm glad you told me, Miss. It's not good to keep too much in your head. I do that sometimes, and, well, it ain't good."

"I came back to the city expecting to see both my parents. And now . . . ?"

"But like you said, your mum and dad may come back."

"Do you really think that's possible?"

"I believe lots of thin's are possible," replied Charlie eagerly. "It's not just believin' that they *can* happen. It's more unnerstandin' there's no good reason they *can't* happen."

"But right now, I really don't have anyone," said Molly.

"Well, you got me."

Molly turned to look at him. "And you have me, Charlie. So we have each other. That means an awful lot, doesn't it?" she said, as though to buck up her own spirits.

"It's loads better than bein' all by yourself. Havin' someone to talk to, and all."

"We will survive this. I know that we will. Don't you feel the same?"

"I'm startin' to," said Charlie quite truthfully.

The next moment their hands reached out, and held firm as they both turned back to stare solemnly at the resting places of the dead.

The wind picked up and rattled the aged trees that ran along one side of the graveyard. The fragile leaves, preparing to end their existence shortly, rippled as slender, weighted branches flexed and bent. Dozens of birds on these shaken limbs lifted off as one and raced headlong into the face of the breeze, clinging to invisible thermals, seemingly unconcerned with where they might next locate a perch. It was a case of sudden independence, and truly something to behold on that drearily cold morning with both recent and aged death all around.

Behind one of these trees, a willowy maple with pointed dangling leaves, stood Ignatius Oliver. His old coat covered his lanky frame, his battered and stained hat rode on his head. He took a moment to wipe clear his specs on the sleeve of his coat. As he settled the glasses back on the bridge of his nose, he looked to the sky, where the birds still soared, looped, and dipped, living kites free of gravity's harness.

He had gone to Charlie's flat to check on him and learned of his gran's passing. He had next gone to the firm of Wilkinson & Dunn because a neighbour of Charlie's had seen that name on the hearse. That was where he had discovered the funeral date and location, and also of Molly Wakefield's involvement. He had come to pay his respects, but to do so without intruding on Charlie's privacy. Yet Oliver had heard all that had just transpired between the two children.

The last time he'd been at a cemetery Oliver had stood and looked at the spot where his beloved Imogen should have been laid to rest for all eternity, with him to lie right beside her when his end came. On the other side were the graves of Imogen's parents.

While the birds artfully rambled above, Oliver walked slowly away.

He had learned something else today. Molly Wakefield was indeed being followed, because Oliver had seen the two men lurking behind some trees on the other side of the small cemetery. They were clearly there to observe the girl, and it made Oliver wonder why.

He slowly walked off, thinking that things were becoming as complicated as one of his encryptions.

All Madness Lies Therein

"WOULD YOU LIKE ANOTHER cup of tea, Charlie?"

Charlie glanced up to see Molly looking at him. They were seated in her father's study, in front of a slowly dying fire.

"No, Miss, I'm full up."

The swirling rain beat down outside, pelting the glass and making the chimney howl.

"I used to sit here with my father when it was cold or raining outside. We'd have a fire and he would read to me. My mother would be lying down."

Charlie looked at her. "Did she lie down a lot?"

"It didn't seem so at the time, but then I had nothing to compare it to. But looking back I can say that it probably was quite a lot, yes. I've come to learn that she is rather . . . fragile."

"Will you go to Cornwall to see her?"

"It would be very difficult. You heard what Mr. Oliver said."

"But she might do better if she can see you. She might come home even."

"The thing is, Charlie, my mother nearly burned this place down by accident because she was a bit off in the head."

He shrugged. "My grandfather was gettin' forgetful like and

sometimes seein' what weren't there. Gran just let him be and he come back right after a time." He paused. "If you did end up goin', how would you get to Cornwall, Miss? By train, like Mr. Oliver said?"

"I suppose so, yes. I'm just not sure how much it would cost."

He looked around the elegant room. "But surely you got plenty of money."

Molly looked at him uncertainly. "My father left some funds, but they're running low."

Charlie glanced guiltily at his teacup and set it down on the table. Then he stared at the cast-off shoes she'd bought him like they were terribly expensive things instead of costing a few odd shillings.

"My mother loved me very much. Perhaps too much."

"You said that before, but I still don't know what you mean by it," said Charlie.

"Do you know the word 'obsessive'?" she said cautiously.

Charlie shook his head.

"It's when someone cares so deeply about another that it affects their mind. They can do things that will actually be harmful to themselves and the ones they love because of it."

"And you think your mum is like that?"

"I think she might be. I just couldn't see it before. But I'm much older now and I can understand things more clearly."

"Well, even if she was this obsessed thin', it's still hard not to be with her. I'd give anythin' to have my mum back."

"I feel the same way, Charlie. My parents mean everything to me."

Charlie looked into the flickering flames. "You'd think your father would want to be round to help you. And her."

She shot him a glance. "Y-yes. There must have been something very important for him to go off like he did. To *abandon* us like that."

"He don't sound like that kinda bloke."

Molly said in a strained voice, "But he just walked out, Charlie. Without a word to me."

"I don't want to say it, Molly, but . . ." He looked at her warily.

"I *know* he might be dead. But he wasn't dead when he left home, obviously. He could have communicated with me, but he chose not to. That was not right!"

"What if he don't come back?"

"Things will become . . . complicated. Even more so than they are now."

They fell silent and listened to the rain as the wind continued to hurl the drops against the glass. Molly turned her head slightly to gaze at Charlie. He looked both far younger, and, in a certain way, older than she. They had both lost their parents—he permanently so, while there was no guarantee that the result for her wouldn't be the same as the one Charlie now endured.

"My mother's family is originally from Yorkshire," she said abruptly.

"Yorkshire?"

"Yes. It's in the north. Quite far away, nearly to Scotland, in fact. It's the largest county in England. So large, in fact, that it's divided up into all sorts of boroughs and *ridings* and the like. It's quite famous. It was where the War of the Roses took place."

Charlie gave her a confused look. "Eh? Blokes fightin' over flowers?"

"No. The House of York versus the House of Lancaster. The red rose was part of the Lancaster coat of arms and the white rose that of the House of York. They were fighting for the throne of England."

Charlie shook his head miserably. "Where did fightin' get anybody, eh?"

"I read up on it after Mrs. Pride told me my mother was from there."

"Hang on. Mrs. Pride told you? And not your mum?"

"That's right. The Tinsdales. That was their name. They were apparently quite well off."

"You reckon you still got family there, Miss?"

"I might."

"You could go and see 'em then."

"Why would I do that?" she said, glancing sharply at him.

"If they got money they might be able to help you and your mum, that's why. And they even might be able to help find your dad."

Molly pondered this for a few moments as Charlie watched the fire.

"And yet if I travelled to Yorkshire and Father came home, or perhaps a letter would arrive about Mother, then that would not be good."

"You could write to the place where your mum is," Charlie suggested.

"That's right. Perhaps I can have Mr. Oliver help me word the letter properly. He seems very smart and informed. And very kind."

"Y-yeah, I guess," mumbled Charlie.

She looked at him. "Is something the matter?"

He shrugged.

"Charlie, tell me."

"It's just that I seen Mr. Oliver doin' . . . well, doin' quite odd stuff."

She frowned. "What do you mean?"

He told her about the man and the packet of pages. "He said it was a man-u-scrip or some such."

"A *manuscript*. Like a book before it's a book. Well, that seems perfectly normal for someone who owns a bookshop to be receiving manuscripts."

"But then I seen Mr. Oliver go to some place in an alleyway and he come out with papers. And the same man was there."

"Was it a publishing house?"

He shrugged again. "Dunno. It were just a door in an old buildin'. And he looked sort of, well, nervous while he was doin' it. And so did the bloke that give him those papers. He looked, I dunno, shifty, like he knew he were up to somethin' no good. And it was long after midnight when I seen 'em the first time."

Molly looked disturbed by this information. "That is not when one would expect to drop off a manuscript. Do you remember where this other place is?"

Charlie nodded and picked up his cup. "Yeah, I think so."

Molly thought for a moment and then came to a conclusion that astonished her. Well, not exactly. She was feeling she had no control over her life right now. She was sick with worry over a mother she couldn't visit. She felt abandoned by a father she had adored. But with this she could take charge, even if it meant finding out that Oliver was simply visiting a friend.

She stood. "Well, let's go there and see what we can see. Mrs. Pride has already gone to her room. We can nip out now and she'll be none the wiser."

Molly found wellies and raincoats for them both, and a large umbrella.

Charlie was about to open the front door when Molly suddenly stiffened and gripped his hand to stop him.

"What?" asked Charlie.

"If those same men are watching the house, I don't want them to follow us."

Charlie nodded in understanding. "Right." He ventured to the back door, opened it, peered out, and saw the fence that surrounded the rear yard.

"Can you climb a fence?" he asked Molly.

"I'm sure I can."

"Okay, follow me then. Keep low, eyes away from the street, in case somebody flashes a torch. Your eyes reflect, see?"

They slipped outside and, keeping low, slunk over to the fence. Then Charlie gave Molly a boost up and over. He tossed her the umbrella, clambered over the fence, and dropped gracefully to the ground on the other side. Grasping her hand, he led her through the rear yard of the neighbouring house, where he once more helped her over a fence before nimbly scaling it and landing easily on his feet. Charlie then led them at a brisk pace, zigzagging through streets, and with him abruptly turning around every so often to check for followers. They reached another street and he slowed his pace.

"I think we're okay now."

Molly said breathlessly, "You're quite practiced at this, um, *skullduggery* business."

"Don't know what that word is, Miss. But if you mean I don't like blokes following me, well, where I'm from, you sort of have to be that way."

A Delivery in Darkness

They hurried over to the next corner and caught a bus that Charlie said would take them very near to where they were headed.

"How do you know the city so well?" Molly asked as they took their seats on the bus.

"Just gets about. Now, I don't take many buses, 'cept when I rides on the back of 'em."

Molly looked startled. "Wait, do you mean on the *outside*?"

"Yeah, I can teach you if you like. Just got to have strong fingers and get your weight and balance just so and keep your head down and be ready to jump if need be. Saves you a lot of coin."

"I would never do such a thing. It's not legal."

"Well, I don't know 'bout that," he retorted.

"It's *illegal*, Charlie. It's why they sell *tickets*."

He stared out the window at the storm and didn't respond.

After twenty minutes of rumbling through London, Charlie pulled the cord, and led Molly off the bus when it stopped at a junction.

Under cover of the umbrella they walked for a few minutes in the rain, though it was easing a bit.

"Down this way," he said.

They turned into an alley and took up position behind an old crate across from a battered door squatting in the middle of sad and grimy brick.

"That's the place," he said in a low voice, cupping his hand against Molly's right ear, though with the wind he could have shouted and still been in no danger of being overheard.

They waited a full hour and were about to leave when Charlie said, "Someone's comin'." He had noticed the tiny bit of light at the opposite end of the alley.

They ducked down lower behind the crate.

The air warden appeared wearing a glow cape and a slickened waterproof under it and gas-resistant clothes below that. A small torch with a shield was in one hand.

As the man walked by he stopped at the door in question, and gazed around. Then he reached into his pocket, pulled out an envelope, and slipped it through the door's letterbox.

As he passed them by, they both saw that it was Ignatius Oliver.

Molly started to call out to him, but Charlie put a hand on her shoulder and shook his head. When Oliver was out of sight Molly said, "Why did you stop me?"

"Somethin' ain't right 'bout this, Molly."

"He might simply be delivering a letter, Charlie, that's all."

"This late at night?"

"He's making his rounds as an air warden. You saw his uniform. And the man you saw here was the same one you saw at the bookshop. They're obviously friends. He might just be saving the price of a stamp."

Molly led them out of the alley, while a worried Charlie looked back at the door through which the envelope had gone.

A Risk Taken

It had been several days since Molly and Charlie had seen Oliver slipping the envelope through the letterbox. They once more sat in Molly's father's study staring at a poor fire that flickered and provided scant warmth. Both of them had rugs over their laps and legs. While it was still cold, at least the rain had passed; the skies were clear, and the wind was calmer.

"We need to see about your school, Charlie. Is it back in Bethnal Green?"

He said, "I'm fourteen, Miss. I'm done with school."

"But when Mr. Oliver gave you that pen you said you were still in school."

"Right, but I turned fourteen the next week and left," he lied. "Law says I can. And I learnt all I needed. Now it's time for me to work."

"Well, hopefully next year I'll sit my exams to see if I qualify for university."

"Is that what you want?" he asked, looking surprised.

"I want to be a doctor, actually."

"Can girls do that sort'a thin'?"

"Of course they can," she replied irritably.

"Speaking of, have you done the letter to that doctor in Cornwall yet?" asked Charlie.

Molly glanced at him and shook her head. "No. As I said, I was hoping that Mr. Oliver would help me with it."

"Then you should go ask him."

"I plan to," she said. "But now I need to go see about lunch. I'm famished."

She left him there and Charlie stood and walked around the room, admiring all the books and furniture and fine implements. He gazed at the door for a moment, then sat down behind the desk and drew out the pen Oliver had given him.

He pretended to write something with it on a crisp piece of stationery that was imprinted with the name Herbert James Wakefield with this Chelsea address. He was still upset to have lost his book to Lonzo. It had meant five quid, but now that he had given it some more thought Charlie had concluded that he could have written things in it, as Oliver had first suggested.

And read them to Mum, like she used to read to me. Molly had said I can leave here and still never leave my mum. Maybe I can read to her wherever I am. And if I start fightin' the Jerries, I won't be able to stay here. But I'll be doin' my bit, like Mum would have wanted.

As he looked at the pen, he thought about what a nice gesture it had been for Mr. Oliver to loan it to him. And then Charlie felt guilty, because he had never told the man the truth that night: that he was one of the boys who had been trying to break into his shop.

You're no good, Charlie. Here the man helps you and what do you do for him? Try to steal his money, that's what. And now you're thinkin' bad stuff 'bout Mr. Oliver when all he's done is be a friend to you.

He was called to lunch, and when he finished his food he was still quite hungry. He could tell the same for Molly, though she had given him larger portions than hers, just as his gran had. But he had something to do now because he had made up his mind. Charlie put on his hat and coat.

"Where are you going?" Molly asked.

"Just for a walk."

"Do you want company?"

Charlie said, "Umm . . ."

"That's all right," she said kindly. "Sometimes I like to be alone, too."

Charlie set off at a brisk pace. He hadn't wanted to tell Molly where he was headed because he thought she might disapprove. He liked and trusted Mr. Oliver. But he didn't at all like the man he had seen at the bookshop that night. There was just something sneaky about him, he thought. Charlie had been around enough criminal elements to know one when he saw one. Maybe the man was trying to steal from Mr. Oliver or maybe get him to do something Mr. Oliver didn't want to do, like Lonzo had made Charlie do. If Charlie could find out what was going on he could possibly help Mr. Oliver.

Charlie arrived at the alley and hid behind the same crate he and Molly had used previously.

A half hour later, Cedric came out from the doorway of the sad, brick-faced building. He turned left and headed out of the alley.

Charlie had to decide whether to follow the man or not. He made up his mind, and Charlie watched Cedric pass out of sight. Then he hurried over and peeked in the window. The curtains were drawn but didn't quite meet in the middle, so he could see a sliver of a small room, where a dim light was on. He could observe no one inside.

The alleyway was quiet. Blackened windows and drab doors stared back at him.

Charlie studied the lock, then he slipped his tool from his pocket, inserted it, and listened intently as the metal scraped and slithered over the guts of the gear-and-tumbler obstacle confronting him. He finally heard a click, and he gripped the knob and turned it ever so gently. Bucking up his courage with the notion that he was helping a friend, he opened the door and peered inside. The room was dark, and, fortunately, empty.

He slipped inside, ready to run in an instant if anyone appeared. The room held a chair and a desk with a cabinet above. The square rug was dirty and thin. There was only a single lamp on a table. The only other light was from the slight gap in the blackout curtains. There was also a small bed, and pegs on the wall, from which a few pieces of clothing hung. A pair of worn shoes was on the floor next to the bed. There was only the one room, with no kitchen or lavatory.

He opened the desk. Inside were blank paper and a pen and some envelopes and stamps. He used his tool to unlock the cabinet door above the desk.

Blimey.

Inside the cabinet was a locked wooden box. When Charlie used his tool to open it, revealed was something that looked like a typewriter he had once seen in a shop window.

However, this one was quite odd in appearance. There was a set of letter keys below, but there was an identical set of letters above it, but they weren't keys to push. They looked like pieces of glass with the letters showing under them. There were also things sticking out that looked like small gears, and a toggle switch that Charlie had seen on the dashboard of an automobile. And there were wires running through the inside top of the box. And between the lower keyboard and the inside wall of the box was a column of black cylinders jointed into the machine.

Most strange of all, there was no place to wind the paper in.

He looked more closely and saw a bit of white along one edge of the machine and the inner side of the box. He dipped his hand in there and managed to retrieve the single sheet of paper.

Charlie could not read or speak German, but he had seen words that he knew were German. And these were German words, he was sure of that.

He put the paper back and placed the box back on the shelf. That was when he noticed the book that was set next to it. He plucked it off and looked at the cover.

"Con-sway-low," he said slowly, reading off the title. He opened the book and gasped. Only the outer rims of the pages remained, leaving a large hole in the centre.

He looked at the inside flap of the book and gaped. Stamped there was:

THE BOOK KEEP
COVENT GARDEN

He slowly closed the novel and put it back next to the funny machine. Then he locked up the cabinet and left, after checking from the window to make sure it was all clear to do so.

What is Mr. Oliver involved in?

Revelations

Back at Molly's house, Charlie told her everything he had found.

She looked mortified. "That was so dangerous, Charlie. What if the man had come back?"

"I know, Miss, but I thought the bloke was tryin' to hurt Mr. Oliver or make him do somethin' he didn't want to do. But now . . . I don't know what's goin' on."

Molly looked thoughtful. "A funny-looking typewriter. And the insides of a book that has been cut out? My goodness, that could be a place to hide something!" she suddenly exclaimed.

"What I thought, too."

"What was the book again?"

"By some man named George somethin' or other. George *Sand*, that was it. And it come from The Book Keep. Its name was in it."

"And the paper you saw was in German?"

"I think so, yeah. And Mr. Oliver's got this thin', Albert's . . . um, *dish* or some such. Thin' is, he says it's for sendin' *secret* messages."

Molly looked distraught by all these revelations. "I'm not certain what to do, Charlie. It's not like we have proof of anything."

"We could call a copper and he could find that funny machine. *That* could be proof."

"I suppose so," said Molly hesitantly. "But you would have to meet with the police and tell them what you saw. But then they would ask you what you were doing inside the man's room. And they might ask you *other* questions."

Charlie had paled as soon as she had noted that he would likely have to meet with the police. He said, "Then . . . I think we need to wait a bit."

"There could be a perfectly innocent explanation for all of this," Molly said slowly, though it didn't appear she believed her own words.

"Right," said Charlie absently. He was distracted by envisioning himself being led to the gallows.

That evening they were huddled in the study listening to a programme on the wireless, when the door opened and Mrs. Pride poked her head in. "Molly, there's a gentleman at the front door asking for you."

Molly looked surprised. "Excuse me? A gentleman?"

Mrs. Pride held out a card. "He gave me this. I don't like letting strangers in the house. Your parents would surely not approve." She stared piercingly at Charlie as though to place an exclamation point on this opinion.

Molly looked down at the card. "Oh, it's Mr. Oliver."

"Should I tell him you're busy? He seems an odd sort."

"No, you can show him in here. I know Mr. Oliver. He's . . . a friend."

Mrs. Pride's face became pinched as she said, "Are you sure?"

"Quite sure, thank you."

They heard her reluctant footsteps heading down the hall.

"What do we do?" said a panicked Charlie. "With what we know?"

"We remain calm and . . . *normal*," replied Molly, though she looked to be neither.

A few moments later, Oliver appeared at the door and then closed it behind him, his hat in one hand and his waterproof shiny with raindrops. "Thank you for seeing me."

Molly, barely looking at him because she was so nervous, said, "Of course. But I wasn't aware that you knew where I lived."

"You were in the telephone book, or at least your father is listed."

"I would imagine there are many Wakefields," she said suspiciously.

"I saw his Christian name on the letter from the Beneficial Institute."

"Ah, of course."

"And you mentioned he worked at the Ministry of Food. I have a friend there."

Now that Oliver had mentioned it, perhaps he could enquire with his *friend* about what had happened to her father, Molly thought. "I hope you didn't walk here in such weather."

"A rumble in the rain is actually invigorating." He glanced at Charlie. "It was a very fine service, Charlie."

Charlie and Molly both gaped.

Charlie said, "Service?"

"At your grandmother's funeral."

"You was at Gran's burial?"

"I was behind the line of trees. I would never have dreamt of intruding on such a private affair, but I nonetheless wanted to come and offer my respects."

"But how did you know she had passed away?" asked Molly.

"I went by to see Charlie at his flat. A neighbour told me what had happened. I didn't know he had come to stay with you though."

Molly nodded, "So you came to see *me* then? Since you didn't know Charlie was here?"

Oliver stood next to the fire, warming his hands there. When he turned to them, his features were clearly troubled.

"Yes, I did, Molly. You see, I worked briefly for the government."

She and Charlie exchanged glances. "Really? What did you do there?"

"Things I'm afraid I cannot tell you. There is a law, you see. The Official Secrets Act."

Molly and Charlie exchanged another startled look before resettling their gazes on Oliver.

"Yes, I know that I don't seem the type, but I guess that's sort of the point." He gave her a troubled look. "When I was at the graveyard, I saw two men watching you, Molly. So you were quite right about that."

Molly glanced sharply at Charlie for a moment. "Do you know who they were?"

Oliver said, "If I had to speculate, I would say government types. Security people. Have you ever heard of MI5, also known as the Security Service?"

They both shook their heads.

"Its existence is not a secret. Basically, its job is to protect Britain against its enemies, spies and such."

"Were you part of this MI5 then?" asked Molly.

"I really can't say."

"But why would these men be following me? I've done nothing."

"When I spoke to my friend at the Ministry of Food, he told me something interesting."

"Does he know what has become of my father?" she said eagerly.

"Become of him?" said Oliver. "You said he was just working long hours."

"Um, well, that was not entirely correct. He actually . . . went away and has not returned. I'm sorry I didn't tell you before."

"Well, I also must make a confession. At the graveyard I actually heard you tell Charlie of your father's absence."

"Then why did you pretend you didn't know?" said Molly in an annoyed tone.

"I was just making sure, that is all. It is a difficult world right now and nothing can be taken for granted. When I saw the men and overheard you tell Charlie that your father had vanished, that is when I began making enquiries."

"I see," said Molly, her gaze drifting to the floor.

"I *was* puzzled why you were asking me about your mother and having me read those letters if your father was still at home. Well, I *have* found out some news of him."

"What?" Molly exclaimed, looking up.

"That your father has *never* worked at the Ministry of Food."

Molly had just then picked up her teacup. She was so startled by Oliver's words that the cup slipped from her fingers and fell onto the Wilton rug.

Charlie stared down at the few drops of tea leaching into the carpet before raising his amazed gaze to Oliver.

"Your . . . your friend must be wrong then," said Molly slowly. "Or perhaps Mrs. Pride misunderstood my father. Yes, that must be it," she said, brightening and turning to Charlie. "That's why he wasn't at the ministry that night. Mrs. Pride just got it wrong."

"But that letter got the Ministry of Food's name on it," Charlie reminded her.

"That's right, it did," said Molly, looking confused once more. "So what else do you know about my father, Mr. Oliver?"

Before he could respond, Oliver's gaze lifted to the ceiling.

Charlie's eyes darted to the window.

Molly said, "What is it?"

"Air raid siren," said Oliver. "I'm off duty tonight and don't even have my gas mask. How very stupid of me."

"You can use my father's. And I have mine and Charlie can use my mother's."

Oliver took charge. "Follow me. A tube station is the nearest best shelter. Quickly. We haven't much time before the next siren sounds, and it's a bit of a walk."

They hurried to the front door and grabbed the masks off the pegs along with umbrellas.

Molly said, "Wait, where is Mrs. Pride?"

They quickly searched the house, but couldn't find her.

"She must have gone out," said Oliver. "She might already be at the shelter."

The warbly sirens were growing louder and louder.

Oliver's expression turned grim as he listened to the sirens. "Hurry, children, hurry."

All Fall Down

As they joined streams of people rushing along, Molly looked up to see if the German planes were really coming. This was an entirely new experience for her and the anxiousness she felt echoed that reality.

Oliver caught her look and said, "They're not here yet, Molly. Another siren will sound, and then we'll have around ten minutes or so before, well . . ."

They passed a demolished "street shelter," which had been mass-erected early in the war and designed to hold fifty people, protecting them from "bomb splinters." However, they had a serious design flaw, namely that a bomb blast would suck out the walls, leaving the nine-inch-thick concrete roof to fall on the unfortunate inhabitants. Oliver had happened on one such catastrophe during his air warden duties, and seeing the result had made him and his fellow air warden retch.

Ten minutes later, they raced down the steps of the tube station along with many other worried-looking people.

Oliver identified himself as an air warden to another warden in uniform who was on duty, and they both helped to get everyone in and situated before securing the entrance to the tunnel.

When he was done with this, Oliver settled next to Charlie and Molly on the station's platform and waited.

"Do you think they're really comin'?" Charlie asked Oliver.

"While it is cloudy and raining, the wind is calm, so there is a possibility. And the civilian watchers have become very good at their jobs, unfortunately from so much practise." He looked reassuringly at Molly. "We'll be all right. This station is quite deep."

Tense minutes slipped by after the second warning siren had gone off. Then the drone of plane engines could be heard. So many that everyone looked up in surprise.

It was so eerily quiet down here that they heard one man mutter, "Come on, you bastards, just chuck it at us and be done."

Oliver slipped his arms around the children, pulling them together and down and hovering over them, as though his slender body could shield them from what was coming.

The sounds of the aircraft engines thudded ever closer, and the anti–aircraft guns commenced firing. Each blast of the weapons made Molly's body jerk. And then came the whine of falling bombs, shrieking higher and higher as they drew closer to the earth.

As the first munitions struck, the explosions seemed to reach right through the top of the station as though an earthquake had just breached London.

Oliver bent lower over the children and grunted in pain as a falling piece of ceiling tile hit him on the shoulder. Another bomb struck nearby, and the floor under them seemed to shift violently with the impact. Farther down the Underground line they heard screams and what sounded like a wall collapsing. Thick dust and smoke shot through the tunnel, making them all gag.

Molly had her hand clenched around Charlie's. She had never been this frightened in her life. She wondered at how Charlie and Mr. Oliver could have endured something like this on an almost nightly basis for months on end during the Blitz.

She managed to catch Charlie's gaze. Molly could tell he was scared. Yet he smiled bravely at her and said, "It's all right, Molly. The Jerries don't aim too good most times."

She nodded and managed a weak smile in return, but, in truth, she felt nauseous and her pulse was throbbing in her ears.

As more bombs landed, the explosions were interlaced with sirens, screams, and sounds of panic from above. Inside the tube station babies shrieked, and children cried, as did some of the adults. A full two hours passed with nearly unrelenting explosions that shook all of them to their souls. Molly thought that nothing in hell could ever match this experience. And then the whines and impacts and explosions slowed, and then abruptly ceased. Everyone sat paralysed in seeming disbelief that it was over and they were still alive.

After ten minutes of quiet passed, Oliver slowly straightened and let go of Molly and Charlie. He rubbed his injured shoulder where the tile had struck him.

"Okay, we should hear the all clear soon," he said. "But we must wait until then. They could be sending in a second wave."

Molly looked at him with a stunned expression. "A . . . s-second wave?"

"But perhaps not tonight," he said in a reassuring tone.

Two minutes later the all clear siren mercifully sounded. Some started to make their way to the exits, while others settled down to spend the night underground just in case the Luftwaffe returned to try to kill them.

When they reached the surface, they could smell smoke and hear screams and sirens, and an explosion or two, probably as ruptured gas lines ignited. Flames rose high into the sky, turning night into near day and heating the air so much they could all feel the enhanced warmth on their skin and the smoke in their lungs.

They watched as firemen battled numerous blazes with hard streams of water and people rushed past them in all directions.

"Looks like they hit us pretty badly," said Oliver dejectedly.

"Help me! Please!" someone nearby cried out.

They rushed towards the sounds and found a man lying amid some heated, smoky rubble. He was bleeding and his face was ashen.

"Children, go and get help while I see to him," said Oliver as he knelt next to the injured man. "As a warden I've had first aid training."

Instead, Molly pushed past him and ran her gaze over the man. He was holding his arm where blood was soaking through his ripped shirt sleeve. She examined the wound and the ominous blood flow.

"Mr. Oliver, do you have a torch?"

He produced one and shone it where she directed, on the man's arm.

She told the man to count to ten and that this would hurt a bit, but she had to do it. She glanced at Oliver and Charlie and said quietly, "If you could hold him still."

They did so while she took the torch and then inserted her gloved finger inside the wound. The man cried out and would have thrashed around had he not been held tightly by Charlie and Oliver.

"Okay," said Molly. "I'm done. You can let him go."

"What did you do?" whispered Oliver.

She whispered back, "I managed to nudge a torn blood vessel back in alignment. It won't fully stop the bleeding but it slowed it considerably. Had I not, I doubt he would live. Now I need to slow the blood loss even more."

She took off her hat, tore the sash from around it, and looked at Oliver. "I need you to hold his arm very tightly while I wrap this around it." She turned back to the wounded man and said firmly, "You must remain very still. Do you understand? This will not hurt like before, but it is necessary. All right?"

He nodded, his pale features in anguish.

Oliver held the arm where Molly told him to and she very carefully chose the location before slowly wrapping the sash around the man's upper arm, and tying it off to form a tourniquet. She then checked the blood flow and was relieved to see that it had diminished quite dramatically.

She looked down at the man. "You're going to be fine, but you need to remain quite still. Charlie, run and get help. He needs to go to hospital straight away."

Charlie raced off and came back a minute later with a policeman. Molly told him what was needed, and he rushed off blowing a whistle. While he was gone Molly checked the tourniquet and wiped the sweat and blood off the man's face. She had also used a clean handkerchief from her pocket to pack the wound. "Close your eyes and breathe in and out slowly and calmly," she advised. "That will lower your heart rate, which will slow your loss of blood. Help will be here soon."

"Where did you learn to do all that?" asked an amazed Oliver.

"At hospital in Leiston."

The constable returned with an ambulance and two medics. Molly told them her diagnosis and that the injured man needed to remain very still and the tourniquet kept in place.

Out of earshot of the wounded man she said, "Before you transport him you'll need to bind the injured arm to his body. I resettled the artery as best I could but it's still damaged. And I had to apply the tourniquet quite tightly because of the volume of blood loss. Remember to tell the surgeon it's the *brachial* artery. When he gets to hospital he will require immediate surgery. You can't keep such a tight tourniquet on indefinitely or else the lack of blood flow will permanently damage the limb, and it might need to come off. Now, do you have morphine?"

One of the medics, who had listened to her with growing incredulity, said, "Yes, but—"

She interrupted. "Then let me have a syrette of it to give to him. That will sedate him for the trip to hospital and also for his surgery."

The medic blurted out, "Give you *morphine*? You're just a child!"

Oliver stepped forwards and said, "Um, I'm a doctor, and my *daughter* is just repeating what I said before you arrived." He looked at Molly, his expression embarrassed. "She wants to be, um, a *nurse*, when she grows up."

The medic looked much more at ease. “Ah, right you are. Do you want to give him the shot of morphine then, Doc?”

Oliver became quite pale. “No, you chaps go right ahead.”

After they took the injured man away, Charlie said, “That was amazin’, Molly.”

Oliver added, “I’m sorry about all that, Molly. He thinks I’m a doctor, but you were the one who saved that man’s life. I carry first aid material when I patrol and I know how to patch and bandage, but nothing like you just did.”

“I just hope he’ll recover. I tried to sound confident in front of him, but the wound was quite serious.”

They walked back to Molly’s home.

However, they found it no longer existed.

Gone by Equal Measures

The fire brigade and members of the Civil Defence's Heavy Rescue Division finally managed to pull Mrs. Pride's body from the rubble of what had once been the stately Wakefield home. Oliver, Molly, and Charlie stood numbly by as the dead woman's body was placed into an ambulance and taken away. It would be determined later that nearly a hundred people were killed during this raid, five hundred more injured, and more than a hundred homes and buildings destroyed, many of them in the posh areas of Chelsea, Knightsbridge, and Mayfair.

"But she wasn't in there when we left," said Molly, still in shock at losing her nanny, her home, and all her possessions in a few hours' time.

"She might have gone out and then come back for some reason," said Oliver. "And then decided to shelter there. It is very tragic." He looked up and down the street. All the other structures in his line of sight had remained largely undamaged aside from Molly's and the one next to hers. He well knew there was never any rhyme or reason as to why one place was hit and another one wasn't.

As they stood there another constable came over. "You lived there, lass?" he asked.

"W-what?" she stuttered.

"You lived there with the dead woman? The lady over there said so. Said Mrs. Pride was your nanny."

"That's right."

"Where are your parents then, luv?"

Molly froze but only for an instant. "They . . . they were not at home. I expect them back tomorrow."

"All right. Do you have some place to stay until they get back?"

Oliver stepped up. "She can stay with . . . with my wife and me. We're friends of the family. We were here visiting Molly while her parents were gone. We went to the Underground when the sirens sounded."

The constable glanced at Charlie. "And you, lad?"

"He's my son," answered Oliver promptly.

"Right then. Well, good luck to you all."

He hurried back over to where Molly's home had once stood.

Molly said, "Where do Charlie and I go now? An orphanage?"

She glanced at Charlie, who stared dully back at her.

"I think we can allow that discussion to wait for another time," said Oliver.

"Mrs. Pride must be given a proper burial, but I'm not sure how to manage it. What little monies we had were inside the house."

"Does she have family?" asked Oliver.

Molly slowly shook her head. "None that I know of. Her husband died before she came to work for us. She never mentioned children."

"Siblings, perhaps?"

"I don't know. It seems quite stupid on my part but we never talked about any of that," she added guiltily.

"Well, let's go to the bookshop and we can think things over. We'll come up with something."

They walked off through the smoke and destruction of the night's bombing, past fresh rubble, and bodies under bloody sheets, and the wounded being loaded into vehicles, and slowly made their way to Covent Garden and The Book Keep. Oliver unlocked the door and ushered them in.

"I have a spare room that you and Charlie can use. Imogen kept items from her younger days that I still have and that might fit you, Molly. And I had a cousin's son who lived with us early on in the war and who was around your size, Charlie. He left some odd bits of clothing behind."

It was evident to both Molly and Charlie that Oliver was trying his best to remain optimistic in the face of such stark challenges.

"I have food . . . um, enough," he added feebly. "And a good deal of tea."

Molly gasped. "My ration book. It was in the house."

Charlie said, "Gran had my book. It's long gone by now."

Oliver said, "It only costs a shilling to replace a lost ration book. However, it might be . . . difficult, since you both would have to appear in person to claim a new one. And there would be troublesome questions. Oh, before I forget, we should talk about your schooling."

"I'm of age, all done," said Charlie immediately.

Molly added, "I am as well, but I hope to sit for my exams next year when I turn sixteen."

"All right," said a relieved Oliver. He rushed off to make tea, while Charlie found himself staring at the repaired front door. Molly caught his eye.

"Charlie, is something wrong?"

He turned to her with an angry look. "Pretty much everythin' is wrong, for both of us. Don't you *see* that? We *are* orphans. Least I am, and you're close to it. They'll put us in some place with a bunch of other kids nobody cares about."

"That's not how it works, Charlie."

His features tightened and he snapped, "It *is* how it works. I got mates. I know what happens to . . . to people like that." He glanced at the door again, and his anger faded to melancholy.

Oliver returned with the teacups and a few biscuits on a tray.

They drank the tea and Charlie had two biscuits, while Molly had one. She ate it with a detached air, as her gaze ran mindlessly over the shelved books.

Oliver peered over his cup at each of them in turn. The weight of what he had just decided to do was clearly pressing down upon his slender shoulders, compacting him into perhaps a lessened version of himself. He turned to look at the till and seemed to be calculating how much money was in there.

Not nearly enough, his sober expression proclaimed. A widower without children now had two, and in contravention of the law. Orphaned children were sent to orphanages. He knew that better than most. He and his brother had gone to an orphanage when their parents had been killed in a railway accident near Doncaster.

"I really can't believe that Mrs. Pride is gone," said Molly. "Aside from my mother she was my only companion, really. My father was always so busy."

"I'm sure he loves you very much, Molly," said Oliver.

"But he left without a word to me. No telegram, no letter. It's . . . it's inexcusable. And my poor mother's in a sanatorium. I have no home. I have nothing, only the clothes on my back, literally." She paused and glanced over at Charlie, who was watching her closely as he finished the last biscuit.

"I'm sorry, Charlie. I know that you have had to manage with far less than I have."

"You lost your home tonight. And your nanny. You got good reason to be mad. I was mad when Gran died. I'm *still* bloody mad," he added sharply.

She took some time finishing her tea. "If only I had an idea of where my father is." Molly eyed Oliver. "Before the sirens started you were talking about my father and the men at the graveyard. But it has nothing to do with me, does it?"

"No, not directly."

"It has to do with my father, you mean? You mentioned this Secrets Act. If he didn't work for the Ministry of Food, where *was* my father working?"

Oliver slowly set down his cup of tea and rubbed his thigh where one of the burns he had suffered previously had begun to ache.

"The person I spoke with said he thought your father had also signed the Official Secrets Act."

"And why would he do that?"

"There are many reasons. If he was involved in the war effort and was privy to confidential information would be one of them."

"Could it be he was, I don't know, a spy working against the Germans?" She glanced sharply at Charlie, who was watching Oliver closely. "I know he travelled to the Continent quite often before the war, but I was never told why."

Oliver said uncertainly, "It's *possible*, Molly."

"Has he been captured by the Germans then? Has . . . has he been killed?"

"I really have no idea," said Oliver. "I'm sorry."

She persisted. "But can you find out more, considering what you used to do? And the men watching me? Maybe they would know something?"

Oliver looked at her uneasily. "I . . . I can try."

"I would appreciate that very much, thank you."

Oliver cleared his throat and said, "I did look up the Beneficial Institute. It's on the coast near Falmouth in Cornwall."

Molly said eagerly, "Is there a way to get there?"

"There is no bus service right now. The GWR *has* train service to Falmouth. But with wartime restrictions, it takes about ten hours, and the trains do not run regularly. The military takes precedence and all that. And the Germans routinely bomb the train tracks, so there is that impediment as well."

"But can I still make the journey? I really need to see my mother. And she may know where my father is."

"There *is* the question of the price of the tickets," said Oliver slowly, once more glancing at the till. "And you'll need food and clothing and money for lodging and other essentials."

"I can earn money," she said. "I . . . I can work in your shop."

"Yes, you could. Though sometimes days go by without a customer coming in."

"Well, I could tidy up the place."

"Absolutely. Yes, you can."

She looked at Charlie, who was intently watching the nervous expression on Oliver's face. Unlike Molly, who was so focused on finding the means to reach her mother, he could evidently sense the man's misgivings on the subject of paying wages for "tidying up."

"And Charlie could work here, too," said Molly brightly.

"For room and board," said Charlie. "But I'll work someplace else for pocket money."

Molly looked confused by this and Oliver said, "Charlie, there's really no need. I'm sure I can find the means with which to pay you both."

Charlie shook his head. "You should only pay us, Mr. Oliver, if you need us to work for you. Otherwise, it's just charity, and Gran never liked to take charity and she taught me the same. And you only got the one ration book for the three of us. Gran had both of ours, and it still weren't enough food."

Molly looked crestfallen. "I can find work elsewhere too, I'm sure."

"But you're just children," protested Oliver.

Molly said briskly, "I'm no longer a child, Mr. Oliver. And there's a chemist's shop down the street. I did a great many prescription fillings at the hospital in Leiston. I can see if they need an assistant."

"There are age requirements surely, Molly," pointed out Oliver.

Her voice rose to a tremulous level. "I just saved a man's life tonight, for God's sake. And I can make enquiries, can't I?"

"Of course you can," conceded Oliver. "But for now, I think a good night's rest is required after all the shocks you've endured. Things will look better in the morning."

Neither Molly nor Charlie looked like they thought that was remotely possible.

And neither, really, did Ignatius Oliver.

The True Beginnings of Something

It was dawn and Oliver had barely slept. Wearing a tattered robe, he moved through the shop touching this book and straightening that one. He removed a bit of dust from a shelf, and a finger mark from the front window with his sleeve.

He then looked down and saw water coming in under the door as the poorly draining cobblestones flooded from all the rain and then sought a pathway into his shop. He hurried to the toilet, seized an old towel, and stuffed it against this gap.

He next walked down the flight of steps, moved over to the doorway, took out the key, unlocked his wife's study, and went inside.

Some writers preferred early mornings to work their craft, others were inspired with the lateness of night. Still other ambitious scriveners wrote all the time.

Imogen had preferred the late afternoon or early evening to work on her novel, when a day's other labour had been completed and the events during that time and her corresponding thoughts comingled into a stream of inventiveness that would make the prose resonate, the characters compel, and the story spark. This did not always happen, she had told him. Indeed, it often didn't, but that did not defeat the logic of her approach.

Writing is often drudgery, she had told him. And no matter how long you did it, the process never became easier. It simply became more bewildering, as though you knew there was a secret to it all, and you'd come close to finding it at times, but right when you thought you had it, the bloody thing just skittered away into the dark recesses of your mind, like the remnants of a slippery dream. But, she had said, in that perplexity and frustration one could sometimes see growth, improvement, and a desire to keep going, which was more than ample reward. Though she had attended lectures where prominent writers claimed to always be in a "perfect" state of self-confidence, Imogen had noted, "such a foolish conviction is like a loaded gun to one's head, and you are but a single false belief away from never placing credible thought to paper again."

Overconfidence in his storytelling abilities was not something with which Oliver was the least bit concerned.

He sat down at the desk and stared at the blank page in the Crown typewriter, his longtime nemesis. Having the presence of two children with him now had no doubt added to his anxiety to produce something of worth.

He lifted his gaze to the ceiling, where directly overhead Molly and Charlie were hopefully in peaceful rest. It was quite ironic. Imogen had never wanted children, perhaps more out of insecurity than anything else. She had confided in him her utter disbelief that she could ever measure up to the standard her mother and father had set with her.

Oliver *had* wanted to be a father, but he wanted Imogen as his wife even more. And now he had a son and a daughter. At least for a bit.

I suppose it's fortunate that they're not small children, as you would be sorely out of your depth. But people their age are not an easy lot to deal with, either. Indeed, they are infinitely more complex than the youngsters. They make the most intricate encryptions pale by comparison.

He stared at the paper and it stared contemptuously back. In desperation, Oliver turned to the tin of typed pages and picked up the first few.

The early chapters had been riveting. The war, the struggles and hardship, the deaths, the unending anxiety from looking to the sky every few minutes awaiting the shriek of the air raid siren and then later the scream of the falling bombs.

Further into the story, he read about families divided and lost. Hope gone, day-to-day survival with a dwindling amount of resources available. Anger and dissatisfaction grew, particularly among those who had never felt the government, even in peacetime, could do anything worthwhile. If the state could not help when its citizens most needed it, what use was it? That was a straightforward and thus powerful argument, and was thematic throughout the unfinished novel.

Imogen had taken on that issue deeply and sensitively, and ultimately pushed back against the notion that anarchy or dictatorship was better than a government made up of the will of the people. They had both heard the talk at the shops, pubs, church, and in myriad other places where one listened and learned about what was on people's minds. There were more than a few here who grudgingly admired the brutal efficiency of the German war machine, the superficial advantage of having one strongman dictate everything for all, in lieu of the unwieldy ebb and flow of compromise required in a democracy.

But for Oliver, as even a casual observer of history could say with complete confidence, such one-man governing structures *never* ended well for anyone, not even the strongman.

Humans make poor gods. We're just not up to it.

Imogen had written that as the opening lines in Chapter Eight. It was one of his favourite epigrams.

But then, both of their lives had been transformed in ways Oliver would never have imagined. And maybe that was why Imogen had never finished her book. Yes, that clearly was the reason she had not. And it was also the reason she had died.

He put the pages on top of the tin box and sat back in the old, worn, and uncomfortable chair. This was intentionally so. Imogen did not like to write in comfort. She wanted to feel on the edge of pain as she wrote, so that she could authentically transfer that emotion to the story.

Pain was a universal connection; everyone felt it at some point in their lives, physically, mentally, and/or emotionally. No one, rich or poor, young or old, was exempt from its claws. However, the resulting ache in his back from the unyielding chair prompted no grand ideas from Oliver. His fingers did not even reach for the typewriter keys. He felt inadequate and overwhelmed.

Distracted and dismayed, he looked up at the doorway to see Molly and Charlie staring at him, their faces puffy from disturbed sleep.

He clumsily rose as they entered Imogen's old sanctum.

Looking around before settling her gaze on the Crown typewriter and the stack of pages Molly said, "Are you a writer?"

Oliver came around to the front of the desk and perched on the edge, blocking their view of both the machine and the pages. For several reasons he felt deeply invaded, a long-kept secret abruptly lost.

"My wife was. A very good one, in fact."

"Are any of her books here? I'd love to read them."

"She was writing her first when she died."

"Oh," said Molly.

"I didn't think you'd be up this early," said Oliver.

"The rain woke us," said Charlie.

"Really? I found the sound quite relaxing," said Oliver, though he was, of course, wide awake.

"I mean the water was drippin' on my head," explained Charlie.

He and Molly were sharing the small spare bedroom that held twin cots.

"Ah, yes, I've been meaning to fix that leak for ages."

"This is a very nice room," said Molly timidly, as though she sensed they had disrupted a treasured privacy. But then she stared at the *typewriter* and her expression changed. She edged forwards.

"Yes, I like to come in here. Usually not this early, but . . ."

"Are you . . . have you been trying to finish the book for your wife?" Molly drew still closer to the desk, saw that it was indeed a typewriter with a blank page wound in, and her features relaxed.

"What . . . um, no," he fibbed. With far more candour he added, "I have neither the talent nor the discipline to do so. I'm much more comfortable with numbers. They are what they are, and they always add up the same way. I prefer that sort of consistency. I do not like unpredictability in the least. Yet that seems to be all there is anymore, which is why the world is so bewildering to me presently." He stopped abruptly as though chastened by the fact that he had revealed so much of a personal nature.

"Could I read what she has written?" Molly asked.

He put a hand protectively on top of the pages. "That wouldn't be fair to Imogen. I mean, a story only half finished?"

He led them from the room, closed the door, and locked it.

"Now, would you like some breakfast? I have two eggs, a strip of bacon and a slice of ham, and some bread and margarine and Golden Shred. I'll need to go to the shops today with my ration book for more provisions. While you're eating I can take a look at that ceiling. I think a well-placed cloth or two will suffice. Or perhaps moving the cot?"

He went off to the small kitchen to prepare their meals.

Molly said, "I'm not sure he was being truthful. But that *was* a typewriter."

"But that don't mean he's not doin' somethin' . . . bad."

"But he just doesn't strike me as the type. And he said he worked for the government. He knows about this Secrets Act thing."

"I can't figure it out," admitted Charlie.

"Do you think we should go to the police? I don't want to believe that Mr. Oliver is . . . doing anything illegal. But we do have a duty as British citizens."

When she had mentioned the word "police," Charlie had involuntarily glanced at the door where the towel was now soaked through.

Molly followed his gaze. "I wish you'd tell me what's bothering you."

He shot her a look and his face reddened. "Right now, everythin's botherin' me. We got no parents. We got nothin'."

"But we're here."

He pointed to the door. "There's a lady over there what runs that tea shop. She'll find out quick enough that we're livin' here and then what do you think she'll do?"

"What?"

"Call the coppers. She knows Mr. Oliver ain't got no children. They'll put us in an orphanage."

"You can't possibly know that."

"I *do* bleedin' know that!"

"Well, maybe an orphanage wouldn't be so very bad," she retorted.

"They are, too. I got mates what got sent to them."

"What mates?"

"Never you mind about that. Just mates." *And now one of them's dead*, thought Charlie. And he had no idea where Lonzo had got to. Maybe he *had* joined the army as Lonzo had suggested at their last meeting.

Charlie couldn't know that Lonzo would try to do so, only it would go horribly, horribly wrong. For both Lonzo *and* him.

For King & Country

"How old did you say you were again, lad?"

The rigid man in the military uniform looked up at Lonzo, who stood before him with his soiled cap clutched in nervous fingers, but his expression resolute. He had washed up with a stolen bar of soap, and water from a public fountain, and then nicked a set of second-hand clothes from the back of a shop. His worn-out brogues had been replaced by a pair of shoes he'd found after the most recent bombing. The owner had apparently been blown right out of them, leaving the shoes a bit singed but still far better than what Lonzo had.

"Eighteen," answered Lonzo promptly.

"You don't look it," said the sergeant major in His Majesty's Army. He was missing his left arm below the elbow, and his right eye where a black patch now lay. They were the reasons he was sitting here recruiting others to fight a war he no longer could. His trim moustache ran straight as a ruler over his firm upper lip.

Lonzo stood as tall as he could manage. "Just need me some proper food and a uniform and I'll look my age all right. Fill out, I will."

"And your address?"

Lonzo said immediately, "Flat Four-a, Thirteen Dapleton Terrace, Bethnal Green, guv."

"East Ender, eh? You blokes make good fighters. And you may call me *sir*."

"Been fightin' for a while now, *sir*. On the streets, I'm meanin'." Lonzo grinned.

"Fighting in a war is a very different thing, young man."

"Right, guv, er, sir."

"Parents?"

"Dead, sir," replied Lonzo.

"How?"

"Me dad in the war. Somewhere's in France, least I think. Mum in a bombin' near the docks. She did the charrin'. The Jerries got 'er then."

"And you live with whom?"

"Me gran. But I don't need 'er to say it's okay, 'cause I'm of age."

"You have papers to prove that? Birth certificate? Registry card?"

"Got lost in a fire." He wiped his runny nose and wouldn't look at the sergeant major. "But it was a B card, sir, 262 was my number, I swear it."

This indicated Lonzo was born in the second quarter of 1926 and was thus eighteen. The B card was issued to those between the ages of sixteen and twenty-one.

"Full name?"

He stood up straight and recited, "Alonzo Sylvester Rossi. Folks call me Lonzo."

The moustache dipped a bit. "Rossi? You foreign?"

"Me dad was from Italy and me mum got some Spanish blood in 'er."

"So, Benito Mussolini and Francisco Franco foreign, then."

Lonzo eyed the man steadily. "Me mum were born in Stepney, same as me. Me dad come over 'ere when he was young. And 'e joined up and died fightin' for the British, sir, so's 'e weren't foreign when it come to pickin' sides. I ain't know nothin' 'bout them other blokes you spoke of."

The sergeant major cleared his throat. "You'll need to pass a physical, have the doctors look you over, eyes, ears, feet, chest."

"I'm 'ealthy as a 'orse."

"Can you read?"

Lonzo didn't miss a beat. "Nuns taught me."

"Nuns?"

"At the school where I went."

"You Catholic?" The sergeant major said this as though that also might be a problem.

"Just smells and bells to me, sir," said Lonzo offhandedly.

"Let's fill out the papers, shall we? And then you can take a seat over there."

"Right you are, sir."

Lonzo, with the sergeant major's assistance, did the necessary paperwork, and the soldier instructed Lonzo to wait. As he was reviewing some documents the man looked over a list that had been provided to him, along with a description of someone. He ran his eye down it and then glanced up at Lonzo, who appeared to be dozing in his chair.

The sergeant major quietly stepped away and made a phone call from another room.

Fifteen minutes passed and then someone tapped Lonzo on the shoulder, waking him.

He saw the official warrant card and the stern-looking man holding it.

"Detective Inspector Willoughby. You'll need to come with me, boy."

Lonzo looked wildly around, but two burly constables with their shiny buttons and tall helmets barred any escape.

"I ain't done nothin'."

"No one said you had, son," replied Willoughby. "Did they?"

With a constable on either side of him, Lonzo was marched out as the sergeant major watched for a moment before ripping up Lonzo's papers and tossing them in the dustbin.

"Next," he called out to an assistant waiting at the door.

DI Willoughby

THE RIDE TO THE police building in the official motorcar was swift. One of the constables and DI Willoughby took Lonzo to a small room with an overbearing electric heater that made him sweat, and barred windows that made him fear.

The constable pushed him down in a hard chair set at a wooden table and then settled his bulk in front of the only door. Willoughby slipped off his overcoat, placed it on a peg, removed his hat, lit up a cigarette, and offered one to Lonzo, who accepted.

Willoughby was fifty and tough-looking, with wide hips and meaty, brutish shoulders. His features were mostly impassive, but he had the look of a man who had seen far too much of life that was horrible, and it had changed him, and not for the better. There was no compassion or empathy or anything else like that left in him. He eyed Lonzo as one would a prize to be turned into an even more valuable one.

As they smoked, Willoughby loosened his tie and opened a file he had placed on the table. He leisurely read over it and then lifted out a picture and placed it in front of Lonzo. "Recognize him?"

Lonzo glanced down at the photograph before quickly looking away, his expression one of revulsion. "No, I ain't never seen him."

"His name's Eddie Gray. Surely you know him, Lonzo. You two *were* mates."

"That ain't look like Eddie to me. And, 'sides, I ain't seen 'im for a while, 'ave I, guv?"

"That's because he's dead. Surely you can see the way his head is all crushed, can't you? And all the blood?" He pushed the picture closer. "Take another look."

Lonzo shook his head. "No, I ain't want to."

Willoughby leaned across, ripped the cigarette from Lonzo's mouth, gripped the back of his head, and forced it over the picture. "Look at your friend, Lonzo. What's left of him. Look at the *mate* you left to die."

Lonzo cried out, "I ain't know nothin' 'bout that. Swear it on me mum's grave."

The detective inspector released his grip and sat back. "We're going to have a little identity parade in a few minutes, boy. The lorry driver saw you clearly. He's here to finger you as one of the other *criminals* there that night. And let me remind you that a constable died. He had a wife and young children. The wife no longer has a husband and the children have lost their father." He pointed a finger at Lonzo. "All because of you."

Willoughby looked up at the constable and nodded.

The next instant Lonzo's face was slammed into the wood of the table. Then he was viciously punched in the head and knocked to the floor.

"Careful, boy, you'll hurt yourself." Willoughby lit up another cigarette and lazily blew smoke out while a bloodied, bruised, and clearly dazed Lonzo sobbed and put his hands over his injured face. One of his eyes was already starting to swell shut.

The constable jerked him off the floor and thrust him back into his chair.

"Is . . . is this a 'angin' job?" asked Lonzo in a whimper.

"It could very well be. A constable *did* die. But if you tell me who the other boy was, well, I might be able to do something for you."

"You . . . y-you could?"

"No promises, mind you. But if you tell us the truth, then I could help you, yes." He stubbed out his smoke, swiped back his hair, and leaned across so that he was only inches from Lonzo. "What was his name?"

"Ch-Charlie. Charlie Matters."

"Where is he?"

"Dunno. His gran died and he had to leave his flat in Bethnal Green."

"Parents?"

"Dead."

"And you have no idea where he is now?"

Lonzo shook his head. "No, guv. I swear."

Willoughby took out a notepad and pen. "Describe him."

Lonzo did so. "C-can you still help me?"

Willoughby finished writing and looked up. "You've really told me nothing helpful, Lonzo. Lots of boys like Charlie in this city. Does he go to school?"

"No."

"Does he have any other family?"

Lonzo shook his head. "Dunno."

Willoughby grabbed one of the boy's hands and twisted Lonzo's index finger until it broke. Lonzo howled in pain.

"Don't lie to me, boy, you won't like it."

He let go of Lonzo's hand and the boy jerked back, holding his damaged finger.

Lonzo wailed, "He ain't got no family, I swear. His gran was all he had, and she died. They buried her over in Stepney. At the church."

"What were you doing breaking into a shop? And why *that* shop?"

Lonzo swallowed and looked down at the table. Out of his one good eye he watched for the constable sneaking up on him again. "We heard it had some money in the till."

"How did you hear that?"

"Just did."

Willoughby pointed to the door. "When we walk out of here and you get picked out of the identity parade, the next stop for you will be prison. And they *will* hang you."

"I never saw that lorry till it 'it Eddie. I swear. Didn't mean to 'urt nobody."

"The law doesn't care what you *meant*, Lonzo. It only cares about what you *did*. Now, I'll ask you one more time. Why that bookshop?"

Lonzo gazed warily at the constable, who had now taken a step forwards, holding his wooden club and tapping it menacingly against one wide palm.

"Ch-Charlie knew 'bout it. He stole from the bloke before, but the git took the money back."

Willoughby's brows knitted in confusion. "Wait, are you saying this Charlie Matters took the money he stole back? Why the devil would he do that, boy? You taking the mickey with me? I don't like that."

"He said the bloke had it bad and needed it. But Charlie had a book that got no writin' in it. He got it from the shop. Said he was goin' to sell it."

"Did he?" barked Willoughby.

Lonzo was not about to add the theft of the book to his list of crimes. "Got no way of knowin' that, do I?"

"Bollocks!" exclaimed Willoughby as he nodded at the bobby.

A punishing strike landed on the back of Lonzo's head from the constable's club, which once more knocked Lonzo to the floor. His head bleeding badly, Lonzo threw up on the floor.

Willoughby cried out, "Jesus, boy, get a hold of yourself. You were going to join the army? By God, you would have lasted all of ten minutes against the Germans. Now get back in your chair before the constable is forced to 'help' you."

Willoughby drummed his fingers against the table and waited while Lonzo picked himself up off the floor and sobbed quietly into the wood of the table.

"You said he got the book from the shop. Did he steal it?"

"He said he bought it with the shillin's he stole from the shop. But that were a lie 'cause he give the money back."

"So *did* he nick it, then?" persisted the detective inspector.

"Dunno. But he didn't want us to go round to the shop. He tried to stop us. Maybe he was a friend 'a the bloke's."

Willoughby glanced at his notebook. "This Ignatius Oliver?"

Lonzo rubbed his damaged nose and touched the wound on the back of his head. His fingers came back all sticky with his blood. "Dunno, maybe. But Charlie ain't want us to steal from him, I can tell you that."

Willoughby sat back and thought this over. "Okay, Lonzo Rossi, the *foreigner*, that will be all."

Lonzo peeked up at the man. "C-can . . . can I go now, guv? I . . . I wanted to join up, fight the Jerries, see?"

The detective inspector looked at him incredulously. "The only place you're going is to prison."

"But you said—"

"A constable has died," interjected Willoughby. "While this country was at war and needing every able-bodied man in either a policeman's or a soldier's uniform. And you and this Charlie Matters as good as killed him. If I have any say in it, and I do, you and he will grow old and grey in prison. That is unless they hang you, which would be *my* preference."

Lonzo started to blubber and Willoughby impatiently waved at the constable to drag him away.

When Willoughby was alone, the man had one overriding thought: to find this lad, Charlie Matters. And he knew just the place to start searching.

Tomorrow he would head to Covent Garden. To The Book Keep.

Nurse Auxiliary

The whiskered, aproned man in the chemist's shop politely declined Molly's offer to mix the powders, but commended her proper English spirit in trying to do her part in the midst of a global conflict.

"And you tell your mum I said so," he added in an encouraging tone.

I wish I could, thought Molly.

She trudged down the street feeling dirty and unkempt. She had searched through Imogen's old clothes, as Oliver had suggested, only to find them full of mold and mildew from water leaks in the flat. So she had sponged her clothes as best she could, and used a few articles of Imogen's to shape her hair and clean her face and the rest of her body. But her shoes were stained and her stockings were beginning to droop and her hat had been squished in on one side, what with all the jostling in the Underground that night.

Two more chemist's shops rejected her request, and neither was nearly as gracious about it as the first. The last fellow actually accused Molly of wasting his time while playing an obvious joke on him before sending her off with a flea in her ear.

"Get on with you before I say something you won't soon forget, missy. Don't you know there's a bloody war going on? A belt to your shins would be the ticket if you were my daughter."

She tried other places, shops and markets and emporiums and cafes and anywhere else that had a POSITION NEEDED sign. But the folks inside always found some reason to deny her employment. Perhaps it was her age, or her clothes—which were, though a bit grimy now, evidently once costly. They might be saving the jobs for those who they believed truly needed them, she thought.

Even though I truly do.

She had been about to give up when she saw a sign and wondered how she had missed it: COVENT GARDEN MEDICAL CLINIC BRANCH.

It was posted outside of a brick building with one door and four windows facing the street. She peered in one of the windows and saw beds with sick and injured people lying in them, and nurses in skirts, capes, and hats rushing around with bottles and trays and anxious looks.

Then, when she drew away from the window and stepped inside the small vestibule, Molly saw the placard: NURSE AUXILIARIES NEEDED. ENQUIRE WITHIN.

She squared her shoulders, righted her dented hat, gripped the door handle, and prepared herself to enquire within.

Molly was met by a slim nurse in a dark pleated skirt and white rubber-soled shoes. Thick worry lines etched her forehead.

"Yes?" she said. "Are you here to visit someone?"

"No, I'm here to apply for the position as a nurse auxiliary."

The woman frowned. "What? I do not have time to waste with silly—"

"I have medical training and I want to help."

"You are a child!"

"No, I'm not. I'm *sixteen*."

"That's still far too young for this position! Special training is required. For your information we are affiliated with the British Army and have been sent here to help with bombing victims and the like. Many of us have served in combat hospitals at the front lines."

"Sixteen-year-old women can marry in England, and have children," countered Molly. "People my age are working in factories and on farms raising crops, and doing a great many other things for the war effort."

"Well, be that as it may, that gives you no right to come in here and pretend to know how to treat the sick and injured. We don't bloody well pick cabbages here, young lady. We had a bombing recently and are overrun with casualties."

"I know about the bombing," said Molly. "I was there. I saw . . . death."

"Then you should know better," bristled the nurse.

"I'm telling you that I was trained to assist the sick and wounded."

"Where?" demanded the nurse.

"In Leiston, where I was enlisted to help at the local hospital. It had been turned over for war use. Many of the wounds were very serious. The vicar's sister, who I was staying with, was an exceptionally trained senior nurse who would assist the doctors in operations. She taught me. As did one of the doctors stationed there. I performed nursing services, from bandaging wounds to even frequently assisting in surgeries."

"Rubbish," snapped the nurse.

"How would you treat a serious infection, then?"

The question did not come from the nurse.

Another woman, tall and formidable and wearing the official markings of a Principal Matron—equivalent to the rank of an army major—stood in the doorway and had evidently overheard this part of their conversation. Her pale, stern features seemed cast from marble.

The nurse looked at her in surprise. "Matron Tweedy, I didn't see you there."

"I'm sure, Sister Helen." She looked at Molly. "Well, *child*?"

Molly looked up at her. "A serious infection?"

"Surely you know what serious infections are if you spent any time treating wounded soldiers," said Tweedy, giving Molly a penetrating stare. "Come, come, for such an *experienced nurse* the answer should be an easy one."

Molly said, "All right. We would use sulfanilamide as a disinfectant, or else shots of penicillin. Both were excellent at killing lethal bacteria, which, as you know, can quickly enter the bloodstream and lead to death by septicaemia. That happened far too often. As did gangrene, of course. We had to amputate many limbs. It was really quite awful, but necessary to save lives. Because once the infection spreads, it is very difficult to stop. Death is often the result."

The superior smile that had been playing over Tweedy's lips vanished. "You know about penicillin and sulfanilamide, do you?"

"Sister Cooper told me that penicillin was invented by Alexander Fleming, and sulfanilamide was discovered by a researcher at the Pasteur Institute. Those medications have saved a great many lives during the war. As has plasma. It's far more stable than actual blood, and doesn't go foul nearly as quickly. Wounded men obviously lose a great deal of blood, and plasma works exceptionally well. And one couldn't very well ask injured men who had lost a great deal of blood themselves to donate more. And excessive blood loss can quickly lead to shock, which, in turn, can kill rapidly. Our only problem was we could never get enough of the plasma. It was in very limited supply. I don't know about the situation here."

"It is quite dire here as well. And soldiers in great pain?" Tweedy said slowly. "How would you handle that?"

"We used syrettes to inject standardized dosages of morphine into the bloodstream. It rendered the men unconscious so that they could be properly administered to without struggling about and doing themselves even greater harm. We would pin the syrette to their collars to alert everyone that they had been given a dose, because morphine is quite potent and an overdose could easily kill. The hospital was quite chaotic at times, particularly when the troop ship docked and all the wounded started arriving, so we did all we could to avoid any mishaps like that."

Sister Helen and Tweedy exchanged an astonished look.

Tweedy said, "I'm sorry that I doubted you. You evidently *did* help with the wounded."

"My apologies for doubting you, too, Miss," said Sister Helen.

"I suppose I *am* quite young for work such as that," said Molly, more to herself than to either of them. "But they needed my help while I was there and thus I helped. It was the least I could do, you see. The men had sacrificed so much." She eyed Tweedy. "So can I help here?"

Tweedy glanced at her colleague. "Well, these are extraordinary circumstances which perhaps require extraordinary measures. I was redeployed from the continent six months ago because of the injuries and disease proliferating through London presently. And we *are* quite short-handed, which is why we are seeking additional help. And the fact is the hospitals only provide nursing auxiliaries fifty hours of training before they go into service, and it sounds like you have had far more experience than that."

"I often worked more than fifty hours in a single week."

"I'm afraid that we can't pay much. Four pounds a week, but we have a small canteen here, breakfast, elevenses, lunch, and dinner. It's nothing fancy, of course, but it is good, healthy food."

"That will be fine."

"Where do you live?" asked Tweedy.

Molly almost said Chelsea, but caught herself and replied, "Not very far from here at all."

"I'm afraid, because of your youth, we will need a letter from your parents authorizing you to work here."

Molly didn't hesitate. "My father will be glad to do so. Now that I'm back in London, he encouraged me to help with the skills and knowledge that I have."

"Very public-spirited of him, too," commended Tweedy. "Sister Helen here will take some information from you and then you can bring the letter from your father tomorrow and we can go from there. Does that suit you, um . . . ?"

"Molly, Molly Wakefield. It suits me very well. Thank you."

"No, thank *you*."

An Inspector Calls

Molly couldn't stop from smiling all the way back to The Book Keep. Now she only had to convince Mr. Oliver to write that letter. If he wouldn't, Molly trusted that she could imitate her father's handwriting well enough. And Matron Tweedy would have nothing to compare it to.

As she turned down the alley she noticed the burly man at the bookshop's door. He wore a creased hat and long brown trench coat, along with a stiff, official posture. Mr. Oliver was standing in the doorway and the man was showing him what looked to be a photograph. As Molly approached them, Inspector Willoughby turned to her and doffed his hat. "And who might you be, young lady?"

Oliver said quickly, "Inspector Willoughby is with the police, Molly. He is here enquiring about a boy named Charlie Matters. He thinks this boy might have attempted to break into my shop with some other lads. And when they ran away one of the lads and a constable chasing them were hit by a lorry and killed."

Molly's face turned pale as Oliver continued, "I told the inspector we don't know this Charlie Matters, and had no idea he might have attempted to burgle my shop."

Willoughby, who was watching both of them closely, said, "And what's your relation to Molly here?"

"She's the niece of one of my cousins who lives in the country. Molly is staying with me for a bit."

Willoughby, eyeing Molly, said, "May I ask why you're in London?"

Molly said quickly, "There is a private girls' school here that my mother is thinking of sending me to."

"Which one?"

"St. Elspeth's."

"What, in Chelsea?"

"That's the one." Molly had selected that one because before she had left for the country, it had been arranged that she would attend there. "Do you know it?"

"I know it costs a packet. Chief Constable Quigley's granddaughter goes there. So your family must have money," he added.

"Well, my maternal grandfather did rather well in . . . pigs . . . and *crops* before the war. And my other grandfather was quite keen on manufacturing things. And my mother considers education to be the cornerstone of one's life. Indeed I hope to become a doctor one day."

"You mean a nurse," corrected Willoughby.

"Oh, yes, no doubt that's what I meant," said Molly pleasantly.

"So you don't know this lad, Charlie Matters?"

"I only arrived in London a short time ago. I haven't had a chance to really meet anyone."

"R-right," said Willoughby, who was still looking suspiciously at both of them. "How about another lad named Lonzo Rossi? Here's a picture of him." He showed it to Molly.

Molly recognized the name from when Charlie had told her that was the boy who had stolen his book. But she shook her head at the photograph. "I've never seen him," she said quite truthfully. "Who is he?"

"One of Matters's mates." He turned to Oliver. "I gave you a description of the boy. If you see him, ring me straight away at this number." Willoughby handed him a card.

"Certainly, Detective Inspector. Certainly."

Willoughby walked off, but looked back once. Oliver waved to him. After he was gone, they went into the shop.

Molly said to Oliver, "So that's why Charlie has been so miserable. It was his friend who was killed."

"And his other mate obviously talked to the police."

"Lonzo Rossi."

Oliver nodded. "Yes. He's in jail right this moment, or so Willoughby told me. They caught him when he was trying to enlist in the army."

"Charlie mentioned Lonzo to me before. Lonzo stole the book you gave Charlie."

"I see."

"What will the charges be?" asked Molly fearfully.

"He mentioned rather a whole assortment, I'm afraid. Perverting the course of justice, wasting police time, but the more serious ones were contributing to the death of a constable, attempted burglary, and evading arrest. Inspector Willoughby said it would mean many years in prison."

Molly looked horrified. "That's preposterous. Charlie's only a boy."

"Nevertheless, the law says otherwise, I'm afraid, since both boys are in their teens. And it's wartime now and apparently different rules apply."

"And yet you lied to the inspector, as did I," pointed out Molly.

"I feel quite guilty having involved you in it. But I didn't want to give the game away."

"That's all right, Mr. Oliver. I would never have done anything to betray Charlie."

"But the inspector is clearly suspicious."

"Where is Charlie?" she asked.

"Like you, he left to find gainful employment. I really wish he wouldn't feel as if he had to do that. I can provide for you both."

"Well, I've just been hired as a nurse auxiliary."

"Really? Where?"

"The Covent Garden Medical Clinic."

"Really? As an air warden, I've often taken injured people there. They're quite good."

"Now, I need you to write a letter, as my father, to give me permission to do so."

"See here, Molly, do you really think that's necessary? I can—"

"It pays four pounds a week."

Oliver gaped. "Four pounds? A *week*? Are you serious?"

"And they provide meals as well."

Oliver put a finger to his lips and glanced at the till, where there was less than twenty quid left after paying assorted bills. "Well, um, if you're quite sure."

"I am. But, Mr. Oliver, we need to make absolutely certain that Charlie and Inspector Willoughby *never* meet."

Revealed

First came the boat, or schooner, or whatever the man called it. What Charlie called it was filthy and the man paid him and other lads half a crown each to shovel things off it and let them fall into the Thames to join the other sludge.

After that Charlie ate an apple that happened to tumble off a stand outside a shop with a bit of a nudge from him. Then he collected horse manure from the hauling wagons and carried it in burlap bags to community garden allotments for fertilizer. That brought a few more shillings. And he later received a crown from a grateful father with two small children in exchange for Charlie's crawling through the rubble of their bombed-out house to find a puppy half buried under stone and dirt. The thing was very much alive and miraculously uninjured. It was so happy to be rescued that it gave Charlie a slew of licks on the nose and clutched tightly to him, clearly unwilling to be alone again. Charlie had never had a pet and was reluctant to give it up until he saw how thrilled the dog was to be reunited with its family. He watched them carry it off, all now happy as could be despite no longer having a home.

Charlie rinsed his face, hands, and clothes at a tap, and followed up the puppy rescue by nicking a pair of handsome leather driving gloves and a nearly brand-new Homburg hat from an unlocked Rolls-Royce that was parked at the kerb in front of an elegant mansion in very tony Belgravia. He sold the items to a shady chap in an alley near the BBC building next to the Langham Hotel, who Charlie knew conducted a good business in "found" items like that. That put three whole guineas in his pocket.

Now Charlie had somewhere to go that had nothing to do with shovelling sludge or nicking for money.

He hitched a ride on the back of a lorry and jumped off very near Chelsea. He walked the rest of the way to where Molly's home used to stand in luxurious elegance.

Charlie searched through the debris and found the Conway Stewart pen wedged between two pieces of split brick. It was in surprisingly good shape and he pocketed it. After that was revealed a curved cherrywood pipe. Some coins, and pounds wrapped with a rubber band, were in a tin box that was under a mound of debris. They went into another pocket. He was quite surprised to find them because usually after the bombs dropped, blokes like him or else the firemen, wardens, Heavy Rescue men, or coppers made off with items like this. There was a hairbrush that he thought he recognized as one Molly had used on him. And finally he found a photo in a frame with the glass cracked.

In it were Molly and, he supposed, her mother and father. She looked, to Charlie, to be around six years old. He wiped it as clean as he could on his trousers and thrust it into another pocket.

He looked up and was surprised that he had not noticed it before.

The garage behind the house had not been damaged. This was akin to a miracle, but Charlie was used to such things. He had been in a building one time when the bombs fell. Both structures on either side of his had disappeared, while his building remained undamaged with nary a window shattered.

He made his way over the rubble to the garage and peered through the window. There was the Singer, yellow with a black top and a long, boxy bonnet.

He looked around and, seeing no one about, he used his tool to defeat the door lock and slipped inside. It smelled of oil and petrol and dampness. There were elaborate spiderwebs spun in all the garage's crevices. He approached the noble Singer with reverence, as though he were in the presence of a divine monarch.

He ran his eye along the long bonnet and then drew up the courage to touch the metal husk. It felt cool and solid. Charlie opened the driver's-side door. It smelled of old leather, and the buttons on the dash gleamed like stars in the sky. He sat and gripped the steering wheel, his fingers curling and uncurling around the sphere. He didn't know how to drive a car, but here Charlie Matters was sitting at the wheel of a Singer!

He eyed the back seat, where he imagined Molly and her parents would ride, perhaps with a picnic hamper next to them full of wonderful things to eat.

He opened the glove box and fumbled around until his fingers touched something metallic. He drew out the key to the car and another key that most likely was to the garage door. Goggle-eyed, he looked at the ignition and the starter button, but then his courage fled. He did pocket the keys because he knew some bloke would happen along here who had the skill and courage and the Singer would be long gone.

He got out, used the key to lock all the doors, and left the garage after securing it, too, using the other key. He hopped onto the rear bumper of a delivery van and rode it halfway to Covent Garden. When he finally reached the alley he spied the man talking to Oliver. He saw him show Oliver something that Charlie couldn't make out. Then Molly appeared from the other end of the alley and they both spoke with the man.

While staying out of sight, Charlie clearly heard his name mentioned several times. And then the name *Lonzo Rossi* came up.

The man had the look of a copper. Charlie had seen enough of them to know. Lonzo had surely told on him.

After the policeman left, and Molly and Oliver went inside,

Charlie slunk forwards and peered through the window into the shop. Molly and Oliver were talking and looking very worried, and he could understand why. His shameful secret was now fully revealed to them. He was a criminal, a murderer in fact, destined for the gallows.

Only a few minutes before, thrilled with the money he had earned and the possessions he had recouped for Molly, and the excitement of sitting in the Singer and imagining all sorts of possibilities that did not include a noose around his neck, Charlie's spirits were now full the other way.

He rushed off into the growing darkness.

Charlie wasn't sure where he was going to go, but he could not go back to The Book Keep. He could not meet the eye of Mr. Oliver and especially Molly. He remembered what she had said after reading the news account of Eddie's and the constable's death.

Well, I hope they catch those other boys. And I hope they feel terrible about what happened.

I do, Molly, I surely do. But I can't do nothin' about it now. Eddie's dead. Lonzo's nearly dead for sure. And I'm next.

He had never felt so lost, or miserable. He had thought his mother's death followed by his grandmother's passing would be the worst things that ever happened to him. But now that his own survival was at stake, the fear in him was all-consuming. And he felt terrible guilt for being so selfish that his own life was more important to him than his dear mother's, who would have willingly sacrificed hers for his without a second thought.

You ain't even worth a farthin', Charlie. Honourable? You're no better than you ought to be. You're no better than Lonzo. You steal and you get folks killed. You deserve the rope.

Even as he thought this the tears leaked from his eyes and his throat constricted, as though the hemp was already around it.

You're not a boy, Charlie. You're a man. Act like it.

But though he said the familiar mantra in his head, it did nothing to change how he felt, which was scared, cold, and hungry. He had money in his pocket, but he could never spend it on himself.

He made a sudden decision and crept back to The Book Keep. He gave a searching look through the glass to make sure no one was about.

Oliver had forgotten to lock the door, so Charlie held the bell still, slipped inside, placed the money and the things he'd found at Molly's ruined house on the counter, and fled.

He looked back once at the little shop that held the only friends he had left in the world. This placed another prodigious lump in his throat, because Charlie realized he would never see them again. He was nothing but trouble, and friends did not bring trouble to their mates.

He picked up his pace and then broke into a sprint. Charlie had always been fast. Running from potential disaster all the time just did that to you.

A Glum Discovery

Later, both Molly and Oliver stared in dismay at the money and other items salvaged from Molly's home that were resting on the counter.

"Charlie was here," she said pointedly. "These things are from my home." She opened the tin box, revealing the money inside. "This was our household funds." She lifted the photo of her and her parents from the pile and studied it, as Oliver rubbed his chin, evidently lost in thought. He glanced at the doorway.

"Do you . . . could he have seen us speaking with the inspector and perhaps deduced what that was about? Or possibly he overheard . . . ?"

"And then he left this here and . . . ?" said Molly, looking to be near tears.

"It would explain things, surely. And then he might have run off, not wishing to bring any trouble upon us."

"We *have* to find him, Mr. Oliver. We have to tell him that we know he had nothing to do with what happened to that boy and the constable."

"But it seems as though he *was* here that night, Molly."

"You can't believe he wanted that boy and the constable to die."

"Absolutely not. Charlie is a good lad. But he . . . well, he . . ."

"What?" she said sharply.

"He actually did pinch some money from me one night."

"What!"

"But he brought it all back the next day. I mean, he came all this way to bring the money back. Now *that* is a good person."

"Yes, it is," said a relieved Molly.

"But in the eyes of Inspector Willoughby, he was at the scene of the crime and then ran, which, in itself, makes him culpable."

"Then what can we do?"

"We need to find Charlie and make sure he's safe and that he knows we believe him to be innocent and that we will . . . shelter him."

"But isn't that a crime?"

Oliver looked deeply troubled. "It could be considered such, but I am the adult and will thus be held accountable. Because of your age you will not be."

"*Charlie* is younger than I am, and yet he is being hunted by the police for a crime, so I'm not sure your position regarding me is accurate," countered Molly.

"You are absolutely right about that," conceded Oliver, sighing.

"But I don't care about that. Charlie is my friend. In fact, you two are the only friends I have. So how do we go about finding him?"

"The first place to look is his old flat. He might have gone back there. However, it may already have another tenant living in it. With housing scarce, these things tend to happen fast. We'll go there straight away."

Molly picked up the money Charlie had left behind and handed it to Oliver. "You should have this. It's . . . partial payment for us, at least now for me, to be staying here. Until Charlie returns," she added quickly.

They headed off. The pavements were fairly empty because a thick fog was filtering in; the air was bracingly chilly. They each had a gas mask with them, and they used the white paint on the kerb, trees, and lamp-posts to see their way.

"So an auxiliary . . . what was it again?" he said.

"A nurse auxiliary." She explained to him about her medical experiences in Leiston.

He shook his head. "My goodness, Molly, to do that sort of work at such a young age. I've never heard of another such case as that. And the way you dealt with that injured man? It's remarkable, truly."

"Young people *are* capable of a great deal if the need is there," she replied with spirit.

"Quite so, yes."

"And you must write that letter to Matron Tweedy tonight."

"I promise that I shall."

After a considerable walk resulting in tired, pinched feet, they reached Dapleton Terrace. Enquiries made within to several of the residents revealed that not a single one had seen Charlie since his grandmother had been taken away. They also learned that while the flat had been let, the new tenants had not moved in as yet.

They walked up the stairs and down the hall to Charlie's old home.

She glanced at him. "You never told me how you knew where Charlie lived."

"I dropped off something for him. Something he had lost near my shop. It included this address. But I have not been inside. Have you been here before?"

"Yes, once when Charlie and I went on a picnic, and a second time when we came looking for the book that you gave him. He had accidentally left it behind."

"I see. And this Lonzo chap nicked it, you said?"

"Yes."

The door was unlocked and they quietly entered. Oliver snicked on a light, and the feeble illumination allowed them to look around.

Molly showed him the cupboard where Charlie had his bed box.

Oliver stood there for a few moments looking down at the compartment that was barely large enough for a toddler much less a lad Charlie's age.

In Gran's bedroom Molly saw the photograph on the wall. "Surely, he would want that."

"Yes," said Oliver, drawing closer. "They look to be his parents."

He took the photograph off the wall and slid it into his coat pocket.

"I would imagine his grandmother had a purse or some such," said Molly. "But I don't see it anywhere. Or the ration books. I should have thought to look for them when I came here with Charlie the last time, but he was so upset about Lonzo taking his book that it never occurred to me."

"I'm afraid that both her purse and the ration books are long gone by now."

"Do you think he could have gone back to where I lived?"

"There would be no reason to. He obviously already went there to search through the rubble and found the items he left at the shop."

"He did mention that Lonzo had been, well, expelled by the families that took him."

"Where did he live, then?"

"Charlie never said."

He looked around despondently. "I'm afraid, Molly, that unless we are quite fortunate indeed, we might very well have to wait for Charlie to return to us."

Her face fell. "But what if he never does? What if he tries to join the army, like Lonzo?"

"Charlie would know that would be impossible. This Lonzo might have been able to pass as a young man of volunteer age, but Charlie simply cannot."

They found a bus that would take them back to Covent Garden. When Molly had admonished him over the price of the tickets he said, "I'm tired, my feet are very sore, as I'm sure yours are, and I still have to make my air warden rounds tonight. And you are going to work in the morning. And I have a letter to write for you. And then I have another letter to write."

"Who is the second letter going to?"

"A chap I know in the War Office. He might know something of your father. I would ring him up on the telephone, but he never answers it. Against strict regulations or something. Quite annoying." He gave Molly a weak smile.

They settled back for the ride to Covent Garden as the rain began to fall and the wind to bluster; the chill scooted right inside the bus and clutched them tightly.

Molly watched as Oliver pulled his thin coat more snugly around him, tipped his hat downwards, and shut his eyes.

She and Charlie had never found out what Oliver was doing with the man who had German papers in his flat along with a funny machine. Yet Molly could not believe that Oliver was involved in anything criminal.

If I can't believe in him, who can I believe in? I have no one left.

The Hiding Place

Charlie blew on his hands and ignored the ache in his stomach. He'd just missed the closing time of a nearby mobile canteen, although the lady there had taken pity on him and slipped him a wedge of Government Cheddar and a days-old ginger biscuit that tasted quite foul but he devoured, nonetheless.

He now lay on the cracked leather back seat of the Singer and huddled into his coat. He had thought about where to stay after leaving The Book Keep. There weren't many choices, but he had settled upon the Singer. If he couldn't drive the car, clearly the next best thing would be to sleep in it. Only he had thought it would be much warmer.

For a moment he fantasized about starting the car and turning on the heater, but that was no good, he realized. It would make too much noise.

Around about midnight—he knew by the ringing of a nearby church bell—he decided that lying here cold and hungry was not the best-laid of plans. He locked up the Singer and slipped out of the garage.

After a long, weary walk, he arrived at Gran's old bakery shop, the one that had cut her wages in half and then failed to pay her what she was owed.

He nimbly picked the old lock on the back door, filled his pockets with all the rolls he could, and also swiped a jar of honey and one of jam. He had never thought of robbing this place while Gran worked there. Now he felt like he was doing it in her memory. But he really wasn't, because Gran would never have approved of him stealing.

As he sat under an awning in an alley and devoured two large rolls with honey and jam smeared over them, his belly grew less annoyed with him.

Charlie decided he could not stay in the Singer night after night. He would have to find new digs. And now would be a good time to address that need. He dusted the crumbs off his britches and ran off into the rain.

Lonzo and Eddie's old place was a bombed-out building in Stepney, near the docks. Or where the docks used to be. He turned the last corner as a bolt of lightning shattered the sky. The resulting rumble of thunder followed him as he ran along the darkened streets.

He crouched at a corner and warily eyed the half-destroyed building. It had just occurred to Charlie that the police might be watching the place. He waited there for half an hour, shooting glances all around. He also peered into the shadows looking for the silhouette of a burly bobby, or someone who looked like the stout copper at The Book Keep.

Finally, concluding there was no danger about, he slipped through the rear door, or where a door had once been before the Luftwaffe had come and forcibly removed it.

He knew that the space Eddie and Lonzo had used as their digs was at the very top of the building. Lonzo explained that the air was nicer up there, and the rats didn't seem to want to venture that high. Charlie had been here many times before, when they had been out hunting together late at night. They would divvy up their spoils before Charlie had headed back to Dapleton Terrace.

Charlie looked down at the twin berths on the floor, no more than wads of filthy cloths, blankets Eddie and Lonzo had nicked, and two burlap sacks with balled-up newspapers in them for pillows. He sat next to one of the beddings and imagined Eddie by his side, starkly alive with his brooding eyes and quiet, resourceful manner.

Charlie eyed the other items lining the floor. A stub of candle, a matchbox, some pilfered magazines, stacks of newspapers—probably for a fire or to use as warming covers for sleeping—an iron pan with the stiffened remains of long-ago cooked food, an empty bottle of Highland Queen Scotch whisky, a foldable spoon and fork in a little leather pouch that Charlie knew Lonzo had stolen from a pub, and a belt with fresh holes punched in it as waists became slimmer from hunger. There were also empty cigarette packs, a pair of worn-out socks, a pile of empty tins and small boxes, and . . . Charlie could barely believe his eyes.

He slid across the floor and picked up the journal that Oliver had given him and that Lonzo had stolen from Charlie's flat. As his fingers closed around the leather, he felt something cold grip him.

I just trod over a grave.

Eddie *was* dead. Was Lonzo? Had they already hanged him?

Charlie slid back over to where he'd been and sat there, his knees drawn up to his chest, the granular coolness of the journal's cover slowly leaching into his hands.

He opened it and saw that Lonzo had written something on the fly leaf. The scrawl was childish—Lonzo had had very little formal schooling, he knew. But Charlie could easily read the two words.

Sawree, Edee.

Charlie mouthed these two words, not simply parroting what was written, but perhaps with the understanding that he was talking to his deceased mate.

Sorry, Eddie.

He put the journal down, rose, and went over to a window that had no glass in it. The cold swept in off the Thames, sending a raw, miserable chill through him, even as drops of rain invaded the inside of his new home.

Charlie looked over the city of his birth, and also likely the place of his death. It was a broad, complicated plain of buildings and people, most who were good, and some who were not. And some, like him, who had elements of both. But he knew that they were all fearful of what was to come.

Charlie could die by bombing tomorrow, or be hit by a bus that lunged out of the foggy darkness at him. Or he could be hanged for crimes during wartime. He knew that he had taken a father from his children, a husband from his wife.

And poor Eddie's head had been crushed beneath that lorry's dirty wheel.

It was awful, and terrible and far beyond his youthful ability to fully comprehend its magnitude. Yet firmly within the spectrum of the narrow moral compass he had set for himself, Charlie had done wrong. And this terrible wrong could never be righted. He could not simply return nicked things, or shrug off a lie or two to his grandmother.

His penance would be the life he must now lead. Even at war's end, no matter the victor, he would be Charlie Matters, the killer.

He staggered over and fell on top of Eddie's old bedding. He did not want to cry. But he did anyway, with the vision of his dead mother steadfastly in mind. When he'd done his fill of weeping and wiped his eyes and face with his dirty sleeve, he told himself:

You're a man, Charlie Matters. No more time or use for tears, mate.

A Night of Missives

WHILE MOLLY DOUBTLESS SLEPT fitfully in her room, Oliver—who had completed his air warden duties during a night in which, thankfully, no sirens had sounded—opened the door of Imogen's study and sat down at the desk. He would not be fruitlessly attempting, as he normally would, to add to his wife's novel. He would be composing a letter for Molly.

He decided that pen and paper would be more appropriate and took up these elements, his only light a candle.

As instructed by Molly, Oliver addressed the missive to Matron Tweedy. He thought intently about the best words to use to convey his complete confidence in Molly's abilities, as well as his approval of her helping in the war effort. It wasn't that difficult to conjure the phrasing, as he had seen her obvious skill on display in quite a desperate situation with the wounded man and his bloody arm. He almost signed his real name at the end of the letter before instead stroking out a fine, bold *Herbert James Wakefield.*

A small deception for the best of reasons.

He blotted the letter, folded it over, and placed it inside an envelope and then sealed it.

Now he had one more letter to compose. And this one he would carry out on the Crown typewriter.

He settled his fingers on the keys and tapped away. The letter was addressed to Major Scott Bryant, his contact at the War Office. Oliver was enquiring as to the whereabouts of one Herbert James Wakefield, lately of Chelsea and an apparent signatory to the Official Secrets Act. Oliver did not set forth why he was interested in Wakefield, or that at this moment he was hosting the man's daughter in his spare room. If they found out, someone from the Ministry of Health might be over in a thrice, he knew, to relieve him of the girl.

But he *was* curious as to why people had been watching Molly. Oliver seriously doubted it could be connected to Molly or her mother, which left the missing father as the cause, and also probably the reason for the man's disappearance.

He obviously did a bunk and they want to track him down. The only question is why.

He ended the letter with the usual platitudes and thanks and affirmation of secrecy and the like. He cranked the letter out of the Crown and signed it. He wrote out the address on another envelope and placed this letter inside it. He would post it in the morning.

His tasks completed, Oliver put out the candle, locked up the study, and placed both envelopes on the front counter. He opened the till and glanced at the cash inside. He knew the amount down to the shilling, and the money Charlie had found at Molly's home had been a significant contribution. He knew those who really had nothing.

Like Charlie.

He walked over to the window and edged the blackout curtains apart.

Oliver had once asked his wife why her father had not located his bookshop at Paternoster Row, in the City of London. That was where most of the leading bookshops were, along with the massive wholesaler, Simpkin & Marshall, from which Oliver purchased much of his book stock. Paternoster Row was a special place, he felt, with quite an interesting history as to its naming.

Centuries ago the monks and clergy of St. Paul's would march down the street reciting the Lord's Prayer, and "Pater Noster" were the opening words, in the original Latin. The words had been combined over time to give the street its unusual name. There had been a spillover effect as well, since nearby were the religious-inspired names of Ave Maria Lane and Amen Corner. It made him smile that from such divine sources had come memorable historical references that had persevered to this day.

His wife's answer to his question regarding the location of The Book Keep had been simple and direct:

"My father said that we must spread the wealth of books around, Iggy. Concentrating them in one place means that others will be deprived of the experience of opening a tome of wonder. No, we must be where the people who need us are. And the people who need books are all over this great city, not simply in one exalted place. And where there are enough books that more people read, places naturally become exalted in the best possible sense, they become exalted of the individual mind *and* spirit."

He remembered those words so clearly. And her father's decision had turned out to be a prescient one for them, but devastating for others. In 1940 on one perilous night around the Christmas holidays, the Germans had bombed the sector containing Paternoster Row with such ferocity it seemed that they knew exactly what was contained down there.

An American politician, Wendell Willkie, had visited the remains of Paternoster Row the following month and remarked that the Germans had obliterated where truth was told. Oliver knew very little about Americans, but he thought Willkie had hit the nail right on the head.

Books filled with truth, turned to ash, and turning minds the same in their absence.

Even before the main bombs had fallen that night, the crackling and popping magnesium clusters attached to parachutes had ignited in the streets, turning a peaceful lane of books and buildings into a conflagration. It burned so hot and there were too many of the clusters, so sand, usually a reliable foe to magnesium, was rendered useless. And if one put water on magnesium, it simply exploded. Added to the problem was the fact that the German bombs had also blown out the water mains. And the attack had happened at low tide, which meant drawing water from the Thames was nigh impossible.

In the end the fire brigades were simply resigned to let Paternoster Row burn itself out.

And it had.

Simpkin & Marshall, in particular, had flamed with an intensity perhaps never before seen in the city. The inferno had been fed by its inventory of millions of books. And more tragically, many people had died, some incinerated in their beds. It had been deemed the Second Great Fire of London, after the one that had occurred nearly three centuries earlier. The entire city was at risk of burning from the mass of incendiary bombs dropped on that cold night in December, but the fires had eventually been extinguished, and nearby St. Paul's Cathedral had once more been spared.

Oliver and Imogen had ventured one day to Paternoster Row and seen the devastation. Both had openly wept at the losses. His wife had been near inconsolable, as the ashes of destroyed books still filtered through the breezy air, covering them like the detritus of an apocalyptic eruption.

The casualty list posted to the borough's town hall ran to several pages, Oliver recalled, including over a dozen firemen who had perished fighting the blazes.

He remembered watching Imogen staring, dead-eyed, at the loss of books and people, her two favourite things in life, and then she had slumped to the pavement sobbing. He had held her as tightly as he could. Yet nothing he could say was consoling enough, and his beloved wife was racked with sob after sob for well over an hour.

When Imogen rose she did so unsteadily, but then his wife

looked at him in a way that she never had before. It was as though a different person was standing before him.

"War is never the answer, Ignatius," she said. "*Never.*"

And then she had walked off. As things turned out, that had been a defining moment for Imogen Oliver. For both of them, really.

Oliver felt tears gather in his eyes at this wretched memory.

He looked at the Secret Garden tea shop across the way. Desdemona Macklin would no doubt describe Oliver as someone who kept himself to himself. But she was also observant. She seemed to note every visitor that he had. And one in particular—Cedric. That was not good.

He drew the curtains. During the Blitz most shops closed at four so that folks could get some sleep before their nightly shift began as volunteers with, among others, the fire brigade, the air wardens, or the Heavy Rescue Division, the latter comprised of men driving battered lorries whose thankless job it was to search the rubble for survivors, but more often finding the dead. These squads were routinely comprised of those in the construction industry who used their knowledge of structures and load points and the like to safely burrow into collapsed buildings.

He rolled up his sleeve and looked at one of the burns he had suffered when a magnesium cluster had landed on him. It was as though electrified fire had been injected into him. Had his fellow warden not been there to assist him, Oliver knew he would be no more. This fellow warden had died the very next night when a wall had toppled on him. Oliver had been a dozen steps behind, only because he had stopped to pick up an injured cat. He had taken off his gas mask to see better and proceeded to knock the burning embers off the poor animal's coat. He looked up to witness the wall collapsing on his mate.

He had not been on duty, but had been near the Marble Arch Underground station on Oxford Street in Westminster when a bomb had come through the station's ceiling. Those not killed by the initial blast had been ripped apart by the tiles sheared off the walls and hurled through the air at them like thousands of spinning knives.

Coming upon that scene he had picked not through bodies, but body *parts*. He and a dozen other wardens had worked for hours helping to clear the mess. Though he knew there were survivors, Oliver had never personally seen a single one.

Part of his air warden training had involved a plea for detachment, a level of sangfroid that Oliver found logical and necessary while being instructed on it, and impossible to employ in the heat of the moment. Any warden who could coolly and dispassionately walk through devastation and death was not a human being he desired ever to meet.

Oliver's official report forms, in which wardens documented all incidents on their watch in order to build a knowledge base of enemy activity, were regularly stained with his tears.

His thoughts turned to Charlie. He was out there somewhere, and in a city of millions and hundreds of square miles and God knew how many buildings and places to hide oneself, he was certain they would never find him. They would have to wait for Charlie to return to them.

If he ever managed to.

A Good Man?

"The letter seems to be quite in order," said Matron Tweedy to Molly the following morning. She folded it up, placed it back in the envelope, and secreted it in a drawer of her desk. She stood and said, "Now, let's get a proper uniform for you. Last night I had one of our volunteers alter one we had for a nurse who was around your size. I think it will work well enough."

She took Molly to a changing room and presented her with the outfit: white skirt and blouse, cap and a blue cape, and rubber-soled shoes and white stockings.

"Now go ahead and change and I'll start you on your duties. I thought at first you could work with some of the WVSes in rolling bandages and the like and then we can have you follow nurses on their rounds, to get your legs under you as it were. How does that sound?"

"It sounds fine," said Molly, who was pink-faced with excitement, but also suffering from a severe case of butterflies in her stomach.

She quickly donned her uniform and met Tweedy in the hall. "I've heard of the WVS, but wasn't exactly sure what they did."

"Yes, the Women's Voluntary Service. They do so much. Running field kitchens and canteens, clothing centres for the homeless, and performing domestic work in clinics, like this one. They even darn socks for the army. I don't know how we would manage without them. They're paid nothing, of course, and even have to buy their own uniforms."

Molly was led to a room where a small group of women in their official livery of grey-green tweed skirts, red jumpers, and felt hats was sitting at a long table, rolling bandages and filling kits with medical items and other essentials. Some were darning socks, as Tweedy had already mentioned. Still others were heading out of the room with mops and buckets and rags and long checklists on clipboards.

Tweedy introduced Molly. Several of the women seemed quite surprised to see Molly in a proper nurse auxiliary's uniform.

"How old are you, my dear?" said one.

"In war or calendar years?" replied Molly, who had been keenly prepared for that query.

This broke the ice as all the ladies tittered over her response. Molly rolled bandages for several hours, actually teaching the women a quicker and more efficient way to do so.

"Marvelous," opined the lady who had queried Molly on her age. "How clever. Where did you learn to do that?"

"In a hospital in a town called Leiston. It's in Suffolk."

"Well, I've never been there, but they seem quite up-to-date with the modern ways."

"Yes, they are."

After a hasty lunch in the clinic's canteen, Molly followed another nurse on rounds. Molly could tell that the woman gave her specific tasks and watched her closely to gauge her level of skill and knowledge.

Later, she said, "You have a nice touch, and quite a bit of experience, Molly, and a good bedside manner. You instill confidence, which is really half the battle."

"These patients have very serious injuries," Molly said.

"Yes, they do. And if the hospitals weren't completely full up, they would be there. And we only have the two doctors making rounds."

"Only two?" said a surprised Molly.

"And they're both quite old and don't know the new ways and such. The young doctors are full-time at the hospitals, or else in uniform. Or else they were killed in the bombings. It's terribly desperate."

"But they have nurses, like you," said Molly stoutly.

"And like *you*, Molly," replied the nurse kindly.

Later, an exhausted Molly, having finished work for the day, walked slowly back to The Book Keep, where Oliver was shelving some newly arrived tomes.

"How did it go?" he asked, looking over her shoulder and seeing Desdemona Macklin staring at them through her front glass. He waved at her and she hesitantly waved back.

Molly looked that way. "Charlie mentioned that that woman was very observant."

"Her name is Desdemona Macklin, and yes, she is. Imogen couldn't stand her. She doesn't miss much. She'd actually make an excellent intelligence officer," he added, drawing a sharp glance from Molly.

She said, "Well, today went very well, at least medically speaking. But the patients there are quite injured and sick. And the resources we have to help them are far from adequate."

"Molly, I think you have just accurately summed up the whole of Britain's chief problem," said Oliver. "But let me put the kettle on. There are few experiences in life that a cup or two can't help. Do you want dinner?"

"No, I ate at the clinic's canteen. Can I make you something?" she added doubtfully. "Although I'm quite hopeless in the kitchen."

"I'm fine."

"And thank you for the letter. It was very well written."

"Imogen must have rubbed off on me," he called back as he disappeared behind the curtain.

Molly set down her bag in which she had placed the clothes she had worn to the clinic and took off her cape, hanging it on a peg next to Oliver's threadbare coat.

It continued to bother her that Oliver seemed to be forever channelling his deceased wife's thoughts and opinions, rather than sharing his own. That he held Imogen out to be this perfect fount of knowledge and wisdom while belittling his own accomplishments and talents. Her mother had been obsessive with Molly; that was now clear to her. But was Oliver obsessed with the deceased Imogen? Was that healthy? Molly didn't think so.

And what was he doing with the odd chap that Charlie had seen, and who had a strange machine and documents in German in his lodgings? Molly knew she should try to find out more about this, but the fact was, she was afraid to. Not that she thought she would find out anything unpleasant or corrupt about Mr. Oliver. But that discovering the truth might somehow cause her to lose him as a friend. Right now, he was all she had. It was an awful feeling, to be so dependent on one other person.

But then Mr. Oliver might feel the very same about me.

Molly looked around the bookshop, and the dishevelled landscape was still quite comforting to her. She took out a book here and there and read off a line or two. Then she looked up and spotted a volume by George Sand. She glanced at the curtain, but she hadn't heard the kettle purr yet, so she would have time. She plucked the book off the shelf and opened it. She was both relieved and disappointed to see that it had not been gutted like the book Charlie had found.

"Looking for a good read?"

She glanced up to see Oliver at the curtain.

He said, "Tea will be ready shortly and I have a few biscuits." He came forwards. "Ah, George Sand."

She watched him closely to see if there was anything strange about his expression, but she couldn't decide if there was or not.

"I've never read it." She glanced at the title. "*Little Fadette*?"

"*La Petite Fadette* in the original French. It's a complicated tale of twins in the rural French countryside. Writers often have a fascination with twins. Shakespeare, for example—twins are littered throughout his work. *Twelfth Night* immediately comes to mind. And the American Mark Twain often wrote about them."

"Interesting. Has Mr. Sand written other novels?"

"George Sand was actually a Frenchwoman named Amantine Dupin. She wrote in the nineteenth century."

"Why use a man's name then?" asked Molly.

"I suppose in that time writing was not thought to be a suitable endeavour for a woman. As Imogen once told me, for most of history 'Anonymous' was a woman."

"If I were ever to write a story I would do so under my own name and be proud of it. I imagine it is a great deal of work."

Oliver glanced at the door to his wife's study. "I can attest to that." He added hastily, "But only because Imogen often spoke of what the ordeal entailed."

Molly frowned at his once more bringing his wife into the conversation. She decided to finally speak up about it.

"Mr. Oliver, do you realize that you always seem to talk about Imogen as though you have no thoughts or opinions of your own, but only your recollections of what she said or did?"

He seemed struck by this observation, and at first Molly was unsure what his reaction would be. Anger, perhaps?

However, his expression softened and he leaned against the wall. "Do I?" he said wearily.

"I think you know that you do," she said firmly. "You told me you were rather good with numbers. That is quite a unique talent. I suppose you were better at that than Imogen."

This seemed to give Oliver pause. He looked down. "I . . . am quite good with . . . maths and such. I don't think Imogen had any interest."

"Perhaps because she wasn't as good at it as you are."

He did not reply to this.

"But one can't be good at everything, can one?"

"No," said Oliver quietly. He glanced up at her. "I appreciate what you are trying to do, Molly. But when you have loved someone as much as I loved Imogen, and then you lose that person?" He shrugged, his expression one of the saddest she had ever witnessed. "I think the one thing you try to do, above all, is to keep that person alive in your thoughts and words. You . . . you want to make sure that the person resides with you at all times. So . . ."

"So you have no opportunity to forget them?" said Molly.

He nodded and said, "And when one also feels guilt about another's passing. . . ?"

"Why would you feel guilt, Mr. Oliver? I mean, I don't know how she died, but there was nothing you could have done, was there?"

"There is always something one can do, Molly. Always. In fact, if I had acted, she might still be alive."

A startled Molly blurted out, "What do you—"

The kettle sounded off and a clearly uncomfortable Oliver said, "Ah, tea." He rushed away before she could finish.

Over their cups of tea and biscuits Oliver said, "Now, Molly, I did want you to know that I wrote the War Office about your father. As soon as I receive a reply I will share it with you."

"Thank you. I'm also going to write to the Beneficial Institute in Cornwall. The letters Dr. Stephens sent me were lost in the bombing, but I remember the address. Now, what are we going to do about Charlie?"

He explained to her about the impossibility of finding their friend. "I dearly hope that he will return here at some point."

Frowning, she said, "But he's out there all alone. Something may happen to him. There are . . . bad people in this city who can exploit defenceless children."

He looked at her in alarm. "Molly, are you speaking about anything specifically with regard to Charlie?"

"Being back here and seeing the destruction and desperation, I just mean that it's not a good situation for a boy to be in all alone."

Oliver looked guilty. "You are quite right and I feel ashamed that I took the position I did. We must make all efforts to find him." He glanced at her. "That is, *I* must. You have a job. I will map out a plan to look for Charlie and will execute upon that plan while you're at work."

"But you run a bookshop!"

"Most of my customers come in before lunchtime. I will work until then and after that my time will be devoted to finding Charlie. Now, if you will excuse me, I have a few things to do before my air warden duties tonight."

"Mr. Oliver?"

"Yes?"

Molly desperately wanted to ask him about the circumstances of Imogen's death and what he could have done to prevent it, but she merely said, "Never mind. It's not important."

The Hitch

"INSPECTOR, SIR, WE MIGHT have a wee problem."

DI Willoughby looked up from his desk at the bobby who had helped in the arrest and violent interrogation of Lonzo Rossi. Framed in the doorway, the bulky constable looked quite unsettled.

"What are you talking about, Higgins?" growled Willoughby, who was attempting to correct some reports that were long overdue. He had never much cared for the job's paperwork.

"It's the Lonzo Rossi lad."

"What of him?"

The constable came in and shut the door behind him. He approached the desk timidly. "He don't seem to be wakin' up, does he?"

Willoughby lit a small, hand-rolled cigarette and blew smoke off to the side. "What the deuce do you mean he's not 'waking up'?"

Higgins shrugged. "Just that. He ain't eaten much since we brung him in. And he seemed drowsy like when we put him in the clink, shufflin' and such and losin' his balance. Threw water on him before to get him up. But now, he won't wake up a'tall. Tried to rouse him to have his bit 'a dinner, but no luck."

"Damn! Take me to him."

A minute later, Higgins slid back the cell door peephole and the

DI peered in. Lonzo was on his back on the hard bed, one arm dangling limply over the side.

"Open the door," ordered Willoughby.

They both went inside. The DI knelt down next to Lonzo and checked his pulse. "He's still alive at least, if barely." He slapped Lonzo hard on his battered face several times. "Here now, boy, wake up. Oi, stop pretending. Lonzo!"

Then Willoughby saw the blood hardened in the boy's nostrils, and on his hair and scalp. He pulled back his eyelid to peer into the unresponsive pupil.

"Do we need to get the doc?" asked Higgins nervously.

Willoughby thought quickly. This was the third prisoner who had been seriously injured during interrogations conducted by him. His superintendent had already given Willoughby a caution about that. If this boy died while in his custody, he might be demoted back to uniform.

"No, we do not. This lad is for the gallows anyway."

The big constable shuffled his feet and looked down at the stained floor. "But not really, sir. I mean, he didn't kill nobody hisself. The lorry done."

Willoughby eyed him severely. "Do I really have to remind you that one of your brethren died? Does that mean nothing to you, Constable Higgins?"

The big man took a step back. "Of course it do, sir. Ambrose Tapper was a good bobby, a fine one, in fact. None better."

"Well then?"

The man looked nervously at Lonzo. "But if enquiries are made, how he come by his injuries, sir. People might . . . you know? I don't want to lose my job," he added, with an anxious glance at the DI. "I mean, none of us do, do we?"

Willoughby rose and looked down at Lonzo. After a moment's thought he said, "The bombing the other night?"

"What of it, sir? Wireless says they may come back tonight."

Willoughby rubbed his stubbly chin and said, "Well then,

tonight we're going to take this lad back to the scene of his crime. And if the Germans do bomb, this might work out all right."

"But, sir—"

"You will either do your duty, Constable, or be written up."

Higgins gave a halfhearted salute. "Yes, sir. How will it be done, then?"

Willoughby began speaking quietly.

One Night in Hell

Ignatius Oliver was dressed in his air warden's uniform. He carried his overly large gas mask with massive eyeholes and a built-in speaking system so that he could address a crowd with instructions that might save their lives. He had a coil of tubing over his shoulder that would be used with a bucket and pump stirrup, which his comrade tonight, Lee Parker, would be bringing. He slipped his training manual into his pocket because no one could remember every line of instruction. He had a torch with a special covering so as not to be an unintentional beacon for the Luftwaffe. Even so, he would keep it pointed down. That and his gas rattle and first aid kit completed his equipment.

Oliver recalled that before the Blitz his uniform consisted merely of dark blue overalls and a steel helmet with "ARP," standing for Air Raid Precautions, imprinted on the front. Things were a bit more complicated now.

He opened the door to Molly's room and saw that she was already fast asleep after her long and tiring day. Still just a child, really, but nonetheless carrying the burdens of adulthood on her youthful, if capable, shoulders.

He set off to meet up with Parker and commence their rounds.

The sky was clear and the wind was quite calm. Both those factors gave him grave concerns. And the moon, while not a bomber's moon, was full and bright enough to be potentially disastrous for the British tonight. And the BBC had repeatedly warned of a possible attack.

He passed an intersection where an official sign hung on the wall instructing:

WHAT TO DO WHEN I HEAR GUNS, EXPLOSIONS, AIR RAID WARNINGS

Oliver went through the official litany in his mind: *Do not rush about like a madman terrifying others, but keep a cool head and take cover in appropriate facilities with your gas mask. Do not try to have a bloody "look" at the bombs falling. Keep in mind that certain noises can be good noises, like our boys firing back with their ack-ack guns. And lastly, the odds are largely in your favour not to be blown to bits.*

How terribly reassuring, he thought.

He met up with Parker, a man of about fifty with a lopsided smile and a flask of water, with perhaps a touch of something added, always on his person. Oliver noted that Parker had the stirrup pump and an empty bucket, which, when paired with the tubing Oliver had brought, could be used to fight small fires. The problem was the fires they encountered were rarely small.

Parker said matter-of-factly, "Appears London's going to get a hiding tonight, all right. Well, let's get on then, shall we?"

They started their sector rounds, which took them past the Covent Garden Medical Clinic. Their blackout curtains were drawn and secure, as were all the others up and down the street. There was virtually no traffic.

They made rounds for an hour, and it was drawing close to ten o'clock when the whine of the first sirens ended the quiet. The radar stations and watchers had obviously spotted the enemy coming from across the Channel.

They both looked to the sky, though they knew nothing could be seen as yet. Oliver also was aware that all over the city, anxious gunners were running to their anti-aircraft batteries, and soon their booms would herald projectiles heading skywards.

He and Parker sped into action as folks started spilling out into the streets.

They blew their whistles, spoke through their gas masks' amplified equipment, and corralled the citizens into orderly groups. Oliver was grateful to see that a sleepy-looking Molly was among them. There were several public shelters about, and Parker and Oliver split up, leading the groups to those respective places as quickly and efficiently as possible. Others with back yards or gardens would be scurrying into their half-buried Andy bomb shelters and lie there hoping not to perish. Oliver knew that many Londoners refused to go to the Underground stations for shelter. Many had told him that they thought hiding beneath the earth showed a lack of moral courage. Desdemona Macklin had been one of those to so inform him. "A hidey-hole?" she had said with disgust. "No thank you. If I'm to die let it be in my own home."

The red alert sounded as he worked away. *Twelve or so minutes to attack*, Oliver thought with a relative calm that belied what he was actually feeling.

Oliver took down the names of everyone at his shelters, then rushed out and compared his list with Parker's. There were a number of people unaccounted for, for whom they had responsibility. They once more split up to track them down.

Oliver managed to get to four of the five fairly quickly. Two had no occupants; the third was Desdemona Macklin. She came to the door, refused to leave as usual, and went back to her basement refuge. The fourth was an elderly woman who was a bit dazed, but Oliver managed to get her to a shelter. He crossed her name off the list and was rushing to the fifth and last home when he felt it.

This was his own personal early warning system that he had discovered during the first attack he had ever endured. It was the inordinate humming and vibrating under his feet, as though a million bees had taken up residence in the pavement. The disturbance, in fact, was coming from the collective force of the fleet of propeller planes thousands of feet above them. And if the sheer force of what he was feeling and hearing was any indicator, this was not going to be a good night for the British.

A hiding indeed.

Oliver began to run. The house he was going to was just around the corner. A Mr. and Mrs. Ramsey, elderly and not always responsive to the sirens. The vibrations became so intense, it was as though he were being lifted off his feet. He looked up again and felt his heart leap thrice in rapid succession. The sky was blotted out. All he could see were dark, oblong shapes. The Luftwaffe force above was truly beyond comprehension. Next, the planes' bay doors opened, and now came thousands of bombs plummeting towards London.

Oliver listened closely to the whistling sounds the falling bombs were making. He knew from experience that if the notes became deeper the bomb was heading away from you. If the pitch started to rise, however, the opposite was true. Unfortunately for Oliver, the pitch soared.

He sprinted around a corner and dove behind a pile of sandbags set ten deep in front of a small hotel. Oliver kept his chest off the pavement so that his ribs would not be crushed by the vibration of the bombs' detonations. The first explosives struck around the corner, and the next thing Oliver knew there were no sounds in his ears. It was like he'd been tossed off a pier into deep water. He could hear nothing except a murky, dulled semblance of disquiet.

He felt his body jerk and roll and hit something hard. Objects fell all around him, hot and burning and sharp and stabbing. Then, with a rush of pulsation in his head, he could hear again; part of him wished he couldn't.

He gasped and looked up as the very air seemed to ignite. Long, silvery threads of electrified molecules were descending like miniature, flaming enemy paratroopers.

Magnesium clusters.

The Luftwaffe had changed up its tactics. The bastards must have recognized some advantage of sending the bombs first and the clusters next, he thought.

He ripped open a sandbag with the utility knife that all wardens carried. He poured the sand everywhere the clusters landed. He had to be careful because the Germans had started adding delayed maiming explosives onto the incendiary bombs. When his dulled knife would no longer open the sandbags, he simply laid his steel helmet on top of the flaming devices to cut off the oxygen supply that fire required.

Oliver looked behind him and paled. The entire façade of the building was wavering, as though deciding whether to stand or fall. The stacked columns of sandbags had been blasted open in one section and he dove through them, rolled on the pavement, came to his feet, and ran for his life.

A few moments later the wall collapsed behind him. The concussive force of its disintegration engulfed him from behind and, Pegasus-like, he was lifted into the air on its tendrils and catapulted across the street, where he collided with a lamp-post. He gripped it momentarily as bricks and shards of exploded windows plowed through the air. Thankfully, he lost his grip and fell to the pavement as this angry horde of debris sailed over him like a murder of crows.

He lay stunned on the pavement for a few moments, trying to regain both his wits and his breath. He slowly stood and remembered where he had been going.

The Ramseys, Neil and Dorothy.

Yet the cries for help and the screams of the wounded and the dying came at him from all directions. He saw people, their clothes ripped off them, staggering from the hotel. They were bloody and dazed, and two dropped to the street as he watched. He ran over to help, only to find they had already died.

The sirens were still screaming, the whines of Jericho's Trumpets were ubiquitous, and the ack-ack guns were delivering their withering response. Oliver watched as thousands of rounds of flak and sledgehammer shells were slung upwards. The velocity with which they were hurtling burned colourful contrails across the dark horizon.

And still the damn bombs fell and clusters of waterproof fire ignited the landscape, and all the darkness and evil of hell was forcefully and cruelly visited upon the earth.

A Curious Victim

Oliver watched as explosion after explosion ripped across London's horizon. Buildings toppled, streets heaved up like ocean waves, parked cars burst into flames or were tossed about like toys by the massive detonations. The sounds of ambulances and fire engines overlay the cacophony of apocalyptic noise.

It was as though a volcano had erupted in the middle of one of the largest metropolises in the world, and all Oliver could think of was Pompeii.

He managed to turn the gas main off for the hotel, as well as two others down the block. He used his gas rattle to warn folks of the dangers of escaped methane. Using the microphone in his gas mask, he shouted instructions to people who could barely stand, much less listen. The hotel looked like a doll's house with its entire front sheared right off, allowing him to see directly into dozens of rooms. Fires roared everywhere, and desperate people were jumping from upper-level floors now, choosing a quick death over being burned alive.

He assisted a group of firemen as they clutched a large, round tarp. They positioned it next to the hotel and beneath a man who was clinging precariously to the ledge.

"Jump," screamed one of the firemen.

The man shook his head in terror as the flames behind him crept closer.

Oliver called out, "We've got you, mate. Haven't lost one yet. Buy you a pint after?"

The fearful man suddenly laughed at these remarks, closed his eyes, and jumped.

Oliver and the firemen all tucked their chins and didn't look up after making sure they were positioned to catch the falling man. That would prevent their necks from being jerked back when the jumper hit the tarp, possibly cracking their spines.

The burned man landed safely and was handed off to an ambulance crew.

Oliver next ran to those who had already leapt to the streets, and found only two were still breathing. He did what he could with his first aid kit, and when the other ambulances and hospital buses arrived, he directed the medics to these victims.

One of the medics called out, "Do we need to take you to hospital?"

"What?" Oliver said, startled.

"Look at yourself, guv."

Oliver glanced down and saw that his cape and tunic had been ripped off and his shirtsleeves and pant legs were shredded. Both arms and legs were covered in blood, and bits of glass shone in his skin like flinty diamonds in the medic's torch. His adrenaline now receding, Oliver felt an odd pain in his right leg; his hearing was also coming and going, as though people were alternating between shouting and whispering.

"I'm all right," said Oliver, who suddenly remembered the Ramseys.

He limped to their house only to find the door blown off and the windows gone. A fire was raging inside. He only had his tubing; Parker had the bucket and stirrup pump.

He cried out, "Mr. and Mrs. Ramsey. Are you in there?"

He knew they had an Andy bomb shelter in the back garden. Perhaps . . . ?

He hurried around to the rear, his teeth gnashing with every step from his injured leg. He saw that the Andy with its corrugated top and sides—which gave the structure its strength—was covered with dirt. That was intentional, he knew. But a section of wall from the house behind theirs had fallen on the Andy, partially collapsing it.

He threw himself down at the entrance to the shelter and pushed bricks and wood and shattered glass away from the opening, cutting his hands in the process.

He saw one shoe and then a hand. The shoe was a man's, the hand a woman's. He edged farther into the Andy and shone his torch around.

The Ramseys were there, all right. They had died together, and from the extent of their injuries, it looked like they had perished instantly. During wartime that seemed to largely constitute God's mercy.

He limped back to the hotel, where he found Parker helping the wounded and dying.

Parker said, "Everyone in my shelters is okay. I think the planes have passed over us now." He suddenly fixed on his fellow warden. "Bloody hell, Ignatius, you're wounded."

"I'm fine actually. The stirrup?" said Oliver.

"Oh, right." He filled the bucket from a hose pipe, and, using the stirrup, they doused people covered with burning embers, and put out modest fires that had sprouted up in several spots. When the fire brigades arrived, they helped the men to put out the rest of the flames in this sector. Then the search for people in the rubble began in earnest as the Heavy Rescue Division showed up to perform work no person should ever have to do.

They found far more dead than living.

A half-cremated young couple still in their bed in the hotel. Oliver later learned they had been on their honeymoon. The man still standing at the front desk, his hand fused to the reception bell by the flames and his lungs crushed by the concussive force of the detonation. He actually looked fine despite being dead. A waiter in the restaurant. A cook in the kitchen. Why they had not heeded the warning sirens, Oliver didn't know. They had paid for that decision with their lives.

They could still hear bombs exploding in other parts of the city. The horizon was so full of smoke it seemed the entirety of London was aflame.

Three hours later the all clear sounded, and Oliver had never been so relieved to hear it. He knew that many damaged but still standing buildings would need to be demolished.

He had taken members of the Heavy Rescue Division to the Andy in the Ramseys' rear garden and shown them the bodies. The unfortunate couple's remains would be removed and their family notified. That constituted normal these days.

The bomb disposal unit had been called in to take care of several unexploded munitions that had landed in buildings and yards.

He and Parker worked steadily until they had done as much as they could. Then they had some coffee and food to eat at a mobile canteen, including some hot soup from a large vat. After the men filled out and delivered their incident reports, they slowly walked back to their homes.

"Oh my Lord!" exclaimed Parker. "Is that another body?"

They rushed forwards and came upon the person. He was battered. And unconscious. And for some reason he looked familiar to Oliver, who felt for a pulse and found it. "Quick, the ambulances are all busy. The clinic's a block over. We can carry him."

Between them he was not heavy, and they made it to the Covent Garden Medical Clinic in short order.

Parker rapped on the door. The sisters came, and the lad was duly transferred onto a stretcher and taken away for examination. Oliver ventured farther inside and noted people in various states of injury lying in the beds lining the walls, with some also on temporary cots and still others simply huddled on the floor. One of the sisters, who had noted his injuries, came over and said, "Do your wounds need cleaning and dressing? We would be glad to do so," she added wearily. Her face was streaked with grime, as was her starched uniform, which was also covered in blood. She looked dead on her feet.

He looked at the mangled bodies writhing in pain and waiting for help.

"No. I think they need you more than I do."

Oliver said goodbye to Parker and trudged back to The Book Keep.

He let himself in, went to the bathroom, undressed, cleaned himself up, and used a pair of tweezers to pick out as many pieces of glass from his limbs as he could. He bandaged what he could and put on fresh clothes.

He checked in on Molly's room and found her back home and sleeping soundly. He knew she would surely need her rest for what faced her tomorrow at the clinic.

Unable to sleep, he made a cup of coffee from days-old grounds. He used a set of interior stairs to climb to the top of the building where The Book Keep was located, carrying with him his trusty pair of binoculars. He took a sweep of the city and was gratified that he didn't see nearly as many flames as he thought he might. But the smoke was ominous, and the gaps where buildings had stood before last night more ominous still.

Will this damn war never be over?

The general theory was that day bombing raids were bad, but those that came at night induced widespread terror. Oliver thought they were both awful.

What was the phrase he had heard once?

Dante had nothing on Hitler.

He stood there as the sun began to leak through the clouds. His arms were so weary, his legs the same, but his mind was the most tired of all. He had never viewed a dead body until 1939. At least not one already in a pine box. Now he had seen more corpses than a person ever should. In all states of death. No, not all. Never in peace. Not once.

His dear Imogen had not died in peace. She had died with much of importance unresolved within her. He knew she would be an impatient, unruly spirit.

He sipped his coffee, whose only redeeming quality was its warmth, and looked out over the city. Transformed, blighted, attacked, wounded, but not beaten. Not if he had anything to say about it. And he did, if just a minor bit.

When the sun began its ascent, he went inside and started breakfast for Molly.

It was nice to have someone to cook for again.

And she would need her beginning meal of the day, meagre though it would be, to get her through the rest of it.

As they all would.

A Fact of Devastation

"His injuries seem different," said Molly as she looked at the patient that Oliver and Parker had brought in the previous night, though she didn't know that fact. Oliver had not told her much about what had happened, and he had tried to cover his wounds. Yet Molly had seen the pain on his face and the way he limped on his injured leg.

And, like Oliver's reaction had been, the patient's face seemed familiar to Molly.

Matron Tweedy was examining the lad closely. "If I had to venture a guess, Molly, I would say this boy has been beaten. The wound on his head looks like it was done by a blunt instrument. And on his face by a fist. I certainly saw these injuries on the front lines. And his finger is broken."

"How did he come to be here?"

"The duty report says that two air wardens brought him in early this morning."

"Air wardens! Do you know who?" asked Molly.

"I wasn't here."

"Do we know who the boy is?"

"Look in his trousers over there," suggested Tweedy.

Molly picked up the trousers and looked for an ID tag on them but didn't find one. However, she froze when she pulled out the registry card from his pocket.

Alonzo Rossi? That was why he looked familiar. He was the boy in the picture Inspector Willoughby had shown me and Mr. Oliver.

Tweedy glanced at her. "Any luck?"

"Um, it says Alonzo Rossi. Will he be okay?"

"He's still unconscious. His head wound had not been treated and was severely infected. It's now been thoroughly cleaned and he's been given penicillin. But the wound was deep—the infection might have already spread and he could have also sustained a brain injury."

"Oh my goodness."

"If there is damage to his brain, I do not hold out hopes of his recovering. We don't have an X-ray device, and the doctors who make rounds here are not brain surgeons. I doubt there are many left in all of London."

Another nurse came to the door and asked for Tweedy's urgent assistance with another patient.

"Just finish up here, Molly, and I'll meet you when I can."

"All right, Matron."

After they left Molly bent low and said, "Lonzo, can you hear me? Lonzo? Do you know where Charlie is? I'm a friend of his. Lonzo? Do you know where Charlie Matters is? We're looking for him."

Lonzo did not answer. Lonzo did not move. Lonzo did nothing.

Molly meticulously cleaned his wounds again, rebandaged them, and arranged his bed covering and pillows. She then stood at the foot of his bed staring at him. One of Charlie's mates. The one who had been with him on that night. But then where was Charlie? Had he been beaten as well? Was he lying somewhere injured or . . . ?

After her workday was over, Molly, with Tweedy's permission, had brought home bandages, antiseptic, and wound ointment. She had told Tweedy that her "father" was an air warden who had sustained injuries during the bombing.

"Then you take good care of him, Molly. We will surely need him in the future."

When Molly arrived at The Book Keep she put her things down, waved to Mrs. Macklin across the way as the woman stared pointedly at her through the glass, and then went in search of Oliver. He was not in his bedroom, but she looked down in horror at the remains of his warden uniform that was lying, bloody and shredded, on the floor next to his bed.

Dearest God, thought Molly. *How did he survive?*

She hurried downstairs and over to Imogen's old study. She knocked on the door. "Mr. Oliver? It's Molly. I have bandages and medicine to treat your wounds. Mr. Oliver!"

There was no answer, and she was now worried that he might be lying in there unconscious from the result of his injuries. She tried the door but it was locked.

Thinking quickly she raced up to Oliver's bedroom and after a quick search found the key she had seen Oliver use before to secure the study door. She rushed back downstairs and unlocked it.

Once she got inside it was readily apparent that Oliver was not here. Molly should have left then and there, but her curiosity got the better of her. She looked in the tin at the stack of typed pages representing the unfinished work of Imogen Oliver's book. Reading several of them, Molly concluded that the dead woman had been quite the extraordinary wordsmith. She put the pages back and continued her search. In one desk drawer she found the George Medal. She reverently ran her fingers over the engraved image of their current king.

As she returned the medal to the drawer Molly noted that there was another photograph of Imogen on the desk. She knew because it was the same woman in the crepe-covered framed photo out front.

Oliver was standing next to her. He looked younger and carefree. He was staring at the woman beside him with the utmost adoration. Molly could only hope that the man she married one day would look upon her with even half that level of admiration and love. Imogen was very pretty, with long, thick, luxuriant hair, but Molly was inexorably drawn to her powerfully intense eyes. Molly was quite intimidated simply by the woman's look from the photo. She imagined it would be altogether something more to experience Imogen Oliver for real.

She noted the letter that lay next to the photo. Molly hesitated, but only for a moment. She unfolded the paper and quickly read it.

It was addressed to Oliver and was from the constabulary in Cornwall. As Molly continued to read she gasped and then hurriedly put the letter back where she had found it. The official communication had detailed the circumstances of Imogen's death.

She had *killed* herself. In *Cornwall.*

Distressed, Molly glanced wildly around the room. She flinched when she saw another George Sand novel on a shelf, this one titled *Jacques*.

She took the book down and slowly opened it.

Her expression filled with despair when she saw that its guts had been cut out, leaving a compartment where something easily could be hidden.

She put the book back, left the room, and locked the door.

The Busybody Beckons

When Molly returned to the front of the shop after putting the study key back in Oliver's bedroom, her mind was awhirl. Why had Imogen taken her own life? Then she thought back to something that Oliver had said—that he felt guilt for her death. If he had acted she might still be alive, he had told Molly. Had Imogen taken her own life because she couldn't live with whatever Oliver was involved in? And was that why Oliver had felt guilty?

She looked up to see that Mrs. Macklin was outside now, sweeping but really watching. She motioned to Molly, who opened the door and came outside.

"Hello," said Mrs. Macklin. "I don't believe we've met, luv. I'm Desdemona Macklin. This is my tea shop."

"Hello. I'm Molly Wakefield."

Macklin set her broom aside and lit a cigarette from a pack pulled from her apron pocket. She sucked in smoke and then exhaled directly at Molly, who irritably waved it away.

"And how do you know our Mr. Oliver?" said Macklin, ignoring Molly's displeasure.

"He's the cousin of my mother," Molly said automatically.

"So they don't live in London then?"

Molly said, "No, in Suffolk. That's why I'm staying with Mr. Oliver."

Macklin eyed her uniform. "Surely, that's a sister's outfit. But you can't be more than fourteen or so."

"I'm older than I look. And I have medical training, you see. I'm a nurse auxiliary at the Covent Garden Medical Clinic. They need all the help they can get."

"Yes, yes, I'm sure they do," said Macklin, shooting her suspicious glances. "And very good of you, too," she added, though her tone was distinctly lacking in sincerity.

"Do you know where Mr. Oliver is?" asked Molly.

"He left the shop around one. Didn't say a word to me. Just a wave and then he was gone. He looked like he was limping."

"The bombing last night. He was injured."

Macklin made a clucking sound that, Molly thought, did not have much actual sympathy behind it. "Poor man. Yes, last night was a corker all right. Thought the ceiling was going to come down on me."

"You didn't go to a shelter?"

"I have a basement here. As good as any shelter, I reckon. And I don't like hiding in the dirt. Doesn't show proper spirit."

"Well, if one is dead it doesn't do much for one's spirit. Now, I must be off."

"I did notice what looked to be a police inspector here the other day talking to Ignatius?"

Molly slowly turned back around. "Yes. Someone tried to break into his shop, but nothing was taken."

"Oh my, those hooligans. Here now, was that tied to what happened with that constable and the lad that got struck by the lorry?"

"I believe so, yes."

"My, my, how terrible."

"Yes, yes it was."

"I also noticed through the glass that you went into the study, Imogen's study, I always called it. Her father, Mr. Bradstreet, once told me it was her favourite place in the whole bloody world."

"Yes, I'm sure. It *is* very nice."

Macklin gave her a cagey look and said, "So did you find what you were looking for in there?"

Molly was disturbed by the woman's obvious probing, but did her best not to show it. "I was looking for Mr. Oliver. So you knew her father and Imogen?" asked Molly. Yet her unspoken thought was, *You know, the woman who thought you an insufferable busybody?*

"Oh yes. The bookshop passed to Imogen after her father died. That was when she and Ignatius came to live there."

"And then she died. How very sad," said Molly, looking enquiringly at the woman. Molly was now doing some delicate probing of her own.

"Yes, yes, it was quite sad. Now, we didn't see eye to eye on much. She was Labour and I'm a Conservative, as was my father and grandfather. She liked to read all the time, but I think books can do odd things to folks. Look at that one Hitler wrote, I forget the name. You think he didn't change some minds with that rubbish?"

"But other books thoroughly refuted all of which he argued," countered Molly.

"I guess it comes down to what you read and what you believe from what you read, eh?"

"Yes, I suppose it does."

"And it seems Germany believes *him*," said Macklin.

"I think some of them may not have a choice in the matter."

"Murderers, all of them!" exclaimed Macklin. "Look at last night. Bloody heathens."

"Um, did you go to Imogen's funeral?"

Macklin placed a malicious stare on Molly. "There was none."

"I'm sorry?"

"There was no funeral because there was no body to bury."

"I don't understand."

"You mean Ignatius never told you?" she said, obviously enjoying this.

"No."

Macklin took a puff of her cigarette. "Well, perhaps he thought you too young. Though you're a *sister* and all," she added disdainfully.

"So what happened?" asked Molly, ignoring the other woman's ugly tone.

"I'm not sure I should tell you if Ignatius thought not to."

Molly realized by Macklin's body language and expression that she was simply dying to convey what she knew. "I can assure you that I am mature enough to be told the circumstances of her passing."

"You sound like you read lots of books, too," said Macklin in a way that was clearly not a compliment.

"I've been known to pick up one or two," Molly replied diplomatically. She had faced individuals like Macklin who, though she ran her own business, thought that a woman should probably never open a book, but only cook, sew, clean, and make babies. "But if you'd rather not tell me, that's fine. I have some things to do." She started to turn back to the bookshop.

Macklin tapped out her smoke on the cobbles and drew closer to Molly, her expression one of ill-concealed delight at what she was about to communicate. "Well, she took a train to the coast, Cornwall, I believe it was."

Molly faced her. "And Mr. Oliver?"

"He *said* he had no idea she was going there. Anyway, she apparently walked all over the place till night fell. Then do you know what Imogen did?"

"What?" said Molly breathlessly.

"She went up on one of them cliffs there and . . . jumped into the sea."

"Oh my God."

Molly's visceral reaction was real. While she had just learned that Imogen had taken her own life in Cornwall, she did not know the exact details because the letter had not mentioned them.

Macklin's eyes danced merrily at Molly's stricken expression. "Oh yes. Now, folks saw her do it, and tried to stop her. That's how we know what happened. The tide was fierce and they never did recover her body. There were ships and mines, and U-boats all over. And, well, she was done for anyway, right? No sense in risking more lives to bring back a dead body. Especially one what done herself in."

Molly let out the breath she had been holding. "How horrible."

"Took her own life, she did. A mortal sin." Macklin made the sign of the cross, kissed her fingertips, and looked to the sky. "Poor thing," she added, with far more relish than sadness, at least to Molly's thinking.

"Mr. Oliver must have been devastated."

"Man didn't leave his shop for weeks, except to do his air warden bit. I did what I could after he told me what happened, brought him some food and such. But the man was clearly in pain. Thought he might go out of his mind, actually. But he finally come round. And I'm sure it's done him good having you here, dear. Men shouldn't be alone. They get all sorts of *wrongheaded* notions, don't they?"

For one awful moment, Molly suspected that Mrs. Macklin knew something about Oliver that might be very damaging. "Yes, I'm sure he does like having me here. He is so very kind and gentle . . . and patriotic. You know, his George Medal and everything."

Macklin just stared at her without comment, which was odd in itself, but perhaps not, if the woman knew something.

"Well, I must be going," said Molly.

"Yes, and I must finish up here. Work, work, it's never done. Now, don't go telling Ignatius what I told you. It'll be our little *secret*. Seems to be lots of *those* floating around these days."

With Macklin's Parthian shot still ringing in her ears, Molly went up to her room and lay on the bed, her mind full of worry.

"Our little secret"? And "lots of those floating around these days"?

Molly felt terrified that she might very well end up losing both Oliver *and* Charlie.

And then I'll truly be all alone.

A Second Reveal

Later, when she heard the door open, Molly rushed downstairs and saw Oliver walking in.

"I was worried about you," she said tersely and with a trace of annoyance.

"Oh, I'm sorry, but I was out looking for Charlie, as I said."

Molly's frown vanished. "Oh, what an idiot I've been. Of course you were, I forgot."

He waved a letter. "I did receive an answer from my friend at the War Office, though."

"You did? What did he say?"

"I thought we could read it together."

Molly looked quite frightened at the prospect.

Noting this, he said, "Are you all right?"

"What?" she said distractedly. "Yes, yes, I'm . . . fine. Um, but before we read the letter you, um, you must let me attend to your injuries. I brought supplies from the clinic."

"But I'm not injured."

"Mr. Oliver, I am a trained nurse auxiliary. Yet even if I weren't it would be only too obvious."

"But the letter?" he said, waving it enticingly.

"Will still be there when I am done."

Molly cleaned, applied ointment to, and bandaged the wounds to Oliver's arms and legs.

"I feel quite embarrassed having you do this, Molly," he said.

"I do it for strangers every day."

She then tested his calf and ankle, probing and fingering certain spots and eliciting grunts of pain and tensed features from the man.

She pulled out a splint and tape from her bag. "You have a mild sprain. This will help keep the joint immobile while it heals. But you should keep off it for a few days."

"Molly, that is quite impossible. After the last bombing all air wardens have been ordered to work every night until further notice."

"Well, do the best you can, then."

"I have a stick I can use. And now, you have waited long enough." He pulled out the letter and unfolded it.

She looked resignedly at the missive as she slowly put her medical supplies away.

He caught her expression and said, "Do you not want to hear what they have to say?"

"Of course I do."

"But?" said Oliver.

"But up until this moment I had hopes that my father would come back. Yet I suppose it's better to know than to remain ignorant."

"Now that I think of it, I believe you should read this alone."

"No, I will need your advice for additional steps. So let's read it together."

They sat side by side and went through the letter. Molly was a bit faster than Oliver and tears welled up in her eyes as she got to the end. As Oliver finished, he glanced at her in surprise.

He said, "I'm sure there must be a misunderstanding."

"I don't see how there can be, seeing as how the War Office says that my father is a criminal who is now in hiding from the authorities."

Hermes

"Eh, how old are you again, boy?" asked the snowy-haired man with the sharp white collar, the stiff black jacket, and the name Arthur Benedict.

The not-yet-fourteen-year-old Charlie looked up at him and said with authority, "Sixteen."

Charlie was in a postal office because he had seen that they were hiring telegram messengers.

"You're a bit small for sixteen."

"Haven't hit my growth bit yet, guv."

"If you're sixteen why haven't you sat your Civil Service exam then?"

"Who said I ain't?"

"Well then?"

"With the war, not many jobs even with that. I need to earn money."

Benedict's expression softened. "What's your name?"

"Ignatius Oliver."

"That's quite a name."

"Named after a saint. Bunch of wild beasts ate him."

"Yes, yes, I've heard about *him* from my vicar. Well, it's true we need the help. Lost four lads to the army just last month and another to one of them unexploded bombs that decided to go off when the poor fellow was riding by. Do you have your own bicycle?"

"Do I need one?"

"No. We have a couple you can use. But it's just you get paid for mileage if you have your own. Otherwise, you get a weekly wage."

"How much?"

"Sixteen shillings and four pence," said Benedict.

"And if I got me my own bike?"

"Four pennies a mile on top."

"I got me my own bike," said Charlie promptly.

"Good lad. Now, it does help if you know the lay of the land hereabouts. Our customers expect swiftness. You ever heard the ancient tale of Hermes?"

"Was he a saint that got et, too?"

"Oh, never mind, boy."

Benedict asked Charlie questions about various locations and the fastest way to them. Charlie answered all of them quickly and correctly and clearly impressed Benedict with the cleverness of several of his shortcuts.

"You've clearly been out and about," noted Benedict. "Almost like you've learned 'the knowledge' that the cabbies have to. And that takes several years."

Charlie looked around the postal office. Most homes in Britain did not have phones. And with the war and the bombings, even those that had phones found they did not always work. Thus, telegrams had become quite popular once more, particularly in London.

"So, do I get the job?"

Benedict peered at him from behind black square glasses that magnified his pupils into fearsome things. "When can you start?"

Charlie had seen a bike lying abandoned in a pile of rubble around the corner. "I just got to . . . run an errand. Be back in a jiff. I can start after that."

"All right. We'll get your uniform and you can work with one of my other boys today, so he can show you the way we do things. Then tomorrow you're on your own. Hey now, are your parents okay with this?"

"My dad died at Dunkirk. My mum needs all the help she can get. There's five mouths to feed."

"Good lord, lad. Your poor mum. Well, go run your errand and I'll get things organized."

Charlie was back in less than two minutes with "his" bike. He had to use a postal pump to put air in the tyres, and he and Benedict had to straighten the handlebars, but it was otherwise fine.

"Now, your equipment and your uniform get inspected daily. I'll give you a pass today on the bike, but clean and shine it up good like. Same for your shoes, belt buckle, and everything else. We have a public image to keep up," he added proudly.

"Yes, guv."

"Good lad."

Charlie's uniform consisted of a navy blue suit with red piping on the jacket cuffs, down the pant seams, and around the collar and edging. The pillbox hat had similar piping and a red button in the crown's centre.

Benedict said, "Now, we provide boots and a coat for winter and proper shoes for summer, along with a cape and leggings for the rain, which this country has more than its share of, so help me God. We'll find the ones to fit you proper. Now, as to your schedule. Starting tomorrow I'm putting you on the eight a.m. to eight p.m. route. But for today you'll get off at five, let you get your legs under you, so to speak. But you be here sharp in the morning, boy."

"Right."

"Now, when you deliver the telegram you wait for them to read it in case there's a reply, which you *always* ask if there is." He added in a warning tone, "Mind you, there's no pushing it through the slot and scarpering off. No muckin' about like that. We're professionals."

"How does that work then, this reply thin'?"

"I'll tell you. In this leather pouch, which you will carry on your belt, are spare telegram forms, envelopes, and business cards. If no one is home, you leave your card to show an attempt was made and what time you will try to deliver the message once more, which you will scribble on the back of the card with this pencil. If they are there and wish to reply, they fill out one of these forms you will present them."

"Okay, I got that bit. But how do they pay for it, guv?"

"They pay *you*. In the rule book here, which you will also carry, the charges are set out. Basically, a nine-word telegram—which includes the address, mind you—is six pennies, and a penny for each additional word. Greeting telegrams come in pale blue envelopes, like this one here, and are six pennies extra. Priority telegrams are delivered first and also cost an extra six pennies. Now, are you good at maths, Ignatius?"

"Real good, least when it comes to countin' money."

"Excellent, because you have to get it exactly right or else it comes out of your wages. And a reconciliation of your takings is done at the end of each day. Now, under penalty of law you are not allowed to accept gratuities of any sort." Benedict stared pointedly at Charlie, then made a show of looking over his shoulder before turning back and adding, "Now, I have no earthly idea how they manage to enforce that particular rule, but I am bound to tell you, son." Then he winked.

Charlie nodded with a knowing look. "Right, guv."

That first day Charlie worked with a young man named Peter Duckett. They both delivered telegrams issued by the office, but Duckett also told Charlie that they could solicit business on the streets by approaching folks about sending messages on the official forms they carried and collecting the money owed. Customers would use the boys' backs as desks to write down their messages and pay at the same time, Duckett told him.

"But if we get paid the same wage each week, why try and drum up more business?" asked Charlie. "What good's it?"

"They give out bonuses the more telegrams we get," explained

Duckett, a thin, reedy-necked fellow of eighteen. "And mileage on our bikes, too. More messages is more miles, see?"

"Right," said Charlie. "Four pennies a mile."

"And folks tip, too. So the more customers the more tips. Guess old Benedict told you we ain't supposed to take *gratuities*."

"He did," confirmed Charlie. "But I don't think he means it."

"You're right, he don't."

Duckett told Charlie he had failed to qualify for the army because of something odd in his chest. "Didn't do so well on my Civil either, but this ain't a bad job."

"Is the Civil hard?"

"Well, it ain't easy, mate, I can tell you that. You got to label all these counties and rivers and whatsis on a map 'a England. Then you got to list down what the government does to get folks to buy War Savings. Then you got to know alls 'bout a gent name of Ma-cow-ber. And then they ask you questions about this quite odd woman from She-lott who keeps lookin' in a bleedin' mirror."

"I don't know none 'a that," said a befuddled Charlie.

"Me neither, mate, why I'm ridin' this here bloody bike." He paused and his expression turned sombre. "People look at you funny, though," he said. "For not bein' in the fightin', I mean. Think I'm a damn coward. But it's not like I can show 'em pictures of my chest. I didn't ask to have no funny heart." He glanced at Charlie with an anxious look. "Least I'm in some sort of uniform. Right, mate?"

"Right," said Charlie.

"Eh, how old are you anyways?" asked Duckett as they rode back to the postal office for fresh messages to deliver.

"Old enough for this job," replied Charlie.

Once Seen

The next day Charlie worked alone, whizzing all over London to deliver messages. His wages obviously weren't due yet, so he got a cup of milk and fried Spam and some chips from a WVS canteen as his only meal of the day.

Outside the postal office he had taken considerable time to thoroughly clean his bike with a rag and some water and a bit of noxious cleaner Benedict had given him. After he was off duty he rode to Covent Garden and made it to the alleyway. He parked his bike and ducked down by the large window. The shop was dimly lit as he watched through a crack in the blackout curtains.

He was startled when he saw Molly in what looked to be a nurse's outfit. And then there was a stiff-legged Oliver slowly moving across the floor to pluck a book off the shelf before turning to Molly and saying something.

Part of him wanted to rap on the door and announce to them both that he was fine and now had a paying job. But they surely would have been told to report any contact they had with Charlie to the police. And if they didn't they could be arrested.

He turned to leave and froze. The woman across the way was at her door and staring at him. He could tell by her expression that she recognized him from their earlier meeting. He dashed away on his bike.

Later, Charlie carried his bike up the steps of his digs and collapsed onto his bedding. He didn't feel entirely safe here. If Lonzo had told the police about this place they might come searching. But wouldn't they have come before now? And granted these lodgings weren't much, but it was better than anything else he had, and if he didn't have to leave them . . . ?

The warning sirens had jarred Charlie from a deep sleep that night and had driven him to a nearby tube station. The smells and the heat of so many comingled bodies had made him nauseous, particularly on a mostly empty stomach.

A woman had noticed Charlie's thin features and offered him a bit of bread and cheese. He had gratefully accepted, and when he wolfed it down, another lady offered him some of her provisions.

When the all clear sounded, Charlie had trekked back to his place around four in the morning. A few hours later he rode to the postal office to begin work.

Benedict looked kindly upon the clearly tired and overly thin Charlie and said, "I'm offering new lads partial wages, Ignatius, if you're interested. Just a bit of pocket change."

"I'm 'nterested," replied Charlie immediately.

He put the shillings safely away and headed out.

For weeks on end Charlie rode through the streets with abandon. He was also becoming quite good at talking folks into availing themselves of his services, especially businessmen.

"Just a bit of coin for gettin' your 'portant messages where they need to be," he would spiel. "Why, just 'magine how good it'll make people feel to hear from you."

That line worked more often than not. He had taken to riding by the Ritz and the Dorchester hotels, and other such places where the well-heeled folks could afford to stay. He made pounds instead of pence there.

And Arthur Benedict was very pleased. "You have a knack for

this line of work, you mark my words, son." He quietly placed an extra crown in Charlie's weekly pay. "You could teach the older boys a thing or two, you could."

When Charlie got back to his digs that night and changed out of his uniform, he knew immediately that something was off. His things had been gone through, and some of his possessions appeared to be missing.

Charlie had all his money on him, so that was all right. And he had hidden the journal under a loose section of wainscotting that looked solid enough. He plucked it out and gathered up what he could and left, thinking of where he might go.

He had just reached the street with his bike when someone cried out, "You, boy, you stay right where you are."

The man yelling at him was the same stout man he'd seen at The Book Keep talking to Molly and Mr. Oliver—the copper.

Charlie did not stay right where he was. He rode swiftly away, while the slow-footed Inspector Willoughby and Constable Higgins ran futilely after him.

It took Charlie ten seconds to disappear into the streets of a city he knew better than most.

Willoughby and Higgins finally stopped running and bent over, sucking in one deep breath after another.

The DI looked in the direction of where Charlie had vanished and muttered, "I will catch you if it's the last thing I ever do, boy."

Frankness on Display

Molly, with Oliver's permission, had used Imogen's typewriter and The Book Keep stationery to compose her letter to Dr. Thaddeus Stephens of the Beneficial Institute. She had got Oliver's comments on several handwritten drafts until she believed she had struck upon the right tone. She had duly posted it early one morning, and had walked back to the shop to prepare for work.

She had previously told Oliver about Lonzo Rossi's having come to the clinic.

He had said, "My God, I helped bring him there that night. I thought I recognized him but I couldn't remember from where."

"Sister says it looks like he was *beaten*."

"Yes. The thing is, the inspector told me that they had arrested Lonzo."

"Do you think he might have escaped?"

"I don't see how he could have possibly managed that," replied Oliver.

"But then how did he sustain—" She paused and then exclaimed, "But surely the police wouldn't have . . . would they?"

Oliver had looked at her uncomfortably. "Before the war, Molly, there were certain things I would not have believed. But after what I've seen, I'm afraid that is no longer the case."

Molly had thought back to what had happened to her mother at that shelter. "I guess I feel the same way." She added, suddenly horrified, "You don't mean that . . . that Charlie . . ."

"I don't know, Molly. I just don't know."

Molly came out of these depressing musings and looked out the window for a moment. "Your friend at the War Office?"

"Major Bryant, yes?"

"He must be wrong about my father. He can't be a criminal."

"I would think as you do, Molly, but I also know Bryant. He is not known for making unsubstantiated allegations like that."

"But what crime is he accused of committing?"

"I have no idea."

She said doubtfully, "I know he worked in money matters in the city before the war and travelled quite a bit."

"Perhaps some missing funds, then?"

"I suppose it is possible. I mean, he *has* disappeared." Molly looked utterly crushed.

"But if that is the case, I wonder why the War Office is involved."

"Did you write your friend back?" she asked.

"I would not, without your permission."

"I simply can't leave it as it is," said Molly.

"Then I will make further enquiries."

"Thank you." She nervously twisted her fingers. "Do you think that would explain why those men were watching my house?"

"It certainly could, Molly."

The following weeks went by rather quickly, and thankfully there were no more bombing raids. Each evening, Oliver told Molly of his efforts to locate Charlie.

"I've been everywhere I thought he might be," he said. "So far, I've had no luck. But I will keep trying."

"What if he *was* arrested?"

"I think we would have heard, I really do," he said.

Each week Molly had duly given him, despite his protests, her entire salary. "It's not much, I know, but it's something."

"It's more than something, Molly, it's quite substantial, in fact, and I will pay you back when I am able."

"Please, without you I would have no home."

"And I did write Major Bryant for further particulars. I will let you know as soon as I receive a response."

As Molly sat and ate the dinner Oliver had prepared, and watched him bustle around the tiny kitchen, she was thinking about how Imogen had died.

She decided to broach the subject with him. "I happened to meet Mrs. Macklin."

"Did you now?" said Oliver in surprise as he sat down across from her with a cup of tea.

"She was outside several weeks ago and called to me one evening. She . . . mentioned she knew your wife. I mean, I already knew that because you had told me."

"She also knew Imogen's father, who owned this bookshop before her."

"Yes, she mentioned that as well. Mrs. Macklin also talked to me about . . . Cornwall."

Oliver set his cup down. "Cornwall? Indeed. Wait, do you mean . . . ?"

Molly's face paled. "Yes, she told me what happened. I didn't ask about it, I promise."

He looked down. "As I told you, Imogen and I spent our honeymoon in Devon. It was such a happy time for us. Thus, it did puzzle me that she would choose nearby Cornwall to do what she did."

"And you had no idea she had gone there?"

He shook his head. "Imogen said she was travelling by rail

to Bristol to visit an old school friend. When the police came round . . . Well, it was quite impossible to believe what they were saying. I made myself think they had got it all wrong somehow. But when I rang the friend in Bristol, and found that she knew nothing of a visit from Imogen, and then the fact that Imogen never came back? Well, it became rather self-evident, didn't it?"

"Perhaps it was an accident? She might have—"

"No, no, I was told that the witnesses were quite clear in their statements. She . . . jumped."

"Did you . . . did you never go there and see things for yourself?"

"I thought I would have done. I planned to go, in fact. I never got the exact location from the police down there but . . . I . . ." He halted.

"I know this is so very difficult," interjected Molly, her features full of compassion.

"I finally decided not to make further enquiries because what would have been the point? I could not bring her back. They could tell me nothing other than that they saw her jump, which I already knew to be the case. And . . . and I simply could not bring myself to go to the place where she . . . died." He looked up at her. "Do you think that wrong of me?"

"I can't judge you, Mr. Oliver, having never been faced with something like that." She played with her napkin as she seemed to be mustering courage. "Did you ever think why she might have done what she did?"

"Yes, I have given it a great deal of thought."

"You said that had you acted she might still be alive. But you never explained that."

As she said this Oliver's eyes closed and tears seeped from under the lids.

Molly looked alarmed. "I'm so sorry. I never should have brought it up. I just didn't want Mrs. Macklin to mention to you what she told me. I thought it better for you to hear it from me."

He lifted his specs, wiped his eyes with his napkin, and said, "I do appreciate your telling me, Molly. As to why Imogen would have done that, all I can say is that she was a *complicated* person. A loving, caring, quite dear woman, but . . . complicated, nonetheless. And when the truth came fully round, I think she couldn't accept . . . things."

"The truth? And what things?" she asked. Molly's mind was returning to the cut-out book and the mysterious visitor and the strange machine Charlie had found along with the paper in German. She couldn't believe that Oliver was involved in anything criminal or suspicious. But she also couldn't understand what *was* going on. Had Imogen killed herself because she thought her husband was . . . a traitor? Her stomach uncomfortably clenched.

When he looked at her, there was something there she couldn't quite identify at first. Then she hit upon it.

Fear.

He got up and walked out without answering her, which did absolutely nothing to curb Molly's growing anxiety.

The following morning Molly readied herself for work as Oliver prepared her breakfast. He had insisted, despite the canteen at the clinic, on making her breakfast and dinner each day.

Molly's mind could not stray far from their very candid conversation from the previous night. Imogen Oliver had killed herself because the truth had fully come around and she couldn't accept "things." And Oliver felt guilty. And he might have been the reason she had jumped off that cliff in Cornwall. It was all so bewildering.

She ate her breakfast, put on her nursing cape and hat, and left the shop.

Mrs. Macklin was outside sweeping the cobbles. Molly sensed she had been waiting for her to leave for work.

"Off to nurse the sick and injured, are we?" Macklin said with a hint of sarcasm.

"Yes, I am."

"Least no more bombings for a bit."

"Yes, thank goodness."

"How is Ignatius?"

"He's fine, quite nearly healed."

She was about to say goodbye and walk on, when Macklin said, "Just so's you know, I saw that lad around here again."

Molly froze and turned back around. "What lad?"

"The lad that was here with you. Seen him in the shop with you and Ignatius. I talked to him before. He said he wanted a job with Ignatius, but I don't think he was telling the truth."

"When did you see him?"

"Oh, a while back. Weeks it was. Do you know him?"

"I . . . I don't know if we're talking about the same person."

"See, the thing is this Inspector Willoughby, I believe was his name, came by to see me, probably the same time he talked to Ignatius. There was a lad and a bobby killed down that way, you know, like we was talking about before. That inspector was keen to find one of the lads. Said his name was Charlie . . . Matters, yes, that's right. Could have sworn he was the same one in there with you and Ignatius. Fit the description and all."

"I'm sure a lot of boys look alike, Mrs. Macklin."

"What's your lad's name then?"

"Tommy, Tommy Barnwell," said Molly immediately. It was the first name that came into her head. It was actually the name of a boy she had met in the country, the son of a farmer, with a thick shock of red hair.

"So where is he now?"

"He left us and we haven't seen him since. So it's quite surprising that you saw him outside the shop. I wonder why he didn't let us know he was here."

"Yes, yes, that is quite puzzling," said Macklin slowly. She clearly did not believe a word of what Molly was saying. "And where is he from?" she asked.

"Um, somewhere around here, I believe," Molly said cautiously.

"Really? The boy told me he was from the East End."

"Oh, yes, that's right. I got mixed up."

Macklin gave her another incredulous look. "Thing is, this last time I saw him, the boy had on one of them messenger uniforms."

"I'm sorry, *messenger* uniforms?"

"You know, the telegram lads? Riding their bicycles around in their smart uniforms and pillbox hats, with the pasteboard flapping around their necks saying, 'Why don't you send a telegram to your cousin in Brighton for a shilling and make him smile.' I know who'd be smiling, all right. It'd be the one with all them shillings." She looked wistful. "I haven't sent a telegram in years. Have nobody to send one to. But they do a nice business with the war and all, so I've heard."

"Oh, well, are you sure it was Tommy?"

"I just know it was the same lad what was there before. I can't tell you his name." She looked sharply at Molly as she said this.

"Yes, well, thank you, Mrs. Macklin. I hope you have a good day."

"It *will* be a good day, if the damn Germans don't show up and ruin it."

The War Office Roars

It was Saturday, and Molly had the day off, though she was due to work on Sunday. She had planned to get up early and make breakfast for Oliver, but he had beaten her to the pan and kettle. She had earlier told him about Charlie's peering in the window, and about Macklin seeing him wearing a messenger's uniform.

"That certainly narrows things down for my search," Oliver had said. "I just wish he had talked to us."

"He's probably afraid he'll get us in trouble."

"No doubt."

Now he was standing by the cooker wielding a skillet.

"A real fried egg, and bacon and ham sound good?" he said. "And a pint of cold milk. Not condensed or powered, mind you. The liquid that comes from actual cows."

Molly looked astonished. "Bacon *and* ham? And a pint of real milk? *And* a real egg? For one meal?" Ever since she had come to live here, Molly's expectations for food had been radically altered.

"New rations for the week and a bit of a flutter. I mean, why not?"

"Sounds lovely. If you think it's not too much."

"I wish I could provide you with a lot more food, Molly, particularly with the important work you do. The troops get hot, fresh food in cookhouses when in camp. On the front lines that's not possible. They have to rely on preserved food in Bully Beef tins and the like. Well, I consider you to be part of the war effort, and you must be fed properly."

"And you too, with your air raid duties."

He smiled. "Well, I might have a bit of the bacon and ham then, too."

They sat and ate. Molly swallowed a mouthful of eggs and looked at him keenly. "You know, you, Charlie, and I, we've all lost people we loved."

"Your nanny's death was truly tragic, but your father may turn up. And your mother is in Cornwall."

"I seriously doubt my father will ever return home, Mr. Oliver, if the charges against him are true. And he might not even be alive." This was a statement that Molly could not have even contemplated uttering a short while ago. But with everything that had happened, it just seemed the practical thing to do was confront the real possibilities life threw at you.

"He might not," agreed Oliver.

"As to my mother, I've done some research into the medical terms that were in the letters from the Beneficial Institute using books that are at the clinic. It is extremely unlikely that she will ever fully recover."

"I am very sorry to hear that."

"But if I hadn't happened upon Charlie, and we both hadn't found you, I'm not sure what would have become of us."

"I can say the same, Molly. My life was terribly lonely. For around a year now it has just been me. And . . . and memories of Imogen. I can see now that that is not the healthiest manner of living. And it was you and Charlie who helped me to see it. That I had more to give, additional friendships to form. I mean, if life doesn't contain that, what is the point of existing, really?"

"Please don't say that that was something Imogen told you."

He smiled in a self-satisfied way. "No, that bit was actually all mine."

The tinkle of the bell interrupted their pleasant breakfast a few minutes later.

Oliver looked at his watch. "I wonder who it could be at this hour on a Saturday?"

They passed through the curtain and stopped abruptly.

Through the window they could see a man in military uniform standing outside the door.

"H-has someone . . . died?" said Molly with dread in her voice.

"It's my friend from the War Office, Major Scott Bryant. The one I wrote the letter to about your father."

He let Bryant in.

The major was tall, broad shouldered, and inflexibly constructed with a trim moustache and a proper gloved grip, which he extended to both Oliver and Molly. He carried an attaché case and held his official cap under the same arm.

Oliver said, "What can I do for you, Major?"

"I'd like a word with Miss Wakefield here."

Oliver looked startled. "How did you know that she was here? I didn't put that in my letter, merely that I was enquiring on her behalf."

"Please, Ignatius, it's my business to know such things."

"Have you found my father?" Molly exclaimed. "I know in the letter you said he had committed some crimes, but that can't possibly be right."

"Shall we go into the study?" said Oliver quietly.

"Fact is, Ignatius, I would prefer to speak with the girl *alone*."

Oliver glanced at Molly. "Are you all right with that?"

She nodded.

Oliver unlocked the study and ushered them in, then closed the door.

Bryant glanced around and took the seat behind the desk. "Sit down," he said curtly.

She did so and waited expectantly as Bryant opened his attaché case and took out a file.

"When was the last time you saw your father?" he asked in a brisk tone.

"When he put me on the train to go to the country in 1939," she answered promptly.

"And did you go alone?"

"Yes. My mother was . . . not up to it and my father was working."

"Did he write to you?"

"Very occasionally."

"Do you have those letters?" Bryant asked.

"I brought them back with me, but then our house was bombed. They were all burned."

"Pity that."

"The house, or the letters?" Molly replied icily. She had taken a dislike to the man and his blunt manner.

"Both, of course."

"Why do you ask about the letters?"

"It might have been something for us to go on," he said.

"They were just the usual things that a father writes to his daughter."

"Right," he said with a suspicious glance aimed at her.

"Did you also open my nanny's letter? She told me that—"

"Standard operating procedure," interjected Bryant. He opened the file and looked through it with a nonchalance that was severely grating on Molly. "We've been following you, did you know that?"

"Yes, or at least I suspected. But then Mr. Oliver confirmed it."

"Oh, he did, did he?"

Molly was suddenly fearful that she had got Oliver into trouble, but Bryant pushed on.

"We also talked to the Coopers in the village where you lived outside of Leiston."

"Why?"

"To see if your father had visited you there."

"I could have told you that he hadn't," replied Molly.

"But he might have told you *not* to tell us."

"I would not lie on behalf of anyone, even my father."

Molly knew she had done so on Charlie's behalf with Mrs. Macklin and Inspector Willoughby, but, to her mind, that didn't count.

He scrutinized her. "Well, that's quite nice to hear, but we can't take chances."

"Why do you think he committed a crime?"

Bryant glanced at the file. "Your mother is at the Beneficial Institute in Cornwall." It wasn't a question.

"I haven't been, but I was told she was there."

"Told by whom?"

"My nanny, Mrs. Pride. She was killed in the bombing that destroyed my home. But I have read the letters the doctor there sent my father."

"Were those letters lost in the bombing as well?"

"Yes," replied Molly.

"Do you remember the contents? Anything at all?"

"I . . . I remember they said she had social phobias and neurosis. They are mental diseases, I've come to understand."

"You may as well know that we have been to the Institute."

"What? Why?"

"To see if your father had visited there after he disappeared."

"And had he?"

"I can't get into that."

"Did . . . did you see my mother?"

He glanced up at her now, his features less stern and more sympathetic. "Yes, Miss Wakefield, very briefly. She was, sadly, not capable of answering our questions."

"I . . . I see." Molly looked down, her spirits sinking through the floorboards.

"I understand that you are a nurse auxiliary. Bit young for that, aren't you?"

"War makes us all grow older, faster," was Molly's taut reply.

Bryant smiled. "In his letter Ignatius said that you were mature beyond your years."

"So I can understand complicated matters, such as my father's situation."

Bryant's smile faded as he put his elbows on the desk and leaned forwards. "I'm afraid there is not a lot I can tell you."

"But that implies there is *something* you can tell me."

"Has your father contacted you in any way since you've been back?"

"No, I've heard nothing from him."

Bryant sat back. "Your father worked for us, for many years. Even before the war. And did an excellent job, as a matter of fact. Quite brave and resourceful."

"He *worked* for you?

"For Britain, rather."

"I know that he travelled a good deal outside of the country when I was young."

"Yes, he was on assignment. His cover, at first, was business, you know, international transactions, money, that sort of thing. Then he was *placed* in a position at the Ministry of Food to continue his work for us. That was a cover, of course. He never really worked there. But then, he stopped working for his country."

"I don't understand."

Bryant drew a long breath. "I do not mean to unduly distress you, Miss Wakefield, but, to put it bluntly, your father murdered three British soldiers in cold blood."

Molly simply stared at him for an uncomfortably long moment before she burst into tears, raced from the room, brushed past a startled Oliver, and fled behind the curtain.

Secrets

A FEW MOMENTS LATER Oliver poked his head into the study. Bryant was still seated behind the desk, looking disturbed.

"I could see that did not go well," observed Oliver worriedly.

"You could say that, yes, and a sight more."

Oliver closed the door and sat down across from the major. "What crime did he commit?"

Bryant told him.

Oliver said, "Cripes, and here I thought it was something to do with money." He glanced at Bryant. "But British soldiers? That explains why you're interested. What proof do you have? And why would he do that?"

"As to the proof, we have a letter from the man admitting his guilt."

"What!"

"Yes, quite remarkable."

"Did he say what his motive was?" asked Oliver.

"Only that if we could not administer justice, he would."

"Any idea what he meant by that?"

"Not the foggiest. Ignatius, can one get a cup of tea in this *book-shop*?"

"You know it's strictly against government regulations to have tea in the morning. But I can provide you with a simply disgusting cup of what the government deems to be coffee."

Bryant glared at him.

"Molly was left quite badly off," noted Oliver in a serious tone. "She's making do as best she can, but it's not been easy."

Bryant nodded. "Murderous father on the lam, mother in the looney bin, house now a pile of rubble, yes, quite badly off, I'd say. Look, I'll have the Ministry of Health take the girl off your hands. I should have brought them with me, in fact."

Oliver leaned forwards, his expression tense but focused. "I would consider it a great personal favour if you would do nothing of the kind, Scott. I really would."

The man eyed him in surprise. "What's all this?"

"She is vulnerable and hurt and confused. And she is also helping the war effort through her superb nursing skills. I think we should allow Molly to continue to do just as she is, and she can remain here while she does so."

"But she's not even sixteen."

"She's far more mature than many an adult of my acquaintance."

Bryant watched him keenly. "Is she the daughter you never had, Ignatius? Is that what this is about?"

"It is about letting someone do her duty for her country whilst she is trying to cope with untold personal tragedy. I would argue that she could do that far better here than in an orphanage."

"You and your brother were placed in an orphanage for a while, if I remember correctly."

"Yes."

"And he's a highly competent surgeon, and you turned out all right."

"We turned out all right in *spite* of our circumstances, not because of them." He glanced hopefully at the major. "So, can you just let this rest? Please?"

After a few moments mulling over this, Bryant said, "As a favour to an old friend, yes, I can." He gazed around the study. "You ever think about the old days at university?"

"Not too often, no. I have other things to occupy my time," replied Oliver. "You know, the *war*?"

Bryant smiled briefly at the remark. "It was quite lucky for us that the Germans didn't stick to only bombing the East End. We might have had social chaos otherwise, poor versus rich, that sort of thing. But they bombed everywhere."

"Which of course drew us more together," said Oliver. "Something I have witnessed firsthand in my official duties."

"And how is the air raid warden bit coming along?"

"The recent lull has been nice."

"Unfortunately, there are darker days ahead."

"Oh, really?" said Oliver dully.

"You know of course of the Germans' V-1 rockets? They started chucking them at us this summer. First one hit on the Kent coast, but London has been targeted as well."

"The doodlebugs? Yes, I've actually witnessed one or two of the bloody things whizzing across the sky."

"Made from sheet metal and plywood. They can fly four hundred miles per hour and carry a bomb payload of nearly a ton. Killed over six thousand people in southern England. They can't reach the north, limited range. But we learned that by banking a plane sharply while flying close to the V-1, we can alter the flight path and drive the damn things into the ground."

Oliver watched his friend's tense features closely. "I take it the Germans have come up with something else of concern?"

Bryant sat forwards, lowering his voice. "Have you heard any whisperings of the V-2 programme?"

"No, can't say that I have."

"Good, no need to inspire fear amongst the public."

"Well, please feel free to inspire it in me," said Oliver brightly.

"It's a new type of bomb the Germans are readying to hurl against us."

"I would have thought they had far too many of those already."

"Like the V-1s, the bombs aren't dropped from a plane. They have their own propulsion and advanced guidance systems, internal gyros, and external rudders and the like. They're thirteen-ton missiles, really, and the damn things can fly thousands of miles an hour, with a payload of a thousand kilograms. They'll be launched from the Dutch coast. They'll strike here, of course, and perhaps Birmingham and Coventry as well, if they have the range."

"And just when I thought things were going so splendidly. So when will they be coming?"

Bryant looked nervous. "I shouldn't tell you this, but . . ."

Oliver looked expectant.

"They've already launched them against us. But we . . . meaning the government, have deemed them to be gas main explosions. Don't want to panic the public and all, you see."

Oliver did not look pleased by this. "Yes, I do *see*."

"The only saving grace is you'll never hear the damn things coming, and you'll be dead before you know it."

"How reassuring."

Bryant keenly studied his old friend. "You ever regret not going to work at Bletchley, Ignatius? They wanted you badly, you know. Your head for numbers and puzzles and all that. And your paper on cryptography outlining the possibilities of separate divisions of labour, mirrored with a shared purpose and folks from many different backgrounds and intellectual capabilities, is one of the reasons why they initiated a scheme like Bletchley in the first place. 'Poets and physicists,' I think you called it."

"Careful, Major, you don't want to run afoul of the Official Secrets Act."

"Since it was on my strong recommendation, I know they had you down to work there," Bryant replied. "And you could have helped the war effort far more effectively than being an air raid warden."

"Well, I had Imogen to consider."

"Poor Imogen," noted Bryant, no longer looking at him.

"Yes, poor Imogen," repeated Oliver, staring at the blank page curled in the Crown typewriter.

Angels of Death

Charlie rode his bike across the bridge to Clapham, passing the famous green along the way. He was excited, because there would be nearly eight miles to be paid for this one delivery.

He turned down a narrow street and, counting numbers, he pulled to a stop in front of a small brick house with dark shutters set behind a wrought iron fence that looked very much like its neighbours on either side.

He climbed off his bike, passed through the gate, and hurried up to the front door. He had many more messages yet to dispense, and the day was getting on.

He rapped on the door and waited. Presently, he heard the click of heels and the door opened, revealing a woman in her early twenties with soft brown hair and large, luminous eyes. She wore a calf-length, hunter-green dress.

"Yes?" she said.

"Telegram, ma'am," said Charlie. "Are you Eleanor Drews?"

"Yes, I am."

Charlie handed her the envelope.

She tore it open, glancing anxiously over his shoulder, and started to read.

"Will there be a reply, ma'am?" asked Charlie.

Drews screamed and threw the message at Charlie; then she started to slap and punch him. His pillbox hat came off with the flurry of blows and he fell back, lost his balance, and nearly toppled off the porch.

She struck him on the cheek, knocking him down, and Charlie could feel his skin start to swell. Drews staggered back and stared down horrified at the bruised and battered Charlie. Her eyes fluttered, then she let out a low moan and fainted in her doorway.

Charlie, breathing hard, rose and looked down at her, unable to process what had just taken place.

"Ma'am?" He knelt down and nudged her arm. "Ma'am. Are you okay?" He looked inside the open doorway. "Hullo, is anybody in there? Hullo, we need some help here. Help!"

He could hear the sounds of footsteps rushing towards him and an older woman came into view inside Drews's home.

"Ellie!" she exclaimed.

She ran forwards, knelt down, and gripped the other woman's hand. She looked sternly at Charlie. "What happened? What did you do to her, boy?"

A frightened Charlie backed up and said, "I ain't done nothin'. I just give her a telegram and she started hittin' me."

She focused on his messenger uniform and gasped. She looked around and saw the paper where Drews had dropped it. She snatched it up, read off the few lines, and dropped it again, her face pale and her limbs trembling.

"Josh?" She called back into the house. "Josh! Come quickly."

A man about her age came hurrying to the doorway, a pipe in hand. "What is—Oh my God. Ellie."

He rushed to the woman's aid. "What's happened?"

"Message came," said the older woman, indicating Charlie. "I'm afraid it's Bill. The worst."

"Oh dear Lord."

Drews was coming around by this point, and they helped her up and led her back inside, leaving the door open behind them. They apparently had forgotten that Charlie was even there.

He stooped, retrieved his pillbox hat, and picked up the crumpled message.

> FROM AIR MINISTRY 77 OXFORD ST W 1 PC 687
> DEEPLY REGRET TO INFORM YOU THAT
> ACCORDING TO INFORMATION RECEIVED THROUGH
> INTERNATIONAL RED CROSS CHANNELS YOUR
> HUSBAND F/SGT WILLIAM EVERETT DREWS LOST
> HIS LIFE AS THE RESULT OF AIR OPERATIONS
> ON NIGHT OF 30/10/44 STOP AIR COUNCIL
> EXPRESS SINCERE SYMPATHY STOP LETTER TO
> FOLLOW SHORTLY STOP...

Charlie slowly folded up the telegram, closed the front door, and carefully pushed the paper through the slot. He got back on his bike and rode across the bridge and back into the city.

While other messengers had warned him of it, that was the first "death" telegram he had ever delivered. He wondered if his mother had received such a message when his father had died.

Deeply regret to inform you that Private Robert Charles Matters lost his life as the result of . . . STOP

His mother had never spoken of receiving such a telegram, but she must have, Charlie thought. Yet she had obviously spared him from knowing about it, until she had sat down one day and told him of the sacrifice his father had made.

"He was so heroic, Charlie. All the soldiers are. He fought for you and me and Gran and Granddad. He wanted so much to come home and be with us, he loved you so dearly. But . . . he just couldn't. But we will always remember him and what he did to keep us all safe."

It was only after his mother had died that Charlie had actually thought about what she had said to him that day. His father *was* a hero. He had given his life for them. He would never be coming home. But they would never forget him. The only thing that made any of this bearable, at least for Charlie, was that he had a half dozen East End mates who had also lost their fathers in the war. Their mothers had all received that telegram. So, Charlie wasn't alone in that loss, even though he quite often felt that he was.

He finished his deliveries for the day, conscious now of seeing if any more were from the service branches. Luckily, none were. But tomorrow was another day for regrets to be sent to suddenly widowed women and fatherless children.

It was the end of another week, so he collected his wages, with a nice bonus thrown in because Arthur Benedict liked him and Charlie was a hard worker with the skill and talent to ring up more business. In his spare minutes he had taken to hanging out at the Savoy, where the American journalists stayed. They were always sending telegrams, and they tipped quite liberally. All Americans, apparently, were rich. And Charlie had ventured inside the hotel on several occasions to see finely dressed folks eating at linen-clad tables and being served by proper-looking staff. And the food they were putting in their mouths? Charlie didn't even know such meals existed. He recalled Gran telling him about caviar and hors d'oeuvres being served there, though he had no idea what they even were.

"See you in the morning, Ignatius," said Benedict as he put the money Charlie had collected in the till. Then he focused on the boy's battered face.

"My word, what happened? Did you fall off your bike?"

Charlie looked up at him. "Do all them telegrams read the same, Mr. Benedict?"

Benedict gave him a funny look. "What telegrams are you speaking of, son?"

"The . . . the ones that . . . tell the family that their . . . that he's dead."

Benedict closed up the till and came over to Charlie. "Did you deliver one of those telegrams? There were quite a few in the bin for today."

Charlie nodded.

"Is that how you got scraped up, then? I suppose I should have told you. But I guess I was afraid you wouldn't want to deliver the damn things, and they have to be delivered. Families *have* to know."

Charlie simply looked at him without speaking.

"Yes, well, the fact of the matter is, Ignatius, that there are so many such . . . messages . . . that . . . well, the government apparently believes that some *uniformity* is . . . necessary." He glanced nervously at Charlie. "In other words, yes, they pretty much all read the same, except for the names, of course." He paused. "Your father . . . You said Dunkirk. So your mum received . . . one?"

Charlie was no longer listening. He turned and walked out, leaving Benedict to awkwardly study his hands.

Sorry, Eddie

Charlie rode through the darkness to his new "home." It was in the basement of a partially collapsed building. It was near the telegram office, and off a street that had once been a busy thoroughfare, but that had gone quietly dormant during the war.

He rolled his bike down the steps and pushed open the door. A painted sign warned of dangerous poison gas inside. He'd found the sign in a dustbin by the river and reckoned it would be a good way to keep curious people away from his digs.

For his dinner he had bread, cheese, a link of fried sausage he'd bought from Peter Duckett for a few pence, a raw carrot, and a cup of water from an outside hose pipe. Then he carefully unfolded the wax paper and looked down at the boiled raisin cake, popularly known as War Cake. He carefully measured out a slice equal to the width of his thumbnail, took one bite, and then another, and let the lump of confectionary rest in his mouth until it was almost dissolved with his saliva. He believed it was real sugar in there. He wrapped it back up and put the remainder in his bag. He'd purchased it from a Sainsbury shop clerk using some of his mileage money. Before the war Charlie had once had a bit of Jaffa Cake and he had thought nothing could be better than that. But the War Cake had come close, if only because his expectations had diminished so.

It was after ten now, and his legs were tired from pedalling and his face still hurt. But the young woman who struck him had lost her husband. His wounds would heal; hers, he reckoned, never would.

Charlie lay on his bedding and took up his book and the pen that Oliver had given him. He opened the journal and looked at the words Lonzo had written on the flyleaf.

Sawree, Edee.

Yeah, sorry, Eddie, Charlie thought. *You should still be here, mate.*

He had filled in many pages of the journal already. He usually wrote at night, since sleep never came easily to him. By candlelight, with the sounds of the city just outside his door, Charlie usually laboured for quite a long time, as though he desperately needed to get things out of his head and onto the paper where he could make better sense of them, perhaps.

When he was done, he looked over what he'd written and found nothing exceptional amid the poor spellings.

But you ain't special, Charlie, six a shillin' you are. Everybody says so, 'cept for Gran and Mum. But they're dead now. So . . .

He supposed that Mr. Oliver and Molly might think him somewhat special. After Gran's death he would have been lost without Molly's help. And he and Molly would have been living on the pavement or else chucked into an orphanage without the aid of Mr. Oliver. The three of them together seemed to have a chance to make it. And yet now he could never be with them again. And that hurt far more than Charlie thought it would. He had always assumed he could get along fine all by himself. Yet he also supposed that people weren't really good at being alone, at least not all the time.

Via an interior staircase, he ventured to the top of the damaged building. There Charlie looked down onto a city that was so different in parts it actually seemed to be several countries haphazardly stitched together. He could ride past Buckingham Palace as free as he liked, but he would never be allowed inside. And men in suits and fancy motorcars could go to the East End to throw someone out on the streets who was behind in his rent. But these men would never be accepted or liked or respected in the East End. The war had brought folks together for a bit, but it wouldn't last, thought Charlie. Then things would go back to his lot, as always, being on the short end of pretty much everything.

Unless we're all talkin' German.

Lost & Found

"Hello, might I have a word?" said Oliver as he walked into yet another postal office in his ongoing search for Charlie.

Arthur Benedict turned to look at him. "Yes, sir, is there a problem with something?"

Oliver approached the counter. "No. I was just wondering about your telegram boys?"

Benedict's expression turned apprehensive. "What about 'em?"

"I was actually trying to locate one."

Benedict warily looked him up and down. "Why, is the lad in trouble?"

"No, nothing like that. It's just that his mother got back into town and we can't locate him. We do know that he's a telegram boy, but that's all we know."

"I don't understand. Wasn't he at home?"

"That's just the thing. He is not at home and his mother is terribly worried about him."

"Name?"

"Charlie Matters?"

"No, got no lad with that name here."

Oliver edged forwards a bit and started speaking in a confidential tone. "The thing is, the boy might be using an alias."

Benedict blanched. "An alias! What, is he some sort of criminal?"

"No, things were not exactly happy at home, you see. His mother had to leave for the country to take care of her sick sister and . . ."

"And the lad didn't like that?"

"That's right. It was actually a terrible fiasco. But she wants him home now and is desperate to find him."

Benedict pulled a paper from a drawer. "Well, here's a list of all my boys."

Oliver ran his eye down the page until it came to rest on Ignatius Oliver.

"See anyone you recognize?"

"I do indeed. That's him." Oliver indicated the name.

"Ignatius? He's a right good lad. One of my best. Works hard and has a way about him."

"Yes, yes he does."

"He probably won't be back for several hours."

"I tell you what, let's have a bit of a surprise for young *Ignatius*. When he returns, can you send him out with a telegram?"

"Well, sir, that *is* the business we're in."

"Of course." Oliver filled out the telegram form and paid over the requisite amount.

"It'll be sometime this afternoon, sir. Say around four or so."

"Splendid." He handed Benedict a crown. "Make that one Charlie's last message of the day, can you? So his mum can spend time with him. Fix things up?"

Benedict took the coin and put it in his pocket. "Surely, sir, surely."

"His mum will be thrilled. But not a word, eh?"

"As you say, sir. *Mum's* the word."

"Molly, dear, are you all right?" asked Matron Tweedy.

"What?" said a distracted Molly breathlessly.

"Those are dirty bandages you're rolling up. The clean ones are in that bin."

"Oh my goodness, I am so sorry."

Molly put the dirty bandages back in the proper bin and thoroughly washed her hands at the sink.

"Are you sure you're all right?" said Tweedy.

"Well, actually, I received some bad news about a family member, and I guess I was thinking about that. It won't happen again, I promise."

"That's all right. We're all only human. Is there anything I can do?"

"No, Matron. I wish there were, but there's just not."

"Do you need some time to deal with things?"

"No, I'd much prefer to work. We're so busy now and it helps me take my mind off other things."

"Certainly. As you wish."

Tweedy left her there, and Molly started rolling the clean bandages. But her thoughts were directed to her father, the alleged murderer. This all made sense now. Her father leaving like he had. No communications to her. The mental image of her father walking up the steps to the gallows made her want to retch. She put the rolled bandages away and settled her face in her hands.

It was clear that her beloved father was lost to her. And her mother? In a sanatorium with mental disease. It had been quite some time and yet Dr. Stephens had still not written back to her. She wondered if he ever would. Perhaps he didn't share information with a child.

But I'm not a child. I'm a nurse auxiliary. I'm doing my part. And she is *my mother.*

After meeting with Major Bryant, she had fled upstairs, flung herself on the bed, and had a good cry. Or a bad one rather. So bad, in fact, that she had nearly stopped breathing.

Get hold of yourself, Molly, she had told herself afterwards. *This does no good. You can't change any of it with tears.*

Mr. Oliver had done his best to cheer her up, but it was a hopeless task. Her life, so perfect before the war, was now utterly destroyed. As much cast in rubble as her old home.

She spent the rest of the morning tending to patients, taking care that she made no more mistakes. The wards were full, the injuries serious, and the pain being endured by those in the clinic crushing to all of them, patients and their caregivers.

She had nursed Lonzo every day, hoping that he would tell her something of Charlie. But though he was sometimes conscious and could eat and drink a bit, he looked muddled and didn't even appear to recognize her.

She hurried to The Book Keep later that afternoon to collect the latest post, something she had started doing after writing her letter to Dr. Stephens. Oliver had given her a spare key, and she opened the door and picked up the letters the postman had put through the slot. She noticed that one of them was addressed to her. Then she gaped. It was from the Beneficial Institute!

She eagerly opened it and read the letter at the counter.

Dr. Stephens acknowledged the receipt of her letter and was sorry to tell her that her mother's condition had deteriorated quite recently and rapidly.

As Molly read through the letter her spirits dropped even further. Dr. Stephens did not seem to hold out much hope.

> *I'm afraid that her issues are deep and troubled and despite certain treatments, we were not able to make any progress. She is also experiencing some grave internal disorders, and frankly I'm not sure how much longer she can survive. I'm sorry to have to tell you this, Miss Wakefield, but felt that you ought to know.*
>
> *Sincerely . . .*

Molly carefully folded up the letter and slid it back into the envelope.

She returned to the clinic in a daze and bumped into someone in uniform at the front entrance.

"Charlie!" she screamed, breaking out into a broad smile. She hugged him.

"M-Molly!" exclaimed Charlie as she squeezed him tightly. "What are you doin' here?"

"I work here."

Oliver came around the corner of the building, beaming. "Ignatius Oliver the telegram boy, eh, Charlie?"

"How'd you know that?" said an amazed Charlie.

Oliver explained what he had done, and that Charlie had the rest of the day off.

"You must come home with us, Charlie," said Oliver.

"I can't. That copper."

"Charlie," said Molly. "Your friend Lonzo is in the clinic. It looks like he was beaten."

"Beaten! Can . . . can I see him?"

"Yes, but I'm afraid he might not recognize you."

& Lost

MOLLY LED CHARLIE TO the ward where Lonzo lay on his bed.

Charlie took off his pillbox hat and sat down in a wooden chair next to his friend. He hadn't seen Lonzo in quite a while, and his old mate looked near death.

"Lonzo, it's me, Charlie."

Lonzo didn't react to him at all.

Charlie looked over at Molly and Oliver, who were standing by the doorway to the ward.

He turned back to Lonzo and pulled something from his pocket. It was the journal. He had taken to carrying it with him. He would write in it when he stopped to eat his lunch.

Charlie opened it. "'Sorry, Eddie,'" he said, holding the book up so Lonzo could see it. "You wrote that, Lonzo, to *Eddie*, your best mate."

Lonzo's right eye twitched and then his left one seemed to shiver a bit in its socket as the pupil focused on the book.

"E-Eddie?" he said in a frail voice.

"That's right, Lonzo. Eddie, our friend."

"He's d-dead."

Charlie lowered the book. "Yeah, he is." He looked Lonzo over. "Who did this to you? Who beat you up?"

"C-coppers done it."

"Coppers?"

Charlie looked over at Oliver, who had clearly heard this.

Lonzo said, "That . . . that Will-bee bloke. He and that constable wh-what-is done it. Hit me in the head. P-put me in de cl-clink, then they th-throwed me in the s-street."

"DI Willoughby," Oliver grimly said to Molly. "Excuse me." He stepped away.

Charlie gripped Lonzo's hand. "They had no call to do that. We never wanted nothin' to happen to Eddie or that copper. And I bet it ain't no hangin' job, either. He was lyin'."

"I'm s-sorry, Charlie. I t-tol' him 'bout you."

"It's okay, Lonzo. You rest easy now. I'll be right here, mate."

Lonzo closed his eyes and his breathing actually seemed a bit steadier.

Charlie looked over at Molly. "We never meant no harm, Molly. We just run 'cause we was scared."

"I know, Charlie, I know. I'm just glad you're safe."

An hour later Molly was astonished to see Major Bryant march into the ward together with another uniformed man. Also with them was Oliver, who was whispering something to Bryant; the man was nodding in agreement.

Bryant spoke quietly with Charlie and Lonzo for a bit. Then, with Charlie's help, Lonzo signed a piece of paper that Bryant presented to him.

"That's a good lad," said Bryant.

He rejoined Oliver and Molly. "After you rang, Ignatius, I checked, and this chap Willoughby has had numerous complaints against him, bad egg all around. He even beat up one of *our* boys after a public drunkenness charge landed him in a cell. I've had Lonzo sign a paper making out a formal charge. He said that a constable also hit him. That bobby will turn on Willoughby quick enough when we put the screws to him. I won't stand for this. Lonzo was trying to join the army when they grabbed him, he said, even though the lad was not of age. Lonzo also told me what happened at the shop, and he said he forced Charlie to go along. Willoughby tried to make it out to be a hanging job, which of course it wasn't. I think I can safely guarantee that neither Charlie nor Lonzo will have difficulties over this, unless you want to press charges for Lonzo trying to break into your shop, Ignatius, seeing as how he's now confessed to it."

"I have no wish to press charges," said Oliver quietly.

"Thought as much."

He and the other soldier left. When Molly and Oliver looked over at Charlie, tears were trickling down his face.

"Charlie!" exclaimed Molly, rushing over and then stopping abruptly.

Charlie was looking at Lonzo, whose eyes were open and unseeing.

"He's gone," said Charlie miserably. "Lonzo's gone."

The Breach Once More

The fire crackled in the fireplace of Oliver's study. They had just returned from Lonzo's funeral service. He had been laid next to his mother. The police had taken care of the arrangements and paid the undertaker's bill. DI Willoughby and Constable Higgins had been arrested and charged in Lonzo's death, and were being held for trial.

Charlie was wearing his telegram boy's uniform, while Molly wore a faded black dress that she had borrowed from one of the other nurses. Oliver had on his only suit. They had all drawn close to the fire because the weather had grown quite cold.

Charlie had refused any dinner and sat there with a cup of tea cradled in his hands. He hadn't yet taken a sip while Oliver and Molly watched him closely.

"It was a nice service, wasn't it?" said Molly, glancing nervously at Oliver.

"Yes, yes it was," said Oliver. "Wasn't it, Charlie?"

Charlie simply nodded.

Molly suddenly remembered something. "Oh, Dr. Stephens wrote me back from the Beneficial Institute!"

"Really? What did he say?" asked Oliver.

"It's . . . it's not good, I'm afraid. My mother is not doing well at all. He fears for her life, actually."

"Oh, Molly, I am so sorry," said Oliver.

"Yes, well, I would like to see her before . . . the end. But I'm not sure I can."

"I wish I had a way for you to get there," said Oliver. "I *did* check. The trains are not taking civilians to Cornwall presently. Most passenger lines have been damaged and the railway lines still in service are strictly for military purposes."

"Yes, of course."

And then it happened.

The air raid sirens started to blare.

Oliver shook his head and closed his eyes for a moment.

Why the hell do you have to come tonight, you bastards?

They rushed pell-mell from the room to grab their coats and gas masks. Oliver had got a new warden's uniform, and he quickly donned it. "Come, quickly now," he said. "Before the red alert sounds."

They hurried through the chill and gloom to the nearest shelter and Oliver got them safely inside. He then met up with Lee Parker at the designated place, and they began rounding up those on their list and getting them to the correct shelters.

They had only a few more people left to find when the familiar humming commenced in the pavements. They both looked up to see the dark cigar shapes in the skies above. The ack-ack fire started and the lethal rounds soared skywards as a fresh battle began.

"Looks to be quite a few of the damn things," Parker calmly noted over the noise of the guns and the engines roaring above them.

"Yes," said Oliver grimly. "It does."

They dashed off in different directions to fetch the remaining people who needed corralling.

When the first bombs struck, Oliver was knocking on the door of The Secret Garden tea shop.

"Desdemona. It's Ignatius. It's not safe to remain in your basement anymore. Please come with me."

There was no answer.

He rapped harder. "Desdemona! It's Ignatius. You must come with me to the shelter." He tried the door but it was locked. He gave a searching look both ways down the alley just as more bombs exploded in the distance.

"Desdemona!"

Damn the woman.

The government had finally announced the truth of the V-2 rockets. More than a hundred had already been launched against London, and they hit without warning and obliterated everything in their path; no building or person aboveground was safe because they flew so fast that no real warning was possible. And while the sirens and the planes above indicated that a conventional air raid was looming, the V-2s could still strike at any time.

Oliver put his shoulder against the wood and pushed hard. It popped open and he burst into the tea shop's front room.

"Desdemona!"

He searched everywhere around her shop, and then upstairs where her living quarters were, just to make sure she had not fallen asleep in bed and not heard the sirens. He then ran down to the basement. While many Londoners, like Macklin, preferred to shelter in place, he also knew that Macklin had rheumatism and bad lungs, and thus he always tried to get her to come to the shelter. She almost never consented to go, but this was the first time she had not answered his knock.

He found her in the basement. And it was now clear why she hadn't come to the door. She was dead, and her death had not been natural. He was not speculating on this; the knife was still sticking out of her chest.

He knelt beside her. "My God."

Her limbs were heavy, her skin still somewhat warm, but cooling rapidly. An explosion that rocked the tea shop brought the shocked Oliver back to the present.

He grabbed a blanket from a small cot in the corner and covered her body with it. He ran back up the steps and out of the shop, and sprinted down the alley as more detonations sounded in the distance.

He had one more person on his list. But the house where he lived was empty. The man must have headed to the shelter. At least Oliver hoped so. He looked up again; the sky was filled with aircraft, and the ack-ack raining upwards was so intense that what had been a clear night sky was nearly opaque with smoke. He could hear the rapidity of machine-gun fire and the scream of aircraft engines, and he knew that meant RAF pilots were thousands of feet up there engaging the enemy.

As he rushed towards the shelter, two planes suddenly swooped low out of the dark sky. One he recognized as a British Beaufighter, the other a German Messerschmitt. The Messerschmitt was in the lead and the British plane was racing to catch up.

"Go get 'em," Oliver called to the RAF pilot.

The German pilot must have spotted the uniformed Oliver because he pointed the Messerschmitt in his direction. A blistering salvo of bullets then raced at him, forcing Oliver to dive headlong through the glass door of a shop. He slid across the shard-littered floor, slammed into a counter, and lay stunned, as the two planes shot down the street, barely twenty feet off the ground.

Oliver rose and slip-slid over the broken glass to poke his head out of the shattered doorway. In the distance he saw an explosion. It was not a bomb; he had just seen the German plane veer out of control and slam into a building, as the Beaufighter soared upwards to take on the Luftwaffe fleet once more.

Oliver breathed deeply and gingerly felt his sore arm. *Before this war would I have ever imagined seeing two planes engaged in combat flying down the streets of Covent Garden!?*

He walked to the next street, turned, and a minute later was in the shelter, closing the door securely behind him. He found Charlie and Molly, who were seated in a far corner.

"You okay, Mr. Oliver?" asked Charlie, eyeing the man's dirty and cut-up clothing.

"Fine, Charlie, considering the alternative would have been extremely unpleasant."

Hours later, when the bombing was over, Oliver took the children back straight away to The Book Keep and then made a phone call.

Thirty minutes later the police showed up along with what looked like a doctor with his bulky medical bag. While Molly and Charlie watched in confusion, Oliver led the men over to the tea shop and inside.

When the police finally departed, Oliver returned to the shop, where both Molly and Charlie assaulted him with queries.

He calmed them down, locked the front door, and led the pair into the study. "All right, I will tell you what happened. The fact is that, well, someone killed Mrs. Macklin. I found her body in the basement when I was checking on her for the air raid."

"Bloody hell," exclaimed Molly, causing Charlie and Oliver to shoot her a surprised look.

"Yes, it is quite shocking," Oliver said.

"Was she robbed?" Charlie asked.

"It didn't appear to be a robbery."

"Who would want to harm her?" asked Molly.

"I'm not sure. Certainly crime has increased in the city since the war started. It could be put down to that. They might have thought she would have been in a shelter. Then she may have stumbled upon them and they . . . did what they did."

For some reason Molly glanced over at the bookshelf and her gaze came to rest on the copy of George Sand's *Jacques*, with the cut-out pages, which was the only item on that shelf. When she looked back at Oliver, his gaze slowly came round to her.

The man did not seem pleased at all.

A Crisis of Discovery

A FEW DAYS LATER the tap-tap on the glass came right at the stroke of midnight. There was something mystical about that hour, Oliver thought as he slowly walked to the door. Both in the pages of a book, and sometimes in real life.

Oliver drew aside the blackout curtains and saw Cedric standing there. He unlocked the door and motioned him in, but put a finger to his lips and whispered, "Please keep very quiet, I have others here with me."

"I know that you do, Ignatius," hissed Cedric. "And I do *not* like it."

Oliver led Cedric to the study, closed the door, and turned to his visitor. "Well?"

"What are those children doing here?" demanded Cedric.

"Don't worry. I'm looking for a place for them. Now, tell me about Mrs. Macklin."

"Who?" said Cedric.

"Busybody across the alley who ran the tea shop."

"What of her?"

"She's dead. Someone stabbed her."

"Interesting."

"You're saying you know nothing of it?" said Oliver incredulously.

"Well, if someone did kill her, you might have already struck upon the reason. Perhaps she saw things that had nothing to do with her. And something had to be done before she could take her foul suspicions and do damage with them. Damage to *you*, I might add. I am, of course, just speculating here. I really know nothing of the matter."

"Do you really think she suspected me?" asked Oliver.

"Let me put it this way. If certain enquiries were made, discreet ones, and those enquiries indicated that the woman might have been preparing to alert the authorities about certain things she had seen, certain people she had witnessed doing certain suspicious-looking things, then, yes, I think there was the potential for important plans to be disrupted. And, of course, that could not be allowed."

"I see. Well, the police *did* come. And the questions were *very* uncomfortable."

"And what do the police think?" Cedric wanted to know.

"I told them about the attempted robbery of my business. But it would have helped if her till had been raided." He stared pointedly at Cedric. "That would have made my theory more plausible."

Cedric shrugged and gave a superior smile. "I never thought of that. You see, there is no crime in Germany. Der Führer will not allow it."

"How commendable. So what do you want now?"

"As you know, D-Day caught us by surprise. And now with the Allies having retaken France, Belgium, and most of the Netherlands, we have lost nearly the whole of western Europe. And your latest offerings have not been particularly illuminating. You must, how do you say, enhance your performance."

"Firstly, the German debacle at D-Day was not my fault. My previous reports strongly hinted at the *correct* location of the attack all along."

"Only we did not see the *hints* until it was too late. Next time be more *direct*."

"*Secondly*, if I am *too* direct it'll be my head in a noose on the gallows, and I'll be of no use to you a'tall."

"But an Allied offensive began in September in the Baltics and is ongoing, and the odds are not looking good for Germany. If that campaign succeeds, the only thing standing between the Red Army and Germany is Poland."

Oliver stared grimly at the man. "Ironic, as Poland was the first victim of Der Führer's Blitzkrieg. But I see your dilemma. The Americans take POWs. The Russians shoot them."

"If Stalin defeats Germany we'll all be communists," retorted Cedric brusquely.

"Well, we can't have that, can we?"

Cedric said, "So, the intelligence I seek, do you have it?"

"I think your superiors will be very pleased. Indeed, I believe this will turn a blundering negative into a brilliant strategic triumph and forevermore enshrine you in the hallowed halls of German spycraft. I congratulate you, Herr Cedric Axmann."

"You British are such fine orators. Put a British accent on an idiot and he sounds like he quotes Shakespeare, or better yet, Goethe."

Oliver smiled. "Yes, but then he's still an idiot."

"Now, the information? I am in a hurry."

Oliver strolled over to the bookcase, pulled down the *Jacques* novel, and handed it to Cedric, who glanced at the spine.

"Another book by George Sand, the French female?" Cedric said derisively.

"Imogen was quite partial to her."

"I do not much care for her affinity for the French, but your wife is missed."

"Yes, Imogen is. Very much," replied Oliver, his casual manner vanishing.

Cedric tensed, then rushed over to the door and wrenched it open.

And there stood a terrified Charlie and Molly.

Reversal of All

The grey four-door Humber Snipe drove slowly through the darkened, empty roads with Cedric at the wheel. Next to him was Oliver. In the rear seat, a tall, thick-shouldered man in dark clothing held a Luger on Molly and Charlie.

Cedric looked in the mirror at them. "This does not make me happy in the slightest, Ignatius. I have children of my own."

"You think it makes *me* happy?" retorted Oliver. "I'd grown rather fond of them."

"But this was *your* fault. You brought them to your home. And now they have eavesdropped. That leaves us no choice, you understand this?"

"I understand all too well," Oliver replied quietly.

"Mr. Oliver," began Molly in a pleading tone.

He held up a hand for her to stop speaking. Oliver looked at Cedric. "Next left. It's wooded, quiet, and the river bends at the right angle for our purposes. The current is very swift there and they'll be past Southend-on-Sea in very short order."

Molly started to quietly weep while Charlie looked at Oliver in disbelief.

Oliver gave Cedric further directions, and he pulled the Snipe to a stop in a small clearing well outside of London where the rush of water could be clearly heard.

They all got out and Oliver looked at Cedric. "Down by the riverbank. It can be done there."

The man with the Luger eyed first Molly and then Charlie. "No pain. You just go to sleep, little ones."

"And you can go straight to hell." This came not from Charlie, but Molly. It was not directed at the man who was about to kill them, but rather at Ignatius Oliver.

An impassive Oliver said to Cedric, "Right through the gap here."

They had walked only a few more steps when they were hit with flashes of intense light from multiple torches.

"Police!" cried out a voice. "Hold it right there. What are you doing with them kids?"

"What is going on!" screamed Cedric, pulling a gun and waving it around.

Oliver snatched it away, tugged Cedric close, and said, "Don't be stupid. It's just the bloody police. They must have seen us put Molly and Charlie in the car and followed. Get them to the river, I'll hold them off."

He fired at the torch lights. As did the other man.

Then multiple shots rang out.

The large man next to Oliver dropped his Luger, clutched his stomach, and toppled to the ground.

Molly had fallen to her knees and watched in horror as the shots were fired. She saw Oliver flinch once and then again, his body twisting with the impacts. He cried out in pain and his gun fell to the dirt.

"Get away from them kids!" screamed a uniformed man, appearing in the light. "You damn slavers."

Oliver's mouth sagged and his hand gripped his chest, where his shirt was fast turning crimson. He looked at Cedric in desperation. "The b-book. R-run. Back to the . . . c-car. B-before it's all scuppered." Blood was leaching from Oliver's mouth, as Cedric fled into the trees.

A swaying Oliver looked at Charlie and Molly. They were staring back at him in disbelief and shock. "I-I'm . . . so s-sorry." Then he dropped to the dirt and lay still.

A uniformed man rushed up to Molly and Charlie. "You okay? Nothing hurt?"

They shook their heads, both their gazes fixed on Oliver's body.

"Where'd the other bloke go?" someone shouted as the sound of a car starting up reached them.

Charlie and Molly pulled their gazes away from Oliver's body when Major Bryant stepped into the clearing and shone a light on them and then on himself, so they could see him.

He looked down at the dead, Luger-toting man, and then at the bloody Oliver lying there, before glancing at Molly and Charlie and saying quietly, "It's all right, children. You're safe now."

"Mr. Oliver was working with the Germans," Charlie cried out.

"They sh-shot him. He's d-dead," added Molly tearfully.

Bryant's trim moustache twitched. "Okay, the coast is clear, you can be resurrected now."

Oliver slowly sat up and wiped the "blood" off his mouth with a handkerchief. He stood and said, "I trust Cedric made his escape?"

Bryant nodded. "We have him on a short leash, of course."

Oliver then looked guiltily at the dazed Charlie and Molly. "Perhaps this can all be better explained back at The Book Keep."

Poor Imogen

Oliver, the children, and Major Bryant were all seated in the study.

Oliver had passed out warm blankets before settling in a comfortable chair in front of a roaring fire, courtesy of several pieces of wood provided by Major Bryant's men.

Bryant began by saying, "Now, just to be clear, there is not much we can tell you. The law and all."

"That's rubbish," blurted out Charlie. "You owe us the whole bloody truth, you do."

Bryant began in a severe tone, "Now see here, young man, while I understand—"

"They're right, Scott. I know you can see that," interjected Oliver.

"What I can see, and what my oath of secrecy dictates, are two very different things, Ignatius," Bryant countered.

"Still, we can tell them *something*. They've been through a truly horrific experience. They deserve to know certain things."

Bryant let out a sigh. "Oh, all right. But you both must swear to carry all that I tell you to the grave."

Molly and Charlie quickly nodded.

Bryant settled back and began. "I operate an intelligence programme with the Security Service called the Double-Cross, a counter-espionage and deception scheme. The Germans have continually dropped spies into our midst, by plane, boat, submarine. Almost all of them were ill-trained, inept—worthless, really. We had broken the German Enigma code and other ciphers before Germany started sending spies here. Indeed, we'd often pick the gits up as they walked ashore! So the Germans got very little out of it. But we began exploiting that advantage by *turning* those very same agents and feeding to the Germans false or, more accurately, some truthful intelligence mixed in with enough tosh so that it looked like their spy effort was working. And we gained quite valuable intelligence on the German spy network in the bargain. But that's not to say the Germans didn't keep trying. And this Cedric bloke was better than most. In fact, we'd never have got on to him without help." He looked at Oliver as if to say, *Okay, mate, I've done my bit.*

Oliver took up the account. "When the war started, Imogen was as loyal as anyone to her country. Then, when the Blitz happened and so many died, including some of her dearest friends, something changed inside of her. When Paternoster Row with all its books was incinerated, that change became complete. I don't know why that particular event did it, but I think she saw the collapse of all she loved in the destruction that happened that night. And she began going to meetings, and those meetings led to her consorting with certain people, who were determined to exploit connections that she had."

"What sorts of connections?" asked Molly.

Bryant said, "Her father, John Bradstreet. Before he retired and bought this bookshop, he was a long-serving statesman of the top tier, including at the War Office, the author of serious political works, and a welcome visitor in the homes of many distinguished public servants. After he died, Imogen was still very much a welcome guest in those places. She was astonishingly bright and as engaging a conversationalist as you would ever encounter." He looked once more at Oliver.

"Yes, well, it got to the point, you see," said Oliver, "that she began working for the Germans."

When Molly looked shocked, Oliver said quickly, "Oh, she had no love of Hitler and his disgusting fascism, Molly. She had convinced herself that she was doing the right thing by *Britain*. By helping Germany so that the bombings and the destruction and the dying . . . would stop. Remember, this was before the Americans entered the war, and we were fighting virtually alone. She truly believed that Britain would remain free and autonomous even if the Nazis took over all of Europe."

"I see," said Molly. "But this information helped Germany. People died because of it."

"Yes, they did, Molly, a fact that Imogen had to eventually confront. Anyway, she performed this work for quite some time. And I was apparently too much of an idiot to see it. But she was ever so much smarter than I am."

"You probably could never believe that she would do that," said Molly quietly, watching him closely.

"I certainly couldn't equate the loving, caring, highly intelligent woman whom I loved dearly being complicit with the Third Reich." He paused and rubbed a hand over his forehead. "And then one day she had me come in here and sat me down in this very chair. And she took my hand and she told me . . . everything. All of it. Her spying, her treachery, all of it."

He looked up at Bryant, who stared stolidly back at him.

"A shock for you, old man," the major said.

"And incredibly painful for her to confess," noted Oliver.

"What did you say to her?" asked Molly.

"I don't quite remember, Molly. It's all rather a muddle in my head."

"What'd you *do*, guv?" asked Charlie.

"It was not so much what *I* did, Charlie. But what Imogen proposed that I do."

"What was that?" asked Molly.

"Help her spying efforts."

"I . . . don't understand," said Molly, clearly taken aback by this statement.

Oliver glanced at Bryant.

The major said, "Imogen was one of only a very few *British* spies working for the Germans, at least that we knew of. And the Germans needed people like her. They exploited her, but now Imogen, having gained their full confidence, was going to exploit them *back*."

"That sounds like a very dangerous scheme," said Molly.

Bryant said, "It was. But Imogen could be a very formidable opponent in her own right. We all attended Oxford together. In fact, Imogen was in the first class of women to be awarded a degree from there. We would hold informal debates at university, the ladies against the gents. Imogen regularly wiped the floor with us. Right, old man?"

Oliver smiled weakly and said, "Yes, quite regularly in fact. She used these skills to convince Cedric and others that I had been working with her all along. We met with them and they became convinced of my loyalty, because Imogen knew exactly what she and I needed to say to make them feel that way. You see, she had read the Germans like a book, just like she read all other books. So I began 'working' for them, too."

Bryant said, "But the difference was that Imogen also came to me and explained the whole plan."

"Including what she had done previously?" said Molly.

"The *whole* plan, Molly," interjected Oliver. "The last thing Imogen was trying to do was avoid the consequences of her earlier actions. She just wanted to make things as right as possible by now working *for* her country."

"Why'd she change her mind?" asked Charlie.

"I actually think it might have had something to do with me," said Oliver thoughtfully. He touched his arm where it had been burned. "As an air warden I very nearly died one night. I remember her sitting beside my bed in hospital while I recovered. Just holding my hand and saying how sorry she was. And when I was finally able to return home, she told me the truth. I can't begin to imagine how much courage it took for her to do that."

"You really must have been quite stunned," said Molly.

"I was many things, Molly, and, yes, that was one of them. So working with Major Bryant here, we regularly fed false information to Cedric and he, in turn, communicated that to Germany. And Cedric would bring me and Imogen false intelligence with the understanding that we would pass it on to Major Bryant, who he knew we were close with. Which we did, but we also told him it was rubbish, of course. And we continued to disclose to the major all we knew about Cedric and his operation. After Imogen . . . died, I kept 'working' with them on my own."

"We knew something was up before tonight," said Molly.

Oliver shot her a puzzled look. "How could you possibly?"

Charlie said, "Like I told you, I saw that bloke, Cedric, here late that night when I come 'round. He gave you some papers. And when you come to my flat the next day I followed you, saw you meet with Cedric at his place. When you come out you had some papers you was puttin' in your pocket."

Molly added, "And very late at night we saw you slip an envelope in his letterbox when you were wearing your air warden uniform."

"My God," said a shocked Oliver.

Charlie added, "And I got into his place and found the book with the pages cut out, and this machine what looked like a typewriter, but ain't."

An amazed Bryant said, "It's the device the Nazis use to send encrypted messages via radio signals." He paused and smiled. "Blimey, if you were both a bit older we might just enlist you for MI5."

Molly said, "We didn't know what to do. But we couldn't believe you were involved in anything bad. Or if so it was against your will."

"Well, thank you for that. And I used the books with the pages cut out to hide secret documents," said Oliver.

"I found one of 'em in Cedric's flat," said Charlie. "Con-sway-low."

"Yes, *Consuelo*, by George Sand." Oliver looked at Molly. "You were staring quite hard at *Jacques* that night. I wondered about that, though I never dreamed you two had penetrated my secret so deeply."

"I had looked inside it when I was searching for you that day. Charlie had told me about *Consuelo*. And the pages were also cut out of *Jacques*."

"It grieved me enormously to desecrate books like that," said Oliver in a depressed tone.

"And Imogen?" said Molly. "Her death?"

Oliver looked at her. "She got me firmly established as a spy in my own right. And then told me she was going to Bristol. Instead she went to Cornwall and ended her own life."

"Why do you think she did that?" asked Molly.

"'Cause she couldn't live with what she done," said Charlie, drawing everyone's attention.

"Yes, Charlie," said Oliver earnestly. "I believe you are quite right about that."

"But you let Cedric go tonight," said Molly. "Why?"

"We let him go only *after* he saw Ignatius *die*," said Bryant. "And we made it seem that it was simply the police that had seen them with children, and suspected the worst. That way he will believe that Ignatius's status as a spy remains unknown. And he will tell his handlers in Germany that the intelligence just provided is perfectly good to use. But the intelligence won't help Germany at all. In fact, we hope it will lead to one of the worst defeats the Nazis will suffer in this war and hasten its end. And when it's time to pick up Cedric, we will. As I said, a short leash. He will not escape. His life will end on the gallows."

"But how did you manage to show up so quickly tonight?" said Molly.

"We have a man who follows Cedric when he comes here. So when you left with Cedric, he reported it and we followed. They must have had someone else kill Mrs. Macklin, and used the cover of the bombing raid that night to do the deed."

Oliver took up the story. "And the place I took us to is the prearranged spot when something is amiss." He glanced at Bryant. "Secret communications do not always necessitate a machine or a series of esoteric numbers; sometimes it is simply what someone *does* while being observed."

"Quite so," agreed Bryant.

Oliver continued. "I was to be shot with a blank gun and Cedric would manage to escape."

"But you was bleedin'," said Charlie.

"Just a little capsule I keep for such occasions, Charlie. Slipped between my teeth and cracked open, and one has instant blood. And then I simply rubbed it across my shirt. Which means I'm down to just the one clean one now," he added, ruefully looking at his ruined garment.

Bryant rose. "And now it's time that I was off."

He left them there in front of the now-dying fire.

Molly and Charlie came to sit on either side of Oliver as he continued to stare at the winking embers.

Molly said, "When you were 'shot' and dying you said 'sorry' to us?"

"Yes. I felt truly horrible for having placed you and Charlie in such danger."

"I'm just glad you're on our side," said Molly, as Charlie nodded. "And I'm so very sorry about Imogen."

He took their hands and squeezed them. "We all have each lost a great deal in this terrible war. But amidst all this destruction and despair, we managed to find one another. As a mathematician I can tell you the odds of that happening are staggeringly long. But here we are, together. As though it were somehow preordained. Now, I want you both to know that so long as I am here, you will always have a home. Never question or doubt that. Promise?"

They both nodded, and said together, "Promise."

Words of a Feather

At dinner the next night Molly could barely stay awake. Oliver filled their plates with what he had managed in the way of food. Their teacups were up to the brim at least. Charlie looked as tired as Molly. His eyes were half-closed as he forked some potato and then a sliver of parsnip into his mouth.

Oliver sat down and eyed them both. "Rough days, I take it?"

Molly stirred. "Three patients died today, and I would be very much surprised if we didn't lose a similar number tomorrow."

"That is awful, Molly," said Oliver.

"I delivered four more 'a them telegrams," said Charlie. "'We deeply regrets to inform you . . .'" He put his fork down.

"Did the people have someone with them when they got the messages?" asked Molly.

"One didn't. She went right down to the floor. I hugged her till a neighbour come along. Couldn't think 'a nothin' else to do."

"I'm sure it was of great comfort to her, Charlie," said Oliver.

Charlie shrugged. Next, he rose and did something he had never done. He left the table without finishing his food. He went to the room he and Molly were sharing and closed the door.

"He's upset," said Molly.

"He has a right to be. He's lost his entire family to this damn war. And look at what you have to confront on a daily basis. It's not fair. None of it."

"War doesn't care about what's fair. It's like a virus. It only wants to invade and do harm." She put her fork down. "I do have a question."

He settled an anxious gaze on her. "All right."

"When you told me about Imogen and the decisions that she had made, it caused me to think about what my father had done, the decisions *he* had made."

"And what exactly did you think about?"

Molly composed herself and told Oliver about her mother being savagely attacked by the men in the bomb shelter.

"God. What a bloody, foul thing. People coming for safety and finding just the opposite."

"Perhaps . . . perhaps he killed the soldiers because they represented the government that refused to help him," she said, glancing nervously at him for Oliver's reaction to her words.

"That could have been the case. But killing innocent people is never right, Molly."

Her features crumpled. "I know. And he blamed himself for what happened to my mum, I'm sure of it. Poor father."

"A terrible, terrible guilt to have to bear," noted Oliver quietly.

"Do you . . . do you think he might have gone off to . . . kill himself, like . . . ?"

Oliver looked deeply troubled with her query. "I really have no idea, Molly. Any answer I could give would be based on pointless speculation."

"I mean, it would explain why he's been gone all this time. Why he's never written or tried to contact me."

"People are very complicated. And your father had your mother and her maladies to worry about, *and* your welfare to think about, too. And remember that he did work for Britain and from what

Major Bryant told me, he was very good at his job. Very brave. It's just that—"

"—he made the wrong decision."

"As did Imogen," replied Oliver.

"But she tried to make amends, while my father—"

"Yes," said Oliver. "Quite so."

Later, Molly got into a pair of old pyjamas that had once belonged to Imogen, and went to her room. Charlie was lying, still fully dressed, on his cot, staring at the ceiling.

"Charlie, it's late. You need to go to sleep."

He said nothing, as was usual when he was like this, she knew.

She sighed, got into bed, and turned off the small lamp.

Later, she awoke and noted the glittering of a light.

It was coming from a candle resting in a holder on the table between their cots.

Charlie had his pen, and his journal, and he was writing in it.

Molly had seen him do this before. "What are you writing tonight?" she said sleepily.

He glanced at her. "Just this and that. Muckin' round."

"Will you ever let me read any of it?"

He glanced at her with a smile. "You need to stick to real books. They're better for you. Learn thin's."

"Yours could be a real book one day that I learn from."

"I doubt that. I can't even spell good," replied Charlie.

"Someone can spell everything quite nicely and it still wouldn't be worth reading. I've read books like that. Or *tried* to."

Charlie grinned as he looked at her again. "You got a wonderful heart, Molly, like my mum. I'm glad we're friends."

She smiled warmly in return. "Comparing me to your mother is an amazing compliment, so thank you very much. And we'll always be friends, Charlie. No matter what happens."

She turned over and fell back to sleep.

Charlie looked at his page and silently read what he'd written.

Of awful messages delivered to families unprepared to receive them. But as Arthur Benedict had pointed out, the families deserved to know, and it was Charlie's duty to bring them that information. He supposed he should feel good about that, but he really didn't.

Later, he put his pen and journal away, and picked up the photo of his mum and his dad that Oliver and Molly had brought back from his old flat.

"Good night, Mum. Good night, Dad. Love you both."

Four hours later the phone rang.

A Desperate Summons

"Hello?" said a sleepy Oliver into the phone receiver. "Yes, this is The Book Keep. What? Molly Wakefield? Who is . . . Dr. Stephens? Yes, I'll take the call. Hello, yes, Dr. Stephens? Yes, my name is Ignatius Oliver. Just a moment and I'll get Molly."

Molly was already at her doorway, along with Charlie, when Oliver climbed to the top of the stairs.

"What is it?" she said. "Who rang?"

"It's Dr. Stephens, from the—"

Molly flew past him and raced down the stairs.

She snatched up the phone from behind the front counter and said, "Yes, this is Molly Wakefield. What's wrong?"

"Your mother, Miss Wakefield." The voice on the other end was slow and ponderous when what Molly desperately required was information as quickly as possible.

"Yes, yes, what about her? She's . . . she's not . . ."

"No, no she's still alive. I rang to tell you that she just now asked for you."

"She . . . she asked for *me*?"

"Yes. I'm glad that you included this number in your letter when you wrote to me. It's much faster than the post. The lines have been tricky as of late, but the operator was able to get me through just now. I apologize for calling so early in the morning, but I was looking in on your mother and she suddenly rallied and asked for you, and I've found that early morning trunk calls have a greater chance of going through. Now, I do not know if you can arrange things, Miss Wakefield, but I think it would be very . . . um, *good* if you were to come and see her. As quickly as possible. She . . . she's not doing a'tall well, as I mentioned in my letter."

"Of course, of course I will. I will make arrangements straight away. Can . . . can I speak to her now?"

"I'm afraid she is not strong enough to come to the phone. When can you be here? I would like to tell her."

Molly looked up to see Oliver and Charlie staring anxiously at her.

Molly glanced at the clock on the wall and saw that it was nearly six in the morning. "You can tell her that I'll do my very best to be there tonight."

"Very good. We will see you then. Oh, is the gentleman who answered the phone, Ignatius Oliver, related to *Imogen* Oliver by chance? I saw her name on the letterhead you sent me. The Book Keep, is it?"

"Yes. Imogen was his wife, why?"

"Just put him on, please."

Molly handed the phone to Oliver. "He wants to talk to you. About Imogen."

"Hello?" a puzzled Oliver said into the receiver.

"Mr. Oliver, I wanted to let you know that I have information about your wife's death."

"How could you possibly know anything about that?"

"She killed herself by jumping off a cliff on our grounds."

"What!" said Oliver as he clutched the phone with both hands. "I . . . I knew that she had done so in Cornwall, but I had no idea it was on *your* grounds."

"If by chance you'll be accompanying Miss Wakefield, I can tell you about it when you get here."

"Yes, yes, of course. But why didn't you contact me before now?"

"I knew her name, but nothing else about her until I saw it on the letterhead. And I didn't know that you were her husband until Miss Wakefield just told me."

"But can't you tell me about it now?"

"I think it would be far better to do so in person. Safe travels."

Dr. Stephens rang off, and Oliver slowly put the phone down.

"What did he say?" asked Charlie.

"Just that he knew some things about Imogen, and how she died," he said vaguely. "He'll tell me when we get there."

"Blimey," exclaimed Charlie, while Molly stared anxiously at Oliver.

The thoughts rushing through Oliver's mind were both vague and unsettling. He knew that Imogen had jumped to her death. But learning that Imogen had killed herself on the Institute grounds? The same place where Molly's mother currently was a patient? It seemed too stark of a coincidence, but then again, if Imogen had been seeking help? She had loved that part of England and perhaps the Institute was the only such facility in the area. But if she had sought help there, why had she ended up taking her own life?

He looked at Molly and said apologetically, "I'm sorry, my mind was just in a muddle. What did he say about your mother?"

"She asked to see me. It doesn't look like she has very long now."

"Then we *must* think of a way to get there and we will! I can check the trains again, or perhaps a bus—"

Charlie slapped his forehead. "Wait a mo'!"

"What is it, Charlie?" exclaimed Molly.

Charlie ran up the steps and was back down in a jiffy.

"We can drive there," he said breathlessly.

"Drive? In what?" said Molly.

Charlie held up two keys. "In your Singer, that's what."

Oliver immediately rang Major Bryant and explained the situation. The major was able to arrange official travel papers necessary to get them to Cornwall, and a map with directions. He got the car and garage keys from Charlie and sent off a couple of men to fill the Singer with petrol, pump up its tyres, and make sure the motorcar was in good working order. They then delivered the Singer to The Book Keep later that morning.

Bryant had added a caveat to their travel plans. "At this point in the war, and on that part of the coast, no one can move about freely without complications. Thus, if you do get stopped, Ignatius, these papers may not be enough. So be prepared to talk your way past any questions."

Oliver closed up shop, and Charlie had rung the postal office and got time off by telling Mr. Benedict that his mum was sick. Molly had already gone to the clinic and explained things to Matron Tweedy, who was very supportive and wished her the best.

"I just assumed it was destroyed in the bombing," Molly said, as they loaded their luggage and provisions into the Singer. "How did you know it wasn't, Charlie, and why did you have the key?"

"I slept in it some, and I nicked the key so's nobody could nick the car."

"Well done, you," said Oliver enthusiastically.

"Can you drive a motorcar, Mr. Oliver?" asked Molly as he settled behind the wheel.

"At Oxford I learned to drive my brother's little Austin Seven. And Imogen's father had a Bentley. He didn't like to drive, so he let me do the chauffeuring. I think I can get the hang of this in short order."

Oliver started the car and they drove off with only a limited gnashing of gears.

"When Imogen and I travelled to Cornwall we went by train, Molly. So you can be my navigator, as it were."

Molly had the map and directions spread out on her lap. Once they were out of London, Oliver turned west, with Molly giving him prompts along the way.

From the back seat Charlie said, "How long do you reckon it'll take us to get there?"

"It's about three hundred miles, Charlie. That's why Major Bryant gave us extra petrol."

"Three hunnerd miles! Ain't we be in America by then? Or France even?"

Oliver chuckled. "Not quite. When Imogen and I went for our honeymoon to Plymouth it took many hours by train, what with all the stops in between. But with the war and everything, the trip by car, I fear, will be even longer."

If we make it through, he thought.

A Wartime Odyssey

They drove steadily for hours on narrow, winding roads and then stopped at a rustic village to stretch their legs and eat the food they had brought. Oliver also filled up the fuel tank using the petrol cans stowed in the Singer's boot. The curious locals stared wide-eyed at the exquisite vehicle and the three strangers inside it.

They later passed a downed German Junker aircraft that children were playing around. They had to stop several times to allow military columns of men and equipment to pass, and there were many detours and slow travel over damaged roads. A few hours later they stopped once more to stretch their legs near a Yank encampment that was next to a POW camp. There, German prisoners of war worked on the farms and also in the mines and quarries in support of the Allied war effort.

At the encampment young women from the surrounding area were gathered around the security fence. Smiling American soldiers tossed boxes of chocolates and packages of nylons and cartons of cigarettes to the excited women, while a guard at the gate watched, smoked, and grinned.

When Charlie saw the German POWs, he moved closer to the outside fence and glared at some of the men, who stared silently back.

When Molly drew next to him he said, “They look like ordinary blokes.”

“I guess they had to fight for their country, too.”

“I s’pose. But that don’t mean I got to like ’em,” replied Charlie.

The darkness had long since fallen as they detoured around yet another bomb-strafed road. They had already passed numerous military checkpoints where the papers provided by Bryant had allowed them safe passage, but with each stop the scrutiny and questions had increased.

Oliver explained, “The closer we get to the coast, the nearer we come to some very sensitive military installations. The Home Guard maintains a heavy presence around here. And there are considerable coastal defences employed: trenches with field guns, anti-tank cubes, pillboxes, fields of concertina wire, and mines in the water, of course.”

“Fightin’ a war seems quite hard,” observed Charlie.

“And just imagine if all that ingenuity and money went into peacetime pursuits,” said Oliver, right as a soldier stepped into the road, blocking their way.

Oliver slowed and then stopped the car. He rolled down the window, his papers at the ready.

Another soldier joined the first one as they approached, their features tense, their weapons at the ready.

Oliver said, “These papers will explain everything.”

He handed them to one of the soldiers. He barely glanced at the papers before passing them back. “Got to turn around. No one’s allowed past here at the moment, not even Churchill.”

“But the papers—”

“Turn around. Now. Or else you’ll have a problem, sir.”

Molly leaned across Oliver and said, “My mother is a patient at the Beneficial Institute in Cornwall. She doesn’t have much longer to live. I must see her.”

“I’m very sorry about your ma,” said the other soldier sincerely. “But we have our orders. There’re military actions going on past this point.”

"Is there really no way we can be let by?" asked Oliver. "We've come all the way from London."

"Not unless you can convince us of your trustworthiness. And a bit of paper and a story about a dying mum ain't going to do that, mate," said the first soldier.

Molly sat back, looking helpless.

Oliver reached into his pocket and took something out. "Will this do?" He handed one of the soldiers his George Medal.

They both looked at it. "You got this?" said one.

"From the King, yes." He held out his ARP warrant card. "I'm an air warden. I . . . it was awarded for bravery. Though I was just doing my job, like you are."

"Well done, mate," said the soldier, handing it back. He looked through the window at Molly. "Lost my mum last year. Got leave, though, and said my goodbyes to her." He looked at the other soldier. "What do you think?"

The man shrugged and nodded.

"Okay, good luck to you then," said the first soldier, waving them on.

As they drove off, Oliver said, really to himself, "First time I'm happy I won that thing."

"We go left at the next road," said Molly, reading off the dim interior light.

Later, Charlie saw the signpost first.

"The Institute's that way," he said, pointing to the left.

"Indeed it is, Charlie, good eye," said Oliver.

They drove on as the rain started to fall.

Oliver said, "My word, the place is really right on the water. You can see the Channel over there through the trees. And just across the water is France."

"I heard 'a the White Cliffs of Dover," said Charlie. "I know they're on the Channel. My gran went there once on holiday and told me 'bout them."

"Yes, but they're clear on the other side of the country, south-east of London, across the Channel from Calais," replied Oliver. "It's said that every British soldier going off to fight looks back and sees the white cliffs as his last glimpse of home. And when he comes back it's his first sight of England."

"*If* he comes back," said Charlie curtly.

They reached an open gate set on stone posts, turned down the lane, and drove on. They rounded a bend, and sprawling before them was their destination.

The Beneficial Institute

"This place looks more like a medieval fortress than a restful retreat for those ailing," observed Oliver in surprise.

The full bulk of the Institute loomed up out of the dark—it was a structure of formidable scale.

They climbed out of the Singer and approached the door.

Molly suddenly said, "Wait, where are we going to stay for the night? We can't possibly drive back to London."

"We passed an inn on the road coming in here right on the outskirts of Falmouth. I'm sure we can get a couple of rooms there," said Oliver.

"But won't that be expensive?"

"Didn't I say? This entire trip is courtesy of the War Office. It was the very least they could do," he added bluntly.

Oliver knocked on the door, and it was opened by an elderly matron dressed all in white. They explained who they were. She nodded and said, "Dr. Stephens told me of your visit. Please come this way."

They followed her down a long stone hallway dimly lit with a string of bulbs. The interior was vast, high ceilinged, and also cold and uninviting, thought Molly. She could see why her mother had not rallied here. She pulled her coat tighter around her.

The matron rapped on a door marked OFFICE.

A soft voice said, “Enter.”

She opened the door and ushered them in to meet Dr. Thaddeus Stephens. He was a small man with white whiskers and rumpled hair. He was dressed in country tweeds with a bowtie that was a bit askew.

“Ah, Miss Wakefield, so good of you to come,” he said, shaking her hand. He turned to the others. “And you must be Ignatius Oliver,” he said, shaking his hand as Oliver introduced Charlie.

“May I please go and see my mother now?” said Molly.

“Yes, at once.”

He led them through a labyrinth of hallways, their footfalls echoing off the walls.

“This looks like an old castle or fortress,” noted Oliver.

Stephens nodded. “I believe that is exactly what it once was. Abandoned for a long time, but perfect for our patients. Peaceful and isolated. At least it was before the war,” he added in a grim tone.

He led them up a short flight of stone steps until they came to a room with a brass name holder.

Molly read off the name: ELOISE MARY WAKEFIELD. Molly hadn’t yet turned eleven when she’d last seen her mother. *Will she even recognize me?*

Stephens unlocked the door. That it would be locked surprised Molly, but she supposed it was for safety reasons.

He motioned them in.

Molly gingerly stepped over the threshold, as though she were about to enter a venue holding unpleasantness and even terror for her.

The room held a bed, a chair, a table, a lamp, and an old, battered armoire. Molly’s glances shot across the space and fixed on the large monogrammed steamer trunk set next to the armoire. She instantly recognized it as her mother's. It had been bought at Harrods. As a child she had loved to run her fingers along the stylishly threaded letters of her mother's initials.

Then Molly levelled her gaze on the person in the bed.

She blinked several times and still that did not seem to help. She looked at Oliver and Charlie, who were also staring at the woman.

Molly felt something touch her shoulder and she jumped.

Stephens advised, "Why don't you go sit by the bed, Molly? If you speak to her quietly and gently, she might rally a bit."

Molly crept over to the bed and sat down. She thought after Dr. Stephens's warning letter that she would be looking at an emaciated woman with a bony face clinging to life. But her mother looked bloated; her skin, instead of being pulled tight against her facial bones, seemed to float above them, like a full pond with submerged logs.

Eloise Wakefield's hair was shot thickly with grey, the beautiful auburn locks of Molly's childhood gone for ever. Even with the bloat, her mother's face was heavily lined, the etch work like whorls on fingertips. She appeared smaller than Molly remembered. But then Molly remembered that she had grown over seven inches in the interim, while her mother had not only not advanced a jot during that time, but seemed, instead, to have shrunk in stature.

She reached out and tentatively touched her mother's exposed hand. It was puffy and coarse looking, the nails irregular and jagged, nothing like the elegant, refined hand of Molly's youthful memories. And she found her mother warm, disturbingly so.

"Mummy? It's me, Molly."

Her mother's eyes did not open. They were periwinkle blue, and Molly had always loved those eyes.

"Mummy?"

The eyelids quivered now, then opened, closed, and opened once more, holding this time. The pupils drifted from side to side, reaching Molly then passing back before once more swinging to her daughter and then remaining on her.

Molly noted what looked to be crusted, reddened wounds that were present in the corners of both of her mother's eye sockets.

The smile emerged on her mother's face like a crack opening along an eggshell.

"Mummy? Do you recognize me? I'm Molly."

Never did Molly think she would have to introduce herself to her mother.

But the hand she was holding squeezed hers just a bit and her mother's mouth moved, though nothing came out at first. Then—

"M-Molly?"

"Molly, yes. It's Molly. I'm here, Mummy."

The smile broadened and spread across her face, the eyes lifted, the delicate cheekbones raised as the doughy, translucent skin receded a bit. A strand of hair drifted into her mother's face, and Molly moved it back into place.

And that was when she glimpsed the vertical scar near her mother's right temple. It pulsated thick, dark, and brutish against the pale skin.

She was brought back from staring at it when she felt a hand on her face.

She looked down and saw her mother's trembling fingers slowly drifting over her skin, like a blind woman Molly had once seen do to someone she had met for the first time.

But clearly her mother could see her.

"Molly?"

"Yes, your daughter, Molly. I'm here, Mummy." Tears formed in Molly's eyes and then drained down her cheeks. "I've missed you so much, Mummy. I love you so much."

"Missed . . . Molly."

And then the hand withdrew and the eyes closed and that, apparently, was that. Eloise Wakefield fell back asleep.

"She tires very easily, but she seemed quite happy to see you," Stephens said kindly. "I was quite astonished when she asked for you by name. She had not been . . . communicative in a long while."

Molly reluctantly let go of her mother's hand and rose. "That . . . scar at her temple? And those holes around her eye sockets?"

"Yes, yes, we can talk about all that later. I'm sure after your long journey you and your friends need a good night's rest."

"There's an inn near Falmouth that we passed," offered Oliver.

"Oh, no, we have a small cottage here on the grounds for visitors. You're welcome to it."

"Are you sure?" said Molly. "I would like to be as near to her as possible."

"I am very sure. We'll get you settled and, though the hour is late, you can meet my colleague, Dr. Foyle."

He led them out and locked the door behind him.

Molly said, "I wouldn't think she could get out of bed."

"We like to take precautions," said Stephens vaguely. "It is best to."

He led them back down the hall in silence.

The Procedure

Their rooms in the small cottage were utilitarian but clean. The simple meal they had in the staff room was flavourless and overcooked, but it relieved their hunger. They gathered in Dr. Stephens's office afterwards to meet with him and his colleague, Dr. Everett Foyle, who was exceptionally tall and lanky, with curly dark hair, and around forty.

Molly opened the discussion by saying, "She seems quite bloated, which suggests she's retaining fluids. Is there something wrong with the functioning of her kidneys?"

A surprised Foyle said, "You sound like you have medical training."

"I do, actually. I'm a nurse auxiliary at a clinic in London. And I performed nursing services at a hospital in Leiston before that."

"Remarkable," said Foyle, eyeing her intently.

Stephens said, "As I noted in my letter, your mother suffers from some difficult internal disorders."

"She also felt very warm. Is she feverish?"

Foyle shook his head. "It's merely a side effect of her treatments."

"Her eyes also seemed . . . off."

"Yes, we noted that, as we've noted it with other patients who have received treatments," said Foyle.

"So another side effect?" said Oliver tersely.

"Yes, that and the lethargy that you probably witnessed," said Foyle. "But that is preferable to the violent outbursts and uncontrollable seizures that she was exhibiting before."

Oliver looked at him with an expression that clearly said, *Is it?*

"And the scars on her temple?" Molly interjected.

Foyle spoke up again. "Your mother suffers from a complex social neurosis that has taken quite a toll on her. Procedures were done to alleviate the behaviour that such an affliction causes."

"What sort of behaviour?" asked Molly.

"Anger, primarily, as I alluded to just now. She was virtually uncontrollable when she first arrived here. Heavy sedation was required at first."

"What sorts of procedures?" asked Oliver.

Foyle looked at him. "Are you related to Miss Wakefield? Dr. Stephens did not mention."

"No, but I'm her friend."

Foyle made a show of turning to Molly. "The procedure is called a *leucotomy.* I refer to it as a *lobotomy.*"

"I've never heard of it," said Molly.

"Well, it was invented less than a decade ago and is a relatively progressive treatment in Britain. It is used with patients for whom other treatments have not worked. Sort of a last resort, as it were."

"And the scars I saw?" Molly asked again.

"They come from the procedure. I won't get into too much detail, but an incision is made and an instrument is then inserted to manipulate certain connections between the frontal lobes and the rest of the brain."

"Manipulate the *brain*?" said Oliver, looking astonished.

Foyle glanced sharply at him. "Yes. We believe much of the cause of our patients' debilitating issues lies in that arena. Once that connection is broken, the issue is resolved. At least that is the hope."

"And the wounds in the eye sockets?" said Molly.

"Very recently, an American chap pioneered something called the *transorbital* lobotomy. When I read of it, I was instantly intrigued, because it is far simpler and takes less time than a traditional lobotomy, as we work through the thin bones around the eye sockets."

"Isn't that painful?" said Molly.

"We use electroconvulsive therapy to induce a seizure that renders the patient unconscious before they undergo the operation."

"It is much preferred to the old method of administering cardiazol to induce seizures," interjected Stephens.

Foyle added, "And the procedure takes no more than twenty minutes. Quite straightforward."

Oliver looked at Stephens. "And you also perform these *operations*?"

Stephens looked taken aback. "Oh, no. Dr. Foyle brought these new methods to us."

"So all of this was done on my mother, and yet . . . ?" said Molly.

"Well, the success rate is not one hundred per cent, Miss Wakefield," said Foyle. "Far from it, in fact. And I'm afraid that your mother was not as responsive to the treatment as certain others have been."

"But she seemed lucid and calm when I saw her earlier."

"Yes, she has those periods," said Stephens. "Indeed, that is one of the benefits of the lobotomy. It makes people . . . calmer."

"So, is she *not* calm all the time?" asked Molly.

Stephens coughed and said, "That is why we lock the door."

"But why did you tell me that she is, well, practically speaking, not going to live much longer?" said Molly.

Stephens looked at Foyle, who said resignedly, "It has nothing to do with her mental issues, Miss Wakefield. She has an incurable disease in her kidneys. That's the principal reason she is bloated, because of the retention of fluids, as you so sagely noted. As these fluids build it puts enormous stress on other organs, including the lungs and the heart. It has reached a stage where no more medical treatments or procedures are possible to prolong her life."

Molly, Charlie, and Oliver sat there looking stunned.

Foyle said, "I'm very sorry, Miss Wakefield. We really did all we could. Now, I hate to rush off, but I have night rounds to make. I'm sure Dr. Stephens can address any further queries you might have. Again, thank you for coming. I'm sure your mother was very much pleased."

After he left, Molly turned to Stephens. "So how long does she have?"

Stephens looked uncomfortable at the bluntness of Molly's question. "I . . . I would say two weeks or so, if she doesn't take a dramatic turn."

Molly put a hand to her forehead and closed her eyes.

"I'm sorry, Miss Wakefield, we really did try to help her."

"I'm sure you did all you could." She glanced at Oliver before saying, "Has my father been by to see my mother recently?"

"No, he hasn't. That surprised me because he once came quite regularly, even with the disruption of war. But I did write as often as I could to keep him informed."

"I noticed that your letters stopped coming to our home," said Molly.

"Oh, yes, that's right. I received a cable from Mr. Wakefield that directed us to send any correspondence to an address in Scotland."

Molly shot Oliver a look. She said, "So he knows that my mother is dying?"

"Yes, at least he does if my letters reached him."

"Did some men from the government visit here?" asked Oliver.

"Yes, they did, as a matter of fact," said Stephens. "They asked about your father. I hadn't heard from him at that point for many months and told the men that. The cable from your father about the letters going to Scotland came *after* they had visited here." He paused and studied her. "Is there some *problem*?"

"Apparently, but that is not your concern. And how are things being paid for?"

"Your father gave us a large amount that has been more than

sufficient for her care. We should not require any further payment. But we have lost a great many of our nurses to the war effort. I do worry about our ability to adequately care for our patients going forward."

"I would like to help then," said Molly abruptly. "I can assist the nurses you do have."

Oliver said, "Molly, do you really think that's a good idea? I mean, what with your mother's condition? And with everything emotionally you must be going through right now?"

"It would provide something constructive for me to do, while I wait for my mother . . ."

Stephens said, "That is wonderfully generous of you. Thank you. Now, you all need to get some rest. Shall we reconvene tomorrow morning over breakfast?"

"At which time I would like to hear what you know about my wife," said Oliver.

Stephens looked at him sadly. "Yes, of course."

They walked to their cottage and gathered in the front room. Oliver studied Molly, who was sitting in a chair and staring down at her hands. "Molly, I'm so sorry."

"And my father is in Scotland? Is Major Bryant wrong and he's not a killer?"

"What?" exclaimed Charlie.

Oliver filled Charlie in about Molly's father. Then he turned to her and said, "They rarely get such things wrong."

Molly said, "I had hopes for something better for her. And him. But hopes don't always come true, do they?"

"No, they don't," said Oliver. "Especially now."

Another Way

Stephens had not been able to meet with them for breakfast, having been called away on some important matter, one of the matrons told them.

After they ate the frugal meal, Molly had once more donned the garb of a nurse's assistant as she followed Sister Lucille on her rounds. There could not have been a greater contrast between this place and the medical clinic in Covent Garden. The latter involved wounds of the flesh. The folks here suffered from maladies of the mind. And as terrible as the injuries were that she had seen at the clinic, the ravages of mental illness that Molly witnessed here left her stricken and dismayed.

The very first patient she assisted with had been an infantryman in His Majesty's Army. Bernard Hughes was twenty-three and had had munitions explode in front of him, both blinding him permanently and giving him shell shock to such a degree that he had tried to kill himself a dozen times in fits of nightmarish psychoses.

Sister Lucille told her that Hughes had undergone a number of *procedures.*

"But the poor man is gone and he's not coming back. You don't need to have a medical degree to see that, do you? He won't talk, he barely eats. He grunts. He has no energy. He's like an infant, except he's a man. Or was."

There were others who were the exact opposite of Bernard Hughes, screaming and chanting and hurling themselves at padded walls behind locked doors. They could only be administered to when burly orderlies restrained them and sedatives were administered. Still, one had tried to bite Molly as she sought to clean and bandage a bloody and ragged self-inflicted wound.

Later, Molly had just finished helping with another patient and was walking back to the staff room when a masked Dr. Foyle stepped out of a room. His gown was covered in blood, and he appeared quite dejected. Through the open doorway Molly glimpsed a body lying on a metal table with a sheet fully covering it. A nurse stood next to the newly deceased, looking stricken and helpless.

Foyle saw Molly, pulled the door closed, and said, "A difficult case."

"Yes, I can see," said Molly.

"There are no easy problems to solve here," Foyle said as he lowered his surgical mask and wiped some blood off his forehead.

"I'm sure not, Doctor."

"You've been seeing patients, I take it," he said, eyeing her uniform.

"Yes. I wanted to help however I could."

"It's so very kind of you." He looked at the closed doorway. "My father was a patient here."

"'Was'?"

"He . . . I tried my procedure. Unfortunately, it didn't work. He was in the army, you see."

"Surely he was too old to fight in this war."

"He fought in the *first* world war. A mortar round hit within thirty feet of him and he awoke to see a dozen of his mates blown to bits all around him. He survived, of course, but with serious injuries. The external wounds were eventually repaired. But the internal ones, the psychological ones, festered. As a child I remembered that he was always a bit odd after coming home. But then one day he didn't remember who I was. And, as the years passed, there were other strange episodes. Once he . . . took off his shoe and tried to eat it. I was quite a capable surgeon by then. But when my father suffered what he did, I changed my career path. I studied mental disease. I brought my father here because my mother insisted that I at least try. And I did, but to no avail. He had a seizure on the operating table that stopped his heart. He literally died in my arms."

"I'm so sorry, but I'm sure you did your best for him."

An awkward silence persisted for a few moments until Foyle stirred.

"I meant to ask you last night, but I wasn't sure how to broach it in front of everyone."

"Yes?" she said expectantly.

"To better help treat patients it's always important to understand their background, how they came by their disorders and the like. What can you tell me of your mother?"

"Didn't my father inform you of what had happened?"

"Not really. He just said she became violent and uncontrollable. He actually had to administer a sedative to her for the trip here."

Molly told Foyle about the incident at the bomb shelter.

"So she was . . . robbed and assaulted and, um . . . ?"

"Yes. Her clothes were torn . . . She apparently had been . . . She was, understandably, hysterical."

"I see. I am so sorry, but that explains a lot."

"It does?"

"That sort of mental trauma is like shell shock in a way. It does things to your mind. Terrible things. You can never seem to dig your way out of the hole the horrible event has placed you in. Your trust in humankind is also shattered. You see the world solely through the prism of that one awful experience. It becomes your obsession and impacts all aspects of your life. It is as though you can never see the good in people ever again."

"Poor Mother," said Molly. Her cheeks flushed, and tears rose to her eyes.

"I wonder why your father didn't tell us about it."

"I . . . I think he felt guilty for allowing it to happen."

"I see. Unfortunately, that is a common enough reaction. If I had known that, we would have offered *him* counselling as well. It sounds like he needed it."

"I wish he had."

Foyle slumped back against the wall and closed his eyes. "Do you know what I wish, Miss Wakefield?"

"I'm sure I don't know, Doctor."

He opened his eyes. "I hope that one day we come up with . . . another way to help people with illnesses such as your mother and my father."

"I share in that wish."

They both went back to work.

An End-of-Life Admission

While Molly had been performing her nursing duties inside, Oliver and Charlie had been working outside helping to maintain the grounds. Oliver had been told that Dr. Stephens had been abruptly called away to London on important business the morning after they arrived, and would not be back for several days.

He and Charlie also pushed convalescing patients around the paths in wheelchairs and, with the help of one of the groundskeepers, caught some fish from the Channel for dinner.

Charlie viewed that body of water in the daylight the first morning that he and Oliver stood by the shore. Seagulls swirled overhead, looking like bright bits of confetti risen to distant heights.

"As I said before, not that far across the water is France," said Oliver, pointing that way.

"Knew it was somewheres round here," replied Charlie, still looking amazed by this as he gazed out to sea.

"The region in France directly across from here is called, ironically, Brittany. It comes from the Latin, *Britannia*, which means 'Land of the Britons,' and, indeed, it shares a deep history with people from Britain, who settled there. I travelled through France while I was at Oxford, you see. A flutter abroad before the working world beckoned. Quite beautiful, and the food and the wine? Well, let me just say that it was something one does not normally experience on *this* side of the Channel."

They glimpsed the long, blunt snouts of artillery guns pointed to the sky up and down the coastline. And uniformed Home Guard and regular British Army personnel brandishing binoculars continually watched over the waters and skies. Far out in the Channel, British ships lurked, and at far higher altitudes than the seagulls, darted RAF planes.

As they worked away one afternoon on their fourth day here, Dr. Stephens came outside smoking a pipe, and he waved at Oliver, who was collecting some firewood in a wheelbarrow.

Stephens walked over to him and said, "I apologize for not having spoken to you about your wife before now. I didn't want to do so when you first arrived, and the last few days things have been terribly busy. I just got back from London, in fact. Our local MP thought it best if I travelled there and argued my case directly to the government. You see, we desperately need more resources, and as we care for a number of soldiers here I was trying to procure some public funds, and also some additional nursing assistance."

"Were you successful?"

"Unfortunately, no. There is apparently nothing to spare. People or pounds. So we'll just have to make do." Stephens motioned to a path that wound around the grounds. "Shall we take a stroll?"

Stephens took a puff on his pipe as they walked and said, "Imogen came to the Institute one day."

"So she specifically came here? Why?"

"She had heard of us, she said. There aren't many institutions that do what we do, Mr. Oliver. And our reputation is broad enough to have reached London. Indeed, I think that's how Molly's mother ended up here. Anyway, your wife said that a friend had spoken to her about us."

"I see."

"Imogen was troubled. She had, I think, a case of severe depression and she also suffered from undue anxiety. I met with her in my office. I gave her some aspirin to take, along with some meditative breathing exercises, and told her to take a holiday if she could while she was here. The sea air, that sort of thing, take her mind off things. I mean, she certainly wasn't a candidate for Dr. Foyle's procedures or anything. Completely in charge of her mental faculties. She just seemed . . . lost."

Oliver looked out to the Channel. "Do you usually see people who just walk in the door?"

"No—never, in fact. But your wife, well, she intrigued me. Remarkable for intelligence. But, if you don't mind my saying so, she clearly had her demons."

"And she jumped off a cliff somewhere around here, you mentioned?"

"Not somewhere," said Stephens surprisingly. He pointed with his pipe to a spot on the coast where the land rose high. "There."

Oliver looked where he was indicating and inwardly shuddered.

"We had several who saw her go up to that very spot. One person even tried to talk her down. But failed."

"Is that person still here?" said Oliver quickly.

"Yes, it was Dr. Foyle, actually. In fact, I have asked him to meet with you tonight to discuss it."

"I'm so sorry, I didn't make the connection with the name until Dr. Stephens mentioned it," said Foyle, as he and Oliver sat in the doctor's office. It was in the evening after a sparse dinner, and both men looked tired and strained.

"That's all right. But what can you tell me about that day?"

Foyle lit up a cigarette and offered one to Oliver, who declined.

"I actually never smoked until I got here."

"I can understand that," said Oliver.

Foyle picked a flake of tobacco off his tongue and sat forward, his long back bowed. "I had just finished a difficult surgery and was taking a walk, just to unwind a bit. I was heading up to the cliff—I like the view from there—when I saw her. There were several other people about, a nurse or two and a gardener. And a patient getting some air with her attendant. But I was the closest because she and I were heading to the same spot, apparently."

"What drew your attention to her?"

"I didn't recognize her, for one thing. And she was walking with such purpose. I've been dealing with mental issues for quite a while now. And I just read something in her body language that set off warning bells in my head. So I called out to her."

"What did she do?"

"She didn't stop, not at first. She walked right up to the edge of the cliff and then turned to look at me. She seemed coolly defiant, I guess you could say. I drew a bit closer and asked her who she was."

"What did she say?"

"She said she was a 'conscientious objector.' 'To what?' I asked her. 'You're a woman, you're not going to be called up to fight.'"

"And her response?"

"She said she wasn't objecting to the war, although she said she had very good grounds to do so. She said she was objecting to her . . . *existence*."

Oliver's expression became pained.

Foyle noted this. "Yes, quite. Not what you wanted to hear, I know." He paused and puffed thoughtfully on his cigarette before resuming. "I told her that I was medically trained in helping people like her and if she would come to my office I would do whatever I could to assist her."

"And?"

"And she thanked me, most graciously and most eloquently. But she said she was beyond redemption. That was the word she used, 'redemption.' Do you know what she meant by that?"

Oliver shrugged and slowly shook his head.

"And then she told me that if, let me think, right, she said if *Iggy* ever asked, that I should tell him he was the most wonderful thing her life had ever discovered. Quite an interesting way to phrase it. I assume that 'Iggy' was referring to you, Ignatius?"

"Yes, it was her pet name for me."

"She added that if there was any way she could have managed it, she would have gone back to him, or you, as it were. But she never found a way to do so that seemed . . . *equitable*, yes, that was the word she used." Foyle stopped and drew in a deep breath. "And then before I could say another word, or take a step towards her, she turned and . . . jumped. By the time I got to the edge, she had already reached the water." He paused and then added, "I will carry the guilt to my grave that I did nothing to stop her."

"Please don't. If not there, she would have simply chosen another time, another place. When her mind was made up, well . . ."

"Yes, she did strike me as being quite formidable in that way."

"Thank you, Dr. Foyle. Thank you very much."

Oliver went back outside, walked right to the cliff's edge, and looked down more than two hundred feet to where the frothing, rocky Channel was but one fatal step away.

He took a deep breath, filling his lungs with the salty air. In that motion he tried to imagine absorbing the last bits of Imogen's life as she stood here, making perhaps the most difficult decision a person could make. Or maybe the simplest—he didn't know, really.

He could see, in her state of mind, how she could have jumped out into nothing, plummeting down, perhaps just staring out at the sky, her very last glimpse of light and life. And then hitting the water and rocks below at such violent velocity that her end would have come before her mind ever had a chance to tell her it was over and done.

Yes, he could see how anyone might do that, given the right circumstances.

Even me, without my Imogen.

But then Oliver took a symbolic step back when the images of Molly and Charlie entered his mind. It was simply a question of being needed, really. Imogen apparently thought that he could get along perfectly well without her. Oh, how she had overestimated him.

But with Molly and Charlie there was no question.

They need me. Imogen chose death. I must choose life. And, truth be known, I need them.

Oliver turned around to find Foyle standing rigidly only a few feet away.

"I didn't see you there," said Oliver.

"I just followed along, at a discreet distance."

Oliver looked back at the cliff for a moment. "You weren't thinking that . . . ?"

"I was just making sure, that's all. You see, I didn't want to commit the same blunder twice. Once was already far too much."

The men stared across the short distance at each other.

"I appreciate that," said Oliver.

"I have some prewar Armagnac back in my quarters, if you're so inclined. Roman grapes, Celtic barrels, and Moorish stills. I find it soothes most of life's ills, at least for an hour or two. And what more can anyone reasonably expect during times like these?"

The men walked back to the Institute together.

A Dream Gone Miserably Awry

George Eliot's illustrious novel *Middlemarch* was in the Institute's small library. After her dinner each evening, Molly would go to her mother's room and read to her from it. Eloise Wakefield would wake occasionally, recognize her daughter, and say quietly, "Molly luv."

Molly would smile, take her hand, and make soothing sounds to her mother. She would also tell her mother about her time in the country and then in London. She did not tell her of the fate of their old home, or of Mrs. Pride's death, or of the dire situation with her husband. Molly did not have to be learned in the field of mental illness to know that such revelations would not be beneficial for her mother.

Molly also had looked through the things her mother had brought with her, or more likely the items her father had packed for his wife—he was always inclined to oversee tasks like that. In the bottom of the armoire Molly found a picture of her and her mother that she had forgotten about. It had been taken at Hyde Park before the war. They were on a bench looking happy and content. Although, as Molly peered closer into her mother's stilled eyes, she saw perhaps a degree of apprehension that she had never before perceived.

Maybe because I didn't want to see it.

Molly had put the photo in a frame she found and placed it on the table next to her mother's bed. If her mother saw it, Molly reasoned, it might make her . . . remember happier times. It was a simple contrivance, but one never knew. And at this stage Molly would do anything to ease her mother's final days.

"I think she's actually getting better," she told Charlie and Oliver one afternoon. "Do you think it would be possible . . . ?" She halted and looked at them uncertainly.

"What?" said Oliver.

"I was just wondering if it would be completely ridiculous to think about bringing her back to London to spend what time she has left there."

"But where would she stay, Molly?" said Oliver.

"She could use our room and I could sleep on the floor in the bookshop," offered Charlie.

Molly said quickly, "Charlie, I could never ask you to do that."

Oliver said, "And surely she needs hospital care, Molly. And then there's the question of transporting her. We can't simply load her into the car and drive her back."

Molly looked defeated, but then her expression changed. "I think I might have an idea." She rushed off.

Later that evening Molly found Oliver and Charlie and told them what she had managed. "I had Dr. Stephens make some enquiries and he found a telephone number for the Tinsdales in Yorkshire."

"Excuse me, the Tinsdales?" said Oliver.

"Rich relatives of Molly's up north," explained Charlie.

"Yes. They're my mother's family and they *are* quite wealthy. I don't think they've been in touch for many years. Anyway, it took the poor operator three tries, but finally I spoke to Lucretia Tinsdale, Mum's second cousin or something like that. They remembered Mum very well. They had no idea what was going on with her, didn't even know she was still alive. They were extremely concerned when I told them about her condition. And they have agreed to help with her care and also in getting her back to London."

"Why, that's wonderful," said Oliver.

"She could be in hospital in London and I could care for her there. And there might be some treatment for her kidneys. I thought I would go and tell Mum now. Do you want to come with me?"

Charlie said, "I will."

But Oliver said, "I don't want to overwhelm her with my presence."

"All right. We'll talk later."

"Well done, Molly," said Oliver.

Molly had been given a key by Dr. Stephens. She unlocked the door and they went into her mother's room.

Molly drew close to the bed and said, "Mum, I've got the most wonderful news. We're going to take you back to London. And your family, the Tinsdales, are going to help. Isn't that so splendid?" Molly smiled at Charlie, bent down, and gripped her mother's hand.

Eloise Wakefield's eyes popped open and the person revealed behind them was not one with whom Molly was remotely familiar.

The scream resonated down the hallway. Eloise sat bolt upright, grabbed Molly's hair and began pulling and twisting it. She then slapped and punched at Molly, knocking her down.

Molly screamed and said, "Mum, stop, it's me, Molly."

Her mother formed no words. She only grunted and shouted nonsense. Then she saw the framed photo and threw it at Charlie.

Charlie ducked and then jumped back as a punch she aimed at him barely missed. He grabbed Molly's hand and pulled her up from the floor. They ran for the door, got through it, and shut it behind them.

Molly frantically locked the door, as more screams emanated from the room. Molly, her hands over her ears, ran down the hall, tears streaming down her face.

"I'm not sure what I was thinking," Molly said in a trembling voice. She was sitting on her bed at the guest cottage with Oliver and Charlie and Drs. Foyle and Stephens all standing around her. After leaving her mother's room she had found Dr. Foyle and a matron, and they had rushed to her mother's room.

"She has fits like that, Molly," said Stephens. "Not often. Most of the time she is totally calm and placid. But something triggers her and then off she goes."

"She was hitting and punching me and screaming. She looked like she hated me."

Foyle added gently, "I seriously doubt she even recognized it was you, Molly."

"The human mind is an extraordinary instrument," said Stephens. "It is the thing that makes us unique amongst all living things. But because of that when it goes bad, it goes terribly, terribly bad, I'm afraid."

"Has she—is she better now?"

"She has been sedated so she won't hurt herself," said Foyle. "She is resting comfortably."

"I suppose I should ring the Tinsdales and let them know that Mum won't be going to London."

"I think she does need to stay here, Molly," said Stephens. "Until . . . She will be well cared for, I promise you."

"And there will be no more procedures," added Foyle. "Of any kind."

They all left, leaving Molly on her bed, alone.

She slowly took off her necklace and opened the locket, revealing her mother's picture inside. She needed to look at it now because she did not want the image of the raving woman back there to be the last one she had of her mother before she went to sleep tonight.

If *I go to sleep tonight.*

When she finally did start to nod off, she held the locket tightly against her chest.

No matter where I go, you will be right here with me, Mum.

The Final Tear

Molly did not see her mother the following day, or the day after that. She was quite fine now, she had been told by both Foyle and Stephens. Yet every time she ventured near that door, the horror of that encounter welled up in Molly's path, blocking her from moving forwards.

Perhaps I am acquiring my own neurosis.

The suffering of the patients here was truly extraordinary. Molly could never see herself working in this field. There was no real medicine that would help. Only apparently sticking sharp instruments into the soft tissues of the brain. And while that might ease some of their violent symptoms, it often subtracted everything of importance from the person, leaving something less than human.

For her, being a doctor meant the ability to heal, not merely relegating patients to a purposeless stupor. Her mother was doomed, she knew that, and Molly had, to the extent any child could, accepted that fate. But that was not the same as understanding it to be right or fair. It was neither.

I can't help these poor people. Apparently none of us can.

Two nights later Molly found that she couldn't sleep. She rose, put on her robe, and used her key to get into the Institute. She walked down to her mother's room with the thought of just watching the woman sleeping peacefully for a bit.

But when she got there she found the door open and her mother gone.

Molly looked wildly around for someone to alert, but found no one about. She ran back to the cottage and rousted Oliver and Charlie from their sleep. They quickly dressed and rushed outside.

"I thought they locked her door," said Oliver.

"I did too," replied Molly. "But it was open."

"She must still be inside the Institute," he said. "She was surely too weak to make it outside. I'm surprised she made it out of her room unassisted."

"What's that noise?" exclaimed Charlie.

They listened and heard what sounded like a door closing.

They ran to the rear of the building.

When they got there the first thing they saw was an empty wheelchair next to a small grey two-door sedan.

Her mother was sitting in the passenger seat looking placidly out the windscreen.

And someone else was with her.

"Father!" screamed Molly.

Herbert Wakefield turned to look at her.

He looked old, far older than she remembered. He was thin, she observed, unhealthily so. He was dressed in a three-piece suit. His hair was nearly all white and punished by the stiff wind.

He looked at her in bewilderment.

She took a tentative step forwards. "Father, it's me, Molly."

"My God," he said. "Molly?"

She took another step towards him.

"I came to visit Mum." She glanced at her mother. "Where are you going with her?"

He looked over his shoulder at his wife. "I . . . she needs to leave this place. We both do. It's . . . um . . . government business. All hush-hush. I'm sorry I couldn't tell you. Official secrets and all that."

"Father, you can't do this. You mustn't do this."

"I tell you, it's official business. I'm taking your mother to a . . . a safe place."

"I know, Father. I know everything."

"Do you now?" he replied sharply, his features hardening.

"Yes. You *killed* British soldiers."

"You know what *they've* told you, I imagine." He gestured angrily to Oliver. "But not my side of things."

"Now you can have your say."

"And would it make any difference to you, child?"

"You're my father," she said simply. "And I deserve an explanation." He seemed taken aback by this and Molly decided to push ahead. "Why did you never bring me home?"

"Home to what? A barmy mum and a murderous father?"

"But I came home anyway. The money wasn't being paid and even though the Coopers would have kept me on, I wanted to come back to you and Mother."

"The bastards froze all of my accounts," raged Wakefield. "The same bastards who could not bring themselves to even look for the disgusting filth who attacked your mother. But no, they had the time to take my money, to watch my house, to open my letters. Do you wonder why I never wrote to you?"

"Why didn't you?"

"I couldn't have them think you were somehow aiding me, looking for secret codes in my letters. No, I wouldn't do that to you, Molly."

"Mrs. Pride told me what happened to Mother at the shelter."

"She didn't know everything. I couldn't bring myself to tell her."

"What do you mean?"

"The men who attacked her? They were *our* soldiers. Your

mother finally calmed enough to tell me what had happened. She was looking for me after we became separated in the crowd. They offered to help. The next thing, they were in a small dark room beating her, robbing her, doing . . . doing God knows what else to her." He stopped and let out a sob. "The bobby on the beat couldn't have cared less," he added more calmly. "Not to be bothered. Had far too much to do to spend time helping a woman who had been *savaged*."

Molly now could understand why her mother flew into a rage at the sight of the uniformed Mr. John, or the postman or milkman.

"I'm so sorry, Father, so very sorry."

"But I worked for the government. I risked my life for my country. So I *knew* I could get justice for her. I knew that we were a good people! I went all the way to Scotland Yard, with all the facts, and even one of the men's names because your mother had seen it on his uniform. They could have rounded them all up easily. And you know what they told me?"

"What?" said Molly tensely.

"That war was hard on the *boys*. He implied that they were just lads being lads. Surely Mrs. Wakefield could understand that. And if they were arrested for their crimes that would be three fewer men fighting Hitler. And if the press got wind of it? Well, that would be bad for morale, wouldn't it? We couldn't have that, could we?" He paused and rubbed at his face, smearing the tears there. "The assistant commissioner told me to get her some chocolates, and some flowers, and things would be as right as rain. Why hurt the lads fighting for their country? And after all it was her word against theirs." He looked to the dark sky. "Chocolates and flowers," he said numbly. "And then apparently she would be *right as rain*."

He turned and pointed to his wife and screamed, "What about *her* hurt? She hasn't had one minute's peace since then. Not one!" He stopped talking and slumped against the car, completely spent, it seemed. After a few moments he said, "Your mother dug down and somehow found the courage to tell me what had happened to her that night. And as soon as she was done, do you know what I saw?"

Molly couldn't form words for a reply. She could only shake her head, her expression fearful of what was to come.

"I saw the light of your mother's life go right out of her. I saw the woman that I loved more than anything vanish right in front of me. Any trust, any faith that she might have had in others, was . . . gone. For ever." He turned to look at his wife, who was still staring placidly out the windscreen. "And this . . . is all that is left of a good and kind person."

Molly, Charlie, and Oliver could only stare helplessly at the stricken man.

"So if the police wouldn't look for those men, then I would, and did. For years I did. I used all the skills and contacts I had acquired while working for my country. I talked to people at the shelter that night. I followed up leads. I even found the room where they dragged her, and took fingerprints and had a friend check them against records of the enlisted. I ran down every clue I could. It took a long time, but I finally found them, one by one."

"And then?" asked Molly in a tremulous voice.

Her father's features hardened to flint. "I assumed the role of judge and jury. I recounted to them all the evidence I had gathered. I asked them how they pled. They snivelled and cowered and begged for their lives. But not a single one apologized, not even when I showed them pictures of your mum, of what she had become. Not a single damn one. They were only interested in saving their own miserable skins. They cared nothing for her. If any of them had admitted guilt, had shown the least bit of remorse—" he let out a long, tired breath "—I would have spared them. But they didn't, and so I didn't. I killed them, and I would do so again, without hesitation."

Molly teared up with this admission. "Surely, there had to be another way, Father."

"There was no other way, child. This was all I had left, to do justice for your mother."

"How did you get past all the checkpoints?" Oliver asked.

"I was wearing a British uniform filled with medals. Medals I earned, by the way, serving a country that abandoned me and her in the hour of our need." He turned back to Molly. "I took the uniform off before I got here. I will put it back on after I sedate your mother, because she can't stand the sight of a man in uniform, and can anyone blame her? That and forged papers go a long way," added Wakefield.

"And now?" Molly exclaimed. "Where are you taking her?"

"I've made arrangements. A boat is waiting to take us someplace . . . safe. Where we can live in peace for the time we have left."

"Mother is not well."

"I know she's dying. And my life is also over, but I refuse to swing at the end of a rope for killing men who should have been in prison, or worse."

"And you?"

"I failed your mother before . . . I can't leave her to die alone." He glanced sharply at Oliver, and, seeming to think he represented all of the British government, shouted, "Oh, to hell with you!"

Wakefield put his hand on the car door. "Now, we need to go. I . . . I'm sorry about all of this, Molly. Truly, I am."

Oliver stepped forwards. "I'm afraid we can't let you do this, Mr. Wakefield."

Wakefield produced a small pistol from a pocket and pointed it at Oliver, who quickly stepped back. "I think *you* have no say in the matter."

Oliver took another step back but Molly moved forwards. "This will not set things right, Father. And please, don't leave me alone. I . . . I need you. Please." The tears spilled down her cheeks.

Herbert Wakefield slowly shook his head. "I'm sorry, Molly." He added in a kindly tone, "You have your life to live, and I wish it everything you want it to be. You have always been quite exceptional. But my life . . . your mother's life . . . is nearly done."

At that moment they heard sirens blaring and powerful engines racing their way.

"Damn!" cried out Wakefield. He slid into the car and started the engine.

"Father, no!" screamed Molly. "Don't go! Please!"

The sound of her daughter's voice finally seemed to reach Eloise Wakefield. Right as her husband put the car in gear, she looked over at Molly, then saw her husband. She opened the door and toppled out of the car. Wakefield put the car in reverse and made a grab for her but missed.

"Eloise!" he screamed.

Charlie and Oliver raced over to Eloise Wakefield and pulled her safely away from the automobile.

Wakefield looked like he was going to get out of the car and attempt to pull her back in. Instead, he sped off. A moment later he had to steer right to avoid the police cars roaring into the drive, sirens blaring. The police cars turned around to follow him, and the three cars disappeared into the darkness, the jarring sound of the sirens further fracturing all of their nerves.

Molly and the others jumped when they heard the gunshots. Then there came the sound of a horrific crash and, a few seconds after, an explosion. A column of flames leapt into the air, lighting the night.

A sobbing Molly wrapped her arms protectively around her dazed mother.

"You're okay, Mum. You're safe."

Goodbye, for Now

Late December 1944 was cold and blustery in London, which meant it was quite normal weather for that time of year.

Eloise Wakefield had died three nights after the encounter with her husband. They had learned that the police had tracked Herbert Wakefield to the Beneficial Institute, and he had been killed in the ensuing chase.

Molly had been holding her mother's hand as she passed away peacefully.

Seeing her father at the end, and learning that he had killed those men, had shocked Molly. At one level she could understand why he had done what he had. At another level, she could never forgive him. With the deaths of both her parents so close together, she had been left bereft. If it hadn't been for Oliver and Charlie's love and support, Molly knew she could not have survived the twin losses. Still, she had cried so much that when she was done, Molly doubted she had any tears left to shed. Ever.

The Tinsdales, after a call from Molly, had arranged for her parents' bodies to be brought back to London, where they were buried, with Molly, Charlie, and Oliver in attendance after returning from Cornwall.

Later, Molly had travelled north to see the Tinsdales for Christmas. After she returned, she told Oliver and Charlie that the Tinsdales would support her university education.

"They're actually very nice and were quite welcoming to me. I mean, really, I'm a perfect stranger, but they made me feel quite at home. And they're really all the family I have left now."

"You're fortunate to have found them, as they are to have found you," commented Oliver.

There was never any question of Molly's actually going to live with the Tinsdales. She had made it clear that she intended to live with Oliver and Charlie and continue her work as a nurse auxiliary for the remainder of the war.

Charlie was still a telegram messenger, and he was very busy because it seemed that the long and torturous war would be ending soon, and folks were anxious for life to return to normal. Sending season's greetings and well wishes and inflated hopes via telegram seemed to be the ticket. Charlie certainly preferred those to delivering death notices.

The bombings had tailed off considerably, and the newspapers and the BBC broadcasts were filled with the news of one Allied victory after another. The mood in London was much better, although Germany had unleashed more V-2 rocket attacks against select targets in Britain and Europe, but not with the widespread devastation wrought by the traditional carpet bombing raids.

For a while Oliver had gone to the study every day in hopes of finishing Imogen's book, but now, having been to the spot where she had ended her life, it seemed that his creative spirit was even more blighted than before. Finally, he simply stopped going.

On New Year's Eve, they gathered with their fellow Londoners to welcome in the year 1945 with the hopes of peace soon to be ahead.

Walking back to The Book Keep after the festivities, Oliver had said, "Molly, while you now have the Tinsdales, I guess we are each other's families, too."

Molly said, "You both are my *first* family; the Tinsdales are quite a distant second. But please don't tell them I said so." She smiled embarrassedly. "I do so want to go to university."

Oliver said, "And you, Charlie, what dreams have you when this madness is over?"

"I liked seein' that water in the Channel. I mean, I seen water before, in the Thames. But that don't really go nowhere. The Channel now, what comes after that, well, it makes you think about thin's."

"You could become a world traveller," said Molly. "And write about it."

Charlie broke into a smile, a rare thing for him. "Even if I'm the only one that reads it." He glanced at both of them. "It was the worst thin' ever to lose my family. But it woulda been a lot worse if I hadn't met the both of you. I don't think I woulda made it but for that."

"I don't think any of us would have," added Molly.

Oliver said, "Sometimes it simply comes down to the serendipity of whom one meets *and* when."

"Is that Imogen or Ignatius speaking?" asked Molly.

"It's a bit of both actually," he replied with a generous smile. "And isn't that a wonderful thing?"

The days continued to turn cold and bitter. During the evenings they would sit in The Book Keep, Molly reading, Charlie scribbling furiously in a third journal, having filled the first two, and Oliver going over the shop accounts and doing the *Times* crossword.

When the air raid siren sounded in late January, they all looked up from what they were doing. Oliver already had on his uniform and was about to commence his patrol. Charlie and Molly bustled into their winter coats, and they all hurried outside.

At the front door of The Book Keep Oliver said, "Now, go to the usual shelter. I doubt it will be much. The Germans are running out of things to chuck at us. I'll join you there in a jiffy."

They had parted ways and Oliver met up with Lee Parker. The two wardens compared their lists, checked the shelters, and found four people missing. They split that number and set off in opposite directions.

Deep in the basement of a warehouse near the river, Molly and Charlie sat next to each other. It was quite cold down here, but experience told them that the comingled body heat of all the folks here would soon rectify that.

"Do you think it will be bad tonight?" asked Molly.

"Dunno. Last few times it ain't been."

"Do you really think you'll leave England, Charlie, after the war's done?"

"I never been out 'a London, 'cept when we went to Cornwall. I might like to see some of the world before I die."

"You have a long way to go before then."

At that very moment an explosion rocked nearby.

Molly reached out a hand and closed it around Charlie's. He squeezed back.

"It'll be okay."

Molly nodded, but she didn't look like she believed him.

The next blast struck closer and with stunning power. The ceiling above creaked and groaned, and the huge wooden posts holding it up seemed to shiver.

"V-2s," said Charlie knowledgably. "No hum or buzz, with the planes comin' and the bombs fallin'."

Molly nodded. She knew Charlie was extremely knowledgeable about such things.

Another blast hit, even closer, and dust and crud and bits of the place fell on top of them. Some screamed; others scrambled to find cover when there was really none to be had.

Charlie held tight to Molly, and they bent lower as the panicked wails of little children filled the now-smoky space.

"They say these V-2 rockets fly by radio beam," Charlie said in an even, calm voice. "We try to block that signal. And we got pretty good at it."

Molly knew he was doing this to take her mind off what was going on. She appreciated this gesture, but it did nothing to rid her of the terror she was feeling.

"Yes, I heard something like that, too," she said tremulously.

"It'll be okay, Molly, really. We've made it this far."

Another explosion hit so close that one wall of the vast room partially collapsed, pushing dust and dirt and shattered wood in a tidal wave towards them.

Everyone ran from the destruction.

As they huddled against the far wall, with all looking anxiously upwards at the tons of material sitting precariously above them, Molly said quietly, "It just feels different this time, Charlie."

Charlie stared at the ceiling that seemed to be giving way bit by bit.

It does *feel different this time*, he thought.

As Oliver ran along the streets he didn't bother to look up. There was nothing to see. No planes, no howls from Jericho's Trumpets. This was clearly a V-2 rocket attack. It was only metal machines coming to kill them, no flesh-and-blood pilots and navigators and bombardiers required. And you would never see or hear them coming. Like his friend Major Bryant had said, you'd be dead before you even knew you were no longer living.

He had one more couple on his list to find. He pounded on the door of their home. "Mr. and Mrs. Perkins. You must come. Quickly now. Please."

A blast hit somewhere nearby, and Oliver looked up to see a building collapse. He put his shoulder to the door and knocked it in, toppled through, and shoved the door shut behind him as the concussive wave from the blast swept across the street and blew out the front windows of the house. However, the door had not fully closed, and it was hit with incredible force. Oliver was lying on the floor with his feet against the door, but it was blown open so powerfully that he was propelled across the room, where he smacked into a dining room table.

"Mr. and Mrs. Perkins!" He staggered upright and looked in every room. No one was there. He ran back out into the streets and hustled towards the shelter. He had seen plumes of smoke and fire, and they were coming from the very building where Charlie and Molly were sheltering. Another direct hit there, and they would be done for.

They are going to survive this bloody awful war if I have any say about it.

He redoubled his efforts to reach them. He would take them and the others to a safer location. He turned the corner right as a V-2 rocket struck at that exact spot.

A Legacy Given

"He left the both of you The Book Keep," the man in a sombre brown suit, and with a handlebar moustache, said as he looked over the typed papers.

Seated in the study, Molly and Charlie stared dully at the man, who was Ignatius Oliver's solicitor, as he went over the contents of Ignatius Oliver's last will and testament.

Molly stirred. "He did?"

"Yes, in equal shares. When you come of age, it will be deeded in your names. There was also the payment from a life insurance policy he had. It will be sufficient to keep the shop going and to help with your expenses."

"When did he do this?" Molly asked.

"On the day after Boxing Day. He came to me and said it was what he wanted. He said he never wanted either of you to fear you would not have a home."

"That was so very kind of him," she said, while a teary Charlie nodded in agreement.

The lawyer said sombrely, "It was quite sad, what happened. They said he was just a minute or so away from safety. The serendipity of life is quite . . . odd."

Molly said, "Yes, yes, it is."

She then closed her eyes and tried to force her mind to shut down because she simply could not process having lost her friend for ever.

Charlie simply gazed at the Crown typewriter.

The funeral service had been a very private one. Major Bryant was there, as were a few other government types. Some fellow booksellers and a couple of Oliver's friends from Oxford were also in attendance. So was Oliver's older brother, Francis, who looked like his younger brother but didn't have his gentle kindness and empathetic spirit. However, he had told them that he loved his brother very much and that Ignatius had written him about them, and that if they ever needed anything, he would help them however he could.

He had shaken both their hands, glanced at his brother's coffin, and then gone back to his home in Glasgow.

Major Bryant had spoken with Molly afterwards. "I wanted you to know that while I cannot condone what your father did, the three soldiers he killed were a terribly bad lot. They had been involved in thefts and other attacks on both men and women, and were about to be court-martialed."

"And yet the police would do nothing?"

"Heads have rolled, Molly, from the bobby on the beat all the way up to Scotland Yard."

"Then some good came of it," she said.

Bryant glanced back at the coffin. "It's an awful loss, both personally and for the country. He was an air warden when he should have been working on other things for the war effort. He would have made a name for himself, I can tell you that. In his field he had few peers."

"And what field was that exactly?" she asked. He looked at her stonily and she added, "Right, you can't tell me."

"Sorry, goes with the territory, I'm afraid."

"So why didn't he work on these other things?" she asked.

"He would have been separated from Imogen. He couldn't do that."

"He must have loved her very much to have given up his dreams for her."

"You know, they were the oddest couple at Oxford. She was all fire and fury, with ideas that broke through all societal norms. And Ignatius was calm and quiet and—"

"Opposites sometimes do attract," Molly pointed out.

"Quite so."

"He certainly always spoke highly of her. And forgave her quite a bit."

Bryant coughed and looked around at the others.

"Don't worry, I will give away no secrets, Major," said Molly. "I only wish that Mr. Oliver had realized how very special he was, too."

"Yes, well. He was just not the sort to dwell on himself."

"But *his* memory will be carried forward through us."

"You really are quite mature beyond your years, Molly."

"And I am quite fortunate indeed to have known Ignatius Oliver."

After the burial, Molly and Charlie sat in the study, with a small fire warming them.

"When do we go to Yorkshire?" he asked.

Arrangements had been made for them to move to Yorkshire and live with the Tinsdales for the foreseeable future.

"Next week, by train. It's all confirmed."

"Are you sure they want me?" said Charlie.

"They are very sure. And if you don't go, I won't go."

He looked at the fire. "It feels quite odd bein' here without him."

"It will always feel that way, I suppose. He *was* this place, really. You can't imagine one without the other."

"He was truly a good bloke."

"I wish I had told him something," said Molly.

"What?"

"He always talked about how brilliant Imogen was, so much smarter than he, so much cleverer at everything, really. And while he and I talked some about that habit of his, I wish I had told him far more often that he was quite extraordinary, too." She looked earnestly at Charlie. "What do you think?"

"He had to make it look like he was workin' for the Jerries when he was really workin' for us. That's quite tricky. He was really brave, with all he done, the air warden bit and everythin'. I mean, I guess it was brave for Imogen to jump off that cliff. I never coulda done it. But . . . I think it was braver to stay here and keep tryin' to do the right thin'. Like Mr. Oliver done."

"I think you said it far more eloquently than I could, Charlie."

"And he knew that you felt that way 'bout him, Molly. He really did. We loved each other. Only thin' that kept us goin' was that. We didn't have nobody else."

She sighed and looked at the Crown typewriter with the blank page.

"So's we can come back here when we're older?"

"Yes," Molly said. "This is our home, Charlie."

Home Once More

Molly was seated in the study of The Book Keep. It was a fine spring evening with a warming breeze and a mostly cloudless sky. During the war people in London would be looking anxiously to the skies for German bombers on such a lovely night. But now it was just a fine time to be alive.

She was writing a letter using her father's old Conway Stewart pen. She loved the flow of the instrument and the elegance of the ink bleeding onto stiff paper.

She was now fifty-one years old, divorced, and the mother of a son and a daughter, one still at uni, and one who had graduated and was now working at a museum in Amsterdam. Her hair was cut shorter and fashioned in the style of the day. It held more than a touch of grey that she was debating covering up. That decision seemed trivial and absurd after what she had faced during the war. But that was also what made it wonderful to be able to contemplate. Her face was fuller and her frame about two stone heavier than during the war. She was in good health, and the recent jettisoning of her faithless husband had been the best decision she'd made in the previous decade.

She was a fully qualified clinical psychiatrist with a thriving practice, an excellent reputation, numerous scholarly papers, and two medical textbooks to her credit.

She knew that she had chosen this particular field because of what had happened to her mother. Dr. Foyle had desperately wanted something better with which to treat troubled patients. And now Molly and other healthcare professionals had a spectrum of medications to prescribe to those in their care. Sometimes they didn't work; sometimes they did more harm than good. But they were all better and far more humane than poking sharp metal objects into fragile brains.

She understood her mother's condition now. Her psychoses probably could have been managed with modern-day medications and professional counselling. Unfortunately, her mother's condition had occurred too early for those types of remedies. But Molly's current patients benefited from them and from her training and empathic bedside manner, which, as a nurse long ago had told her, was half the battle.

She finished the letter, slid it into an envelope, sealed it, and wrote an address on it.

It was a missive to the Tinsdales. They had been so very kind to her all this time, and she kept in close contact with the family, whom she had visited many times over the intervening years. Molly set the letter aside and looked at the finished manuscript that sat on her desk. She next focused on the names of the two authors of the book set forth on the title page.

Imogen Oliver and Molly Danvers.

This novel seemed as far from her medical writings as possible, but perhaps not. It *was* full of psychology, the human condition, in the most traumatic of times. People did not typically need her help when suitably happy with their lives. They needed her skills when the opposite occurred, as it so very often did in life.

Molly had barely revised the first portion of the novel written by Imogen decades prior. It turned out the dead woman had been a more naturally gifted writer than Molly, but the second half of the novel had more than held its own in the storytelling, at least her agent had told her that. And there were several reputable publishers currently formulating serious offers to purchase the rights to the story.

Out in the shop she heard the bell tinkling and customers coming and going. She had two very good people helping in the shop, and it had prospered over the years.

She rose, opened the door, and stared out into the bookshop area as a half dozen customers looked over various volumes, while a queue of others were having their purchases rung up and bagged at the counter. She had retained much of the untidiness from Ignatius Oliver's days, and customers seemed to like that attribute as they explored the stacks and crevices for new literary treasures.

She also had a special section of the works of George Sand, with not a single one missing any pages.

Molly closed the door, walked back over to her desk, and looked at the framed picture of Charlie and his family that was placed there. He lived in Australia now, where he had a ranch. As a young man he had travelled the world via freighters, trains, and planes, written down all that he saw and experienced, and he was the only one who read a word of it. He now had five children, and his wife, Meredith, was very kind and welcoming. Molly had been to visit once, and Charlie had even taught her how to ride a horse while she was there.

She had been terrified, her heart thudding in her chest, but in his calming voice, which had changed only slightly from his youth, he had said all the right things to carefully wean her from the panic. Even though he lived so far away, she could not imagine him not being a part of her life. He was the godfather to her son, and she was godmother to his oldest daughter. They spoke on the phone at least once a week.

She looked around the confines of the study. It hadn't changed much. Oh, some of the furniture had worn out and been replaced over the years. But the desk was the same, as was the uncomfortable chair. The Crown typewriter was on a shelf now and had been replaced by an IBM Selectric II typewriter. Molly tended to type too fast and the Crown's keys would gnash, like rheumatic fingers all in a dither.

But every time she opened the door and stepped in here, it was like creeping cautiously back into the war years. She could still see Ignatius Oliver hunched at the desk, the smell and haze of a meagre coal fire lingering in the room like a thin fog.

There were several graves to visit in the city and she did so regularly. Her mother and father, Charlie's mother and grandparents, and Ignatius Oliver. He was buried at Kensal Green Cemetery. Her parents were also buried there, and Molly herself had a plot there for when her time came. She was a fan of G. K. Chesterton's poetry and had tearfully quoted from "The Rolling English Road" at Oliver's funeral:

For there is good news yet to hear, and fine things to be seen,
Before we go to Paradise by way of Kensal Green.

If Oliver had not come along when he had, Molly was certain that her and Charlie's lives would have turned out very differently, and not for the better. It wasn't so much the decisions you made, it was simply who you stumbled into while you were trying to work out important matters. Run into one person instead of another, and one's future could be completely altered, as Oliver had said in somewhat different language on New Year's Eve so many years ago.

Molly took her bag, said goodbye to one of her assistants, and walked out into the spring evening.

The war had been over for decades now. London had moved on, of course, although there were many in the city, like her, who had lived through those desperate times.

V-E Day parades were still robustly popular. TV shows and movies were replete with stories of the worldwide struggle. Books aplenty had been written about it, and Molly was about to add hers (and Imogen's) to that pile.

Yet memories faded and other wars had come to replace that one, though thankfully none as extreme or as far-reaching. The 1970s had been quite eventful for Britain. There had been strikes by miners and postal and dustbin workers. A drought in 1976 and one of the hottest summers on record had dampened the spirits of many, but the Queen's Silver Jubilee a year later had lifted the country to a happier, prouder time. That was the way the world worked, Molly well knew. Highs and lows and long periods of a normal existence in between.

The decades-long nuclear arms race between the United States and the Soviet Union was still raging ahead. The British and all the rest of the world were justly terrified about how this struggle would play out between the two superpowers.

Indeed, half of her practice was now devoted to those who were certain the violent end of the world was near. Molly found she could speak with particular knowledge and thoughtfulness to such anxieties, because she had lived them herself. No foreign bomb had fallen on British soil since 1945. She hoped that would remain so, for ever, but there were no guarantees. Life was not about predictability, indeed quite the opposite.

She stopped at the spot on the pavement where Ignatius Oliver had lost his life while valiantly performing his duties as an air warden. It was fronted now by a women's shoe store, a nice one, an expensive one. Molly had never been inside, nor would she ever.

She and Charlie had left the shelter that night and walked back towards The Book Keep, wondering where Oliver was. Then they had come upon a small group of people and another air warden. They were gathered around something on the street. And that something had been the remains of Ignatius Oliver.

Both she and Charlie had fallen to their knees next to him and wept bitterly at losing the very best friend they ever had. As Molly had stared down at him that night so long ago, he had seemed at peace. Perhaps he had joined his wife, who had voluntarily given up her life, while his had been wrenched violently from him. But even with two very different outcomes, they could perhaps find a renewed connection for all eternity; at least she hoped so.

Molly felt herself tearing up at the long-ago but still painful memory, and she hastily moved off down the street. She knew there was a price to be paid with important relationships like that. They were wonderful, but they also had the capacity to exact a punishing price when one in the relationship was gone. Grief, sadness, anger at a loss, and terrible, unrelenting hurt were the costs to be paid for loving and being loved. It felt completely worth the bargain right up until the very moment payment was demanded.

She would never get over the loss of Ignatius Oliver, but she would always benefit from having had him in her life.

Molly looked into the window of another bookshop and then lingered, wondering what it might feel like to see her novel there. And if he had lived, what would Oliver think of her having finished Imogen's story? Would she have done so at all if he had not perished?

Molly actually understood that she had completed the book mainly as a tribute to her dear friend.

Ignatius Oliver had come along at precisely the right time for two young people who would lose everything during the greatest armed conflict the world had ever suffered through.

Despite that, she knew theirs was only one small human story among millions of others.

But this was *their* story. Three people standing together against all the world could hurl at them.

As she looked at the clear sky, Molly's mind superimposed a trio of faces there: Ignatius Oliver, Charlie Matters, and herself. Separately, through no fault of their own, they had been something less than full measure in the face of war's deadly grip. Yet together they had confronted a collective hardship that, at times, seemed beyond anyone's capacity. It spoke well indeed of the resilience of the human spirit when one had friends with whom to share the sometimes calamitous burden of existence.

We all need someone at certain times in our lives. It makes the inevitable pain lessened and the periods of happiness exalted.

With this uplifting thought blossoming in her mind, Molly continued her walk down the streets of lovely London in the warmth, and robust peace, of springtime.

ACKNOWLEDGEMENTS

To Michelle, thanks for reading an early draft and giving great feedback.

To everyone at Grand Central Publishing who believed in this project from the first day I dropped the surprise manuscript into your collective laps. Having such a trustful relationship with a publisher is very rare, and I never take it or all of you for granted.

To Aaron and Arleen Priest, Lucy Childs, Lisa Erbach Vance, Frances Jalet-Miller, Kristen Pini, and Natalie Rosselli. You are the absolute best in the business.

To Mitch Hoffman, whose exemplary editing skills clearly work on both sides of the pond.

To everyone at Pan Macmillan who rolled up their sleeves and got immediately to work when I wrote a story set right in your backyard, albeit eight decades in the past. Your stalwart friendship and brilliant publishing continue to both humble and amaze me. Long may our partnership reign.

To Praveen Naidoo and the wonderful team at Pan Macmillan in Australia, for another record year of publishing my books.

To Caspian Dennis and Sandy Violette, who remain my biggest cheerleaders and two of my best mates.

And to Kristen White and Michelle Butler, who make the wheels on the bus go round and round.

ABOUT THE AUTHOR

David Baldacci is one of the world's bestselling and favourite thriller writers. A former trial lawyer with a keen interest in world politics, he has specialist knowledge in the US political system and intelligence services. His first book, *Absolute Power*, became an instant international bestseller, with the movie starring Clint Eastwood a major box office hit. He has since written more than fifty bestsellers featuring, most recently, Travis Devine, Mickey Gibson, Amos Decker and Aloysius Archer. David is also the co-founder, along with his wife, of the Wish You Well Foundation, a non-profit organization dedicated to supporting literacy efforts across the US.

Killer twists. Heroes to believe in. Trust Baldacci.

THE ONLY MAN FOR THE JOB

Discover David Baldacci's latest series, featuring undercover operative Travis Devine.

Meet Travis Devine.
Framed. Blackmailed.
Accused of murder.
It's just another day
on Wall Street for
the 6:20 Man.

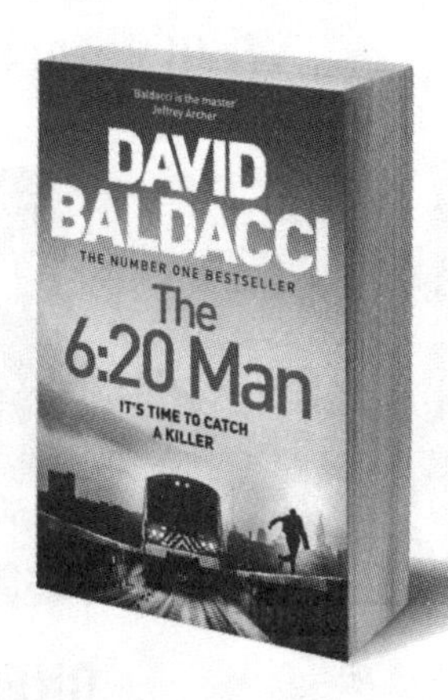

The 6:20 Man is back!
Can Travis Devine solve
the haunting murder of
a high-ranking CIA agent
before his own time runs out?

Trying to escape a skilled
predator who wants him
dead, Devine finds himself
on a job perhaps even
more dangerous than the
one he's running from . . .

In a town full of secrets who can you trust?

Discover David Baldacci's historical crime series featuring straight-talking WWII veteran Aloysius Archer.

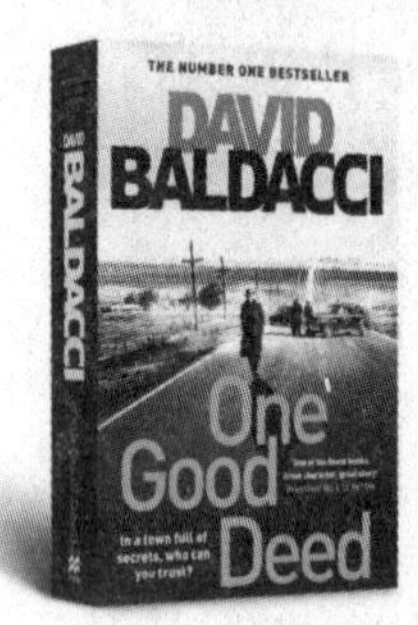

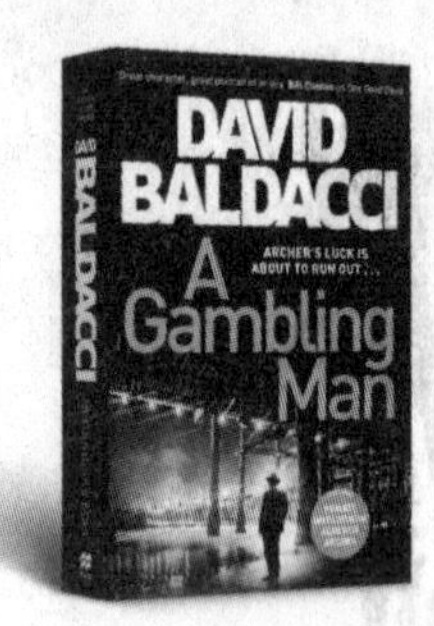

ONE GOOD DEED

Poca City, 1949. Aloysius Archer arrives in a dusty southern town looking for a fresh start. After accepting a job as a local debt collector, Archer soon finds himself as the number one suspect in a local murder. Should Archer run or fight for the truth?

A GAMBLING MAN

California, 1949. Archer is on his way to start a new job with a renowned private investigator. Arriving in a tight-lipped community rife with corruption, Archer must tackle murder, conspiracy and blackmail in a town with plenty to hide . . .

DREAM TOWN

Los Angeles, 1952. Private investigator and WWII veteran Aloysius Archer returns to solve the case of a missing screenwriter during the Golden Age of Hollywood.